Keith
AuG 91"

UNDERTOW

UNDERTOW

TOM FOOTE

KNOCKEVEN PRESS

Published in 1997 by
Knockeven Press
An Imprint of Salmon Publishing Ltd,
Cliffs of Moher, Co. Clare

© Tom Foote 1997
The moral right of the author has been asserted.

ISBN 1 897648 93 6 Softcover

Cover design by Brenda Dermody of Estresso
Set by Siobhán Hutson
Printed by Redwood Books, Kennet Way, Trowbridge, Wiltshire

To Hilary, for her constant encouragement

My grateful thanks to a dear departed friend, Harry MacMahon, who continues to work miracles, and made me laugh when I needed to.

Thank you, Anne Kennedy, for supporting me at the beginning. Thank you also, Sean O'Loughlin, for applying the spur at the final hurdle.

An especial thank you to my publisher, Jessie Lendennie, for going out on a limb, and to Nancy Thompson for her editorial wisdom and infinite patience.

'Yet though their splendour may have ceased to be,
Each played her sovereign part in making me;
Now I return my thanks with heart and lips
For the great queenliness of all those ships.'

– John Masefield

One

'Who am I?' he asked the night wind. 'I know you,' the whine in the rigging replied. 'You are a sailor who respects me, and always have.'

Jim Prendergast chuckled at his fanciful thoughts and ducked his head to avoid another sheet of flying spray as a cresting sea broke over the foredeck and the yacht shuddered in the darkness. Shaking free, she dipped her bow and genuflected to the succeeding wave.

He squinted at the compass. The light from its bowl reflected off the varnished woodwork and illuminated his features, which were half hidden by the hood of his jacket. He stole another glance through the open hatch. It was unfair of him to have insisted on being out on a night like this, he thought. He had forced it on them.

He braced himself as the boat rose to another oncoming wave. He enjoyed the feeling of the boat's movement through his sea-booted feet, but was longing for a cigarette. For a moment he thought of asking Jane to light one for him, but he knew it would only add to her annoyance. She didn't approve of him smoking. Besides, a cigarette would only turn to pulp in the spray that swept the cockpit. He set the thought aside and concentrated on steering through a night that had no stars.

Now and then he caught sight of Jane in the hatchway. Only a single light over the chart table relieved the gloom of the small cabin where she did her best to maintain some sense of order. No matter how much care she took beforehand, loose items were inevitably flung about under the violent pitching of the yacht, and tonight was no exception.

He glanced at his watch. They were now two hours out from Galway and rain squalls lashed out of the darkness, hiding any lights on the shore. He knew Jane was not happy to be out, especially in a strengthening wind that tugged white crests from the wave tops and flung them in their path. Even before the starting gun had boomed from the yacht club balcony, she had said that a long race around the Aran Islands was too much for them, particularly one that would last through the night. The bad forecast added to her concern.

The sound of his daughter retching and scrabbling for the bucket reached him. It added to the general wretchedness of the situation below decks and weakened the stubborn streak that drove him. Susan was only eight. Although she was comparatively warm and snug in her sleeping bag on the lee bunk, she had been seasick since they left. She had yet to complain, and he realised how like him she was.

Jane's clouded face appeared for an instant. Her clothes looked damp and her hair was in disarray. Their eyes met as she forced her shoulders through the hatch. 'Really, Jim, don't you think this is becoming a bit much for us? Susan is very sick.' Her eyes flashed. 'You're being utterly pigheaded about this damned race! You should have done it on your own. I told you that.'

He didn't answer immediately. Caught momentarily off guard, he heaved on the tiller as the yacht again buried her streaming deck in green water. He wished that he had put a second reef in the mainsail before darkness had set in, but now was not the time to ask Jane to take over the helm.

'This should ease off soon,' he shouted. 'It's just a squall, but if things don't improve in another hour or so, I'll run off up into Greatman's Bay.' He tried a reassuring smile. 'We're almost half way to the islands now.'

'I don't really give a damn where we are. We shouldn't be here!' She broke off and looked behind her. 'I think Susan has finally fallen asleep.' She left the hatch and he watched her trying to wedge herself into a more secure position near the navigation station where she sat glaring at the chart in an effort to stay awake.

It's not that bad, he told himself. They had been out in worse. Normally they cruised in the boat, an enjoyable pastime that brought no pressure, but occasionally his competitiveness surfaced and he joined in a race simply to drive the boat hard. He had to admit that there always seemed to be bad weather whenever he did, and although Jane had never told him, he sensed that she hated it. She had told him once that he underwent a personality change. Besides, they were no match for the faster racing yachts with their big crews, and always came last. 'Take a male crew and race on your own, Jim,' she had said that morning at breakfast, but he didn't want that. In his eyes *Larinita* was part of his family. He saw them all as an indestructible unit.

He squinted into the darkness. As always, the big boats were already out of sight, thrashing their way out to the three islands that stretched southwards across the mouth of Galway Bay, almost thirty miles from the port of Galway. 'It's all right for them,' she'd said. 'They don't have kids on board.'

He stole another glance below. He could see Jane's head nodding over the chart where the entrance to their own little harbour at the head of Kiggaul Bay was marked, her long strands of auburn hair touching it briefly. Perhaps she was looking at the spot where *Larinita* normally swung quietly on her mooring in sight of the cottage that they had rebuilt from a ruined pile of stones. Despite its isolation, the Prendergasts had grown to love the harsh beauty of Connemara. Life was good he thought, especially since the birth of Susan. At first he'd seen the baby as an intrusion that would stifle him, but no longer. Instead, his daughter had brought him hope, and a feeling of devotion that sometimes terrified him.

A thunder of noise from ropes and sails warned him that the wind had shifted in direction. He braced himself as he felt the boat rising to a larger wave. Down below, the oven door of the cooker spilled open with a metallic crash, depositing tin trays and the frying-pan in a skidding mass across the already greasy cabin floor. Jane sprang to her feet to retrieve them, but collided into the companionway steps. He read the pain on her face as she glared up at him.

'Everything okay?'

'Yes,' she snapped. 'Try to give us a bit more bloody warning the next time.'

'Couldn't help it,' he shouted. 'I caught a glimpse of the light on Black Head. The visibility is still frightful, but things will be easier now that the wind has shifted. Hold tight while I put her about!'

'You're a pompous bastard, Jim!' she screamed. 'I really believe you're enjoying this!'

Prendergast threw the helm down and drove the yacht through the wind in a welter of driven spray. Fighting with the head-sail sheets he winched them in until the groan of the rope told him it was enough. He glimpsed Jane returning to the security of her perch by the chart table, and saw her lunge just in time to save the sodden chart and the dividers from joining the other debris sliding about in the oily wetness of the cabin floor.

She dropped her head into her arms and he slowly relaxed. Perhaps she would sleep now and leave him to get on with it. The strain on the tiller had lessened and he felt comforted by the knowledge that he had turned away from the foot of the headland. Pity about the visibility, he thought. It remained too overcast for moon or stars to show, and now that the wind had eased, the rain had settled into a steady driving drizzle blanketing any lights that should normally be seen on the shore. He squirmed in his wet oilskins and braced himself against the heel of the boat, trying to find relief for his aching backside on the hard seat.

Night sailing always thrilled him in spite of the cold. The solitude and darkness of the cockpit made it a place to think and dream, where he could let the boat became a living thing, responsive and obedient in his hands. His mind restlessly flicked back, remembering fine crews and ships and the places he had taken them. In spite of over thirty years spent at sea he still loved and valued his contact with it. For him, life without the sea would not be worth living.

This year he would be forty-eight, he realised. A tall man, he carried no excess weight and had yet to show his years. Jane said that he was good looking in a bony sort of way. Once, she had whispered to him that it was his eyes that had first attracted her. They were the colour of a winter sky, she had said, and long ago in Saudi when they had first met, that sky was what she had missed most of home.

It was a little after two o'clock in the morning when the wind eased to a moderate breeze and allowed him to lash the helm. Confident that the boat was capable of looking after herself, he dropped down below for a cigarette and the opportunity it gave him to plot a rough position on the chart. It was relatively quiet in the cabin, except for the noises of the boat working her way to windward. Susan was sleeping peacefully in her sleeping bag held securely in place by canvas lee cloths and Jane had crawled into the quarter berth and had lapsed into a fretful sleep. As he studied them, his feeling of guilt returned. He pushed the thought aside and busied himself boiling some water on the stove to make a cup of hot soup before returning to the cockpit.

Back on deck he saw lights ahead in the mist. First, green then red and green, and finally a single red. He realised that a boat was turning ahead of him, but found it difficult to judge how far off because of the poor visibility. Thinking that it might be a trawler with nets set, he altered course. Soon the lights disappeared altogether and he forgot them.

It was daylight at six o'clock and still very cold on deck. Tiredness overcame Prendergast. The prospect of continuing to race around the back of the islands, especially all through a day that was showing little promise of an improvement in the weather, was becoming less appealing. Perhaps it was time to call it off, he thought. He was still trying to reach a decision when Jane arrived on deck with a steaming mug of coffee. Her face was pinched and he could sense her anger. Perhaps she'll agree to go on, he hoped, just so that we can say we finished it together.

'Good morning,' she said in a flat tone that carried its own meaning. He sensed her feelings and gave in. 'As soon as we sight something that will give me a position fix, we'll pull out of the race.' She gave him a wan smile. 'I'm sorry,' he said. 'I shouldn't have pushed it.'

'Perhaps we could meet up with the others in Kilronan after the race is over,' she suggested. 'They'll all be there before us, anyway.'

Jim smiled ruefully. 'I'll pretend I didn't hear that last remark.' But he had to admit that right now, a quiet anchorage and a warm bunk were uppermost in his mind, too.

'I think I saw land,' Jane said, pointing. 'Over there, on our port bow.'

He held his course until a darker shape in the mist revealed itself. Soon they were able to make out a cluster of low white buildings with the vague shape of hills rising in the background.

'That must be Kilmurvey,' he muttered. 'If it is, we're further west than I thought. Maybe we should tack out again.'

Quickly they came about. They were ready to settle on a new course that would take them away from the shore when the great bass roar of a ship's siren thundering across the water brought them both to their feet. Out of the drizzle on their starboard side appeared the ominous bulk of a freighter. Riding high in the water, she was much bigger than any ship Jim had seen in the bay before.

The ship swept past them about a quarter of a mile away, still sounding her siren. Prendergast could see a vague figure waving at them with both arms on her bridge wing, but as quickly as she had appeared, the ship became lost again in the gloom away to the east.

'Jesus!' he exclaimed. 'She could have run us down!' His knee trembled. 'What on earth is a ship of that size doing up here?'

Jane had no answer as the sonorous blast of the klaxon again shattered the quiet. The ship had turned. She again appeared out of the mist, but from astern of them this time, with a great wall of threatening white water surging at her forefoot. She was much closer now and appeared to be coming straight at them. Prendergast screamed for Jane to release the sheets, but before she could do anything, he put the helm down and tacked away, with sails aback.

The ship passed only yards away. Her towering steel hull, a dirty white colour with battered plates, was streaked in rust. Her only distinguishing mark was a yellow funnel, but he was not able to decipher her name and she flew no flag of nationality. The figure on her bridge was still waving frantically. As they watched, a second man joined him. They appeared to be arguing. She steamed away northwards, her propeller clear of the water and thrashing at the surface. They could vaguely hear the powerful throb of her diesel engine long after she became lost in the fog.

'Maybe she's lost,' Jane offered.

'No,' Prendergast said. 'Ships don't get lost, not with all the navigation gear they carry. If we had a VHF we could contact her. Perhaps she's trying to drop off a sick seaman.' Abruptly, he remembered the navigation lights that he had seen earlier. It must have been the lights of the ship. Whatever she was up to, the freighter must have been cruising about out here all night.

'I think we should continue on for a bit longer before we head back to Kilronan. I don't want to run foul of that bastard again.' Jim paused and smiled self-consciously. 'Anyway, I'm bloody tired.'

Jane touched his hand and smiled. 'Now you're making sense.'

The coastline astern had completely disappeared. They were alone again, and already feeling the Atlantic swell funnelling through the North Sound. 'Maybe this would be a good time to get Susan dressed and on deck with us,' he said. He tried to sound matter-of-fact, not wanting to voice his anxiety.

'I'll try and get us some breakfast while I'm down below.' She looked scared and Jim could understand her fear. Every sailing season brought its rash of reports of yachts that had been less lucky in avoiding rogue ships, particularly in the English Channel. To his knowledge, there had never been a collision on the west coast of Ireland.

He watched her climb down through the hatch, awkward and constricted in her oilskins. Then she turned in the opening and smiled back at him. 'By the way,' she said, 'you really are a bastard at times!'

He gave her a sheepish look. 'Perhaps,' he replied, his eyes glowing with the warmth that he felt for her. 'This is supposed to be fun. I need to remember that.'

Jane gently touched Susan on the shoulder and kissed her on the forehead. 'Wake up sweetheart, time for breakfast.' She lit the stove and it hissed, feeding warmth into the cabin.

Susan dressed herself, chattering gaily. She was no longer feeling seasick, and helped to clean up the debris and mess of the night's passage. Slowly, the cabin regained a semblance of order and the warmth of the stove started to dry out the interior.

Susan crawled up into the cockpit, clutching her teddy bear under one arm. 'Hi Daddy!' She threw her arms around Jim and kissed him noisily on the cheek. 'You look tired Daddy, didn't you sleep?'

Prendergast hugged her with one arm. 'No pumpkin, I didn't have time. Be a good girl and clip on your safety harness.'

She clipped her harness to a ring bolt and glanced at him coyly with lowered eyes. 'Teddy was very sick last night Daddy, did you know that?'

'Yes, I did.' He laughed. 'I heard him.'

'You love Mummy, don't you Daddy?'

'Of course I do.'

'As much as me and Teddy?'

'Yes,' he said, wondering where this was going.

'More than *Larinita*?' she probed.

Prendergast felt taken aback. 'Much more than that,' he said quickly. Certainly, he had feeling for the yacht. He doted on it. But to put the boat in the same category as his wife and daughter was another matter. Just then, Jane poked her head through the hatch and passed up two steaming bowls of porridge. 'Jim, don't you think Susan should wear a life jacket?'

'It's quiet enough up here now, she'll be okay. She's clipped on.' As each minute passed without sighting the ship, Jim's nervousness dissipated. The terror of being run down slowly abated and the annoying twitch in his muscles stopped. Awkwardly, he took a spoonful of porridge, 'God! That tastes good. Come on up and join us.'

Slightly burnt toast and coffee followed before Jane clambered back on deck and wedged a portable radio in a cave locker. She switched it on and they listened silently to the morning weather forecast. It painted a bleak outlook for the rest of the day, with more heavy rain promised, and winds veering north-westerly and increasing to force six or possibly seven. They had made the right decision. Jim reached over and switched the radio off. 'That's it then,' he said. 'We'll get in out of it.'

Suddenly, Prendergast again sighted the ship less than a mile away on their starboard bow. She lay stopped in the water, rolling uneasily in the swell. As he looked for her name, he could make out a number of men working at one of her cargo holds on the foredeck. He gripped Jane's shoulder and pointed at the ship. 'Jesus!' he exclaimed. 'That thing is like a recurring bad dream!'

There was a puff of blue-white smoke from her funnel before they lost sight of the ship again. Before she disappeared Prendergast was certain that a small blue trawler came into view around her stern. Then came a flash of white churning water as the ship's propeller bit into the Atlantic swell. After that, the mist swallowed her and she faded like a ghost into the murk.

Jim broke an eerie silence that had descended on them like the fronds of fog that swirled over the water. 'Christ! I wish we had a VHF radio. Whatever is going on over there makes no sense to me.' He couldn't prevent worry creeping back into his voice.

'Whatever it is, it scares me.' Jane's voice was anxious. 'I'm frightened, Jim. Please let's put about and get away from here. God knows what they're up to.'

'Okay. We'll bear away and run downwind. Ease off on the mainsheet!'

As they started to turn away, the needle-like spire of the

Eeragh lighthouse appeared like a spectre on their port bow. It was only there long enough for Jim to take a quick bearing of it before it disappeared into the fog as though some unseen hand sought to hide it.

With the boat now running comfortably before the wind and lifting her stern to each following wave, even the rain lost its sting, and the spray no longer come flying aft to beat against the cockpit spray hood. 'Here, Sweetheart, take the helm,' Prendergast said. 'I need a break, and I had better plot a course to find Straw Island. We'll be down there in jig time.' He handed Jane the helm and disappeared below.

Crouching at the chart table, he quickly marked a rough position a mile or so north of the Eeragh lighthouse, then pencilled in a course line on the chart. He made a quick calculation. A little over two hours of sailing time would have them safely inside Kilronan harbour. Was it his imagination playing tricks or had he heard something? Satisfied that he knew where they were and had a course that would lead them safely past the protruding eastern tip of the island, he started back up the companionway ladder just as Jane began to scream.

Emerging on deck, he looked aft over the stern past Jane's shoulder. His face filled with horror on seeing the huge rust streaked bows of the freighter appearing out of the mist. As she ploughed towards them the rumble grew deafening.

'Oh my God! Give me the helm!' he shouted, throwing himself across the cockpit in a desperate effort to reach the tiller.

Jane swivelled around, her eyes widening in terror at the bluff thrusting bow of steel less than a hundred yards astern. The ship was so close that they could hardly see the navigation bridge above the towering bow. Jim threw all his weight against the tiller, screaming for Jane to harden in the sheets. Too late, he fumbled for the engine starter button. Caught in a massive bow wave, the yacht rolled over in a welter of spray, her masts and sails flat in the water. His ears filled with the grinding sound of splintering timbers before he was swept bodily into the vortex as if he were some tiny scrap of flotsam.

The last sound he heard was the horrific roar of the freighter's engine. So close it seemed, that he could have reached out and touched it. Then came the thrashing fury of her great four-bladed propeller, smashing down on the remains of *Larinita* as the suction dragged him under.

As quickly as it had started, it was over. The only lingering sounds were the fading throb of a diesel engine and the call of a lone sea bird above the noise of breaking waves.

Prendergast surfaced, choking for breath, frantically trying to jettison his sea boots. A wave broke over him, rolling him under and he panicked, swallowing more sea water. Choking and sobbing uncontrollably he surfaced again and gulped for air. As he filled his lungs something hard bumped him on the back of his head. It was a section of splintered coach roof from the yacht. He held on to it, the buoyancy of the timber helping him to keep his head above most of the waves. He called out but there was no answer. He screamed their names. Again and again he called, sobbing in desperation.

Frightened that his piece of wreckage might capsize and leave him with nothing to cling to, he struggled a little higher, hands grasping at the jagged hole where once there had been a deck-head skylight. A single scrap of blue cockpit cover floated nearby. As far as he could see, nothing else remained of the yacht except for a few shattered pieces of planking. An empty jerry-can bobbed some distance away, but whether it came from the yacht or not, he could not tell.

Of Jane and Susan, there was no sign. No desperate cries for help, and no response to his own.

'God, why didn't I insist that they wear lifejackets when all this started?' He should have prepared them. He was the one who should have known. Then he remembered that Susan had been harnessed to a safety ring bolt in the cockpit. Could she have freed herself or was she dragged down with the sinking yacht? If *Larinita* didn't sink, was it possible that she could still be afloat, damaged but intact and not far away? Why had the ship not stopped? The crew must have seen them. Had they been run down deliberately? Flares, he thought. He should have used flares! The questions flooded his mind, and there were no answers.

He felt desperately cold already. Even though it was summer, he knew his survival time was ticking away, minute by minute. He struggled and managed to free the safety harness built in to his jacket, and with some effort, was able to clip it onto a ring bolt protruding from the splintered decking. After that, he remembered nothing except infinite darkness as he took a first step along death's pathway.

Two

Captain Koumianos Arkides huddled in a corner of his wheel house. The consequences didn't bear thinking about. In just a short few minutes his overweight frame seemed to have shrunk, swamped by the enormity of what had happened. He knew that all the instincts of the seaman had again deserted him; he had deliberately run down the yacht, albeit under duress. Lives had been lost as a result of his actions, he thought wildly, though that mattered less to him than being found out.

His anguished thoughts returned to his last failure when he had abandoned the *Argos Sky* in the Indian Ocean off Port Elizabeth. That dreadful vision never really went away. Now renewed and intensified, it was as vivid as on the day it happened. As the ship foundered he had taken his panic stricken crew with him and left over a hundred passengers to fend for themselves. Fifty of them had gone down with the ship. When the truth became known, the world press was unremitting in their condemnation. It was the end to his promising career. From that moment on, ships like the worn out *Georgios* became his only home. He shivered and moved closer to the windows, fixing his gaze on the mist-shrouded foredeck.

Nearby, Gupta Bose stood at the wheel with legs splayed, his feet planted squarely on a teak grating. He stared at the compass, his features dark and brooding. None of this concerned him, he told himself. His pay was still well below union rates for a seaman. He wasn't paid to think or make decisions. His only worry was that he might be punished.

Gupta made up his mind that he had seen nothing, knowing that his best course of action would be to forget about the accident and keep his mouth shut. He had to safeguard his job and the money he sent home to Madras each month. At sixty years of age he was no fool. A lifetime spent tramping the oceans of the world made him well aware of the risks in knowing too much on ships like the *Georgios*. Nobody would take much notice if yet another Indian deck hand disappeared overboard on a dark night. He spun the wheel in his experienced hands and continued to concentrate on the swinging compass, blotting out what he had overheard, centring his thoughts on his wife and family.

The wheel house door slid open allowing a gust of rain laden wind to swirl through the opening. The Second Mate stepped quickly inside and shook the water from his clothes. Manoli Vlassos felt cold and wet after his hurried visit to the forecastle. 'No damage, Captain, none whatsoever,' he reported. 'The carpenter has sounded the forward ballast tanks. He says the number one hold and fore-peak are dry. We are making no water.'

Arkides stirred himself and turned to face him. 'Were you able to see the bow plating? What about paint scars?' His sharp eyes willed the other officer to make the right answer.

The mate stared back at him with undisguised contempt. 'There are none. I looked right down to the water line. Luckily the boat was built of timber. We drove right over her and she sank without trace.' He wanted to add, 'They didn't have a chance', but he stopped himself. He was conscious that the road that had led him to the *Georgios* was pot-holed. He, too, was lucky to still have his ticket. By good fortune, some owners were still willing to employ officers with a dubious past.

'What about survivors? That's what interests me!' The shriek was in English but the accent was unmistakably Irish.

Manoli whirled to confront a small podgy figure who had burst from the chart room at the rear of the wheel house. He scowled at the man. 'There are none, Mr. Foster. We smashed the boat and she went straight to the bottom. There's little enough wreckage. If there were survivors, we would have seen them.'

Foster was not satisfied. 'I want to be certain,' he said. 'Captain, turn this damned ship around and continue to search.

We can't afford the risk of someone knowing anything about this bloody ship. Christ! That's why we ran the fucking boat down in the first place!'

'Absolutely not,' Arkides snapped. 'I am taking this ship out to sea and we will continue our voyage. If we hang around here any longer someone else could see us, especially now that it's daylight.' He paused for a moment, then added, 'We wouldn't be in this mess if you and your friends had been where you were supposed to be last night. We spent the whole night searching for you. You can't blame me for thinking the yacht was our contact when we first saw her.'

'I suggest you think again, Captain. You've got two cases of our cargo on board and the fishing boat is still waiting for them.' His voice became more menacing as he continued. 'My people need the rest of that cargo. It's vital to them.'

Captain Arkides ignored him. He reached over and rang for full speed on the engine room telegraph. 'Give me a course for Gibraltar, Manoli!' he ordered. 'The fishing boat has gone, Mr. Foster. Get that into your head. You have no choice but to sail with us. We'll drop you off in Ceuta when we refuel.'

'Ceuta! Are you fucking crazy! Turn the bloody ship around and finish what we're paying you for!' The Irishman's eyes blazed with fury.

'Mr. Foster, get the hell off my bridge!' Arkides was almost out of his mind. 'I'll have someone prepare the pilot's cabin for you. There's nothing more I can do. That's my last word on it.' He strode into the chart room to join the second mate, who was already working at the chart table.

The vibration from the engine as it drove the ship up to full speed set up an annoying rattle in the windows, but Foster hardly noticed. He glared through the salt-encrusted glass, seeing nothing except rolling seas that churned in the pit of his stomach. Fuck! Arkides was right. There was no land, and the fishing boat was gone.

Two miles away, the two-man crew of the fishing vessel *Stella Maris* turned for home. They had already waited an hour, one that seemed more like four. Charlie Donovan's craggy features were creased in a perplexed frown. He was a gruff uncompromising man, used to earning a scant living from fishing in the harsh and demanding waters off the Connemara coast. He did not panic easily. But what had yesterday seemed to be an easy way to earn a considerable sum of money had now become an enigma. He could not understand why the ship had cast his boat off and left him rolling in the swell with the job unfinished. Donovan assumed that the freighter must have seen something on radar that frightened them away. There was always the possibility that a Navy patrol vessel had come on the scene. If that was the case, self-preservation was now paramount.

Donovan pressed the engine starter button and the big diesel roared into life. 'There's no point in hanging around any longer. That ship isn't coming back.'

Squeezed beside him in the cramped confines of his tiny wheel house, his deck hand, Harry McDonagh, sucked on an unlit Hamlet cigar. Harry could almost taste his own fear. 'Jesus, we can't leave Foster out there. What about the others, what are they going to say?'

Charlie ignored his protest. 'I don't give a shit about Foster. Something has gone wrong. I tell you, that ship has long gone. We're a bit early for the tide but we can pull a few pots off the Skerd rocks on the way.'

Harry opened his mouth to object but shut it again immediately. There was no arguing with Charlie once his mind was made up. Anyway, he thought, the sooner they got rid of the boxes in the fish hold, the better. The guns would keep the lads ashore happy. And once the guns were off their hands, the shadow of a spell in Portlaoise prison would become more remote.

It was late in the afternoon before Donovan slowly steered the boat past mist-shrouded Golam Head. He carefully skirted Bruiser Rock at the approaches to Kilkieran Bay. Soon they rounded Dinish Island, passing Inishbarra close at hand before following an unmarked channel that led to a crumbling stone pier at the end of a narrow inlet. The wind continued to whip small whitecapped waves off the surface and they could make out the distant peaks of the Twelve Pins as brooding humps in the sky. Cloud and mist swirling down from the slopes made the place look inhospitable and incredibly lonely.

Donovan saw no houses overlooking the pier. The nearest was half a mile away behind a rock strewn hill. Long ago, this would have been a busy little cove, the pier having being built to serve the turf trade. In those days, Galway Hookers carried the turf in their black bowels to the far corners of Galway Bay. He could see them now, magical sailing boats that flitted like brown moths in and out of a hundred such harbours.

The blue hulled trawler crept into the pier. Donovan peered through the wheel house door as he watched the tide mark on the rocks lining the channel, while Harry McDonagh kept careful watch on the echo sounder ticking off the depth as the water shoaled. Nothing moved except a few scraggy sheep grazing on the sparse hillside. The tide was flooding, sucking greedily at the boat as she nudged the pier. They were late, and the incessant drizzle made evening seem even later than it was. Overhead, a scattering of seabirds wheeled in the gloom as though they had nowhere to go, while a lone cormorant, vainly attempting to dry its outstretched wings, watched the boat come to a stop.

Huddled behind a low stone wall in the lane, a man wearing a drenched tweed cap and a waxed jacket watched as well. His eyes were wary. McGinty was normally suspicious. It was his nature. Five years in a British prison had seen to that, not counting months of living rough on the run. He gave a low whistle and a second man dressed in a black raincoat flitted across the lane to join him.

'Keep low!' hissed the man in the raincoat. 'They're so fucking late, who knows if it's them.'

'I hate dealing with amateurs,' whispered the man in the waxed jacket. 'But so long as they've got what we came for ....'
They lapsed into silence and crouched lower behind the wall as a muffled roar signalled that the boat's engine was going astern.

They saw a man in yellow oilskins jump up onto the grass and fasten mooring lines to a pair of ancient stone bollards. He cursed as he stung his hands on an outcrop of nettles, then looked around, squinting his eyes in the drizzle. His voice reached them as he called down to the boat. 'Charlie, there's nobody up here. Are you sure this is the right pier?'

Donovan stepped out on deck. 'Of course it is. Take a walk up the boreen and see if you can see anybody. A lorry should be up there somewhere. I'll brew up a cup of tea while you're gone.'

'Okay, but for Christ's sake, keep the engine running so as we can get out of here fast if needs be!'

The two men behind the wall watched the fisherman approach. When he drew level, the man in the black raincoat stood up, hands deep in his coat pockets, and stepped into the lane. 'Harry, where the hell is Foster?'

McDonagh jumped in fright. 'Jesus, Liam! Are you trying to stop my heart? Something went wrong and the ship took off. Foster's still on board.'

McGinty came into the open, leaping the low wall with his shotgun held at the ready. 'You eejits!' he roared. 'Don't tell me the stuff is still on board the fuckin' ship as well!' He swung the gun in a wide arc towards McDonagh, who heard a click as the safety catch released.

The man in the raincoat lunged forward and depressed the gun barrels. 'McGinty, cool down man, there's time enough for that. Let's get their story first.'

Fear brought a sudden pallor to Harry McDonagh's weathered skin. Talking in the pub was one thing, he thought, but mixing with these people for real was dangerous. He forced his eyes away from the gun. 'Look lads, it's nothing to do with me. Come on down to the boat and let Charlie do the explaining. After all, he's the skipper.'

McGinty relaxed. Lowering the shotgun, he strode off towards the pier without another word.

Liam pulled up the collar of his raincoat. 'Don't take him to heart. These are hard times, and he's strung out. We'll sort it out between us on the boat.'

Charlie Donovan switched off the engine and came through the wheel house door as they approached. 'Come on down lads, tea's in the pot and there's a drop of the hard stuff if you want it.'

'Never mind,' Liam said. 'Let's get down to business. What have you got for us?'

Donovan hesitated for a second. 'Six boxes.'

McGinty rose to his feet so quickly that McDonagh dropped his mug in terror. He watched it shatter on the steel deck at his feet. 'There's supposed to be eight,' McGinty growled.

Donovan shrugged. 'Yeah, but the last two were coming on deck when they cast us off.' He paused and sipped at his tea. 'The ship never came back after that. She went off out to sea and took Foster with her.'

Liam drained his mug and sighed. 'Something must have gone wrong out there. Did you see anything?'

Donovan shook his head.

'Looks like it was no fault of yours. Foster can look after himself, he's well used to it. Let's have a look inside one of the boxes.'

Harry McDonagh opened up the hatch boards to the fish hold and jumped down inside. Standing on the cargo, he looked up at them. 'You'd better not come down unless you've got strong stomachs. It stinks down here.'

'Open one up,' McGinty ordered.

McDonagh fumbled nervously with the catches of the nearest crate and opened the hinged cover. He peeled back a paper wrapping and exposed the top pair of Kalashnikov AK47's, the guns black under a thick coating of grease.

Liam felt a throb of excitement. 'Pass one up.' He hefted the weapon. 'Good bit heavier than the Armalite, but sweet Jesus, McGinty! Look at the folding butt! This is neat, dead neat.' He handed the gun back and stooped to wipe his hands on a pile of nets.

If McGinty was impressed, he didn't show it. He leaned into the hold. 'Are all those boxes the same?'

'Yes,' McDonagh answered.

McGinty's face went blood red. 'I fuckin' knew it! he screamed. 'The bloody bastards still have the ammunition on board. These are as useful as a Johnny with holes in it!'

'I don't understand,' said Donovan, frowning.

Liam spoke very quietly, but there was a steely tone to his voice. 'It's simple. These are Russian guns using 7.62mm bullets. The NATO rounds for the Armalite won't fit, and they are all we have just now. McGinty is right. Without the ammunition these weapons are useless.' He turned to McGinty, his thin lips tight. 'Go back up the lane and fetch the van.'

'You're the boss,' McGinty replied. He leapt onto the pier and loped off up the lane, taking his shotgun with him. Liam turned to McDonagh. 'Help me get this stuff up on the pier.'

The rain had finally stopped by the time McGinty puffed up to the van, sweating under his heavy waxed jacket. The woman in the driver's seat was asleep with her head forward on her chest so that her long blonde hair cascaded over the steering wheel. She awoke instantly as his hand touched the passenger door handle and he found himself looking at a snub nosed Beretta. 'Put it away,' he said. He opened the door and climbed in beside her. 'Down to the pier, no lights.'

Five olive-green boxes were already stacked on deck. McDonagh was balancing the sixth on the capping stones when the van backed to the edge of the pier. Exhaust fumes billowed down over the edge before he could duck, filling his lungs and spattering his face in oil specks. He turned to swear at the driver.

Charlie Donovan gaped at the Mercedes camper van with German licence plates. A surfboard sat incongruously on the roof and two bicycles hung from a rack on the back. His surprise heightened when the driver jumped down from the cab and walked to the edge of the pier. She was tall and slim, with a face that would be beautiful were it not so hard. Her mane of hair was highlighted by a black leather jacket. He looked at her long shapely legs in matching skin tight trousers. 'Jesus!' he whispered.

Liam laughed for the first time. 'Sorry Charlie, you didn't meet Lisa before. She's a foreigner, but you can't blame her for that, can you?'

Lisa didn't smile. Her look was icy cold. Harry McDonagh forgot what he was about to say and closed his mouth abruptly.

McGinty came to the side of the pier and scowled down at the boat. 'Let's get on with it.'

It took them twenty minutes to load the camper. They stowed most of the boxes underneath the bunks out of sight, covering the last two with a coloured blanket. To a cursory glance, the boxes simply resembled a table. When it was done, McGinty climbed into the back of the van with his shotgun. Lisa returned to the driver's seat without a backward glance.

Liam took a small revolver from his raincoat pocket before throwing the coat inside the cab. He returned to the boat, tucking the pistol into a shoulder holster as he walked. At the edge of the pier, he bent down and handed Donovan a brown envelope. 'As far as it goes, well done. I'll be in touch. Keep your mouths shut.' He pointed to McDonagh. 'Charlie, I'll consider you responsible for him.' He strode back to the van. A door slammed and it was gone.

'Fuckin' hell!' Harry's voice cracked in relief. 'We've done it.'

Donovan grunted and threw off the mooring lines. 'Start her up, Harry. Let's get out of here while we still have enough water under us.'

The powerful engine burst into life and they backed away from the pier. Seconds later the boat was only a smudge against the background of rock and weed.

They motored out of the cove. By the time they rounded Dinish Point, the wind had eased to a fresh south-westerly breeze, showing clear skies out to the west. 'It'll be a good day tomorrow,' Donovan said, studying the sky.

'It's been a good day today,' replied Harry. He steered the boat past Muskerry Rock with the dim light from the compass magnifying the fatigue written on his face. Soon the guiding flash from the lighthouse on Croaghnakeela Island blinked in the far distance and he relaxed as familiar waters opened before him. Donovan opened the brown envelope and divided the wad of twenty-pound notes as previously agreed. One third each, and a third for the boat.

'Where are they taking that stuff?'

Donovan reared on Harry. 'I don't know and I don't care,' he snapped. 'Nor should you. Forget about it. It's over and done with, we've been paid and that's the end of it.'

Harry was not ready to be shut off. 'What about those two? What do you make of them? And what about that bitch Lisa? She was something else! Did you see her legs?'

Charlie Donovan whirled on him. 'For fuck's sake, Harry, will you drop it! The woman I don't know anything about, and less I care. We're dealing with strange animals. You heard what Liam said. Keep your trap shut, or they'll stamp on you.'

Harry concentrated on the money and what he could do with it. Secretly, he envied Donovan. Charlie owned his own trawler, but he was just a paid hand. Maybe I'll get my own boat, he thought. He wondered if he would ever have the guts for that, starting to feel nervous at the very thought of it.

It was midnight before they tied up at the inner pier in Roundstone harbour. Above them in the narrow street that overlooked the harbour, holiday makers were spilling out of O'Dowd's pub and the sound of voices drifted down. The money felt heavy in McDonagh's oilskin pocket. He looked at his watch; he was thirsty and in a mood to celebrate. 'Do you think we'll get in for a drink? It's a bank holiday weekend. Twomey might still serve us.'

'Forget it, Harry.' Donovan heaved a box of clattering lobsters up on the pier. 'Put these into the trap for the night, then go home and get some sleep.'

They climbed the steep hill, ignoring the last of the revellers coming out of the pubs on the opposite side of the road. Before they separated at the top of the street, Donovan gripped McDonagh's shoulder tightly in his fist. 'No fishing this weekend, Harry, but we'll go out again on Monday. Don't let that money out of your pocket. Sit on it for a while, until things settle down. I'm giving you sound advice. If you don't take it, you could be a dead man.'

He watched Harry disappear up a dark lane. Below him, the headlights of a car flashed down the street as the village became quiet. He shook his head. I'll have to watch you like a hawk, he thought. This bloody money could ruin us yet, if I don't.

Three

The sea was rougher now. Another wave, larger than the last, broke over Prendergast, and he struggled to maintain his hold on the scrap of decking timber that kept him afloat. The next wave followed quickly, lifting him higher, and for a brief instant, he saw the white spire of Eeragh light house. In spite of his exhaustion he knew he had not imagined it. Have to reach it, he thought. Have to find Jane and Susan. He concentrated on remaining conscious, knowing there was little time left before hypothermia would overcome him.

He kicked out with his legs in a last feeble effort to force himself closer to the jagged outcrop of rocks below the light house. It was definitely closer. He could already hear the roar of surf breaking on the rocks. Then he heard the muffled sound of an outboard engine above the noise of the surf. Another wave rose beneath him and there it was, a small black curragh edging through the inner passage of the rocks. He tried to shout, but could only croak through his cracked lips. As he tried to wave, he passed out.

Colm Conneely nursed his spluttering engine, eyes straining for a lost lobster pot close in under the rocks. It was only a single red pot marker, but to him and his brother Dermot, it meant the difference between earning a few pounds for their day's efforts or returning home empty handed. Keeping outside the line of surf, he skillfully manoeuvred their frail canvas boat through the larger waves and guided it through the foam of the backwash.

They had already passed Prendergast before Dermot glanced

astern and glimpsed a flash of red amongst the waves. He tapped his brother urgently on the shoulder. 'Over there, in under the rocks!' he shouted, pointing his finger.

Colm swung the boat in a wide arc. Seconds later he killed the engine. Prendergast felt strong hands hauling him out of the water and heard the click of his safety line being unclipped. His eyelids fluttered just once before he was heaved into a mess of ropes and sea water. Vaguely, he heard voices and smelled the tarred sides of the curragh before everything went black.

The two brothers stared at Prendergast in disbelief. Dermot tentatively reached out and touched Prendergast's face. It felt cold, like the flesh of a fish. 'Christ almighty, Colm!'

'He's not dead. I saw him move, but he'll die soon if we don't get him ashore. Cover him up, try and get some warmth into him.'

Stripping off their own oilskins, they covered Prendergast. Colm ripped at the starter cord of the ancient Evinrude motor. It burst into life, sprinting them in sheets of spray at full throttle.

It took the Conneelys an hour to reach Kilmurvey. Ignoring the pier, they drove the boat straight up on the beach and clambered out onto fine white sand.

'Take his legs, Dermot. We'll bring him up to the Quinns. That's the nearest.' Colm reached into the boat and grabbed Prendergast's shoulders. Between them they dragged the limp figure out of the boat and staggered up the beach through piles of yellow seaweed. Slipping and sliding through the kelp, their boots squelched through the mess, stirring clouds of buzzing sand flies into the air. Reaching the road above the high tide mark, they made straight for a low stone cottage further along on the opposite side where a curl of welcoming smoke rose above its thatched roof.

It was almost six o'clock in the evening. The kitchen table was already set for the evening meal as Annie Quinn patted a strand of hair back into place and dropped a handful of sausages into the pan. Her husband, Kieran, sat patiently in a corner, reading the *Irish Independent*. At his elbow on the window-ledge a battered radio was tuned for the evening news.

Annie flashed him an amused smile. 'Don't get too settled, Kieran. The tea will be ready in a minute.'

Just as the chimes of the Angelus sounded from the radio, an urgent hammering on the door startled them. Before either of them could reach it, the door crashed open and the Conneelys staggered into the kitchen, panting with exertion as they deposited Prendergast on the flagged floor.

'Mother of God!' exclaimed Annie, her eyes widening. 'What happened, Colm? Who in God's name is it? Is he dead?'

Kieran Quinn dropped his newspaper to the floor and crossed the kitchen in a bound. Bending over the body on the floor, he knelt and put his ear close to Prendergast's mouth, then straightened. 'Help me get him into the bedroom. Dermot, take my motorbike and phone the surgery from the pub. This man needs a doctor straight away.'

Between them they lugged Prendergast into a sparsely furnished bedroom off the kitchen and stripped him of his sodden clothes before lifting him into the bed. His body was already blue-white and icy to their touch.

Annie Quinn wrapped three hot water bottles in old shirts. Returning from the kitchen, she stuffed them under the bed covers. The man's face was almost as pale as the starched white pillow-case, and his breathing was shallow. She placed a motherly hand on his forehead, stroking him. 'That's all we can do until we get help,' she said.

Soaked to the skin, Colm Conneely was shivering uncontrollably. His teeth started to chatter as Annie turned her attention to him. 'You're half frozen yourself, Colm. Get yourself into the kitchen by the fire.'

'Thanks, Annie.' Glancing at the bed he added, 'We picked him up off the Eeragh. Wouldn't have seen him at all if it wasn't for his red jacket. Come to think of it, he was dressed like one of them yachties. We saw a couple of yachts early this morning down off the Foul Sound.'

'He's not from the islands, at any rate. That's for sure. Now go and get out of your wet things. I'll fetch some of Kieran's clothes for you.'

'I've been through his pockets. No wallet, no money, no identification. Nothing except a cigarette lighter.' Kieran Quinn dropped Prendergast's wet clothing and fished in his pocket for his pipe. He dragged a chair over to the bedside. 'I'll stay here and keep an eye on him.' He sat down and started to stuff his blackened pipe with slivers of plug tobacco, his big weathered hands caressing the pipe as he lit it and puffed it into life.

Kieran sniffed the air. 'I think something is burning, woman! Leave him to me.' He placed his pipe on the dresser. 'Get yourself into the kitchen and look after Colm.'

Annie hurried to fetch some dry clothes from the airing cupboard and handed them to Colm in the kitchen. 'Put these on, there's a good lad. There's a dry towel in the bathroom.'

A cloud of acrid smoke swirled above the range and the sausages were burnt black in the frying pan. Annie rushed to the stove and lifted the pan. 'Damn!' she exclaimed, turning to face Colm as he returned. 'I'm afraid they're too burnt, Colm. I'll give you some bread and tea while I put on more.'

'Give 'em to me as they are, Annie. I'd eat a horse right now!' Colm wolfed the sausages, stuffing his mouth with brown bread and scalding tea. Slowly, warmth spread through his body. Annie dropped more sausages into the blackened pan and placed another kettle of water on the stove. Wiping her hands on her apron, she filled Colm another mug of tea. Moth-like, she fussed and flitted about the kitchen, stopping only to peer anxiously into the bedroom where her husband kept his silent vigil.

Dermot Conneely reached the pub a mile down the road a few minutes after leaving the cottage. In his haste, he almost fell off the skidding motorbike as he came to a halt in the muddy yard outside. He threw the bike aside and ran into the pub.

The bar was empty except for a few locals huddled around an open turf fire, nursing their pints. They all looked up when Dermot rushed in, hoping he might be a tourist with a few pounds to throw around.

The barman rubbed at a pint glass with a dirty tea-towel. 'Get out, you bastard!' he yelled, as a black and white collie seized the opportunity to slink through the open door, squeezing past Dermot's legs. 'Jesus, Dermot, would you ever close the feckin' door after you!'

Dermot ignored him. Michael Loughnane's surliness was a byword on the island. 'Mickey, give us some change for the phone. I've no money on me and I have to call the nurse. It's an emergency.'

'Sorry, can't help you. It's busted again, there's a dud coin stuck in it.'

'Fuck it!' Dermot headed back out of the open door. Seconds later he was off down the road in a cloud of exhaust smoke, until the motorbike ran out of petrol and spluttered to a halt about a mile further down the road. Disgusted, Dermot threw it up against a stone wall and started to run the last mile and a half downhill into Kilronan.

Agnes Doyle was working later than usual in her tiny surgery. The evening had been unusually busy. The doctor was away on holiday and a locum had yet to turn up from the mainland. She took a last look around, checking the surgery's tidiness, and reached for the light as the door opened.

'Agnes, we need you over in Kilmurvey. We pulled a man out of the water. He must have been shipwrecked.'

'Let's go,' she said without hesitation. 'We'll take my car.' She grabbed her medical bag and led him outside. 'We should stop and tell the priest on our way. He'll probably want to send out the lifeboat.'

'We might need him anyway. Yer man doesn't look good.'

It was eight o'clock when they drew up outside the priest's house. The rain was back again, and the few stunted trees in the unkempt front garden stirred uneasily in a cold breeze. They knocked at the front door and a housekeeper ushered them inside. 'Father Carroll is relaxing,' she protested. 'He's had a busy day.'

Agnes pushed past her. 'There's been an accident,' she

snapped. 'We have to see him.'

The housekeeper sniffed and stood aside. 'He's in the lounge.' Sullenly, she contemplated the trail of wet footprints on the polished floor as Dermot followed the nurse through the hall.

Father Carroll stood in his sitting room, savouring a pre-dinner whiskey and warming himself in front of a fire that roared at the chimney. Steam rose from his damp clothes in an opaque cloud. He had obviously just come in, and he eyed them warily as he reached for a handkerchief. He didn't speak, but dabbed at his beak-like nose, which dominated his face and seemed to be afflicted by an unremitting drip. Dermot stifled an urge to laugh. The priest's affliction was a source of amusement to the islanders and most of the children who attended the school were adept at mimicking his actions.

'A man has been taken from the sea, Father,' Agnes explained in her clipped tones.

Dermot coughed and butted in. 'Me and my brother pulled him out near Eeragh this evening. He was clinging to a piece of wreckage. We took him to the Quinns over in Kilmurvey. By the state of him, he could be dead already.'

Father Carroll put down his half-finished whiskey. 'I'll have the lifeboat put out first. If there are other survivors, that's my priority. I'll join you in Kilmurvey as soon as I can.'

Agnes Doyle drove to Kilmurvey as fast as she dared. Dermot shivered beside her, his wet clothes steaming the car windows. She wrenched to a halt outside the Quinns' cottage, ran in without knocking, and made straight for the bedroom behind Annie. Annie and Kieran left her to her patient and rejoined the men in the kitchen. 'He hasn't moved since you left, Dermot, but he's alive,' Kieran said. I think you lads saved him.'

Annie nodded. 'You saved him all right, I'm sure of that. Dermot, you're soaked through. There's a pile of clothes in the bathroom. Go and change while I get you something to eat.'

Dermot emerged from the bathroom looking like a rag doll in oversized clothing, and immediately tucked into the food at the kitchen table as his brother Colm nodded off in a chair by the kitchen range. As he finished his meal, a distant explosion from the direction of Kilronan heralded the firing of maroons summoning the lifeboat crew.

Agnes Doyle returned to the kitchen and removed her wire-rimmed spectacles. She washed her hands in the kitchen sink while they all waited for her to speak. She turned towards them. 'He needs sleep and rest more than anything else, but I think he is going to survive. The important thing is to continue keeping him warm. He probably won't come to until the morning. If he's up to it, I'll arrange to move him to the Galway hospital then.'

Colm got up from his seat near the fire, relieved but exhausted. He knew that he would only fall asleep again if he remained any longer. 'That's grand news, Agnes. We'll be off home ourselves. Annie, thanks for the grub. I'll bring over the clothes in the morning.'

'Don't worry about it, anytime will do'. Annie gave him a warm smile and got up from the table to see them out. Kieran accompanied her, opening the door. 'You did well today, lads,' he said. 'I might drop down to the village for a pint later and see what's happening with the lifeboat.' He dropped the door latch after them.

Agnes Doyle re-packed her bag and prepared to leave as Annie peeked into the bedroom. 'I'll sit up and keep an eye on him tonight, Agnes. Just in case he does wake and need anything.'

'Get some sleep, Annie. He'll be fine. Besides, he couldn't have landed in a better house.'

As the nurse backed her car out of the yard, Father Carroll clumped into the kitchen, blowing his nose loudly into his handkerchief as he stooped under the low doorway. 'Where's the patient?'

Kieran nodded. 'This way, Father. He's in our bedroom. Thanks be to God, I don't think he'll need your services.' The priest followed him and stood quietly for several minutes looking down on Prendergast before returning on tiptoe to the kitchen.

'He looks fine at the moment.' The priest blew his nose again. 'As long as I'm here we might as well say the rosary for him, and anyone else that might be out there where he came from.'

Annie felt mortified that she had not had sufficient warning to clean the house. She glanced to the pile of unwashed dishes and the frying pan swimming with congealed fat, hoping he would forgive her. Whatever the reason, a visit from the priest was noteworthy, and one to feel proud about. She nudged her husband. 'We'd like that, Father. God's help is needed right now.'

Kieran sighed and looked at the clock on the wall as he knelt with them on the hard stone floor and fell to studying the droplet already forming on Father Carroll's nose. He wondered if there might still be time to go down to the village for a few pints when the praying was over.

Four

The maroon rocketed into the evening sky over the harbour in Kilronan and shattered the silence that had fallen over the yachts lying to anchor. It had been a long tough race, and cold out to the west of the islands. Most crews, after having a hot meal on board, were sleeping. Only the fittest could hope to partake in the evening's festivities in the pubs ashore.

Bill McGuire, skipper of the yacht *Lone Star*, stuck his head through the forehatch after the rocket exploded overhead. A muffled voice reached him from one of the bunks down below. 'What's going on up there, skipper?'

'Buggered if I know. They're getting the lifeboat ready. The crew is going out to her now.' McGuire slid back inside and slammed the hatch shut .

Willy Fahy, one of his crew, was already out of his bunk and pulling on his trousers. 'Maybe we should go ashore and find out. Are all our lads in?'

McGuire reached for his own clothes. 'It's pissing rain outside, but as far as I can see all the boats are in except for *Larinita*. Rouse out the lads. I'll pump up the dinghy.'

On deck, McGuire fed air into the inflatable with a foot pump and watched the lifeboat preparing for sea. He could see orange clad figures readying themselves for what might be a long and tedious search that could keep them at sea all night. Down below he could hear his own crew tumbling out of their bunks. They were boisterous as they woke, confident that their boat had safely won the race. He had a strange feeling that their elation was not to last for long as the lifeboat powered away from the harbour, the thrum of her engine quickly receding.

An hour later, McGuire sat in the American Bar, contemplating a half-drunk pint of flat and tasteless Guinness. Through a window that overlooked the harbour he could see a series of rubber dinghies making their way ashore from the anchorage. 'It doesn't look good, Willy,' he muttered. '*Larinita* is still out there.'

Willy Fahy sipped his hot whiskey, hoping the spirit would dispel the chill in the room. 'There's time enough yet,' he said. 'She's the slowest boat in the fleet, and the beat up from the south will delay her even more. Take no heed of the rumours.'

In twos and threes other crews sloshed into the pub. McGuire listened to their hilarity draining away as the rumours spread from one to another. He couldn't stand the inactivity. 'I'm going to walk out to Kilmurvey to take a look at this guy they say has been picked up.'

Willie finished his drink. 'I'll come with you. The walk will do me good.'

The two men laboured up the hill through the outskirts of the village, not speaking until they crested the top. From there they could look down over the steely expanse of the North Sound. The sea looked featureless and the far shore of Connemara on the mainland remained hidden. Directly beneath them close in to the shore, the tiny speck of the lifeboat ploughed westwards, an occasional flash of white spray breaking over her decks. They stood for a while, watching the lifeboat as they regained their breath.

Fahy stuffed a piece of chewing gum into his mouth. 'You know, Bill, I hate to say it, but it could well be the *Larinita*. They might easily have gone up on the Eeragh rocks.'

'Jim Prendergast is far too experienced for that, Willy. You know as well as I do that he's not a risk taker. Not with his wife and kid on board. If he was in any doubt, he would stay well out before he rounded the Eeragh. It's more likely that he retired from the race. Too bad he couldn't let us know.'

'It's a pity he didn't fit a radio this year like he said he was going to,' Willy replied. The two men continued on down the road, oblivious to the necklace of latticed stone walls that all around them divided the tiny fields. Under normal circumstances they appreciated the island's beauty, but today the vista was sombre and uninviting. It's a wonder that people can exist here at all, McGuire thought.

Halfway down the hill into Kilmurvey a car approached from the opposite direction, its engine labouring on the incline. The car stopped and the priest leaned from the driver's window. 'Are you on your way out to the Quinns, by any chance?'

Bill McGuire shook his head and shrugged. 'We're from one of the yachts below in the harbour. We heard that someone has been picked up in the Sound. Do you know which house it is?'

'Carry on straight down. Quinn's is the first cottage on the left after you come to the strand. Tell me; is he someone you know?'

'He could be, although I hope not,' Fahy replied. 'One of the yachts that raced out from Galway is overdue.'

The priest frowned and wiped his nose on the back of his hand. 'The men who picked him up thought he might be a yachtsman. Something about his clothes, they said. The island nurse has seen him and he is being well looked after. I'm sorry but I can't give you a lift. I have to get back to the phone.' He put the car into gear. 'You might contact me later when you get back to the village?'

McGuire nodded. 'Certainly. By the way, was there anyone with him?'

'No, no. He was on his own.' The priest sniffled loudly and drove off. With an air of increasing depression Fahy and McGuire trudged on. A few more minutes brought them to the house.

Kieran Quinn opened the door at their knock. He wore a shabby fawn raincoat with a weathered felt hat, as if he was just about to go out. McGuire looked at him expectantly. 'Mr. Quinn?'

'Yes?'

'I'm Bill Mc Guire and this is a friend of mine, Willy Fahy. We've come out from Kilronan to see the man that was rescued.'

'Do you know him?'

'That's what we've come to find out.'

Annie Quinn appeared in the doorway beside her husband, her face anxious. 'Do come in,' she said. She led them into the bedroom. 'Oh my God.' Fahy exhaled a deep breath. 'It's Prendergast.'

Bill McGuire's hand shook as he rubbed his eyes. 'We know him very well, he's from Galway. His wife and daughter were also on the boat with him.'

'Dear God,' exclaimed Annie. 'This must be a terrible shock for you. Come into the kitchen and sit down. I'll make you a cup of tea.'

They moved out into the other room. Kieran took off his raincoat and hat and hung them on a nail on the back of the front door. He looked out the window and wiped the condensation from the glass with the side of his hand. 'If that poor man's wife and child are out there, I hope they're found before much longer.'

Bill McGuire didn't speak until Annie finished pouring the tea. 'You know, I can't find it in me to believe that he put the boat ashore. I think it's more likely that he fell overboard. Jane and Susan are probably safe aboard the boat and searching for him right now.'

Willy brightened. 'You know, that's just what I was thinking myself. If that's the case, the lifeboat will definitely find them.'

Kieran Quinn cleared his throat. 'The Conneely boy told the priest that there was wreckage. I'm sorry,' he added. 'I don't mean to dampen your hopes.'

'That puts a different light on it,' McGuire agreed.

'How old is his daughter?' Annie asked softly.

'Seven or eight, I'm not sure exactly,' replied Fahy.

'Dear God!' Annie Quinn made the sign of the cross.

Mc Guire rose, followed by Fahy. 'We should be getting back to the harbour. Maybe we can be of more use there. Thank you for the tea, Mrs. Quinn.'

Kieran put on his hat and coat for the second time that evening. 'I'll come with you to the village,' he said. 'I have to pick up my motorbike, anyway. Give me a minute while I get a can of petrol from the shed.'

Bill McGuire visited the bedroom again before they left. Prendergast lay perfectly still with his mouth slightly open. A silver tipped stubble of beard rimmed his sunken cheeks and his breathing was ragged and fretful. Suddenly, he started thrashing around under the bedclothes, mumbling incoherently. McGuire bent closer, trying to make some sense of the low babble of sound coming from Prendergast's cracked lips.

'Jim, can you hear me? It's Bill McGuire. You're all right, old son, you're okay.'

Prendergast's eyelids fluttered, then opened wide. His speech was weak and faltering. 'Where's Jane and Susan? Are they all right?'

McGuire shuddered. 'It's okay, Jim, take your time. The lifeboat's gone out for them, they'll be all right. Can you tell me what happened?'

Prendergast's face contorted. 'The bastards sank us.' Bathed in perspiration, he mouthed something and tried to sit up. Then he fell back into the pillows exhausted and closed his eyes as though he wanted to block out whatever vision he saw.

Annie had come into the room on hearing the sound of voices, and McGuire turned to face her. 'He came round for a second or two, but he seems to be raving.'

Annie squeezed out a flannel cloth in a bowl of cold water standing on the dresser and dabbed at the perspiration on Prendergast's face. 'Don't worry, I'll look after him. The nurse might have given him something. She said he wouldn't be right 'til the morning. You go back to your friends. I'll sit by him.'

'You're very kind,' Bill said.

She glanced up at him, her eyes tearful. 'It's the least I can do. We lost a son of our own at sea.' McGuire nodded and left the room.

Fahy looked up from the kitchen table. 'He seemed to wake up for a minute,' McGuire told him. 'He's babbling about someone sinking the boat.'

Fahy stared at him incredulously. 'You're joking!'

McGuire shook his head. 'I'm sure that's what he said. There's no telling what he meant. It's beyond me.' He picked up his jacket. 'Come on. Let's get back to the village. Maybe there will be better news there.'

Although they set a good pace on the walk back, it was nearly ten o'clock when they reached the American Bar. The rain had stopped again and Kieran Quinn was waiting for them. The pub was relatively quiet for that time of the evening. The crews already knew the worst. One of their own crew rose to his feet. 'Jesus, it's terrible news, lads. The Guard has been in looking for you. He says he'll call back later. What're you having?'

'Get me a double Powers,' McGuire replied. 'And the same for this man here.' He motioned towards Kieran Quinn. 'He deserves it.'

Fahy and McGuire slumped into chairs. McGuire felt drained; even his stomach felt empty. He still couldn't believe it. Somewhere he heard a voice in the crowd. 'No news from the lifeboat yet, Bill. We're going to take our boat out and join in the search. Some of the fishing boats have already left.' He nodded.

About half an hour later the priest and a uniformed Guard entered through the back door. Father Carroll looked ominous in his black clothes. 'The rescue helicopter from Shannon will be here before first light,' he said. 'It is delayed by another mission.' He blew his nose and accepted a drink someone pushed in front of him.

The policeman declined a drink. Instead, he produced a notebook and pencil from his tunic pocket and took off his cap. 'Who wants to start? I'll need some details.'

McGuire could see that the Guard was ill at ease. Obviously he was not used to having much more to occupy his time than clearing out the pubs at closing time, or breaking up the odd brawl outside. 'I will,' he said.

'Good. Name and address?'

'Bill McGuire, The Pines, Moycullen.'

'Can you tell me what happened, Mr. McGuire?'

'Not really.'

'Why is that, Sir?'

'Because I know bugger all,' snapped McGuire. 'All I can tell you is that a yacht called *Larinita* left Galway with us last night and she hasn't turned up yet. The owner is Jim Prendergast and he was picked up from the sea near the Eeragh lighthouse this evening. He is presently recovering with the Quinns in Kilmurvey. His wife and daughter were on the boat with him.'

'I'm aware of that, Mr. McGuire. I have just returned from Kilmurvey. I am more interested in what he said to you. I understand you spoke briefly with him earlier.'

'Well, yes, that's true, but what he said didn't make sense.'

'Let me be the judge of that, Sir,' the Guard replied.

McGuire felt annoyed. 'What he said was "The bastards sunk us," but he was almost incoherent and blacked out before he could tell me more.'

' What do you think that meant, exactly?'

'How the hell should I know!' He took a deep breath. 'I'm sorry, I didn't mean to lose my temper. Maybe he was in a collision.'

'With another yacht?'

'No. We would know that. Maybe a ship, or perhaps a big trawler.'

'Did anyone see a ship last night?'

'Not that I'm aware. We certainly saw nothing, but the visibility last night was terrible.'

The Guard stuffed his notebook into his tunic pocket. 'Those are all the questions I have for now, Sir. I may want to see you in the morning before you leave the island. I'm going to phone Galway now and fax my report. This is a sad enough business and no mistake, this thing about the yacht being run down worries me.'

Willy Fahy was in bad humour by the time the Guard left. 'Christ, you'd think that bastard suspects we sank the bloody boat!'

'You'll have to forgive him,' Father Carroll admonished. 'Nothing much happens out here, you know. Perhaps a little mild sinning now and again, but no crime to speak of and few accidents.' McGuire grunted and ordered another round of drinks as Kieran Quinn joined them, his honest face fired by whiskey and his briar pipe belching smoke and ash. By now the drink was introducing its own morbid cloud, dulling their senses. The promise of morning hangovers already loomed.

Concerned that the Guard might come back, the publican called time at exactly on half past eleven. Outside, the road leading down to the Old Pier remained deserted except for a group of teenagers congregating outside a chip shop. Even they seemed subdued.

McGuire relieved himself onto a pile of fishing nets before joining the others in the rubber dinghy, and they motored the short distance out to the *Lone Star*. As they came alongside, the yacht rolled in a slight swell formed in the bay by a south westerly wind. An insistent tick-tacking sound from the mast let them know that a halyard was loose and would need tying off before they turned in to their bunks. They secured the dinghy and one of the crew went forward to do the job. The others went below to prepare for sleep.

Bill McGuire remained alone in the cockpit smoking and watching several sets of navigation lights rounding the Killeaney buoy out near the flash from the lighthouse on Straw Island. Soon afterwards three yachts came in to anchor, and several small fishing boats rafted up at the pier. His hail across the water elicited no real news. They had come in for the night having found nothing. The lifeboat remained out in the sound and would continue searching until daylight.

Finally he went below. Flopping out in the quarter berth he was soon asleep, leaving a half-finished glass of brandy on the saloon table.

One by one the lights went out on the anchored yachts and in the houses lining the shore all the way to Killeaney. Just a few dim yellow lights on the pier cast a glow across the harbour. Kilronan had closed down for the night.

Five

Most of the crew were sleeping as Second Officer Manoli Vlassos took over the watch at midnight for the next four hours. It was a clear night. Already one hundred miles south of Roundstone, the *Georgios* had settled into her sea routine.

Manoli studied the chart. They had recently passed the Skellig Rocks off the Kerry coast without sighting them. Apart from a radar contact showing what appeared to be a fleet of fishing vessels twenty miles further west, they had the ocean to themselves. It promised to be a routine night watch. There would be time to think.

Manoli had seen nothing of Foster since he had gone to his cabin that morning. Earlier he had spoken to the officer's steward who told him that he had taken a tray of fried fish and rice to Foster's cabin soon after the evening meal. The steward said that he had found Foster lying on his bunk staring vacantly into space. He left the tray on the writing desk and backed out of the cabin. The Irishman ignored him and they did not speak.

Manoli felt fairly sure that most of the crew were unaware of Foster's presence on the ship. Of one thing he felt certain; Arkides had not done this without a substantial payment. He began to make his plans to ensure that he would get a share in the proceeds, too.

Gupta Bose spun the wheel and watched the digital readout of the gyrocompass repeater over his head as he kept the ship on course. He had spent most of the day in the crew's quarters, asleep in the twin berth cabin he shared with a Chinese seaman named Yun See. They hardly knew each other, although they had shared the same cramped cabin for almost eight months. Yun See spoke little English and no Hindi. What little conversation they managed was in the pigeon idiom of the Far East. That made it easier for Gupta to keep the promise he had made to himself after the collision: to say nothing. He suspected that the Chinaman did not know what had happened. As the day went on, he found no one else of the crew of twenty who knew anything, either. He felt pleased. The fewer who knew, the better.

Foster paced the worn brown carpet in the pilot's cabin. He alternated between irrational blind fury, seasickness, and cold planning. He had considered using Arkides as a hostage, but he had discarded the thought, at least for the moment. He knew nothing about the workings of a ship. For now, anyway, he was in no position to change anything. To his surprise and satisfaction, his cabin door remained unlocked. Obviously Arkides did not see him as a threat as long as the ship was at sea, leaving him free to move about at will.

He picked at his evening meal. After the steward removed his tray, he pulled out the bottom drawer from a chest fitted in the cabin and secreted a small pistol and silencer in the space between the bottom of the drawer and the floor. If someone searched the cabin, it would be better if they thought he was unarmed. He returned to his bunk as he started to feel seasick again.

When the watch changed at midnight Foster still lay fully dressed on the bunk, staring at the faded paint on the steel deckhead and listening to the unaccustomed sounds of the ship. The cabin was uncomfortably warm and he had been unable to open the single brass porthole, the lugs of which were totally seized up with verdigris. He finally dozed off.

For his part, Captain Arkides became more confident as day became night. Each sea mile that passed under the keel lessened the chance of being caught off his planned route from Rotterdam to the Straits of Gibraltar. Later he would make the necessary changes to the ship's log to cover the time spent on the Irish coast. A relatively simple matter, he thought. A contrived engine breakdown somewhere down off the Portuguese coast would be a sufficient excuse for the loss in time. If the maritime officials should ever check, this would not raise any eyebrows. The *Georgios* was an old ship built in Burntisland in 1950 and long past her prime. Her owner was reluctant to spend more than absolutely necessary to keep her operational. Engine break-downs were by now routine occurrences.

Arkides' only worry at the moment was the two cases of ammunition that remained on board. He could not risk carrying the crates into Ceuta. He would have to jettison them, and the sooner the better.

Having the Irishman on board was another problem. He toyed with the idea that maybe Foster should accompany the crates over the side, but his instincts warned him that the people Foster worked with were far too dangerous for him to get away with that. He would just have to smuggle his unwanted passenger into Ceuta, and devise a way to do so without attracting the attention of the Spanish Moroccan authorities.

For the moment he could see no other course of action. He had been well paid for his services as soon as Foster got aboard that morning and a neat pile of American dollars now rested in the ship's safe in his cabin. He poured himself a large brandy and drank it while he waited until well after the midnight change of watch. Then he dressed and made his way to the bridge.

Arkides found Manoli sipping coffee in the chart room. The electric kettle was still steaming. He made himself a mug of coffee and followed the second officer out into the darkened wheel house. Gupta Bose did not even look up when they came in. Arkides placed his mug on the ledge of the wheel house windows, and lit a cigar. 'We need to get rid of the cargo in number two. Take him with you.' He gestured towards the helmsman.

Manoli made no reply. He had expected it. He adjusted the controls and switched on the auto pilot. Then he beckoned to Gupta Bose to follow him.

As soon as he saw that they had reached the main deck, Arkides went to a switch panel in the corner of the wheel house and switched on the cargo lights, floodlighting the forward deck. He watched from the wheel house windows, ringing for half speed on the engine room telegraph as they started opening up the hatch. An answering tinkle on the telegraph bell was followed by a change in the engine note as the ship started to slow.

Grunting with effort, the second mate and Bose removed half a dozen hatch boards. Two of the cargo derricks still remained topped up. Manoli sent Bose down into the hold. He then released the cargo hook and put the electric winch into gear, guiding the hook and its steel cable into the open hold.

It only took a few minutes to hoist the two crates on deck. They were smaller than the ones that had contained the rifles. The markings on the boxes, distinct in the light from the cargo floodlights, indicated that they had been manufactured in the Czech Republic.

Foster awoke suddenly to the changing note of the ship's engine and realised that the ship was slowing down. Jumping from his bunk, he stepped into his battered brown brogues and pulled on a scruffy blue anorak before slipping out on deck. It took a minute or so for his eyes to become accustomed to the darkness. By the time he reached the wing of the bridge, Manoli and Gupta had the first of the ammunition cases balanced on the top of the bulwarks. With one mighty heave, they pitched it overboard and it disappeared almost without a splash beneath the waves. Foster rushed into the wheel house. 'What the hell are they doing?' he screamed. 'That's our ammunition!'

The captain ignored him and signalled from the window for the second case to go over the side. As soon as it was done he rang for *full ahead* on the telegraph. The engineer responded and the ship started to pick up speed again. Arkides then turned his attention to Foster. 'There is nothing else I can do. I'm not prepared to carry them any further. Certainly not into Ceuta, or into any other port for that matter.'

Foster wanted to kill him. His mind raced. There would be

time later, he thought. 'You'll pay for this.' The words were delivered with no emotion as Foster stalked off in the direction of his cabin.

Arkides felt cold. A trickle of perspiration ran down his back under his grubby singlet. The threat seemed to hang in the air, taunting him long after the man had gone.

Manoli and Gupta replaced the hatch boards, cleated down the heavy tarpaulin cover over the hold, and stowed the cargo der-ricks, after which they returned to the bridge. Gupta Bose resumed his trick on the wheel and closed his ears to the mum-bled conversation between Manoli and the captain. He let his mind wander once again to the shores of India, imagining his return there with a vividness that surprised him.

Arkides placed his hand on Manoli's shoulder in the darkness. 'Thank you, Vlassos,' he said. 'I will not forget your help.' Without waiting for a reply, the captain returned to his own cabin.

Manoli raised an eyebrow. He had never heard Arkides thank anyone for anything. He stared through the windows at the rise and fall of the ship's bow in the darkness. You're right, he thought. You won't. I've got you right where I want you. The captain had ground him down, constantly reminding him that he should be grateful that Arkides would hire an officer who had barely survived a court of enquiry into the stranding of his last ship. It was only recently that he had discovered Arkides was responsible for far worse. Now he, too, had blood on his hands and Arkides would pay for his silence.

Six

The Mercedes camper bumped up the narrow lane from the pier with Lisa Schmitt driving. It was getting dark but they made their way without lights, wanting to reach what passed for a main road without attracting attention.

They drove past the quarry where they had hidden the vehicle during their wait for the *Stella Maris.* Next they passed a small bungalow. A black and white collie launched himself from the gateway and followed them for the next quarter of a mile, barking furiously. Liam had to prevent McGinty from giving it both barrels of his shotgun through the rear door of the van,

'I sometimes wonder if there is anything between your two fucking ears!' he yelled. 'All we need is you shooting up the whole bloody island!'

McGinty reddened but said nothing. As far as he was concerned the whole mission was a dismal failure. He blamed Liam for that. You're the one who is going to carry the can, he thought with some satisfaction.

A product of Long Kesh and the blanket, brutality was McGinty's second nature. He had lost count of the number of times that he had killed, and it no longer mattered to him. If it had been up to him, he would have finished off the two fishermen back at the pier, he thought. Solutions came only from the bomb or the bullet.

Reaching a tarred surface they turned left. Knowing that soon there would be traffic, Liam reached over and switched on the lights. 'Lisa,' he said, 'If we're stopped by the cops, you do the talking. We're German tourists, and I don't speak English,

- 44 -

okay?' Liam swivelled in his seat and looked into the back. 'McGinty, keep your goddamned mouth shut! That Belfast accent is the last thing we need anyone to hear.'

Liam knew he would not relax until they were on the mainland proper and able to select their route at will. That mad bastard McGinty in the back was no help, he thought. He was like a ticking bomb, liable to go off at any minute. Lisa was different. She had surprised him with her coolness. Newly arrived from Germany, she was relatively untested. To be fair, she had not messed up once since she joined the unit. She was promising material and he knew that the link presently being forged with the German group was important to his leaders in the North. Such a connection could only help to further their activities on mainland Europe and facilitate long range strikes against British bases scattered through the NATO countries.

In eight years of active operations in the North and in England, Liam had never been caught. He was proud of that. He knew his anonymity was based on his ability to make sound, reasoned decisions. He knew also that the Army Council in Dublin and the GHQ Staff in the North valued and recognised his track record. That in itself was no mean achievement.

Lisa concentrated on her driving. It was a big vehicle for these narrow roads and complicated by its left hand drive. She didn't want to crash. She missed the autobahns where the powerful Mercedes engine could flourish, kilometres ticking away with every second. Used to meticulous German planning, she was amazed, and sometimes frightened, by the laxness of the Irish. She didn't dislike Liam, but he seemed to be almost soft in his approach. She was waiting to see him face a real crisis.

McGinty was another matter. She was beginning to develop a loathing for the man. His blackened teeth and fetid breath repulsed her. He was unstable, she thought. She was far more professional than either, if not superior to both, of them. She smiled smugly in the darkness.

Soon the road skirted a small landlocked lake glistening in the pallid light of a moon that peeped through the clouds. She noticed with distaste a cluster of skeletal abandoned cars strewn by the shore. It offended her sensibilities that the Irish could wantonly desecrate such beautiful countryside. It would never happen in Germany, she thought.

Soon she slowed the van and turned left at a crossroads marked with a sign to Tir na Fiha. A cluster of houses lined each side of the road and a car passed in the opposite direction. Ahead, a man on a bicycle hugged the ditch as they passed.

Liam sighed with relief as they crossed the bridge from Gorumna Island to Lettermore Island. The road became appreciably better as they sped through Lettermore village. Lisa squealed the brakes at the next bend and swerved as they brushed past a shaggy long horned cow. Beyond it, two companionable goats munched together on the roadside brambles. McGinty cursed in the back as he was thrown across the van, the snick of a safety catch coming off as he prepared the shotgun. 'Jesus, McGinty!' Liam was livid. 'Will you for Christ's sake put that gun away before you blow us all to kingdom come?'

Ahead on the left, the welcoming lights of a roadside pub beckoned. They hadn't eaten since morning. Liam glanced at his watch. They had plenty of time. 'Pull in there on your right,' he ordered.

Lisa brought the camper to a halt in a lay-by that was sheltered by a copse of trees opposite the pub. There were only two cars parked outside. 'Anyone hungry?' Liam asked. 'Make sure you lock the van. McGinty, leave that bloody shotgun behind you.'

At the pub's bar, two men were squatting on high stools, pints of Guinness in front of them, watching a television mounted on the wall opposite the entrance. They looked up and one of them leered at Lisa until Liam's return stare forced him to drop his eyes. Stubbing out his cigarette in an overflowing ashtray, the barman nodded. He was a big heavy man, his shirt stretched taut across a beer drinker's belly. He studied Lisa with interest as they selected a table in a corner by the window overlooking the road. 'Three pints of stout,' Liam ordered. 'And some sandwiches.'

The barman nodded again. 'So long as you don't mind waiting. I'll have to make 'em up. All I've got is ham.'

Lisa sipped her beer, shifting her chair to escape the pressure of McGinty's knee under the table. McGinty drained half his pint in one swallow and wiped the froth off his upper lip with the back of his hand. 'Christ, that's better, I needed that,' he wheezed.

'Don't get carried away, McGinty,' Liam said. 'This is not a piss up. We've a long way to go yet.'

The barman approached with the sandwiches and McGinty reached for one. 'Fuckin' stale bread!'

'Just eat the bloody stuff,' Liam shot back. 'There won't be time to stop again.' He was aware that the barman was studying them. 'Finish up,' Liam ordered. 'That bastard at the bar is showing too much interest.' He paid for the drinks and led them out of the pub.

Lisa started up the engine and backed carefully out into the road. Liam adjusted the back of his seat and said, 'Take it nice and easy, there's no rush. I'll give you a break in a couple of hours.' They could hear McGinty scuffling around in the back as he rolled out a sleeping bag on one of the bunks. A few minutes later they were across the final bridge and had left Lettermore Island behind them. Soon they reached Cashla. The distant lights of the fishing harbour in Rossaveal were visible across the water. Liam switched on the radio and began to hum to himself.

Shortly before dawn on Sunday, as a rescue helicopter began its search of the North Sound, the camper left the main road south of Donegal, taking to the minor roads leading into an area of lake-dotted countryside south of Lough Derg that was known as The Black Gap. The countryside had the appearance of a magical fairyland in the early dawn mist that lay on the nearby slopes.

Lisa had slept for a while in the passenger seat when Liam took over the driving after passing through Sligo. Now she was wide awake and she rolled down her window to sniff the morning air. In that brief moment, the smog-laden streets of industrial Germany seemed a million miles away.

McGinty stirred too, now that they were back on bumpy country roads. He poked his unshaven face through the curtain. They had made great time. He was glad to be back in the familiar surroundings of the border country.

The first rays of the sun were showing when Liam turned into a narrow boreen that led to a dilapidated farm house nestling a few hundred yards from the edge of a lake. Surrounded by trees, the house could not be seen from the road. A scattering of well-kept iron sheds clustered at the rear of the house. Behind them, a forest of fir trees stretched up the hillside until it reached the rocky escarpment of the mountain. The whole place seemed deserted until they turned into the yard where a rusted Ford Escort was parked to one side. Chickens scratched busily in the dust, and from the open door of a barn came the sound of cattle shuffling.

A man appeared in the doorway of the barn as they stopped in the yard. He was short and stocky and wore faded brown corduroys below a ragged tweed jacket. He smiled as he came towards them. 'Ah! Liam, I thought it might be you, but you're like the will 'o the wisp, I never know when to expect you!'

Liam introduced him. 'My brother John. Johnny, this is Lisa, and that ugly brute getting out of the back is McGinty. We'll be staying for a day or two.'

Johnny stared at Lisa and flushed before looking away. 'Come inside,' he said. 'You'll be wanting your breakfast.' Johnny showed them in and started clearing the debris of a half eaten meal from the kitchen table. Lisa judged him to be older than Liam. He was bald, and she thought she caught the smell of whiskey as he passed her. Then she noticed a cardboard box of empty bottles thrown in one corner beside a bucket that overflowed with potato peelings and other kitchen refuse.

Johnny picked up the bucket. He went to the door and threw the contents into the yard. 'For the hens,' he said.

Liam loosened his jacket, making no attempt to conceal the butt of the pistol in his shoulder holster, and flopped into a battered armchair near the big open fireplace that still held the embers of a turf fire. From a pile in the corner, he selected a few sods of turf and threw them into the embers.

McGinty took a seat as Johnny produced a bottle of Black Bush and some glasses from a cupboard over the sink and placed them on the table. 'You'll be wanting a drink. Get stuck into that while I throw on a few rashers for you.'

'You're a gentleman,' McGinty said, filling a glass. Lisa sagged in her chair and sipped at her drink, finding the whiskey smooth and welcome after the long night's drive. They devoured the rashers Johnny placed in front of them. By the time they finished, Johnny was on his third glass of whiskey.

Liam pushed away his plate. 'Thought you were going to lay off that stuff, Johnny.'

His brother's face clouded. 'Sure, you know how it is, Liam, what else have I got out here on me own? You're away all the time enjoying yourself and this farm isn't easy you know, not on your own.'

Liam softened. 'I suppose not, but don't forget one thing, drink loosens the tongue. Anyone been round here lately?'

'No, the Guards haven't been up here for over a year, and then it was only to give me a summons for having no tax on the car. In fact, they haven't really been nosing around since your lot killed Mountbatten years ago.'

Liam scowled. 'You know bloody well we had nothing to do with that. I never agreed with that job.'

'He was a member of the British establishment,' Lisa said haughtily. 'We liked it in Germany.'

'Too bloody right!' McGinty broke in. 'The fucker deserved it!'

'This is a waste of time,' Liam said. 'There's no point in us arguing about it now. Finish your drinks. I want those guns stored away. I'm going to have to go over this afternoon to make a report and we all need some sleep.'

'Ever the boss.' Johnny drained his glass. 'I suppose you'll be needing the tractor? I'll get it ready for you.' He went out through the door and they soon heard the cough of a tractor diesel starting up in the yard.

Liam got to his feet. 'Get it down you, McGinty, it's time for work. Lisa, you stay here. Give the place a clean up, if you feel like it.' He glanced at the sink with its pile of dirty dishes. 'It needs it.'

Liam went out and made a perfunctory sweep of the timbered hillside with a pair of binoculars. There was no sign of movement anywhere. Satisfied, he backed the camper into the barn, waiting until Johnny reversed the tractor inside. His brother switched off the engine and jumped down. 'Do you want to lend a hand?' Liam asked.

'No, I'll leave you to it. You know I don't agree with this shit. I've got work to do.' Johnny left the barn and stomped off across the yard.

McGinty helped Liam to transfer the weapon boxes from the camper into a trailer that they had hitched to the tractor, then followed on foot up a little used track into the forest above the house. Liam finally stopped the machine in a small clearing. There was a delicious smell of pine, and below them the lake sparkled as the sun surprised it. High above in a cloudless sky a hawk hovered for an instant before plummeting on its unsuspecting quarry.

'Nice place,' McGinty said.

'I didn't expect you to notice,' Liam answered. 'Grab a box.'

Slipping and sliding under the weight of the gun boxes on their shoulders, they struggled through dense undergrowth until they were well away from the clearing. 'There,' Liam said, pointing to a natural cavern in the hillside. They brushed away a carpet of pine needles to expose a concrete bunker fitted with a steel lid. Inside, the bunker was dry but musty, lit only by the daylight filtering in through the narrow opening.

McGinty gave a low whistle of approval. 'This is the best I've seen.'

'We've had to learn a lot,' Liam replied. 'With thermal imaging and multi-spectral photography, the Brits have got far too smart. They won't find this one.'

It took them an hour to carefully stow away the cargo of boxes. They refitted the lid and scuffed the deep bed of pine needles until there was no sign of disturbance, then made their way back down the hillside.

Lisa had transformed the kitchen while they were away. Liam laughed at his brother's discomfort. 'Maybe you should marry her, Johnny,' he joked. 'A woman around the house might keep you off the booze.' He regretted the remark immediately, realising it was callous. Johnny flushed. Grabbing the bottle of whiskey, he poured himself another drink.

'I'll have one as well,' said McGinty.

'Leave it,' snapped Liam. 'You slept all bloody night. I want you to store the camper away in the barn, and set a watch up on the hill while I get some sleep.' He turned and walked to the narrow stairs leading upstairs from the kitchen. 'Call me in a couple of hours if I'm not awake by then. I need to leave by two o'clock.'

'I want a bath,' said Lisa.

'There isn't one,' Johnny mumbled.

McGinty stopped in the doorway. 'You'll have to use the lake.' He laughed coarsely as he left.

'I have cows to milk.' Johnny followed him outside.

Four cows moved about restlessly in the barn. Johnny talked to them as he pulled up a stool, picked up a bucket, and prepared to start the morning milking. Perhaps one day he would get a milking machine, he mused. On the other hand, there was a comfort here close to the animals that he knew so well. Maybe a machine would take that away from him.

Sometimes he worried about Liam and the risks that he took. He didn't approve of the IRA, but he would never betray his brother. The German woman was a distraction he felt he could do without. Those tight leather trousers! He wasn't used to foreigners, especially women. When her shadow filled the doorway, he turned and blushed.

Lisa stepped across the warm straw. 'I've never seen a cow being milked before.'

He looked up at her in surprise. She was carrying a bundle of clothes and a towel. She had removed her leather jacket and her breasts were obvious beneath a white cotton blouse. He coloured and returned to his milking, watching the milk splash into the pail. 'Have you ever killed anyone?' he asked.

She hesitated. 'Yes. Why do you ask?' Her face clouded in a frown.

'I know what Liam does. I sympathise to some extent, but it's not for me, that's all.' He hesitated for a moment. 'Who did you kill?'

'Does it matter?'

'Of course it matters!' His strong hands squeezed the teats harder. The cow made a restless movement in the straw and for a moment stopped chewing. Lisa remained quiet for a moment. Her face was in shadow, her yellow hair backlit by the sunshine filtering through the open doorway. 'Just some Israelis,' she said. 'If you must know.'

'Jesus! Just some Israelis? You mean you don't care who you kill? You must think you're much better than the rest of us poor hoors.'

'How could you understand? That's why your people will never bring the British to their knees. You're not adventurous enough.'

'Don't you think we've had enough killing? Where has it got us?'

'Oh come on!' Lisa laughed disdainfully. 'Do you think the British really give a shit about a few Paddys blowing themselves up? Who cares! There's only one way to deal with bastards like the Brits. Or the Israelis, for that matter. Hit them hard, where it hurts. Your people have a lot to learn.'

Johnny moved on to the next cow. 'They are not my people, as you put it. I look after my brother, that's all.'

Lisa stepped back to the door. 'I'm going for a swim in the lake. Perhaps you'll have a different outlook when you see what we can accomplish.'

High on the hill, McGinty settled himself in the grass at the edge of the forest and took a swig from the bottle of whiskey he had

brought with him. His binoculars rested by his side and he cradled the shotgun in his arms. Far below, he could see Lisa crossing the farmyard, his eyes following her as she walked slowly
towards the lake shore. 'High and mighty Kraut bitch,' he muttered. Raising the shotgun to his shoulder he sighted down the
barrel as she disappeared into a copse of trees. 'Bang!' he said
quietly. 'Bang!' he said again. This time he laughed.

Lisa rested for a while in the heather, idly tossing pebbles into
the placid water. This might be a beautiful and peaceful place,
she thought, but it was not for her. She would go mad if she
were to stay here for long. She missed her German compatriots.
Even the language here was taxing. Although her English was
good, the rapid fire accents of the Irish made it difficult for her
to understand them sometimes. Were the Irish really under-
standable at all? she wondered.

Take Liam, she mused. He was wasting his time. If she was
him, she thought, she'd be out there capturing the headlines.
Liam was as weak as his brother, she decided. They had their
misguided loyalty in common.

She glanced around her. Everything was still. She undressed,
conscious of her body's odours, and stepped gingerly into the
water. She gave an involuntary yelp and cradled her breasts in
the freezing water. First, an energetic swim; then, standing in
the shallows, she soaped away the grime of the past few days.
She did not see the flash of sunlight reflected from the binoculars
up on the hill.

McGinty couldn't take his eyes off her. He sucked noisily on the
whiskey bottle and the liquid spilled down his unshaven chin. It
was a long time since he had seen a naked woman, even at a distance. Even longer since he had had one. The last time had
been on a trip to Amsterdam. He felt the surge of an erection
and drained the remainder of the whiskey.

Lisa dried herself roughly with a towel and dressed in clean jeans
and a yellow teeshirt. She lay down again in the warm heather

and stretched. The sun was warmer now. A single fleecy white cloud floated motionless overhead. The air was heavy with the sound of bees at work and she was tempted to sleep. Resisting it, she lay staring at the sky. It was afternoon when she finally moved, refreshed and good humoured. Collecting her discarded clothes, she walked slowly back to the house humming a German love song.

Liam had already left. There was no sign of his brother and both the Ford Escort and the farm tractor were gone. Earlier she had noticed a washing line hanging inside a hay barn beside the milking shed. She washed out her soiled clothing at the kitchen sink and carried them across the yard to the hay barn.

As she was hanging a black lace bra on the line, she heard a sound behind her. She whirled around, instantly alert.

'Very tasty. Do you always wear stuff like that?' McGinty leaned in the entrance, cradling his shotgun in the crook of his arm.

She looked at him coldly. 'I thought you were ordered to keep a watch up on the hill.'

'I came down to stretch my legs.'

Even from where she stood, Lisa could smell the drink and sensed acute danger. She could make out the bulge of his erection against his jeans. So that's what he wanted, she thought. She should have known.

'You're drunk, McGinty. Get out of my way.' She took a step towards him as he raised the twin barrels of the shotgun. She heard a click as he released the safety catch. She froze. Her right hand brushed the hard outline of the spring blade knife that she always carried in her pocket.

Suddenly, McGinty closed the distance. He swung his fist and caught her a glancing but murderous blow on the side of her face, and she fell reeling in the straw. Her vision blurred, she tried to get up and he hit her again. This time it was an open handed slap, but it almost took her head off. As she fell back, his fist bunched in her teeshirt and ripped it, spilling her breasts free.

'Now,' McGinty hissed, 'we're going to have a little fun. Get down on the fucking ground!' He motioned with the gun. 'Face down, bitch! And put your hands behind your back. I know what you need, you cunt.'

Lisa sank to her knees. Her mind was racing as she turned her head to face him.

'Drop your jeans!'

Her fingers plucked at the zipper and she pushed the denim down over her hips.

'Nice,' he said. 'Black suits you.' He jabbed the gun into the small of her back. 'All the way down, you bitch.'

Lisa stretched flat on the soft cushion of straw that lay on the barn floor, listening to him moving closer. Obediently, she crossed her hands on her back, right over left, her brain whirring like a calculator. There had to be a way out. He was so close now that his breath hung over her like a rancid cloud. She felt the cold pressure of the gun barrel as he ran the firearm up the length of her inner thighs, bringing it to rest between the cleft of her buttocks.

'You like guns,' he leered. 'Maybe after I'm done with you, you can have a piece of this one.'

His breathing was ragged as she felt the baling twine touch her wrists. 'No!' she whispered, half turning her head. 'You don't need that.' From the corner of her eye she saw his finger tighten on the trigger. Then he pulled away from her and rested on his knees. Slowly, she rolled onto her left hip, a half smile playing on her lips.

'I know you're fuckin' hot for it, you German bitch!'

He grasped one of her breasts in one hand, squeezing violently. She felt her panties being ripped away like tissue as he frantically tried to disengage himself from his trousers. She turned to face him and leaned back on her elbows.

'Why don't you let me do that?' Her voice was husky and she wet her lips with the tip of her tongue.

He stopped, unsure of himself. His eyes bulged as he let the shotgun slip from his fingers into the straw beside him.

'Just lie back, Liebchen. You're going to love it,' she breathed.

She moved over him, caressing his penis with one hand. She bobbed her head and he gasped, arching his back. He didn't even see the knife. He heard a click and felt a single searing pain. He sat up with a silent scream on his lips. His face contorted with fear as he looked down at the pool of blood welling from his crotch, staining the half discarded clothing.

'Open your mouth, you bastard.'

His eyes dilated with fear. 'You're fucking crazy!'

'Open your goddamn mouth.' She stabbed him in the shoulder and he roared in agony. 'You want sex? Have it with yourself, you son of a bitch!' She forced the bloody member into his open mouth and he gagged on it. He felt like his eyes were bursting from his head. His last conscious thought was of a red roaring torrent that thundered in his brain, as this time the knife slashed across his throat.

Lisa got to her feet and pulled up her jeans before backing away from him, her breath rasping painfully and her breasts heaving under the shreds of her shirt. She felt calm. No remorse showed on her face. One of his legs kicked feebly just before he died. She turned away and walked back to the house.

Seven

The thunderous noise of a Sikorsky helicopter ushered in the dawn on Sunday. Flying out of a crimson glow in the East, its rotors thudded in the still morning air as it swept low over Kilronan before rising steeply over the high ground, its blood red fuselage reflecting the sunrise.

Bill McGuire tumbled out of his bunk on the *Lone Star*, cursing as his bare feet struck the damp coldness of the cabin and the roar of powerful turbines shattered the calm. His head felt muzzy with sleep. Mouth parched, he drained the half glass of brandy left over from the night before in a single gulp before pulling on his clothes. He had slept badly, unable to get Prendergast's tragedy out of his mind.

He climbed on deck, stretching to ease the ache in his back. Sleeping on the boat always seemed to give him a backache. He cleaned his teeth, rinsing his mouth from a mug, and spat over the side. He could see the sandy bottom, and he contemplated a starfish twelve feet down, crawling on some mysterious errand. The wind had died away completely during the night and the sun, only half risen, was already warm. The day promised to be summer perfection.

McGuire roused out his crew. 'Willy, you get the breakfast started. Two of you take the dinghy and tell the others that we'll have a skippers' meeting on board here at nine o'clock. We'll cancel the race and motor back to Galway later when we know what is happening.' It was only fitting, he thought.

He watched the dinghy puttering around the anchored yachts as he shaved. He rinsed out his razor in a bucket and dumped the soapy water overboard before slapping on some aftershave lotion. He began to feel better. He glanced through the hatch and lit a cigarette. Willy was slicing a black pudding, and bacon sizzled in the frying pan. Just for a second, the trip became pleasurable again.

Plummeting down over the pearl white sand of Kilmurvey beach, the helicopter made a wide loop out over the sea. Already in radio contact with the coxswain of the lifeboat, the pilot prepared to make a first searching sweep that would criss-cross the North Sound in an elongated north to south box. The morning light was perfect for his purpose and the sea below stayed flat calm. He could see the lifeboat and a scattering of fishing craft close inshore concentrating their search near the rocks at Eeragh.

The helicopter passed so low overhead that Kieran Quinn felt sure the thatch had blown off the roof. He staggered sleepily out into the yard in his bare feet and scratched at the crotch of his long johns as he watched the chopper become a red speck out to sea. Then he hurried back inside to dress.

Annie Quinn bolted upright in the armchair that she had moved into the bedroom as the aircraft roared over the roof. The noise terrified her. She had spent a restless night, waking each time Prendergast moved in his bed. Now she felt cramped and tired. She checked that he was still sleeping and wandered out to the kitchen to put on the kettle before returning to the bedroom.

Jim Prendergast awoke slowly. His eyes focused on the unfamiliar room. They rested for a moment on a wooden crucifix hanging on the white-washed wall at the foot of his bed, then travelled to the cracked china bowl and water pitcher on a painted wooden dresser. Finally, he saw a woman sitting in a beam of sunlight that peeked through a small window. Surprise and bewilderment etched his features. He tried to sit up, but became racked by a spasm of coughing.

Annie crossed the room to him quickly. 'Lie still,' she said. 'It will pass.' She stroked his forehead. 'My name is Annie Quinn and you are safe in my house in Kilmurvey. You were picked up last evening.' Slowly, everything flooded back into his memory. Susan's kiss was still warm on his cheek and he touched it with fleeting fingers. 'My wife ... my daughter ...'

'Whisht now, everything is going to be all right,' she said. 'The lifeboat is out looking for your family right now.' Annie could see the pain in his eyes. 'Lie still,' she said again. 'I'll get you some tea with honey in it, then we'll see if you are hungry enough to eat something.' She left the room before he had a chance to reply.

Prendergast could hear low voices in the next room but he couldn't make out what they were saying. Fifteen minutes later, as Jim sipped on a mug of strong tea laced with honey, the helicopter located the body of Jane Prendergast floating face upwards just a bare half mile from the rocks at Eeragh.

The radio crackled as the pilot directed the lifeboat to the spot and her crew retrieved the bundle from the sea. The coxswain looked away and blessed himself as they lowered the body gently below deck. The woman's head had been crushed, possibly by a falling mast. She had died before the sea had a chance to claim her.

He picked up his VHF microphone. 'Hotel Oscar this is the Galway lifeboat,' he called. 'It's a woman, I'm afraid she's dead, over.'

A voice from the helicopter issued from the speaker. 'Roger, we'll continue the search. Hotel Oscar out.'

Agnes Doyle arrived at the cottage shortly after nine o'clock. She found Prendergast sitting up in bed wolfing a bowl of sweet porridge, watched over by an anxious Annie Quinn. 'Well,' she said, 'this is a pleasant surprise!'

She waited until he finished, then popped a thermometer into his mouth and studied his ravaged face for a minute. Extracting the thermometer she held it up to the light and smiled. 'You're a tough rooster,' she said. 'But you're going to have to take things easy for a while. I'd like to get you into the hospital for a check up as soon as we can.'

Prendergast shook his head. 'I'm not leaving the island until I have news of my wife and child.'

The nurse frowned. 'I'm not sure that's a good idea. You've had quite a shock.'

Annie interrupted. 'You can stay here just as long as you like.'

Prendergast smiled at her. 'I appreciate your kindness, Mrs. Quinn. But I think I should at least get myself into Kilronan. If there's any news, that's where it will be.' He touched her hand. 'Please don't think I'm ungrateful.' Already he felt stronger.

'I'll drive you into Kilronan. We have to fly you to Galway from there anyway.' The nurse dropped her thermometer into her bag and closed it.

'I'll get your clothes,' Annie said, leaving the room to retrieve the items she had washed and dried. The nurse helped him to dress, steadying him as he stood for the first time. 'I'm going to get you on the three o'clock flight to Galway. It's hospital for you, my lad. Whether you like it or not.'

Jim grimaced as he tested his weight on feet that felt like two swollen blobs of lard. He was unaware of any feeling in his legs as he moved uncertainly towards the door and took his first faltering steps out into the warm sunshine in the yard. He felt groggy and weak but breathed deeply, taking in the fresh smell from the sea just across the road, a reminder of why he was here.

He found Kieran Quinn in the tiny field next to the cottage feeding his geese, watched over by a small grey donkey. 'Thank you for everything you've done for me, Mr. Quinn,' he said.

Kieran waved away his thanks. 'For nothing. Anyone would do the same.' He looked at Prendergast. 'Do you want to tell me what happened?'

Prendergast sighed. How could he forget? 'We were in a race,' he faltered. 'A race around the islands into Kilronan. The weather was miserable, and we had just decided to pull out and go into Kilronan when we met up with the ship.'

'What ship?'

'I don't know. I couldn't make out her name. It was all covered in rust. But she was big, painted white, and had a yellow funnel. That's all I know.' Jim gripped Kieran's arm. 'She ran us down deliberately, Mr Quinn. I'm sure of that.' His face contorted and he started to shake.

Tired and despondent, the life boatmen lacked the exhilaration of a successful rescue. The body, already zipped into a plastic body bag, now lay on a stretcher below decks. Apart from a few pieces of splintered wood planking and a yellow dan-buoy attached to a life buoy, the lifeboat men had nothing else to show for their night's effort.

The coxswain looked up to where the helicopter continued its search over the Sound. He could see the winch man leaning out of the open doorway. Wisps of fleecy white cirrus high in the atmosphere signified settled weather. Further out a number of fishing boats continued to patrol the still waters. The coxswain opened the throttles and moved off, hugging the rocks.

At midday the helicopter, short on fuel, called off the search. The silence on channel sixteen crackled with a final message. 'Galway lifeboat, this is Hotel Oscar breaking off to refuel in Carnmore. If you wish to transfer the body to Galway, I will land in Kilronan, over.'

The lifeboat coxswain acknowledged the message and spun his steering wheel, turning for home. The lifeboat's stern squatted lower in the water as her speed increased. Her crew settled themselves below, trying hard to avoid looking at the pathetic package in their midst as the Sikorsky swept away, flying low along the shore line in a last futile search.

Susan Prendergast had not been found.

A crowd gathered in morbid silence on the pier in Kilronan as the lifeboat returned. News of her grim cargo had already spread after the helicopter touched down on the airstrip in Killeaney. Gently, the stretcher was passed ashore and loaded into a Land Rover for the journey to the airstrip.

The yachts all remained at anchor having delayed their departure to Galway, and their crews now waited ashore in the American Bar for Prendergast to arrive from Kilmurvey. He came into the pub accompanied by Father Carroll. One by one, the crews lined up and pressed his hand, not having the words to express their feelings.

Prendergast had a drink with them in the bar but said little. A short while later he left in the priest's car to catch the scheduled Aer Aran flight to Galway.

It was stuffy and hot inside the Islander aircraft while they waited for take off. The only other passengers, a German tourist and his wife, quickly sensed that their fellow passenger was in some desolate world of his own. Jim stared from the window at the helicopter nearby. As he watched, its rotors started to turn and the whine of the turbines reached a crescendo. The pilot smiled at someone on the ground and gave the thumbs up signal from his cockpit window. Then the machine lifted into the air.

Prendergast tried not to think of what the chopper carried. He swallowed, fighting back his emotions. He hardly heard the engines of the Islander starting up, taking little notice as the plane bumped down the short runway, soared into an azure sky and banked over the harbour.

Far below, the lifeboat cut a swathe in the water as she headed back to sea. A line of yachts motored away from the anchorage. On the pier, a small group of fishermen turned white faces skywards. Prendergast slumped further into his seat as the engines settled to a monotonous drone. He closed his eyes not wanting to see the beauty of the Bay or the magnificence of the Burren hills in Clare. He had already seen too much.

Eight

Liam awoke just before two o'clock in the afternoon. His head throbbed. He lay for a few minutes longer, still half asleep, before he opened his eyes and looked at his watch. There was not much time.

Still, he was reluctant to move. The room had been his as a child and even now instilled in him a comfortable feeling of being home. Outside the open window, the leafy boughs of a nearby tree stirred themselves in a summer breeze while a blue-bottle, trapped behind the unwashed curtains, buzzed in rage. He allowed his mind to wander.

The tree had always offered an escape route for himself and his brother when they shared the room together as boys. Whenever his father returned home drunk from the village, that tree had been their passport to freedom. It gave them the exit that their mother never had.

He squirmed deeper under the bedclothes. His memories of the drudgery and poverty brought back pain. He remembered that there was never enough to go round. The drinking saw to that. Bit by bit the farm became more and more neglected, producing less and less, and their mother, God rest her, seemed to fade with each passing day. Even when his father was finally killed on the tractor, drunk as usual, there was no respite. Their mother simply withered away like a tired, dried up shrub, and followed him six months later.

Liam went wild for a while. He went to England and worked on the building sites of Birmingham and many other cities, none of which he liked. It was there that he first met fringe members of the IRA. Most of them were simple pub patriots who contented themselves with rebel songs and maudlin thoughts of Ireland. Now and again he would tire of the late night talks of violence that never went anywhere and gravitate homewards between jobs, but he always went back. His was a day to day existence, without goals or ambitions. He was young enough not to need any.

He'd never wanted to end up like Johnny. His older brother was more responsible and stayed to work the farm after it was left to him. Slowly Johnny had built it back up, although he'd never get rich on it; no one could. But now he was following in his father's footsteps, and drink was eroding the place again.

Liam was glad he'd avoided that particular plague. Instead, he'd joined the IRA right after Bloody Sunday. For the first time, his life took on some meaning. But the hope and excitement seemed a long time ago. Now he was feeling tired and his resolution had worn thin. Years of violence had scarred him and he felt drained by futility. They never seemed to get any further ahead. Working with the likes of McGinty just seemed to make matters worse, and there were too many McGintys. The senseless killing appalled him, and he despaired as an increasing number of innocent victims became enmeshed in the web of terror that he had helped to spin.

For a while the cease-fire had provided some respite, but it was crumbling now. The cry was again for weapons. He was back on the brink of a precipice. One push was all it would take.

This is getting me nowhere, he thought angrily, jumping out of bed. He dressed and shaved at the kitchen sink. He could see that the tractor had gone from the yard. There was no sign of Johnny. Probably gone to the village, he thought. Lisa was missing, too. Maybe she had gone for a walk.

Finished shaving, he crossed the room to the phone and dialled a number in Omagh. He drummed his fingers idly on the top of the sideboard as he listened to the ringing tone. The voice, when it came, was brusque. 'Yes?'

'It's Liam. I'll be there by five.'

'Good. I'll tell the others.' The phone at the other end went dead as the dial tone returned.

The keys of the Ford Escort were still on the dresser. He would take that rather than the camper. It would be less conspicuous crossing the border.

Liam crossed into Northern Ireland near Belleek where an Irish army checkpoint sprawled invisibly under its camouflage netting on one side of the road. He slowed the car, but a Guard waved him through without making him stop. He was glad. Whether they were Irish or British, the troops at the border posts always made him feel edgy even though he rarely carried a weapon. It paid to be careful. Others had not been so lucky.

On the road to Omagh, he switched on the radio. An RTE news bulletin was in progress but he only caught the announcer's last few words. There was one survivor from a yachting accident off the coast of Galway where a search was still in progress for two other missing crew members.

He reached Omagh just before five o'clock in the evening, but he didn't go directly to the meeting point. Instead, he drove around neighbouring streets, carefully checking before he approached an unassuming terraced council house on the outskirts of the town.

He parked the car some distance away and began to walk. He surveyed the house. Nothing looked out of place. He recognised a powerful Suzuki motorcycle that lay parked on its stand in the pocket-sized front garden. A slight movement of the net curtains drawn across an upstairs window told him that someone had already seen him.

Outside, a group of children played noisily with a football in the street. A mongrel dog growled as he stepped to the door, before dragging the bone it was gnawing out of his way. The door opened before he rang the bell and he went quickly inside. The hall had not changed. There was a pervasive smell of cooking and the faded rose-covered wallpaper retained its greasy sheen.

The woman who had opened the door closed and bolted it behind him before greeting him warmly. 'Liam, you're looking grand! The others are already here. Go through to the back kitchen.'

'You're looking fine yourself, Maggie,' he lied. If anything, she looked worse than the last time he saw her. He wondered how much longer she could hang on to her remaining teeth.

Liam had never bothered to find out her last name. The less you knew of anyone, the better in this game. All he knew was that her husband had been a supporter of the movement until he died from emphysema a few years back. Since his death, Maggie had continued to provide a meeting place or a safe house whenever one was required.

He forced a smile. 'I could do with a sandwich or something, Maggie. I haven't eaten since this morning.'

'Sure,' she said. 'But I have to keep watch upstairs for a bit. Go straight in to the others, and I'll get you something afterwards.'

The kitchen shared the neglect of the rest of the house. Shafts of weak sunlight penetrated a filthy window over the sink and froze a haze of tobacco smoke into stillness. Three men sat at the table. They were drinking tea and talking, but they stopped instantly when he entered the room and pulled back their chairs. The biggest of them grabbed Liam's hand in his beefy palm and squeezed, his florid features breaking into a broad smile. 'Welcome back, old stock!'

Liam genuinely liked Big Jim Hogan, considering him to be the best Brigade Commander in the North. Hogan always thought out his operations and took pains to ensure that his plans were meticulously executed. As far as humanly possible, he left nothing to chance and he rarely took risks. Those who worked for him in the Active Service Units remained devoted to him. Steeped in Nationalism, Hogan had devoted his entire life to the Republican cause. Now nearing sixty years of age, his fervour remained undiminished.

Liam wished the other two men in the room could be more like Hogan. The Intelligence Officer, Harry Trent, was a product of a Belfast slum, and he looked it. Small of stature, with pinched features that rarely saw the sun, he vainly tried to comb his mousy hair to cover his gnome-like skull. Mean and inquisitive, his mind constantly searched for ways to enhance his stature amongst the hierarchy of the movement. Liam knew little else about him except that he had spent a number of years in Long Kesh, where he'd studied Republicanism under Gerry Adams.

'Glad to have you back, Liam,' Trent said. He didn't offer his hand.

Liam nodded. Their dislike was mutual. He had heard rumours of Trent's involvement in the drugs scene since the cease-fire started. The IRA man who had warned him about Trent's activities had died a year ago at the hands of a punishment squad, but Liam had never been able to prove his suspicions that Harry had ordered the killing to silence him.

The second man was a relative newcomer. Originally from Dundalk, Seamus Dunmurray had all the right qualifications. He came from a staunchly Republican family with generations of IRA linkage. Dunmurray was swarthy with dark hair, almost Latin in appearance, and reputed to be a ladies' man. Self-sufficient and confident, he'd risen quickly in the ranks to become Brigade Quartermaster, responsible for weapons procurement.

Liam shook his hand. He seated himself at the table and accepted the mug of tea that Dunmurray pushed towards him. He took two spoons of sugar and stirred, trying to think of how best to convey what he had to tell them. They waited for him to speak.

'We ran into a bit of a problem down in Galway,' he began.

Jim Hogan leaned forward and clasped his big hands in front of his face. 'Tell us about it.'

Liam picked his words with care. He described the arms delivery, finally disclosing that both the ammunition and Foster had been left on board the ship.

'At least you have the guns,' Dunmurray said. 'Where are they now?'

'Back at the farm as planned.'

'That's good,' Hogan murmured.

'There's something else that worries me,' Liam said.

Harry Trent's eyes sparkled. 'What's that?'

'On the way over here,' he said. 'I picked up the tail-end of an RTE news broadcast. Apparently there was a yachting accident down in Galway the same night. The fishermen said nothing about a yacht, but I wonder if there might be a connection. There is one survivor. Call it gut feeling if you like, but it worries me.'

Seamus Dunmurray drew in his breath. 'I doubt if the yacht has got anything to do with it. Off the coast of Galway could mean anywhere. What's more important is that the guns are no bloody use without ammunition, even though we need them badly. We have to come up with a solution to source more ammo if we can't get the other stuff back.'

Jim Hogan waited, but Harry Trent said nothing. 'What do you think, Harry?'

Harry lit a small cigar, fighting for time. 'I don't feel comfortable that Liam has given us enough facts on what really went wrong down there. I'm surprised he's willing to trust the word of a pair of mercenary fishermen, even if they are ones that he brokered.' He focused on Liam. 'Don't you think you should do something to sort it out? After all, Foster is missing and he's irreplaceable, in my estimation. He set up the whole deal. We can't afford to lose him. Do you want everything he put together in Europe to go right down the bloody drain?'

Harry sat back in his chair and puffed at his cigar to keep it alight. He hadn't finished. 'We could be compromised by that survivor from the yacht,' he said. 'Providing, of course, that there is a connection. Liam needs to tie up these loose ends before we go any further.'

Liam contained his anger. It would serve no purpose to show his annoyance. 'The fishermen told me all they could. I'm sure of that. They didn't know why the ship took off, and they never mentioned a yacht being involved. How could I get Foster off – I was on the shore, for Christ's sake! Those two did what they could; they brought back the guns. Foster, as all of you know, can take care of himself. Look, this was a small shipment, a test if you like, and it worked. If it worked once, we can do it again.'

Hogan scratched his jaw. 'Foster will get himself out of this.

We'll hear from him when the ship drops him off. In the meantime, it's probably better that he's still on board. We paid hard cash for that cargo. Foster will work a way to get the ammunition back. It's ours by right. '

Seamus Dunmurray started to say something but the big man held up his hand. 'I'm not finished yet,' he said. 'Liam's right, you know. We've proved that the west coast is wide open for another drop, bigger next time. Foster will see to it, mark my words. Liam, I want you to work on it, too. We need Semtex next time. You may have to hold off until Foster surfaces because you'll need his contacts. And listen – next time I don't want any failures.'

Seamus leaned forward in his chair. 'One major shipment is what we need. Semtex is in short supply now, and for years we've been trying to get Stinger missiles. The Libyans have them, or can get them from the PLO. I don't give a shit what they cost. We should try for them again. Even if we could bring down one Brit chopper, it would be worth it.'

Harry Trent's face tightened. His narrowed eyes appeared flat and cold. He had forgotten the strength of Liam's friendship with Hogan. Careful, he thought. This was not the time to test it. 'Liam, why are you so sure those two fishermen are going to stay quiet? I'm saying this just in case there really is a connection with that yacht you were talking about. If they open their mouths, you can forget the Galway area altogether. I know how hard you've worked on this. It would be a shame to see all your hard work fucked up over a careless mistake. An error of judgment – you know?'

'Piss off, Harry. I wish I had never mentioned the fucking yacht. Our new contacts have been well paid to keep their traps shut. Jesus, do you think they're not scared? McGinty waving that fucking gun in their faces made sure of it. One peep out of them and another visit will take care of it.'

Trent scowled. 'That might be too late,' he replied. 'By the way, what about McGinty? And the German woman?'

'I was about to come to them,' said Liam. He directed his remarks to Hogan at the top of the table. 'Jim, the German seems to be a cool customer, and I reckon she will be useful when she understands us a bit better. To be honest, I'd go so far as to say I'd be happy to see her stay on in my unit, if that's what you have in mind for her. But McGinty is a problem. He's a trigger-happy bastard and you know I don't like that. I think he would have blown away the two fishermen given half a chance. '

Harry Trent pounced. 'That might have saved us a lot of trouble!'

Liam again stifled his anger. 'Harry, you still haven't got it, have you! It would have got us nowhere. There'd certainly be no chance of a second crack at Galway.' He glared at him. 'As I was saying before I was interrupted, I think McGinty is going over the top. He's drinking too much, for one thing. I want him out of my unit.'

Hogan said nothing. There was silence in the room except for the ticking of a clock by the cooker. Finally he said, 'I'll leave the German with you for the moment. She might be useful to you.' Hogan paused. For some reason he looked displeased, then he went on. 'I can move McGinty if that is what you really want, but I can't replace him. If you want to work as a two-man team, that's up to you. Just remember that we don't know too much about this German woman. She might become a handful.'

Liam had a strange feeling that Hogan was holding something back. He studied the big man's face for a moment, then said, 'That suits me fine. I'll take my chances with her, but transfer McGinty out. There's plenty for the likes of him in Belfast or Derry.' He paused. 'You've known me a long time, Jim. I don't like risk takers. That's why I've never done time.' He looked directly at Harry Trent, and saw the hatred reflected in his eyes.

Jim Hogan saw it too. He got to his feet. 'Take a few days off, Liam. I'll talk to you again when we hear from Foster.' With that he left the room.

Trent and Dunmurray left soon afterwards when Maggie came into the kitchen. 'I'll get you something now, Liam,' she said after the door closed behind them.

'Thanks Maggie.'

She made up cheese sandwiches and handed them to him. 'You look tired,' she said, as she sat down.

'I am, Maggie. I'm tired of a lot of things.'

Liam returned to the farm shortly before midnight. He found Lisa in the kitchen, ironing clothes. The kitchen sparkled. Liam commented on it, but she simply shrugged.

'Have you seen Johnny?' he asked.

'Not a sign of him all day.' She pressed down hard on the iron and a cloud of steam sizzled up towards a length of blonde hair falling out of place over her forehead.

'I suppose he's away on the piss again. Is McGinty is still up the mountain, or has he gone off to the village as well?'

Lisa unplugged the lead to the iron and wound the cord neatly around the handle before she answered him. 'He's dead,' she said. 'I killed him.'

Liam stared at her. Her face was a mask. 'Tell me about it,' he said. Another fuck up, he thought. And this time someone was dead, on his watch. Being rid of McGinty wasn't worth the trouble this would cause. Lisa did not mince her words. She described exactly what had taken place that afternoon while he was away. As she brushed back her hair, he noticed the livid bruise on her temple.

'Where is he now?' Liam asked.

'He's still out in the barn. I couldn't move him on my own.'

'Stay where you are.' He strode from the kitchen. As he crossed the yard to the barn, a light flashed at a distant bend in the road. Liam thought he heard the cough of a tractor engine on the still night air. That would be Johnny on his way home, full of drink, he thought.

Liam entered the barn and fumbled for the light switch. The body lay face up. Blood soaked the straw and hay on the floor. McGinty's eyes were wide open and staring; Christ, the mad bitch hadn't even closed his eyes. Liam went on one knee to close the staring eyes. It was then he saw what was in McGinty's mouth. He recoiled from the body in horror.

Someone moved in the doorway. It was Lisa. Liam leaned

forward. ' I thought I told you to stay in the house. Jesus! Did you have to cut his bloody cock off! There will be hell to pay for this. You know that, don't you?' He stood up. 'We're both on the line for this one! There will have to be an enquiry, you realise that?'

Lisa interrupted him. 'Look, that drunken bastard tried to rape me. He crossed the line, and I don't have to take that shit from anyone! Need another reason? He stank. Maybe if he'd taken a bath I wouldn't have had to do it!'

Liam heard the farm tractor swinging into the yard and went to the door. Barely in control of the machine, Johnny fell from the driver's seat. He lost his balance trying to reach for a bottle of whiskey that he had carried home in the dump bucket at the back of the tractor, and fell flat on his face in the yard.

'Christ, this is all I need!' Liam switched off the light in the barn. 'Get Johnny inside. I'll start cleaning up this mess. When you're finished come back and help me lift the body. I'll bury him down by the lake.'

Lisa nodded. With difficulty, she managed to get Johnny on his feet and steered him toward the kitchen. The stairs were an obstacle. She hesitated at the bottom step as he stumbled, losing her temper as his dead weight fell on her. 'Come on,' she urged as she pulled his arm over her shoulder and supported him on one hip. She steered him into his bedroom and left him on his bed fully dressed, already snoring in a way that would see him out until morning.

By the time she got back to the barn, Liam had reversed the tractor inside. 'You take his feet, I'll take his shoulders,' he ordered.

McGinty was heavy. With a heave they dropped his body into the dump bucket on the tractor. Lisa's face showed no emotion as she worked, and Liam found it difficult to understand her composure. 'Fork that straw out into the yard and burn it,' he snapped. He threw a shovel into the dump bucket. 'Then hose down the floor of the barn.' He climbed into the driving seat, started up the tractor and drove off towards the boreen leading to the lake.

The lake was black and strangely forbidding, and the water

made small gurgling noises as it lapped the shore. There was little moonlight, but with the aid of the tractor's headlights Liam hollowed out a shallow grave in the boggy soil. He reversed the tractor and backed up to dump the corpse from the bucket.

McGinty's body adopted a strangely foetal position in the grave, almost as though he were returning to the womb. There was something macabre about it. A chill ran down Liam's spine as he shovelled earth over McGinty and carefully replaced the top turf. When he'd finished, Liam stepped back a few paces and surveyed the site. He had chosen it well. Certainly no one would see it from the boreen or by walking along the lake shore. He climbed back in the tractor and returned to the farm.

Back in the kitchen, Liam poured himself a large glass of whiskey, wondering what to do next. Through the kitchen window he could see flames blazing in the yard as Lisa set light to the straw. He avoided looking at her when she came through the door.

'I'm going to bed,' she said.

He didn't answer. Sipping his drink, he waited for the creak of floorboards upstairs. Then he picked up the phone and dialled a number.

'Hogan.' The voice at the other end was indistinct.

'It's Liam. Something important has come up. I need to see you.'

'Is it urgent?'

'Yes.'

'Okay. Tomorrow morning at ten, in Pettigoe.'

The line went dead.

Johnny appeared as Liam ate breakfast. He looked awful. His face had a greenish yellow hue and his hands shook as he poured whiskey into a glass. Neither he nor Liam spoke. This was not the time to take him to task, Liam thought. He could see that Johnny was too shaky to concentrate or even understand anything he might say to him. Maybe there would be an opportunity later, if Johnny didn't die from the drink first. He left the house, again taking the Escort.

There was little traffic in Pettigoe except for a scattering of farm vehicles and a few disinterested people going about their morning business in the handful of run down shops that constituted the village. A mud spattered Garda patrol car passed him but the driver did not even glance in his direction. Liam watched it turn right and park outside a corrugated iron custom's post opposite the bridge that led over the border to Fermanagh. The morning was fine and dry, with just enough wind to stir the sprinkling of litter in the main square, in the centre of which stood a stone memorial to a 1922 freedom fighter, who defiantly raised his rifle to the sky.

Jim Hogan was in a hurry. He was irritable and wanted to get down to business without delay. Refusing to go for a drink, he insisted that they walk while they talked. He listened intently as Liam unfolded the story of McGinty's death. At the end of it he whistled through his teeth and said, 'People are going to think you've really made a balls of this one. Harry Trent will piss himself in delight. You know that, don't you?'

'Harry Trent can go fuck himself!'

'Don't underestimate him, Liam, he's an ambitious little shit. I've done my best for you, but I don't want this one going any further than it already has. God knows, that bastard McGinty probably got what he asked for, but we're going to have to put a lid on it.' Hogan paused for a moment. 'We're both dead meat if we don't.'

'What do you mean by that?'

Hogan shook his head. 'Things are changing, Liam, and I don't like it. We're not going to see a settlement; the peace negotiations are going to collapse. There are new people on our side who are only concerned with mayhem.'

'What people – who are they?'

'I can't say any more than that.'

'It's Foster, isn't it? And this fucking German thing!' Hogan made no reply.

They stopped briefly before crossing the street, avoiding a young cyclist. Liam felt deflated. 'What else can be done, Jim? The sod is dead and buried, disappeared, if you like.'

Hogan thrust his jaw out and rounded on him. 'You know damn well that's not good enough. It won't satisfy anyone, least of all Harry Trent. There are plenty around who think that McGinty has served us well, and they think enough of him to want to know the full story.' Hogan stopped and faced Liam. He looked him directly in the eyes. 'That's the way it is. I'll go out on the limb for you, but it's up to you to make sure that McGinty goes down on the records as killed on active service. That way, everyone will be happy and your arse and mine won't get kicked.'

Liam stayed silent for a minute. He couldn't believe what he was hearing. 'Are you suggesting I dig him up and get him killed a second time?'

Hogan gave a short laugh, but there was no humour in it. 'You've got it in one. Do it right, and McGinty will win a medal. Then the rest of us can then sleep easy in our beds. After you get it done, track down that ammunition. I'll let you know as soon as Foster turns up. You're going to need him.'

Hogan emphasised his next words. 'I don't care what it takes, Liam. You're on your own now. Sort out this bloody mess – you and the German. That's the best I can offer you.'

Hogan proffered his hand. His handclasp was still firm and warm, but he sounded detached. 'There are changes coming, Liam, that will affect us all.' He gestured at the memorial a few yards away. 'There's few honest ones like that about any longer. Just remember that. Those days are gone. None of us are safe. Don't prove me wrong in you, Liam, not after all this time.'

Hogan ducked into a narrow side entrance between a pair of stone buildings and climbed into a waiting car. A few seconds later it whisked him away towards the bridge leading over the river Termon.

Liam watched the car until it turned the corner in front of the customs post and disappeared from view. He felt dejected and alone. Turning away, he collided with a woman pushing an overloaded pram. He offered no apology. He felt like getting drunk; or better still, making a run for it, away from this whole stinking mess that constituted Ireland and his narrow world.

Nine

Prendergast surveyed his hospital room with undisguised frustration. He had no pyjamas and the green surgical gown that opened down the back infuriated him. Every time he got out of bed he was conscious of his backside sticking out. He felt like a damned fool.

They had lent him a dressing gown earlier, when they brought him to the mortuary. He didn't want to contemplate the identification procedure. The sight of Jane's face, pallid and distant in death, had hammered home the bitter realisation that this wasn't a dream. Even the knowledge that she had died instantly from her head injury was of no consolation. It only meant that Susan had suffered death alone.

He wanted a cigarette badly, and it irritated him that he had none. He had asked the nurse to get him some, but she just wagged her finger, pointing to the no smoking sign on the wall, and left him to suffer on.

At least he had a private room, he thought. That, at least, protected some of his dignity, but he felt tired of being prodded and poked. There was nothing wrong with him and he wanted to get out. He wanted to do something, anything to make something happen, although he didn't know what.

The last time he had been in hospital was when he met Jane. It was in Jeddah, after a shipboard accident. She had nursed him until the sea called him back. He remembered that they had talked a lot because their experiences were so similar. They met at a time when they had simultaneously reached a stage in life that led them to believe that marriage was for other people.

Each of them was resigned to living alone, and selfish enough to think that it contented them. Six months later they married quietly in a London registry office.

There would be no awakening from this nightmare, he realised. He thought of calling the nurse for one of those bright pink pills that she had given him earlier, after he'd told the woman who called from the undertaker's what kind of coffin he wanted for Jane. Oak, he'd said. The best they had.

It was all so matter-of-fact. It wasn't every day that you had to choose a coffin for your wife. He remembered the day that he put the ring on her finger. It was springtime and there was only a handful of guests. They had both spent too much time abroad to make many long-term friends and neither of them had family. Now they had each other, they'd agreed.

He lay back, wishing that this searing pain by some miracle would go away. Shortly, the nurse re-entered the room, carrying his clothes. 'You can get dressed now, Mr. Prendergast. The doctor has said it's okay to discharge you after lunch. A Detective Sergeant Iain McQuaid from the Mill Street Garda station is waiting to see you.' She lowered her voice. 'I think he's Special Branch.'

'Tell him to come in. I don't mind him watching me dress.'

The nurse hesitated. She seemed embarrassed by what she had to say next. 'The other nurses want you to know that you have our sympathy. We are used to dealing with bad news, but we're terribly sorry for you.'

'Thank you,' he said. He turned away, not wanting her to see his face. As he started to pull on his clothes, Iain McQuaid entered. Jim waved him to the visitor's chair near the window of his room.

The man did not look like his idea of a detective, especially one from the Special Branch. McQuaid looked more like a tax inspector or even a bank clerk. He was a short rotund man of middle age dressed in a rumpled suit. When he sat and crossed his legs, Jim noticed that he wore two odd socks and that his brown shoes were mud-stained with tiny cracks running through the leather. He was almost completely bald with a few long wisps of hair plastered across his domed skull.

'Everyone thinks it, including the bad guys. It comes in handy at times,' McQuaid said.

Prendergast looked confused. 'What?'

'That I don't look like a policeman.' McQuaid gave a slow easy smile. 'Don't let it worry you.'

Prendergast warmed to him. 'I'm sorry, I didn't mean to stare. What can I do for you?' He tucked in his shirt and sat on the edge of the bed.

McQuaid's smile faded. 'Firstly I'd like to offer you my condolences on your tragic loss. It was a frightful accident. You have my deepest sympathy.'

Instantly, Prendergast hardened. 'It was not an accident, Sergeant,' he said fiercely. 'It was plain wilful murder! What about my daughter? Have they found Susan yet?'

McQuaid looked uncomfortable. 'Not yet. The islanders are still keeping a look out, but the search has been officially called off.'

Prendergast found it difficult to get the words out. 'Somehow I don't think they ever will. She was harnessed to the boat when it happened.'

McQuaid nodded. 'Divers went down this morning, but they haven't yet found the wreck. The water is very deep and they say that there is thick kelp all around the area.'

Jim sighed and shook his head. 'There might not be much left of the yacht. She must have been severely damaged in the impact.'

'In that case, why wasn't there more wreckage?'

Prendergast frowned. 'You have a point there.'

The detective opened a small notebook. 'I understand your daughter was eight, is that correct?'

'Yes.'

'How old was your wife?'

'I don't see what that has to do with it, Sergeant, but she was forty-five.'

'I'm just setting the record straight. Perhaps you could start at the beginning and tell me as much as you can remember.'

- 78 -

Prendergast stretched out on top of the bed and listened to himself drone on as he recounted the event. He felt as though he was listening to a stranger voicing the same old jumbled thoughts that had been with him ever since he woke up on Inishmore on Sunday.

'You say you had no radio transmitter?'

'No.' Prendergast felt agony at his admission.

'Why was that, Sir?'

'Because ... oh, shit, because I hadn't fitted one yet. I was going to do it this season. Perhaps if I had ...' Prendergast shot him a look of despair.

McQuaid glanced at his watch and closed his notebook. 'It might not have made a difference, Mr Prendergast. If, as you say, the ship rammed you intentionally, you hardly had time to use a radio even if you had one. You're sure you can't remember seeing the ship's name or her port of registry?'

'No. The visibility was too bad.' Prendergast clenched his fists. 'When the ship got close enough I didn't even have time to take a good look at her. I had too much to do trying to get out of her way.' He shuddered. 'It was all over in a matter of seconds after that.'

'You're certain that the ship was painted white with a yellow funnel, though?'

'Yes, I'm sure. Earlier on, when she was further away, there was time to see that. She was white all right, but with plenty of rust stains. She hadn't seen much paint recently.'

'About the fishing boat – can you elaborate on that?'

Prendergast though for a moment. 'She was blue. That's all I remember. The ship was stopped in the water, but when she started to move the boat appeared. She must have been alongside.'

The detective stood up to leave. 'It's not much to go on, Mr. Prendergast. Our best hope is that the ship puts into an Irish port, but if she doesn't ...' He shrugged his shoulders.

'What about the blue fishing boat? She must have something to do with it as well. They weren't just having a morning chat, damn it! They must have been up to something illegal.'

'Like?'

'I don't know. That's your job, isn't it? Drugs? Guns? Maybe both, for all I know.'

'I'll admit that drugs crossed my mind. But guns? I doubt that very much. The cease-fire is holding. The IRA has no need for them now.'

'You really believe that?' Prendergast was scornful. 'Those bastards aren't just terrorists. They're criminals. They'll always have a use for guns. I want you to understand one thing, Sergeant. I loved my wife and daughter very dearly. I know that I can't bring them back, but if I can find any way to avenge them I will. I want the bastards who did this!'

'I can understand your feelings,' McQuaid said. 'We'll do our best, you can count on that. You must realise however, that there are probably hundreds of blue fishing boats around the coast. Without some other identification it's going to be difficult. I have your address and phone number. I'll be in touch if anything develops.'

Prendergast studied the detective's face intently. 'You're not going to find them, are you?'

'I didn't say that. The ship might be difficult. She could be out of our jurisdiction by now.'

'Jurisdiction!' Prendergast was livid. 'That's a convenient rock to crawl under! If I find them, jurisdiction won't be an issue!'

McQuaid frowned. 'I don't advise you to get involved. Leave it to us.' He took a step towards the door.

'Then find the bastards! By the way Sergeant ...'

'What?'

'Have you got any cigarettes?'

McQuaid pulled a squashed packet from his pocket and tossed them on the bed. 'Keep them,' he said. 'You look as if you could do with one.' The detective paused at the door. 'One last question, Mr. Prendergast.'

'What's that?'

'Did your wife have an insurance policy?'

'I believe she had a small one, just a few thousand pounds. I don't ...'

McQuaid smiled. 'Purely routine, Sir. I have to ask it.'

Prendergast listened to the door closing. McQuaid had done little to raise his optimism. He closed his eyes and Susan's face swam before him, her blue eyes appealing and full of love. He clenched his fists as tears came and trickled slowly down his cheeks. He didn't even have a body to bury alongside her mother. He had never felt so miserable and lost.

Ten

Liam returned to the farm in a brutal mood. He cursed McGinty and Lisa Schmitt, but more than that, he cursed himself. He should have seen it coming. Now he had to find a way out of it.

His meeting with Big Jim Hogan in Pettigoe left him in no doubt that he had little time in which to regain control. If not he would be lucky if he didn't join McGinty in a hole in the ground himself. The justice meted out by an IRA court martial would be swift and without compassion. Liam knew that. Such was the rivalry and internal feuding within the ranks of the terrorist group that even a man with the stature of Jim Hogan could not live without fear.

He found Lisa in the yard sitting in the armchair that she had dragged from the living room. She was reading a paper and enjoying the midday sunshine. She wore a white tee shirt and a pair of jeans that she had cut down to make into shorts. The tops of her thighs were already turning pink with sunburn.

'Cover up your legs,' he snapped, as he crossed the yard.

'You sound like one of your bloody priests,' she shot back. 'I think the whole damned lot of you are obsessed with sex in this country!'

'It's sunburn you need to worry about, not sex!' Liam went into the kitchen.

Lisa threw down her newspaper in disgust and followed him into the house. 'I made a cold lunch. There's some left and there's tea in the pot.'

Liam pulled up a chair to the table and started to eat the ham sandwiches she had left out. He hadn't realised how hungry he was.

Lisa sat down and watched him eat. 'What happened this morning?'

He poured a cup of tea. 'They want me to devise a better end for McGinty. They want him to be a bloody hero, and you're going to have to help me dig him up and make him into one. How do you like that?'

Lisa stared at him in disbelief. 'Do you people all want to be martyrs! This would never happen in Germany!'

'Well, thank God, this isn't Germany. It's Ireland, and its time you started to remember it. We'll do the job this evening. I'm going to shift him before dark.' He pushed his chair back. Picking up the telephone on the dresser, he dialled a number.

Liam had never liked using the phone for business, but on this occasion he felt that he had no other choice. He needed to get this thing settled without delay. He made at least three calls before he joined Lisa who had returned to the yard.

'Okay, it's all set,' he said. 'We've just got to get him over the border.'

Lisa handed him a newspaper. 'You had better read this,' she said. Her tone was serious.

Liam took the newspaper from her. His stomach began to sink as he scrutinised the front page of the morning edition.

YACHTING TRAGEDY OFF GALWAY COAST

Yachtsman Jim Prendergast, 48, is comfortable in Galway Regional hospital following his rescue on Saturday when his yacht sank after a collision with an unidentified ship. Tragically, his wife Jane, 45, and daughter Susan, aged 8, did not survive. The Galway lifeboat and the Shannon rescue helicopter were involved in the rescue. Gardai are continuing their enquiries.

Grim faced, Liam handed the paper back to her. 'Get packed. We'll leave for Galway first thing in the morning. This has to be sorted out.'

'Do you think our contacts had something to do with it?'

'I don't know.'

He looked around the yard and noticed that the tractor was missing. 'Where's that brother of mine?'

'Where do you think?'

His anger immediately returned. 'Shit! Take the car and go and get him. You'll probably find him in Murphy's pub down in the village. Either bring him back, or leave the car with him. We need that damned tractor.'

Reaching into his pocket, he handed her a bundle of money. 'If you bring him back, get him a couple of bottles. The less he knows about any of this the better.' He turned and strode off without another word. A few minutes later she could hear him talking on the phone again.

Lisa felt happy as she turned the car out of the yard and bumped down the lane. This is more like it, she thought. We're active again. Liam seemed to be regaining his grip, and it was not before time.

It was late afternoon before Lisa returned with the tractor and evening shadows were cloaking the hills. Liam was waiting impatiently for her. He could see that she was alone.

'Did you find him?'

Lisa switched off the engine and climbed down from the tractor. 'Yes,' she replied. 'He wouldn't come with me. I left him the car.'

'That's just as well. He won't be able to bother us.' He threw a shovel into the dump bucket. With Lisa balancing behind him, he drove off towards the lake.

Liam had chosen the burial site so well that at first he had difficulty finding it. He drew to a halt and carefully looked around. Nothing moved except for a heron wading in the shallows close to the shore. The bird eyed them haughtily before taking off in a slow and ungainly flight across the lake, its wings making low swishing noises over the water until it was lost from sight.

Working quickly, Liam shovelled away the loose covering of soil on the grave. 'Grab an arm,' he ordered.

Lisa helped him to drag McGinty's body from the shallow hole until they could lift it into the dump bucket. It was a distasteful task, and Liam marvelled that Lisa didn't complain. 'You're a cold bitch!' he grunted. He shovelled the earth back and levelled the site. Then he threw the shovel into the bucket and climbed into the cab.

On the way back, he heard the small herd of cows lowing in discontent in a nearby field. They needed milking. Liam cursed his brother and his damned whiskey . The farm was going down the same road that his father had driven it, and to make it worse, there was nothing he could do to stop the slow disintegration.

Reaching the yard, Liam uncoiled a hose and turned on a tap. He dowsed the corpse where it lay. Turning over the body he washed off the earth that clung to it underneath. It surprised him that there was little odour yet, but the corpse was already stiff. Lisa stood off to one side. After he finished, she helped him to load several bales of hay to hide the body.

'You might as well go to bed if you like,' Liam said. 'I won't be back for quite a while.'

She wanted to ask him what he intended to do with the body but he had already climbed back in the driver's seat and the noise of the engine starting up prevented her from saying anything. She watched the trailer disappear down the lane into the twilight and then went back into the house to start packing her things.

Liam drove the tractor off into the fields long before he reached the main road. He didn't bother with lights. To anyone watching, he was just a farmer transporting feed to his animals. He passed through several gateways, until, just before the fading light gave way to darkness, he crossed over the border on an unapproved lane, carefully skirting a rubble filled crater in the road that had been the British army's feeble attempt to restrict passage.

A mile further down the road, he pulled off into a small copse of trees. The moon had not yet risen, but he could see two cars parked and waiting in the darkness. The doors opened on one of them and two men got out. They wore camouflaged combat jackets and black balaclava helmets and one of them carried an ancient Sten gun slung over his shoulder. Neither of them spoke as they went to work. It took the efforts of all three of them to force the stiffened corpse into a semi-sitting position on the front passenger seat of one of the cars.

'I brought a sledge hammer in case we had to break his legs,' Liam said. 'I'm glad we didn't have to use it.'

The taller of the two, carrying the gun, opened the door of the second car and climbed inside. 'That's not a job I'd like to do every night of the week, Liam. You can leave it to us now. We'll take care of it.'

'Just get rid of him as soon as you can. I don't want to have to do it again either, and I don't have to remind you to forget all about it after it's done with.'

He watched the lights of the two cars until they turned a bend in the road, then he reloaded the hay, started up the tractor and drove back the way he had come.

Whistling quietly to himself, he turned into the farm yard shortly after midnight. The Ford Escort was jammed against one of the concrete gateposts, one of its wings crumpled and the windscreen cracked. A thin wisp of steam escaping from the bonnet indicated it had not been there for long.

Lisa came down the stairs as he reached the kitchen. She carried a bowl of water and a stained towel. There were bloodstains on her white teeshirt.

'What the hell has happened now?' he asked in amazement.

'Your brother has just arrived back.'

'I could see that out in the yard.' Liam made for the stairs.

'Don't trouble yourself,' she said. 'He's out cold. I think he might have broken his nose.'

Liam retraced his steps and sank wearily into a chair. It wasn't worth thinking about it anymore.

If either of them had been standing outside the house shortly after midnight, they might have heard the faint echo of an explosion from the surrounding hills, but they would have been too far away to see the flame lighting the night sky.

The car containing McGinty's body exploded at the roadside ten miles away just before a small British army foot patrol came upon it. The soldiers dived for the ditches on either side of the road as the bomb went off, blackened faces in the dew-damp grass, shakily clutching their weapons.

Sergeant Andy Phillips lay prone in a ditch full of muddy water for a full three minutes, his heart pounding wildly. He could feel the cold water seeping slowly into his boots. He raised his head. 'Anyone down?' he shouted. 'No Sarge!' came the answering shout from somewhere on the other side of the road. Thank Christ for that, he thought. Sod these fucking Paddies! Just two weeks more and they would be back on the Rhine. Personally, he couldn't wait for it to end. He didn't want to lose anyone at this stage, not with their tour of duty almost over.

One by one, they cautiously climbed out onto the roadside and approached the blazing wreck, stooping low and ready for an ambush. The grass was burning at one side of the road and threatening to set fire to the briars and gorse. Like ghosts they kept to the shadows away from the light, weapons at the ready.

It was clear that the job was the work of experts. What remained of the car was a blazing inferno. 'Thermite,' Phillips said. The heat was so intense they could not approach close enough to see inside, but they could see the grotesque silhouette of someone's head and shoulders blazing in the driver's seat. Whoever it was, there would be little left of him when the fire burnt itself out.

After a brief radio call to the RUC they scattered to the fields on either side, fanning out across the scrub land in a sweeping search of the surrounding countryside, each of them knowing they would find nothing.

Liam woke Lisa early, just before six o'clock. He was cheerful and felt rested after a night's sleep. It was only when Lisa reminded him of his brother, still upstairs in bed, that the worry returned and his face clouded in fury.

While Lisa finished loading the camper, Liam climbed the stairs to Johnny's bedroom. The room stank. He drew back the curtains and opened the window to let in some fresh air. It was bright outside, where a luminescent bank of mist rose near the lake and drifted in swirling patches towards the farm. He could see from the clouds that rain was not far away.

Standing motionless by the bedside he looked down on his brother who continued to sleep noisily. Although Lisa had cleaned up his face the night before, his pillow and bedclothes were stained with blood and vomit, and Johnny's ruddy face showed the purplish tinge of a massive bruise spreading from the swollen area around his nose.

Liam decided not to try and wake him. You poor bastard. What is going to become of you? he wondered.

Before he left the room he reached out and touched his brother's calloused hand He held it for a moment and muttered, 'God be with you, Johnny.' It was the nearest he had come to saying a prayer for a very long time. He left a tattered wad of money on the dressing table and closed the door quietly behind him.

Lisa was waiting for him outside in the camper with the engine running. He climbed in beside her and motioned for her to move off. Liam stared at the damaged car in the gateway as they drove past it. 'That's going to cost him a few bob,' he said.

Halfway down the boreen a light misty rain started. The windscreen wipers were sticking and started to squeak on the glass. Liam did not look back. He slumped low in his seat, and closed his eyes. Lisa glanced in the mirror once, then concentrated on the road. She felt glad to be leaving.

It was a considerable time before Liam spoke. 'I want to stop in Bundoran to make a phone call,' he said. Lisa nodded. He reached across and switched on the radio. The first news bulletin of the morning had just started. The newsreader went on to announce that the RUC were investigating a car bombing on a country road south of Strabane. The report confirmed that one person had been killed. The RUC believed that the explosion was accidental, and suspected that the car was being used to transport an explosive device that had detonated prematurely.

Liam switched off the radio. 'I've changed my mind,' he said. 'There's no need to stop in Bundoran after all.'

Eleven

At midday, Captain Arkides, who had rarely left the bridge since leaving the Irish coast, fixed the ship's position at a little less than two hundred miles north west of Cape Finistere. Favoured by weather that had remained mostly overcast for the past two days, fog and generally poor conditions continued to cover their tracks on the way south. As far as Arkides could judge, no other ships had seen them.

He studied the chart for a few minutes longer. Today would be perfect for his planned engine breakdown which would cover the time the ship had been off its route. He had already meticulously hidden the deception in the ship's log and felt confident that no investigation would ever uncover the truth. His only nagging worry was the Irishman who remained on board. The sooner Foster was off his hands the better.

Replacing a pair of dividers in their holder, he wrote out a message on a pad before making his way to the radio room. He remained there for fifteen minutes while he made a call to the ship's owners.

Manoli Vlassos was in the chart room when Arkides returned. 'Kalispera, Captain,' he said in greeting. His voice held little enthusiasm.

'Kalispera, Manoli!' Arkides beamed at him. He looked pleased with himself. 'We need to have a little chat, Vlassos. Come with me.'

Obediently, the second mate followed him into the wheel house. They were alone. Now that the ship had plenty of sea room she was running under automatic pilot and no one was at the wheel.

Buttoning up his jacket over his soiled vest, Arkides went over to the radar and spent some time staring intently at the screen. The searching pulses of energy returned no echoes out to the limits of its range. No other ships were within sixty miles of them. He joined Manoli at the forward facing windows.

'You might enter in the log, Vlassos, that we have just broken down.' Arkides extracted a cigar from his top pocket. 'It will take the engineers until morning to fix the problem. He winked as he puffed the cigar alight. 'You can say that it is a fuel pump failure.'

Manoli nodded. It was now or never, he told himself. 'I think we should discuss this matter, Captain, before I do that.'

Arkides raised his eyebrows. 'Are you refusing my order, Vlassos?'

'Certainly not, Sir. I just want to reach an understanding with you, that's all.'

'I see. Then perhaps you will explain what it is, that we need to understand.

'Lives were lost on the yacht. I heard there was a woman and a child involved.'

Arkides shrugged, but looked uneasy. 'It is of no consequence to us, Manoli. Forget you were there.'

'I can do that,' Manoli hesitated for a moment, 'for a price. Captain, before I enter up the log there is the question of payment. I want to share in this business in Ireland.' He broke off for a moment. 'Sinking that yacht could cost me my ticket. As you have pointed out, I suffered a suspension once before.'

The response from the captain took Manoli by surprise. Arkides bellowed a mighty laugh, 'You and I have much in common, my friend.' His belly shook under the rumble of his laughter as he slapped a fatherly hand on Manoli's shoulder. Lowering his voice, he said, 'You're a good boy, Vlassos, a good officer. I value that. I wouldn't have it any other way. You will receive your fair share in Ceuta, have no fear about that.' He clapped the second officer on the back and laughed again. 'Everyone will be happy, eh!' His laughter echoed through the empty wheel house.

Arkides suddenly became serious. 'I've sent a radio message to the owners telling them of our engine breakdown,' he said. 'Now be a good fellow and enter it in the log.'

As the Captain left the bridge, he caught a glimpse of the Irishman in his blue anorak on the boat deck. Arkides felt sure that Foster had seen him, but the Irishman didn't raise his eyes or alter the rhythm of his step. He continued striding up and down the short deck between the lifeboats, intently reading from a small black book. He was totally engrossed in it, his mouth silently forming the words in a way that looked almost reverent.

Arkides tasted bile in his mouth. Cursing the man under his breath, he stepped over the sea step leading into his own quarters. His mood had already changed. That man continued to be a thorn in his side, nagging at him constantly.

Manoli remained standing in the wheel house after the captain had left the bridge. For once, he had the bridge to himself. He was mesmerised by the almost imperceptible rise and fall of the forecastle as the ship ploughed into an undulating Atlantic swell. Money be damned. How could he ever forget what he had done?

Outside, mist shrouded the foredeck and tiny rivulets of water coursed slowly down the windows. A collection of stained coffee cups rattled on a wooden shelf near his elbow. Oblivious to the muffled throb of the ship's engines he dreamed of being elsewhere. He consoled himself with the thought that already the weather was becoming warmer as they travelled further south and soon they would see the sun again.

He returned to the chart room and wrote up the log as Arkides had directed. Tackling the captain had scared him. It had been so easy, he thought. Had it been too easy? Perhaps he had showed his hand too early. His sense of unease returned and he started to regret having said anything.

After two days at sea, Foster was finding the freighter claustrophobic. Fully recovered from his earlier seasickness, his frustration and anger bubbled like lava about to erupt.

He had spent most of the voyage confined to his small cabin, rarely venturing outside except for a daily walk on the boat deck, and eating only when the steward brought him food. He kept himself aloof, avoiding contact with the crew. He needed solitude to plan.

The opportunity he sought came shortly after midnight. He left his cabin as the ship rolled through a dark night, the blackness of which was relieved by moonlight that made fleeting appearances through a layer of low cloud. The threat of rain was in the air, but the wind was out of the south and it was noticeably warmer.

Lurking in the shadows of one of the lifeboats Foster could feel waves of sudarific air emanating from the open engine room skylights. He became aware of someone moving on the bridge, and in the glow of the engine room lights he recognised Gupta Bose coming towards him. He retreated further into the shadows. As the ship rolled more acutely he steadied himself with the heavy steel handle used for swinging out the lifeboat davits.

The Indian seaman passed him, unaware of his presence. As he came to the ladder leading to the afterwell deck, Foster sprang from his hiding place. Just as Gupta stretched out his hand to grasp the rail he heard a scuffled footstep behind him. He half turned, but it was already too late. His eyes widened in horror as Foster leaped out, raised both arms and swung the heavy steel handle with all the force he could muster. There was a sickening crunch as the blow caught Gupta violently on the left temple and propelled him down the ladder onto the steel deck ten feet below.

Foster waited for only a moment at the top of the ladder. He did not have to descend to the deck to know that his victim was dead. A spreading pool of blood on the rusty steel plates glistened in the dim deck light. The body didn't move. He paused only for a minute to wipe the blood from the end of the winch handle with a handkerchief before returning it to its holder. Then he threw the blood stained rag overboard.

Nobody was about. The decks remained deserted. Foster glanced up at the empty bridge wing just for a second before returning along the boat deck to his cabin.

He switched on the light and removed his anorak. Anxiously, he checked the coat for blood stains. There were none. He washed his hands in the small wash basin, staring at his reflection in the mirror. The excitement and satisfaction on his flushed features stared back at him and his mean lips relaxed into a smile of triumph. At last he had started to gain the upper hand. One of his enemies had paid the penalty for dragging him away on this cursed boat.

A deck hand found the body at the next change of watch at four o'clock in the morning. Later when the news filtered through the ship everyone on board believed that it was an accident. After all, Gupta Bose had been an old man. He must have slipped on the ladder, lost his footing and fallen to the deck, crushing his skull as he did so.

Arkides didn't believe it. He knew that this was no accident. He made no appearance on deck when the body was slipped over the side later in the morning; instead, he watched the Chief Officer take charge of the funeral from the safety of his cabin. Outside his open porthole in the warmth of the morning sunshine, he could see the bosun hosing down the afterdeck with a fire hose, the powerful jet of water dispersing any remaining blood stains from the deck.

'Into the deep we commend his body,' he heard the mate intone. Then the body, sewn into a piece of torn hatch tarpaulin and weighted with scrap metal from the engine room, slipped from a hatch board over the side. It disappeared feet first beneath the surface without as much as a splash.

Suddenly Foster came into his line of vision from where he had been watching the burial. As the corpse slipped over the side, Foster made a simple sign of the cross. Then he returned to pacing up and down the deck, head down.

Arkides turned away from the cabin porthole. Was the Irishman's step more jaunty, or had he merely imagined it? He lit a cigar and poured a glass of brandy with shaking hands. He could smell his own sweat as he gulped down the drink, but the fire of the liquid did nothing to take away his fear.

Twelve

Jim Prendergast left the University College Hospital in Galway on Monday afternoon with the final words from the coroner's inquest still echoing in his mind. 'Death by misadventure and accidental drowning.' The hearing itself had been perfunctory, and except for those words, Prendergast did not recall it clearly. Only his rage and bitterness stayed with him; to Prendergast, the statement did nothing to capture the reality of what had occurred.

He stepped outside into a warm summer day, still a little unsteady on his feet, and stood for several minutes on the hospital steps squinting in the bright afternoon sunshine. He saw his neighbour, Mary McGonigal walking towards him and smiling. He returned her wave as he lit one of McQuaid's cigarettes and inhaled deeply. The tobacco tasted good, his first for two days, but it made him feel slightly dizzy. It crossed his mind that now would be a good time to give up smoking, but he shrugged off the idea and drew the smoke more deeply into his lungs.

'Hi, Jim.' Mary came closer. 'It's been an awful shock. You must be going through hell. In fact, you're looking better than I expected.'

'Don't let appearances fool you, Mary. I feel pretty rotten.'

She stepped up and gave him a peck on the cheek. 'Bertie is waiting for us in the car. If we wait here a minute he'll bring it round.'

Prendergast watched the approaching car and dragged on his cigarette. He felt uncomfortable not knowing what he could say, or what they expected to hear. As the car stopped, he threw his oilskins over his shoulder and descended the steps.

'Hi, Bertie, thanks for coming in for me.' He shook hands with Mary's husband and climbed into the back seat of the car.

'For nothing, Jim.' Bertie looked uncomfortable. 'We'll take you straight home. You don't have to talk about anything if you don't want to.'

'Thanks,' he said. 'I would appreciate that.'

They drove through the outskirts of the city as Prendergast wondered what it would be like to get home. It was difficult to imagine that he would be alone. He noticed afternoon shafts of sunlight enhancing the towering cumulus cloud formations marching in from the west, and as they sped along the coast road from Galway the backdrop of distant mountains was never clearer. It was an artist's landscape but for once, it made no impression on him.

Nearing Spiddal where the road skirted the shore, his eyes flicked to the gentle blue waters of the bay before he forced himself to look away. He couldn't bring himself to look at the sea again just yet.

In the past, whenever he drove this way, Jane was always with him. She used to scold him for getting angry as they passed some of the more ostentatious bungalows along the roadside. It always annoyed him that right next-door to some nestled the original family cottage, derelict in neglect. Now, he didn't even notice.

Bertie glanced over his shoulder concerned at his silence. 'Do you want to stop for a drink or anything, Jim?'

Mary answered for him. 'Of course he doesn't. Keep your eyes on the road, Bertie.'

Prendergast said nothing and closed his eyes.

In early evening they crossed onto Gorumna Island and turned left shortly afterwards to Carneg Bay. The car bounced up a grass filled boreen and drew up outside the cottage.

Prendergast held his breath and surveyed the house, steeling himself for what he would find inside. So much had taken place and changed forever in a short few days.

'You'll come in?'

Bertie opened his mouth, but Mary nudged him. 'Later,' she said. 'After the church service. I've made up some food, Jim, so you don't have to bother.'

'That's very kind of you, Mary. I'm sorry I don't have more to say at the moment.' Prendergast felt relieved that they weren't coming inside. Right now, he needed time and space to get used to the empty house. Besides, he knew he was going to cry and he desperately wanted to be alone for that.

Unlocking the front door he stepped into the house. His footsteps echoed back from the wooden floors of the hall. He looked around the living room. A few simple furnishings made the room comfortable, and it was neat and freshly dusted. He could smell furniture polish and he knew immediately that Mary McGonigal had been preparing for his homecoming.

He wandered through the house in a disconsolate mood, not looking at the empty beds in the bedrooms. Returning to the lounge, he poured himself a stiff gin and tonic and stood savouring it at the large picture window overlooking the sea. Modern sliding glass doors gave access onto a small patio paved with Liscannor stone that overlooked the rocky beach below.

He sipped the gin and stared at the unoccupied mooring buoy bobbing like a red fishing float below the house. *Larinita* should be there. His eyes suddenly misted over and he started to sob. He lay down full length on the faded settee by the window and placed his glass on the floor beside him. Susan's face floated before him as tears welled in his eyes and loneliness consumed him.

At seven-thirty, a knock at the door wakened him. It was the McGonigals. Time for the first major hurdle, he thought, the short evening church service that he dreaded. He opened the door. 'Come on in,' he said. 'I'm sorry, but I fell asleep. I'll be with you in a minute.'

Mary McGonigal noticed his reddened eyes and said nothing. She looked at her husband meaningfully and took a seat in the lounge. Jim went into the bedroom and changed into a fresh shirt and a navy blue suit. When he emerged, Mary McGonigal tried to break the tension. 'You look well, so you do,' she said, trying to lift their spirits. 'Bertie, why can't you look like that when you dress up!'

Bertie grimaced, shuffling his feet self-consciously, and straightened his tie. He looked uncomfortable in a suit, and by the way he fingered his shirt collar, it was too tight. His inability to think of anything to say that would help the situation only added to his embarrassment.

Jim forced a wan smile. 'Mary, thanks for the clean up. I wouldn't have been able for that.'

'It's nothing,' she replied. 'I've emptied their wardrobes, too. All the clothes are in boxes. I put them in the spare room.'

'If there is anything you would like to have ...'

'Oh no! I couldn't.' She started to cry.

'Well, at least take Susan's toys for the kids.' He blew his nose into a clean handkerchief. 'She'd like that. Come on. Let's get this over with,' he finished.

They drove the short distance to the church in awkward silence. The church was nondescript and neglected, unlike those nearer to the affluence of Galway city. On the outside, its walls were beginning to peel, crying out for paint. Built at a cross-roads on high ground, it was windswept most of the time, but now it was washed by evening sunshine, and to Prendergast, it possessed a foreign appearance, as though it had been trans-ported there from some southern country. Behind it, dotted with a myriad of rocks and remote uninhabited islands that stretched all the way to Slyne Head, lay the water to the west of Gorumna.

He could see a number of cars parked outside already. Here and there amongst them were farmers' tractors. Inside, the church was cool, though already crowded.

At the back of the church, nearest to the door, the children from Susan's school grouped together, finding solace in their close-packed numbers. A few people turned their heads anx-iously as Prendergast's footsteps echoed down the central aisle. One of his shoes started to squeak, but he still stared straight ahead, trying to ignore what lay in front of the altar.

The priest surprised him by shaking hands when he reached the front pew. The man's warmth and concern was unexpected. Prendergast had never been one of his regular customers. It dawned on him that it was an example of how country people banded together against adversity.

Fortunately it was a short service. Prendergast heard little of it. He sat alone right in the front looking directly ahead, averting his eyes from the oak coffin. Afterwards, shuffling feet heralded the worst part of all, the handshakes and the muttered condolences. He steeled himself and endured it all in numb silence.

Back in the house the mood became almost festive. Mary McGonigal had provided trays of sandwiches and as the drink flowed, tongues relaxed. It was almost like a party, but one that had nothing to celebrate. Prendergast felt as though he was in a trance.

Practically everyone he knew from the Sailing Club was there. Prominent amongst them, the crews who had been in Kilronan gathered around, remembering Jane's role in previous races. Most surprising to Prendergast was the presence of the Galway Harbour Master. He hardly knew Vincent Kelly. They had chatted a few times about shared experiences away at sea, but that was all. That they had all taken the trouble to travel from Galway was in itself remarkable. He had to admit that it brought him a sense of pleasure and lessened his dreadful sense of isolation.

Vincent Kelly was the first to leave. Jim walked to his car with him, glad of the opportunity to get outside into the fresh air. It was a night of clear perfection with just enough of a wind to stir and spread the aroma of the pines that surrounded the cottage. Lights twinkled far across the bay and off to the left a blaze of neon lit up the fish processing plant in Rossaveal.

'Thanks for coming, Vincent,' Jim said, as they reached the car. 'I appreciate it.'

The Harbour Master fumbled for his keys. 'My own wife died a few years ago, but of natural causes. What happened to you is horrific. I only wish there was something I could do.' He stopped to gaze out across the still waters of the bay. 'There's too many rogue ships out there now, Jim, and it's getting worse all the time. It's just a damned pity that you didn't at least get the name of the one that found you.'

'That one wasn't just a rogue, Vincent,' Prendergast responded. 'That bastard ran us down deliberately. That ship murdered my wife and kid, I'm sure of that.' Emotion welled up inside him and it was a second before he could continue speaking. 'The fishing boat that was out there at the time must know something. The police are working on it, but the chances of getting anywhere appear slim. One thing is sure, though, they were all up to no good out there. They're not going to turn themselves in.'

Kelly didn't seem to know what to reply. 'I suppose not. That would be too much to hope for,' he agreed, easing himself into his car. 'But listen. Look me up anytime you are in Galway, and if I hear anything around the docks, I'll let you know. Sometimes I pick up bits of information that would surprise you.'

'Thanks, I'll do that, Vincent.' Prendergast watched the lights of the car until it turned onto the main road from the boreen, then he walked back to the house.

In the early hours of the morning, the last of his visitors left. Jim felt drained and he knew he had drunk too much to even attempt to clear the debris. It would have to wait until morning. He avoided the bedroom and curled up on the settee, too tired to feel the sadness that was eating at him inside.

Prendergast awoke at nine the next morning to the faint sounds of running water and the clink of glasses being washed in the kitchen. He hadn't heard Mary McGonigal sneak in. The windows were wide open and a soft breeze was breathing life through the room, clearing away the smell of stale tobacco smoke.

The radio was on in the kitchen and he could just hear bits of the news. There was something about a car being blown up across the border in Tyrone. It was, unfortunately, becoming a common enough occurrence again, and he paid no more attention to it.

He got up, his back aching and his clothes rumpled. He went into the kitchen and lay his hand on Mary's shoulder, giving her a quick kiss on her cheek. 'You're a saint,' he said.

Mary reached for a tea-towel. 'Enough of that,' she said. She was blushing. 'What are neighbours for? Go and get yourself shaved. Bertie will be up soon to take us to the Mass.'

The funeral mass was almost as crowded as the evening's service before. Kieran and Annie Quinn from Kilmurvey were both there, as were Colm Conneely and his brother Dermot. They had all come over to Rossaveal that morning on one of the island boats. The simple kindness of their presence overwhelmed him.

Prendergast suffered another round of condolences after the Mass ended and it desolated him for a second time. He embraced Annie Quinn outside the church. 'Thank you for coming,' he said. 'It means a lot to me.'

Her eyes were moist. 'I'm sorry we can't stay for the burial, but a boat is waiting to take us home.'

Kieran stuck out his calloused hand. 'Good luck to you, Jim, and God bless you. Our door is always open to you. The lads on the island haven't given up. They'll find your daughter yet, you can be sure of that.'

'I hope so. I can't thank you enough for what you have done for me, but I will come and see you.' Prendergast shook hands with him and walked with them to a waiting car.

Then came the final act. The drive to the graveyard was only a short distance, and most of the mourners walked behind the hearse in the traditional country way. Solemnly, Jim did the same, his ears tuned to the crunch of boots and shoes on the loose gravel. The journey took longer than he expected.

He hesitated only once when he saw the walled triangular-shaped cemetery nestling at a bend in the road, just above the tidal rocks across the bridge to Lettermullen Island. It was neatly kept and strangely peaceful, despite the omnipresent whine of wind in the roadside telegraph poles. Inside the gates, a freshly opened grave beckoned amidst the weathered headstones.

Within minutes the graveside service ended. When it did, after the last lonely prayer finished, Prendergast seemed to sag and grow old as he waited until the grave-digger placed the final shovel of earth on the mound. People milled about him, but he insisted on walking back to the house alone.

Later, in the evening sunset, he returned to the grave and read the cards on the wreaths and on the many bouquets of flowers. One card in particular caught his attention. It came from the Shannon helicopter crew and was in the form of a fouled anchor. As he knelt to read it, the sound of falling stones startled him and he jerked to his feet.

A small herd of rangy black bullocks peered at him over a low stone wall. Standing in their midst on top of the wall was a single white goat, a fine proud animal with curling brown horns. Framed between the goat's horns, in the far distance, was Eeragh lighthouse. He watched its light flash as darkness came, with hatred growing in his heart.

Somewhere out there was the body of his daughter. He pounded the stony ground in anguish, oblivious to the blood that dripped from his split knuckles. 'Whatever it takes,' he cursed, 'I'll find them.'

Someone would pay for this. He promised himself that.

Thirteen

Two days later on Wednesday afternoon the *Georgios* neared the Straits of Gibraltar. Lost among the motley gathering of merchant ships funnelling through the narrow opening to the Mediterranean, she was just another rusty tramp going about a mundane business.

Arkides paced the bridge, enjoying the heat of the sun but wishing away the hours to their arrival in Ceuta. Mount Hacho was already visible. He could see it as a blur on the horizon. Part of the Pillars of Hercules, it dominated the narrow peninsula on which the city of Ceuta rested.

Directly ahead, a warship moved to cross their bows. 'Starboard, ten degrees,' he ordered. He watched the haughty shape of a British frigate sweep past. Her slim pencil-shaped hull cleaved through the calm blue waters as she headed for the naval dockyard in Gibraltar. The Rock itself lay on their port side, a hazy mass in the warm afternoon sunshine.

Arkides walked over to where the second mate was studying the disappearing warship. 'Not long now, Vlassos,' he remarked. 'Once Foster has left us, you will be a rich man.' He chuckled.

'I hope so,' Manoli replied.

Shortly after six o'clock in the evening they picked up a pilot and under his guidance entered a semi-circular bay. A Spanish enclave since 1580, five centuries had given the modern buildings fringing the edge of Ceuta's bay a Spanish, rather than a Moorish, appearance.

The anchor roared away through the hawse pipe as a cloud of

rust-coloured dust shrouded the crew working on the forecastle. Gently, the ship snubbed at the chain as the anchor bit, bringing the sense of finality that comes with the end of every voyage.

Arkides reached for the engine room telegraph and rang *fin - ished with engines.* He could see two boats already speeding towards them. One flew a customs pennant, and the other was the shipping agent. Arkides thanked the pilot for his assistance and hurried from the bridge to greet them.

After the customs officials left, the agent accepted a beer. 'We can't dock you immediately, Captain. Another ship is occupying the refuelling berth, but you will be able to come alongside as soon as she leaves.' He reached into his briefcase and extracted a bundle of mail for the crew. 'There is also a cable from your owners that reached me an hour ago.' He handed over a sheet of paper and waited while Arkides rummaged for his glasses.

Arkides read the cabled note and sat down at his desk. 'They've sold my ship,' he said. 'What do you think of that?' A steward entered the cabin with more cold beers and Arkides handed him the bundle of mail. 'Give these out to the crew.'

The agent helped himself to another can of beer. 'Your orders are to take on three hundred tons of fuel but to remain at anchor until the new crew takes over. Your own crew will pay off here and fly to Athens. You are to join another ship in the Persian Gulf.'

The steward hurried away, excited by what he had overheard. He was eager to impart the news of the sale before he doled out the mail on the afterdeck. Arkides stood up and stared out the porthole in his cabin for a few minutes. Then he returned and sat at his desk. 'We had a death on board during the voyage,' he said.

'Oh?' The agent raised his eyebrows.

'Purely an accident,' the captain said. 'An Indian seaman fell down a ladder one night and was killed. He was an old man and not very steady on his legs at the best of times. He was buried at sea.'

'I will have to inform the police,' the agent replied.

Arkides felt a stab of alarm. 'Is that necessary?'

The agent sipped his beer. 'Purely a formality, Captain, I assure you. They might require a statement, you understand?' He gave a short laugh. 'But seamen die every day, don't they? Especially old ones!'

Arkides smiled. What was he worrying about? Gupta Bose was just a Lascar after all. No one would miss him. He did not mention the Irishman to the agent. There was only so much you could get away with, he thought. 'Very well,' he said. 'I will give the police any information that they may need.'

'I doubt very much that they will want any,' the agent responded.

A row of surprised faces stared back at the steward as he told them what he had overheard in the captain's cabin. Yun See sat on top of the cargo hatch to open a letter from his brother in London. He read it avidly, feeling his spirits lifting with every word. Come as soon as you can, the letter read. The restaurant is doing well and the British emigration authorities have granted your visa. The words sprang from the page, filling him with delight. He felt deliriously happy. He was oblivious to the chattering amongst the others as it dawned on him that the ship's sale suited his plans admirably.

The news also delighted Manoli Vlassos. This was just what he wanted. Armed with his pay and whatever extra he could squeeze out of Arkides, he felt confident that he would have time to find a better ship. He might even have enough to go back to the Marine Academy in Piraeus and study for his master's ticket. He started to clear up his cabin and pack his clothes.

With his packing finished, there was time to pay Arkides a visit before they raised anchor to go alongside the oil terminal. Better to do it now, he thought. Later there would be too many people about and he would lose the opportunity. He made his way across the boat deck to the captain's cabin, while the lights of Ceuta glittered a mile away like a string of jewels.

Manoli knocked lightly. Pulling aside the door curtain he stepped inside. As usual, the captain's accommodation was a muddle of littered clothes and overflowing ash trays. The smell of cigar smoke and stale sweat added to the torporific atmosphere. In spite of a gentle sea breeze coming through the open porthole, the cabin was hot and stuffy.

Arkides was seated at his desk in his underwear, working on some ship's papers. He looked up. 'What do you want now, Vlassos?' he growled. 'Can't you see that I am busy?'

'Excuse me, Captain.' Manoli faltered for a moment. 'But now that we are paying off, perhaps we could settle up on what we spoke about two days ago?'

Arkides swivelled his chair. 'Very well,' he replied. 'This is as good a time as any, I suppose. You'll see that I am a man of my word.' He winked at the second officer. 'Everyone is going to be happy, eh! Just as I said.' The captain rose to his feet and walked over to the ship's safe.

Manoli crinkled his nose and swallowed. The sudden smell of perspiration was overpowering. He wasn't sure if it was his own or the other man's.

Arkides opened the safe. Reaching inside, he produced a bundle of notes and counted them onto a low coffee table in the centre of the cabin. 'There you are, my friend, a thousand dollars. Now, doesn't that make you feel better?' Manoli snatched up the bundle of notes and stuffed them into his pocket. Perhaps he had misjudged Arkides all along. He mumbled his thanks and backed to the door.

The captain eyed him intently. 'Don't forget what it is for, Vlassos. It is to buy a secret. You have never been to Ireland, okay?' He gave a short snorting laugh and said, 'In a day or two you will be on your way home, perhaps even tomorrow. Don't spend it all at once on those girls in Piraeus.'

Manoli stumbled back to his cabin. He couldn't believe his luck. He counted the notes yet again, holding each one up to the light. He smiled. Then he locked his cabin door and took a shower before making his way to the poop deck to take his docking station.

At ten-thirty that night, the *Georgios* secured alongside the oil terminal to begin refuelling. Most of the crew, already in their shore-going clothes, were lining the gangway, eager for a night ashore.

Arkides felt relaxed for once. He re-read the message from the owners and put it away in a desk drawer. Things seemed to be working out quite well. He lit another cigar and slopped a third large brandy into a glass. He was already a little bit drunk, but it was a pleasant feeling that rounded off the day. The police had been and gone. Just as the agent had predicted, they had shown little interest in his report on the accidental death of Gupta Bose. They really couldn't care less, it seemed. A bottle of whiskey to each had helped ensure their quick departure from the ship. He congratulated himself. Outside, a rattle of foot-steps on the gangway announced that more of the crew was heading off for a night ashore.

When the knock came on his cabin door Arkides knew instinctively who it was. For an instant he toyed with the idea of ignoring the knock and feigning sleep. Better to get it over with now, he told himself. In spite of the oppressive heat in the room he pulled on his uniform jacket. The tarnished gold braid on the sleeves gave him enough stature and courage to open the door.

'Come in, Mr. Foster,' he said. 'I've been expecting you.'

Foster stepped into the cabin and closed the door behind him. 'I'll bet you have,' he replied.

Arkides noticed that he was wearing the same clothes that he had come aboard in. His shirt looked as though it had been washed, although not ironed. Over his left arm hung his blue anorak.

Arkides motioned to the bottle of brandy on his desk. 'Have a drink with me. It's safe for you to leave at any time you like. We have cleared formalities with the port authorities. They are not even aware that you came with us. I did not list you on any of the ship's papers.' He forced a smile. 'That was clever of me, don't you think?'

Foster poured himself a drink. 'That's exactly what I wanted to hear.' He swallowed the drink quickly. 'Before I go, there's the little matter of our money. I want it back.'

Foster's tone was not lost on Arkides and he started to sweat under his heavy jacket. 'That's impossible,' he stuttered. 'You people got just about everything I agreed to carry. You lost the rest of it entirely through your own fault. Think yourself lucky that you can walk off this ship in one piece. I could have turned you over to the Spanish police.' Arkides tried to out-stare the Irishman but his bluster did nothing to disguise his fear.

Foster looked at him with disdain. 'Look, you shit, open that bloody safe and hand over what's ours, before you join that little bastard of an Indian over the side!'

Arkides felt paralysed. So he was right all along. Gupta Bose had been murdered. 'All right. Have it your own way, but don't expect anything more from me. You won't find it too easy to get someone to do a similar job for you again. You can sing for a ship the next time you need one as far as I'm concerned.' The captain opened the safe and withdrew a bundle of dollar bills. He threw them onto the coffee table.

'Now count them!' snapped Foster.

'It's all there,' protested Arkides. 'That is, with the exception of a thousand dollars I had to use to buy off the second mate. If we are to keep this quiet, I'll need more for others in the crew.'

'I know a cheaper way.' From beneath his folded anorak Foster produced a pistol. Even Arkides knew what a silencer looked like, and he swore at himself for not realising that the man would be armed. He should have searched his cabin for a weapon. His legs turned to jelly and he collapsed into his chair. He could feel a warm trickle of urine running down his trouser leg.

The bullet hit him dead centre in his forehead at close range. It left just a small hole as his head snapped back under the force of its entry, but the desk and cabin bulkhead behind him blossomed in a sickly pink and grey mass as the back of his head exploded outwards. The trickle of urine reached the carpet and the stain spread over his groin.

Foster calmly pocketed the money. He glanced down at the wet patch on the carpet before he left the cabin, closing the door behind him.

Manoli Vlassos made a fatal mistake. He volunteered to supervise the refuelling instead of going ashore. He had finished his packing when the knock came to his door. All the other officers in the alleyway had gone. He was more than surprised when he opened the door and Foster pushed him roughly aside.

The Irishman held a gun in his left hand. 'Don't waste my fucking time, just give me the thousand dollars!'

For the hundredth time Manoli thought, I knew this was too easy. He knew that to hand over the money was the safest thing to do, and did so. Looking at the gun in the other man's hand, he said, 'There's no need for that.'

'Is that a fact?' Foster smiled. 'It's funny, but that fat slob of a captain probably thought the same thing! You two had plenty of opportunity to dump me over the side. That was a mistake, and mistakes in my world cost lives.'

Manoli's eyes glazed in terror and he threw himself forwards in a desperate effort to seize the gun. He glimpsed a flash of light a micro-second before a dreadful pain erupted in his chest. The force of his forward movement and the speeding bullet brought him to his knees at Foster's feet. He couldn't understand why he had heard no sound from the gun. Clutching his chest he looked upwards, his eyes pleading, as a warm torrent of blood filled his mouth. Foster placed the end of the silencer against the Second Officer's temple and squeezed off the fatal shot.

He unscrewed the silencer and placed it in the pocket of his anorak. He was in no hurry. He scattered a few twenty dollar bills around the floor, making sure they were contaminated by the blood soaking the threadbare carpet. Then he quickly left the ship. Above him in the darkness of the towering poop deck a vague shape moved at the ship's rail. He never saw it.

An hour later he joined a pushing throng of people crowding to board the last ferry to Algeciras. Long before that, he had dumped the pistol and the silencer into the coal black waters of the ferry terminal.

Fourteen

Lisa and Liam parked their camper just outside Roundstone in a small camping site near the beach. Lisa climbed out of the driver's seat, stretched, and looked around. The site was nestled in a sheltered hollow on the very edge of Gorteen strand. It was Wednesday evening. The sun had not yet set and the white sweep of Dog's Bay lay in an arc at their doorstep.

Compared to the rush through the night on the previous trip, it had been a leisurely drive from Donegal. There had even been time to break their journey in Westport. Lisa felt relaxed. This time, it was almost like being on holiday.

Liam seemed to have forgotten the events at the farm. Not once had he discussed McGinty's death. It was as though it had never happened, not that she wanted it any other way.

Lisa was beginning to detect another side to Liam, especially now that he was more free from pressure. He was an attractive man and quite handsome, especially when he smiled, but when he did so, it was in a wistful way as though he longed to be somewhere else. She noticed that the further south they travelled, the more he seemed to be at ease. It was as though he had left his brooding depression behind amongst the granite rocks of the border hills. She had to find a way to penetrate his facade and read what went on in his mind, she thought.

She had one nagging worry, that he might be too soft for what was planned for him. Maybe he didn't have the balls any more. She had made up her mind that unless the IRA showed more aggression, she would not retain her interest in their activities. In that case, a return to Germany was inevitable. For the moment, she decided to stick it out a little while longer.

Liam had indeed relaxed. He felt better now that he had left
Johnny behind and was no longer a silent witness to his drinking. He also felt content that he had taken care of McGinty to
Hogan's apparent satisfaction. A phone call from Castlebar had
confirmed that Jim Hogan had already leaked an admission to
the media that a member of an Active Service Unit had been
killed in action the previous night. Hogan hadn't named
McGinty. It wasn't necessary. The British would find that out
themselves in due course and there was no point in making it
easy for them. McGinty would be buried with full military honours as befitted a heroic martyr just as soon as the authorities
released what little remained of him.

The only plan Liam had for the moment was to check on any
loose ends in Galway while he waited for Foster to surface. The
next few days were simple, he told himself. Nothing more than a
short holiday before he could get things well and truly back on
the rails. He might even visit the Galway Races if there was
time.

He took Lisa for a walk on the beach before dusk.
Wandering through the sand dunes, they fitted in unobtrusively
with their neighbouring campers. Before dark, they unclipped
their bicycles from the back of the Mercedes and cycled in to the
village. They ate a meal of chowder and fish pie in O'Dowd's
pub overlooking the harbour, then Liam led Lisa outside to
where the holiday makers crowded against a stone wall overlooking the harbour.

Liam's particular interest was in the fishing boats tied up
below them at the stone piers. He wanted to talk to the two
fishermen, Charlie Donovan and Harry McDonagh, but
amongst the collection of fishing craft there was no sign of a blue
half-decker. He finished his drink and turned to Lisa. 'No sign
of the buggers. Finish your drink and we'll take a walk through
the pubs further up.'

One by one they combed the scattering of pubs spread out
on a steep hill rising through the village from the harbour. They

were out of luck. Neither of the two men was to be found.

Liam felt a twinge of frustration. 'Let's back-track.'

'To which pub?'

'The one where we saw more locals. Twomey's, I think it was. There were more fishermen there.'

They retraced their steps to one of the bars that seemed to be unpopular with visiting holiday makers. 'This is the last one,' said Liam as they stepped through the low doorway. 'If we don't find them here, we'll give it up until tomorrow.'

Liam shouldered his way to the bar and ordered two pints of stout. Turning to a bearded man wearing an Aran sweater, he enquired where he could find Charlie Donovan. 'Off outside,' said the man, waving his glass towards the solitary window.

'You mean he's just left?' Liam asked, fighting to hide his annoyance.

'Nah! He's away fucking fishin'. Who're you, anyhow?' The bleary-eyed man turned to Liam. He was drunk, and aggressively so.

Liam debated whether to hit him then or later. He didn't need this hassle. He decided not to hit him at all. Controlling his anger, he said, 'I'm on holiday. I met Charlie a week or so ago and he said he would let me have a couple of lobsters. Here! Let me get you a drink, your glass is empty. The man accepted a whiskey and without thanking him muttered to the man next to him, 'Fuckin' wankers!' The other man laughed.

'Let's get out of here!' Liam tugged on Lisa's sleeve. He pushed his way through the crowd towards the door.

Lisa felt a rough hand grasp her bottom and whirled to face her assailant. Before Liam could stop her, she brought up her knee into the man's crotch and he collapsed to the floor in an uproar of breaking glass and loutish laughter.

'Jesus!' exploded Liam, 'You're some bitch! Come on!' He grabbed her arm and forced her towards the door. They reached the doorway but were brought to a halt by a shout from inside. 'Hey mister! If you're looking for Donovan, Charlie's fishing out of Clifden for the past week. You'll find him there.'

Lisa fell off her bike twice before they reached the camper.

She thought it hilarious, but Liam was furious. He didn't like the attention she was drawing to them. Then, in a flash, he realised that it had probably done no harm. After all, this was supposed to be a holiday trip. 'You are well pissed,' he laughed, aware it made them look all the more believable.

Long after he switched off the lights inside the camper, Lisa continued to giggle in the darkness from the bunk opposite his. He was suddenly aware of her nearness and it disconcerted him. She had made no attempt to undress out of sight. It was the first time they had really been alone together and she had done nothing to suggest that she was not available. Liam fell asleep thinking of that. So did she.

They found the two fishermen in Clifden before nightfall the next day. Liam had almost given them up. It was late and they had watched every boat that came alongside the pier that evening as the tide flooded and covered the muddy foreshore.

The last boat to make its approach up the still waters of the river was red, not blue. Liam was about to turn away but Lisa stopped him, 'That's them,' she whispered. Slowly, they sauntered back along the stone-capped quay.

Harry McDonagh stepped lightly ashore holding the blue mooring ropes as the boat nudged gently against the pier.

'Evenin', Harry. Did you catch much?'

Liam's voice had a conversational tone but it startled Harry as he bent to tie a rope to an iron ring on the pier. His face flushed in surprise. 'Jesus, what are you doing back here?' His eyes were wide.

Liam lit a cigarette. 'Thought you might have a lobster or two for us, that's all.'

Charlie Donovan came out of the wheel house onto the narrow side deck showing none of McDonagh's nervousness. 'We can't help you there Liam, but you're welcome to a salmon if you like.'

Liam looked over the boat. 'I see you painted it since we last saw you.'

'Yeah,' replied Charlie. 'I decided I didn't like blue anymore.

Anyway, red seems a safer colour. Ever since that business with the yacht, questions are being asked about blue half-deckers, so there's no point in seeking attention right now.' He grinned disarmingly and pointed at a new set of aerials on the wheel house roof. 'We fitted radar and a VHF as well, since then.'

'Expensive,' said Liam. His voice was disapproving.

Donovan jumped down onto the afterdeck. He rooted in one of the fish boxes and extracted a shining silver salmon. 'Don't let it worry you,' he said. 'The fishing is good this year, thanks to these.' He kicked a pile of nets with his boot. 'They're illegal.' He started to cover up the nets with a scale-encrusted tarpaulin.

Liam frowned and turned his attention to McDonagh, 'What about you Harry? Have you been spending money as well?'

'Me? No. I've got it all tucked safely away. A few pounds on the horses was all, and I was lucky there, I picked a few winners.'

Liam changed the subject. 'What happened out there that morning?'

Donovan looked worried for a moment. 'I don't know,' he replied. 'We didn't see any yacht, but it must have been our ship. From everything we've heard, she was in the right place at the right time. The yacht must have seen her, it all fits.'

Liam lit another cigarette. 'What about the cops, have they given you any trouble?'

'Not much,' replied Donovan. 'The guy in Roundstone came down to us a few days ago and wanted to know where we were fishing that day. I told him we were up around Slyne Head. Haven't seen him since. I painted the boat right after that.'

'Good,' responded Liam, 'I like that. That's why I called. By the way, I might have another job for you in a month or two. There could be a bonus in it.'

'That's why I fitted the radar and the radio,' replied Donovan. 'We might know what's going on the next time.'

Harry glanced towards Lisa who stood a few yards away picking at her finger nails with a nail file. 'Where's that other guy that was with you last time?'

Lisa looked up and flashed him a smile. 'Dead.'

'Dead!' Harry felt sick again.

Liam cut in. 'He got himself killed in an accident. It happens sometimes. You guys should remember that. You do a dangerous job, too.'

His meaning was not lost on them. There was something chilling in the way these two could be so matter-of-fact about someone's death, Harry thought. He wished he had not asked.

Donovan slipped the salmon into a plastic bag and handed it across. 'Here you are, enjoy it, fresh this afternoon.'

'Thanks,' said Liam taking the bag. 'I'll be in touch.' He eyed them intensely. 'Just don't make me come back to check on you two.'

The fishermen watched them walk slowly away until they were out of earshot. Donovan turned to Harry McDonagh, 'Don't even say it! Keep your feckin' mouth shut. There's better money in it than fishing, and well you bloody know it.'

Liam parked the camper for the night just outside Clifden at the edge of a turf bog. They gorged themselves on grilled salmon cutlets. The fish was excellent, and Lisa had never tasted anything so good. To her surprise, Liam helped with the dishes. He was in a good mood and pleased with the outcome of their meeting with the fishermen.

Before midnight they prepared their bunks. Although she was sober, Lisa treated Liam to the same strip routine as the night before, but he seemed not to notice. Before she had even finished undressing he reached up and switched off the light over his bunk. It flashed through her mind that maybe he was queer. The thought amused her as she slipped into her sleeping bag and zipped it up. 'What's on for tomorrow?' she asked.

'We're having a day off,' he replied. He had already turned his back to her and his sleeping bag muffled his voice. 'I'm taking you to the Galway races, now go to sleep.'

Lisa lay for a long time in the semi-darkness watching the moonlight flicker on the panelled sides of the camper. She willed him to cross over the narrow space and join her. She knew he was awake, too. She listened to him breathing and wondered what he was thinking, but he stayed silent and did not move. Finally sleep came to both of them.

The wind rose early on Thursday morning, bringing rain. It gusted across the open moor land and buffeted the camper on the narrow road to Oughterard. By the time they reached Galway it was raining hard enough to snarl up the traffic all the way to the racecourse on the other side of the town.

The rain did nothing, though, to dampen the spirits of the spectators, and they had to fight for a place in the general melee at the tote windows before the second race. Liam fought his way to a window and re-emerged clutching two tickets. 'Your horse is number two! Come on, we'll try to get up in the stand.'

Lisa looked peeved. 'Don't I get to pick my own horse?' She gave him a long hard look. 'Oh! I get it. I wouldn't know how, right?'

Liam frowned at her. 'If you shut up just for a minute, we might have time to get up into the stand before the bloody race ends.' They fought their way through the crowd surging across the mud to the shelter offered by the grandstand.

On the terraces the noise was deafening. Like everyone else, Lisa came to her feet as the horses flashed to the winning post right in front of them, steam rising from their straining flanks as they came under a final onslaught of their riders' whips. Caught up in the excitement of the moment, she forgot her annoyance. Number two won by a head. The rain stopped and the sun came out. Lisa was ecstatic; she jumped up and down like an excited child. 'How much did I win?'

Liam laughed. 'Stay there, I'll go and find out.'

'No, I'll come with you.'

'Look, go and place our bets on the next race if you want something to do. I've just seen someone I expected to find here. I want to talk to him and he won't talk if you are with me. I'll meet you back here.'

He didn't wait for an answer and disappeared into the crowd surging down the steps of the stand.

'Damn you!' she shouted after him.

A huge crowd packed the main bar underneath the grandstand, all jostling and shouting for attention at once. Liam spotted his quarry and shouldered his way alongside a tall straightbacked man drinking at the bar. 'Any tips, John?' he asked quietly.

The other man, startled, turned to face him, the smile fading on his lips. He was tall but thinly built, and the recent drenching rain had plastered his brown hair down over his forehead. His eyes had a furtive look as they hunted through the crowd. 'Who are you? I don't think I know you.'

Liam pushed closer to him. 'No, but I know you. Hogan suggested I might have a word with you, if I was down this way.'

The other man's face paled. 'I don't know who you are talking about.'

Liam gave him a clap on the back. 'Big Jim sends his regards, John. He's the one that pays you every now and again.'

'What the hell do you want from me?' His hand holding the glass shook and he slopped beer down the front of his sports jacket. 'I don't want to be seen speaking to you people.'

Liam laughed. 'No, you just like to take our money, right? No big deal. I can understand that. All I want to know is how the investigation is going into that yacht that was lost, that's all.'

The other man gulped at his beer. 'It's just about dead, if you have to know. The file is still open, but no one is doing anything with it.'

'We want you to make sure it stays that way.' Liam gave him a piercing look. 'Where did it happen, anyway?'

'Out off the Aran Islands. The skipper claimed that he was run down by a ship, but we doubted his story for a while. The detective in charge thought that the guy might have sunk the boat himself for the insurance, but he dropped that idea and put it all down to an accident.'

Liam said nothing for a full minute. It was too much of a coincidence. Foster had to have been involved. 'What happened to the ship?'

'Nothing is known about her, not even her name. She disappeared. Why all the bloody questions? What's your interest in this?'

Liam ignored the question. 'That's all I wanted. Easy, wasn't it? I think maybe you guys get paid too much.'

The tall man frowned. 'I should have known you buggers were mixed up in this. Try a fiver on number six in the fourth race. Now bugger off and leave me alone.' He put down his half-finished glass of beer on the counter and forced his way back into the crowd.

Lisa waited for Liam in the doorway of the bar from where she had been watching the exchange between the two men. 'Who was he?' she asked.

'A cop. A right shit of a cop, but a useful one. He lets us know what the Special Branch are up to now and again. Come on. I've got a tip for the fourth race. If we win, I'll treat you to a swank hotel tonight, one with a real bath in it.'

That night, Liam and Lisa slept together for the first time amidst the opulent surroundings of the Ardilaun Hotel. Liam turned away from a window overlooking wooded gardens that were lit by fairy lights in the trees as Lisa came back into the room. Her hair was still damp from the shower and he watched as she sat at a vanity unit, brushing the strands carefully. She raised her arms and the towel she had wrapped around herself slipped.

She looked up with a coquettish smile that in the soft glow of a single table lamp relaxed the hardness of her features. Her eyes shone in the half-light. 'You want me, don't you, Liam?'

Her voice reached him as a soft whisper and suddenly his mouth felt dry. There had been little time for women in his life. She stood up and walked towards him, allowing the towel to fall in a soft pile. 'Don't be afraid, say it!'

He felt her fingers on the buttons of his shirt, then their warmth as they circled his neck, pulling him closer. The scent of her perfume enveloped him, driving any thoughts of saying no from his mind.

'Say it!' she repeated.

'I want you.'

She bit him lightly on his neck with her even white teeth. 'What are you waiting for, then?'

Fifteen

Foster lost himself amongst his fellow passengers and slipped off the ferry in Algeciras. A nondescript man, carrying no baggage and dressed in scruffy clothes, he made no impression on two Spanish policemen who, without interest, sleepily watched the passengers filing ashore. Eyes darting left and right, he glided away from the ferry terminal and faded into the warm Spanish night.

Directly across the bay, somewhere amongst the twinkling lights of Gibraltar, he knew there was a British intelligence unit who would have given dearly to know of his coming. As yet, C-13, the Anti-Terrorist Unit, only suspected his existence. Right under their noses, quietly and without fuss, one of the most dangerous subversives in Europe had arrived back, unheralded, on the mainland. He chuckled at the thought of it.

Within minutes he had gone to ground in a cheap rooming house close to the port area. There, he slept until morning.

On Thursday night, the train from Algeciras arrived in Madrid, one hour late as usual, and Foster stepped out onto the platform at the Estacion de Atocha. His clothes looked even more rumpled, and a sparse bristle of beard covered his lower features, softening the tight outline of his mouth. He was hungry, dead tired, but almost home.

Too jaded to attempt the crowded metro after over thirteen hours of travelling, he took a taxi to an area south of the Plaza Mayor known as the Rastro. A tough working class area famed for its weekend flea market, it was a refuge of huddled houses and narrow streets. He paid off the cab and walked the last few hundred yards before slipping through a faded green doorway.

By the time he reached the top of a third flight of stairs his breath wheezed in his chest. He was almost at the end of his endurance. The key slipped easily into the lock in a door marked 3B, and he opened the door and stepped inside. He did not bother to switch on the light, but crossed the familiar darkened room and flopped onto an iron framed bed, fully clothed. He lay face down, too tired to sleep, listening to the noises of the building. An argument was going on somewhere downstairs, and from across the street the sound of a jazz saxophone found the open chink in his window. Finally, with one last gasp of relief, he fell asleep.

Foster awoke to the street noises below his garret room. The noon sun was high in the sky, bringing warmth and light to the street below his window. For a few minutes he was not even sure where he was. He lay on the bed for a while longer, feeling hot and sticky in his soiled clothes, slowly collecting his thoughts.

A shaft of sunlight glinted on a large brass crucifix that was the sole decoration on the white walls of the room. The floor was brown tile and there were no carpets. A wooden table and two chairs in one corner stood near a small alcove that contained a sink and an ancient electric cooker. At the other side of the room rested a settee and a well-worn armchair that was showing its stuffing through a split in the leather upholstery. A number of shelves on one wall leaned drunkenly under the weight of numerous books.

Some hooks screwed to a wall substituted for a wardrobe and a couple of suits hung there on wire hangers. A curtain hid the toilet and a shower from view. Apart from a portable radio and an alarm clock on a bedside table, there were no other furnishings.

Foster felt glad to be home, but his recollections of the trip from Ireland diluted his sense of pleasure. After a while, he climbed from the bed and stripped to his underwear before padding barefooted into the bathroom.

For a moment he stood in front of the sink and surveyed himself in the mirror. His face was pallid, the skin blotchy, and a growth of beard aged him far beyond his fifty-ninth year, but the coldness in his eyes still glinted fiercely from his puffy features. He shaved with difficulty, making a mental note to buy new razor blades. Then he spent a full twenty minutes under a shower, washing away two days' grime and sweat, luxuriating beneath the steady stream of water.

Afterwards he dressed in clean clothes and knelt by the bed before the crucifix, bowing his head in prayer for a considerable time. He thanked God out loud for his safe return and the opportunity to continue with the task bestowed upon him. He continued kneeling in silence, his face blank, like an Eastern mystic. He enjoyed these quiet moments when he could give reverie freedom to roam and take stock of his accomplishments.

The makeup of a terrorist was never so complex as in Foster. Deeply faithful to his Catholic beliefs, his convoluted mind was able to justify the disparity between his religious faith and the barbarity that he was capable of. It mattered not to him that he was responsible for the deaths and maiming of many. He was striving for the freedom of his country.

He had long since shrugged off the workings of politicians as empty-worded nonsense. This conviction rationalised his world and enabled him to rub shoulders with his fellow killers, many of whom subscribed to an out-dated Marxist agenda and were fighting for a united Ireland far different to the one he envisaged.

Working largely on his own, his was an isolated existence, but one of his own choosing. He was fluent in a number of languages and this enabled him to flit at will throughout Europe, melding into whatever community he chose. For the past year, he had chosen Madrid.

In that time, without raising suspicion, he had painstakingly put together a network of contacts throughout Europe that had enabled him to tap into sources of illegal arms and to legitimate suppliers of electronic surveillance equipment and timing mechanisms. The arms shipment by the *Georgios* had been his latest effort, one that had proven his ability to infiltrate weapons through the unprotected coastline of the west of Ireland. That it had not been totally successful was a source of chagrin to him, but he was determined to exploit the route again.

Largely due to his unstinting pressure, links had been forged with the surviving break-away members of the Baader-Meinhoff and Red Brigade subversive organisations. Even though their cause was meaningless and beyond comprehension, these people appealed to him because of their willingness to vent their rage on an innocent society. Lisa Schmitt had arrived in Ireland as a result of his efforts in forming that common alliance, but he was aware that the IRA High Command was nervous about these new-found friends. They had deep reservations about becoming involved with radical groups that really had no interest in what happened in Ireland. Because of that he trod warily. He knew that he had only managed to get their agreement by a very narrow margin, but it made him eager to prove himself right in his conviction that pure terror was the only way forward.

Hungry, he got to his feet and scavenged the kitchen cupboard, but there was little in it. The small refrigerator revealed a solitary mouldy piece of cheese and some sour milk. He would have to go out, but that didn't matter. He needed to phone Ireland anyway to let them know that he was back.

Foster locked the door behind him. Directly across the landing, the door of 3A came ajar as he did so, and an elderly lady in a cotton print dress peeked out. Recognising him, she opened the door wide, 'Oh! It is you, Senor. I thought I heard you come back last night but I wasn't sure.' Speaking softly in Spanish, she fussed one-handed, trying to replace a hair grip that had loosened.

Foster gave her a slight bow. It was almost a gesture of dandyism, and his pale linen suit, although stained in places, lent him the quaint air of a southern gentleman. He greeted her courteously in perfect Spanish. 'It is so nice to see you again, how are you? Your sister is well too, I trust? I've been away in Seville on business again, but the weather is far too hot there and I am glad to be back.' They continued to chat for a few minutes and Foster offered to bring back fruit and bread from the market when he returned.

The woman had never known his name. She was far too polite to ask, and he had never mentioned it, but he had always been very kind to her since he had moved into the apartment and often shopped for her. She lived with her deaf and dumb older sister, who now also appeared in the doorway, smiling and nodding as though she understood every word they said. To both of them, Foster had always been both solicitous and chivalrous, even if he was absent a great deal.

'You are so kind, Senor. Fresh bread would be lovely and some oranges, too, if it is not too much trouble. I am finding the stairs are becoming difficult. It is my age, I suppose.' She cackled merrily while her sister continued to nod like a ventriloquist's dummy.

Foster smiled and laughed on cue. 'You are only approaching the peak of your lives, both of you,' he declared, as he headed for the stairs.

On the second floor there were three slightly larger apartments, one of which housed a prostitute who seemed to work on a twenty-four hour basis. He crept towards her door. She had accosted him on the stairs on a number of occasions and derived much amusement from his embarrassment whenever they met. Once, she had even brushed her large pendulous breasts suggestively against him in the hallway. The idea of touching her nauseated him. As usual, he tried to get past her door quickly without raising her attention.

He remembered once being inquisitive enough to look inside her open doorway, where he'd seen the garish quilted bed, the pink shaded lights, and the lingerie displayed on the walls. He had scuttled away in confusion and had prayed for her that night, before masturbating in the darkness of his room.

Perhaps she was busy already. The very thought of it propelled him down the next flight of stairs.

The sunlight in the street outside the building was blinding in its white intensity. He paused on the step for a moment, blinking like a mole leaving its burrow, and donned a pair of sunglasses before pushing his way through the crowds thronging the street stalls.

Foster ate lunch in a small bar where he was known well enough for the owner to greet him as if he had found a long-lost brother. He poured Foster a glass of his favourite sherry without being asked. Whilst on one level Foster enjoyed the attention, it also discomforted him. He had already begun to think that it would not be long before he would need to move on. He no longer felt safe being so well known, but for the moment he was ravenous and in no mood to go elsewhere. He dined on a delicious paella and washed it down with a rough Castilian wine, cheap but very good.

Afterwards, he called Jim Hogan from a call box at the back of the noisy bar. 'It's me,' he said. 'I'm back.'

'Good,' Hogan replied. 'That's excellent news, the best I've had for a while. How was your trip?'

Foster's face took on a black look. 'Not very pleasant,' he said. 'But successful. I retrieved our money.'

Hogan sounded pleased. 'I'm delighted to hear it. I'll let Liam know that you are back. By the way, McGinty met with an accident. He is being buried today.'

The news startled Foster but he made no comment. 'I'll leave tonight.' He put down the telephone. He had not mentioned the murders. That could come later, if ever.

Foster made his way back to the apartment where he delivered his purchases to the two sisters on the top floor. Refusing their offer of a glass of sherry, he returned to his own room and packed a small bag.

Soon afterwards he took a taxi to the Plaza Colon where he boarded a bus for Barajas airport on the outskirts of the city before leaving Madrid at four o'clock on an Iberian 737 to Brussels.

Sixteen

Yun See fretted in his cabin aboard the *Georgios* while awaiting his turn to be interviewed by the detective investigating the killing of Captain Arkides and his Second Officer, Manoli Vlassos. It was already midafternoon and the questioning of the crew had been going on since early morning when the ship left the oil terminal and again anchored out in the bay.

He should be at the airport right at this minute boarding a plane for London, he thought. The thought of it gnawed at his insides as he saw all his dreams disappearing like so much smoke on a stiff breeze. He did not understand what was going on. The killings were nothing to do with him, he thought, and the delay was a threat to his future in England.

When a knock eventually came to the door, the cabin walls suddenly seemed to close in on him, opening his sweat pores to send a rivulet of moisture down his spine. The Filipino cook stood grinning in the doorway. 'You next, Yun See.' Without waiting for a reply, he clumped off down the alleyway, relishing his new-found power. Yun See followed a few paces behind him and crossed the afterdeck , thong sandals flip-flopping noisily on the steel plates.

Felix Valverde perspired in the officer's saloon amidships and perused a single page of terse notes in his notebook. The air was torpid as the midday sun roasted the ship, and the single over-head fan was incapable of doing more than turning it to the consistency of soup.

This was getting nowhere, he thought. At this moment he wished he had never become a policeman. It was bad enough having a double murder on his hands without having to question a rag-tag crew who spoke no Spanish. His knowledge of English wouldn't enable him to order a plate of fish and chips on the Costa del Sol, not to mention question an entire ship's crew. Luckily, early on in the proceedings, he had discovered that the ship's cook was from Manila and spoke reasonable Spanish, even if he did seem to be a half-witted moron.

The cook came into the saloon and glided over to the table followed by Yun See. He ran a finger slowly down the list of crew members. 'Yun See, Hong Kong.' He seated himself at the table and glowed with importance.

Felix stared hard at the Chinese for several seconds, his eyes searching the moon-like face. Something told him that this was going to be another farce. 'Ask him where he was last night,' he ordered.

The cook's grin broadened. 'He was working on board the ship taking fuel.'

The detective glared at him. 'I said ask him. I don't need you to tell me what he was doing.'

'There's no point,' replied the cook. 'He doesn't speak English, only Cantonese, and I know he was on board all night. He never goes ashore anywhere. He saves his money to buy a restaurant.'

The detective sighed and put down his pen. For an instant he contemplated punching the inane grin from the cook's face. He gazed into the mask of Yun See's face. The brown almond-shaped eyes did not waver, but stared back at him with a mirror-like finish that revealed nothing. 'Mother of God!' he exploded. 'How do you give orders to him if he can't understand any language but his own?'

'He knows enough words for working the ship, that's all.'

Valverde felt defeated. What was the point, he thought. 'Ask him if he saw anything unusual last night. Try anyway.'

The cook turned to Yun See. 'Captain boss, second mate boss – all dead.' He drew his finger across his throat. 'You see other sailor-man?'

Yun See fixed his eyes on the top of the cook's head and

stared unblinking at some unseen spot. He remembered that man Foster scuttling away into the darkness as he watched him from the poop deck rail the previous night. He knew this was what the detective needed to hear, just as surely as he knew that his cabin-mate Gupta Bose had not fallen down the ladder from the bridge accidentally. His thoughts drifted to his brother's restaurant in Soho and his visa to enter England. If he said anything, it could ruin his chances. If he told them nothing, absolutely nothing, what could they do about it? He shook his head.

The cook smiled at the detective. 'He says he saw nothing.'

'I gathered that,' Valverde replied. He beckoned to a uniformed policeman standing by another table. 'Get his finger prints, Rocco, and send for the next one.' His exasperation surfaced as his mouth set itself in a thin line of impatience. As if to add to his difficulties someone had switched on a radio elsewhere in the accommodation. The sound of an opera penetrated to the room, annoying him even more.

Yun See returned to his cabin feeling calm and pleased with himself. Maybe tomorrow he would be able to go to London. As he crossed the open deck he could see activity at the oil terminal. A police launch bobbed alongside and a flagged buoy floating on the surface indicated that divers were down searching the bottom of the harbour. He could have saved them the trouble. He knew they would find nothing.

Valverde packed his briefcase as the sun set. Somewhere in the town a mullah was calling the faithful to prayer and his chant carried faintly across the still water as he boarded his police launch.

It was already dark when he reached his office. He left the lights off and stared down from the darkened window to the street below, where the lights of a line of cars snaked their way homewards. The noise of the traffic did not penetrate the closed windows. The only sound in the room came from the hum of the air-conditioner.

The telephone on his desk broke the silence; he switched on

the lights before picking up the receiver. 'Valverde here,' he said in a tired voice. It was the Chief of Police.

'Yes Sir, I understand perfectly.' He replaced the telephone and sat drumming his fingers on the desk. Sleep, he decided, that would erase the frustration he felt. He would go home to his wife. Maybe they would make love, then he would sleep, and the futility of his life would be that much lessened.

A sharp knock on the door to his office heralded a uniformed sergeant. Valverde looked up. 'Sit down, Sergeant. I don't expect you have much to tell me.'

'No, Sir. The divers haven't come up with a weapon. They found nothing at the bottom of the harbour except shit.' He turned up his nose. 'There's plenty of that down there, I can tell you!' Even though the room was cool, Sergeant Carpizo felt unnaturally warm and dabbed a handkerchief at his forehead. He looked tired and his uniform was soiled with mud.

'I can smell it.' Valverde sighed. ' You can remove the guard from the ship tomorrow morning.'

Carpizo raised his eyebrows in surprise. 'What about the finger prints?'

'See that they are processed tonight against the crew records. But you won't find anything there either, I'm sure of that. I've had orders to release the crew tomorrow if we don't come up with anything.' He stopped talking for a moment and gazed at the ceiling. Politicians, he thought moodily, but why should he concern himself over a couple of dead seamen, anyway? Tomorrow's papers wouldn't even print it on the front page. He closed the file on his desk with a loud snap and said, 'It was a robbery, pure and simple, not by the crew but by persons unknown, probably from the shore.' Even as he said it he knew the sergeant didn't believe it, either.

Seventeen

Late on Friday evening, Foster arrived at Brussels airport. As soon as he had cleared customs he made his way directly to a bank of telephones in the arrivals area.

Thirty minutes later, a nondescript blue Fiat Ritmo picked him up outside the terminal building and carried him towards the city.

The Libyan Peoples' Bureau had not changed since his last visit, he noted. Camera controlled entrance gates opened automatically in front of the car, allowing it to crunch up a short gravelled driveway before entering a garage at the rear of the building. Once inside, the doors closed and the driver ushered him into the building through a back entrance.

Colonel Mohammed Ghalboun, a senior intelligence officer at the bureau, was waiting for him in the splendidly furnished library. Foster had never visited him without marvelling at the amount of money the Libyans were able to lavish wherever they established a presence. At the same time there was something decadent about the place. Several long-haired young men in sweat shirts and faded jeans lolled about in the antique chairs furnishing the room.

Ghalboun was a tall, handsome young man of impeccably good manners. He wore a silk Armani suit, expensive handmade shoes, and an open-necked blue designer shirt. Thick black hair softened his angular features, and he sported a black moustache. Indeed, Foster mused, the Colonel looked dashing enough to whisk a romantic dreamer away to some desert oasis.

Ghalboun greeted Foster cordially, immediately offering him refreshments. 'Mr. Foster,' his voice boomed in the lofty room. 'It is so good of you to call and see us again.' He crossed the room in a few long-legged strides and extended his hand. 'We didn't anticipate another visit so soon. I trust you had a pleasant flight.' He selected a crystal decanter from amongst several on a sideboard, and dropped ice into two glasses. 'Scotch, I think?'

It seemed to Foster that in spite of Ghalboun's orthodox Muslim background, the man had developed a liking for good Scotch, along with many other Western pleasures. He wondered how Ghalboun and his compatriots ever managed to re-adapt to the rigours of a strict desert society when they returned home. 'That will be fine, thank you, Colonel.' He glanced at the others in the room. 'But I would prefer if we could talk alone, if you don't mind.'

Ghalboun's smile was dazzling. 'We have no secrets from each other here, but of course, I have no objections, if that is your wish. Perhaps you would feel more comfortable in our conference room?'

Without waiting for Foster to reply, he picked up the amber filled glasses and led the way from the room across a wide entrance hall whose marble floor glinted in the light from a crystal chandelier high on the lofty ceiling. They climbed up an ornate curving staircase.

Foster had been here before. On the second floor, in the centre of the building, the Libyans had constructed a secure room well away from all external walls. The room was windowless and soundproof. More important to the occupants, it was free of electronic bugs and frequently checked with electronic sensor equipment to make sure it remained so.

The intelligence officer opened the door and courteously ushered Foster inside before closing the door behind him. Inside, the room was clinically sparse. All that it contained was a single long wooden table surrounded by uncomfortable metal framed chairs. In spite of electric extractor fans built into the ceiling, it had a stale unpleasant smell. The white neon-lit glare of the interior was unrelieved by any form of decoration and was out of keeping with the rich trappings evident elsewhere in the house. Ghalboun seated himself at the table, 'How can I be of service to you, Mr Foster?' he asked in a low voice.

Foster got immediately to the point. 'We have run into a number of problems,' he began.

Ghalboun silenced him by raising his hand. 'I know all about your problems, Mr. Foster. It has not been as successful a trip as you envisaged, is that not so? Also, that little mess you left behind you in Ceuta is embarrassing, to say the least.'

The directness of Ghalboun's remarks took Foster by surprise. His mouth dropped open. How the hell did the bastard know this already? When he found words to speak, his voice echoed the consternation on his face. 'How on earth ...'

Ghalboun's laughter had a melodious ring to it as he enjoyed the effect of his words. 'Suffice it to say, Mr. Foster, that it is our business to know about most things in which we have an interest or an involvement. We live in a dangerous but interesting world, don't you think? A world in which one has to be increasingly careful.' He picked up his glass and gazed at it for a moment, turning it in his hand so that the crystal picked up the overhead light and reflected it in a momentary metallic flash of blue. He sipped the drink slowly and swirled the glass so that the ice tinkled in the silence. Then he continued. 'We have already taken steps to take care of the problem you left behind in Morocco. The Chief of Police is, how can I put it, a close colleague, so to speak. You can be assured that the affair will be taken care of satisfactorily.'

Foster could not deny that this piece of news was welcome, but it amazed him that the Libyans had got onto it so quickly. 'Obviously, I am delighted to hear that the problem is being contained. I am very grateful to you, but you do understand that I had to do it? I couldn't sit by and allow them to rip us off.'

Ghalboun sighed. 'Messy, very messy, Mr. Foster. Slipshod might be an even more appropriate word. Fortunately for you and your people, you have us to rely on. I have to say, however, that this might not always be the case.'

The hidden threat in the Libyan's voice was not lost on

Foster. Before he could reply, Ghalboun forestalled him. 'I think I know what you will ask of us next.' Ghalboun's eyes had the look of a cobra faced by a mongoose.

Foster felt ruffled. Ghalboun was needling him. His face flushed slightly but his eyes showed little. 'The ammunition for the weapons was unfortunately lost,' he said. 'We need it, otherwise the guns are useless. It's not a question of money. We must replace that ammunition, whatever the cost.

'Exactly,' said Ghalboun. He gazed for a while at the white polystyrene tiles on the ceiling, one hand fondling his moustache almost as though he were stroking a well-loved pet. 'But I'm not sure that we wish to get further involved with you after what has happened. The whole operation was sloppy, and the risks for us are far too great.'

A worried frown clouded Foster's features. This was not what he had expected to hear. 'Colonel, you have got to see this through now. You have to help us in this! If it's money you are worried about ...' He trailed off in midsentence, knowing that he was blustering. He suddenly felt weak and exposed. A stain low down on the opposite wall caught his eye. It looked remarkably like dried blood. His mouth felt parched and he gulped at his drink.

Ghalboun didn't hesitate. '*Got to!* Mr. Foster, there is no such thing as *got to*, I can assure you!' The Libyan clipped his words in a precise steely way. 'If we agree to help you again, there will have to be changes, many changes. There is far more than money involved, I can assure you. We would expect to see a substantial return for our continued involvement.' He paused for a moment, letting his words sink in. 'By that, I mean, Mr Foster, that we would expect to see a concrete result for our efforts. Do you seriously think for one moment that we have any real interest in your petty little Irish squabbles?'

At least there is still hope, Foster thought. The man had not actually said no. He seemed to be offering a compromise. 'Now it's my turn, Colonel. How can we help you?'

The Libyan drained his drink thoughtfully. He set the empty glass on the table and pushed it away as he leaned forward.

'That's more like it,' he said, smiling again. He spoke earnestly and quickly for a long time as he outlined what he was prepared to do. And, more important, what he expected in return.

Foster listened to him and did not interrupt. The plan was far-fetched, incredible even, but it excited him. He was being presented with an opportunity to blow the lid off the peace talks; a chance that might never occur again. He felt his blood pumping as he listened to the Libyan's proposal.

Several hours passed before Foster left the bureau. The same blue Fiat carried him swiftly into the centre of the city. Lost in thought, he slouched in the back seat making no attempt to enter into conversation with the young Libyan driver who manoeuvred the car through the traffic with the verve and dash of a Formula One contender.

Foster brooded, letting his mind go over every detail of Ghalboun's plan, searching for weaknesses, incisively dissecting it and putting it back together again. The more he thought about it, the more excited he became. But how to sell it to his people back home? That was the stumbling block he kept returning to.

When the car entered the Grand Place in the Lower Town he signalled to the driver to stop and he alighted at the next corner. The driver immediately pulled away from the kerbside. There was no acknowledgement between them. He stood for a few minutes watching the rear lights as the car sped away.

Even though it was late, there were still people about in the square. The evening was warm, enticing them to stay, and they dawdled as tourists do, but Foster hardly noticed them. For once, the exquisite elegance of the square made no impression on him. Too many thoughts and ideas crowded into his mind, fighting for space.

Right now he needed food. Afterwards, he would relax in his own special way. It was time for that, he knew. Perhaps it would purge the blackness deep in the inner recesses of his brain.

He had his first really good meal in days in an Italian restaurant not far from the square. Calmed by the influence of a good bottle of red wine, he took a taxi to the Gare du Nord, a tawdry area where he knew he would find what he craved. For the moment, thoughts of terrorism and the cause that his father had weaned him on were the furthest things from his mind.

It did not take Foster long to find what he was looking for. Outside the Kit Kat bar he was soon in conversation with an emaciated youth who clung to life through the daily thread of his heroin addiction. The excitement welled and bubbled inside him again as he stared into the needle-like pupils of the youth's eyes. The youth quoted a price, his voice flat and uncompromising and his eyes steady as he said it. Foster doubled it in American dollars. Straight sex was one thing, he thought. But not tonight. Tonight he wanted more than that.

The young man accepted in resignation. Life was not always simple, and in any case he had travelled the road before. He led Foster down a darkened street to a run-down building that offered rooms by the hour or by the night. In the lobby, a concierge lurking behind a well-worn desk hardly looked up as he passed over a key. He had a face like a dried prune and his breath reeked of alcohol. He stuffed the money Foster handed him into a tin box and returned his attention to a magazine on his desk.

Beneath a glaring naked light bulb in a room on the second floor, Foster handed the money to the youth. Breathing heavily through clenched teeth, he stripped the youth of his threadbare jeans and his black teeshirt with a fluorescent orange Hard Rock design.

The youth's imagination had already transported him far away, away from the onslaught of hands and the stench that permeated the room from the stairwell outside the locked door. Savouring every minute, Foster bound and gagged the rent boy before thrusting him face down on the bedclothes, which were still warm from the previous occupants.

The young man tensed himself, thinking only of the money and his next fix. The first cigarette burn scorched the skin on his bony shoulders and he closed his eyes. More followed, slowly, in succession down the white outline of his spinal column, down to the wasted inner thighs. His teeth clamped tightly on the gag.

In a spasm of agony his body contorted and writhed in silence. He caught a whiff of garlic in the air as the breath of the maniac leaning over him rasped with excitement.

To Foster, this was just the preliminary game, and the feeling of power overwhelmed him. The infliction of pain was the only way to bring about the release that the Irishman craved. He fondled his penis, feeling the organ growing, matching his need.

The boy's muffled sobs finally died as Foster lowered his fat belly to the clenched white buttocks. Parting them, he sodomized the unmoving body.

Minutes later, Foster released him. The boy lay on the bed hardly moving, breathing in quick shallow gasps, not wanting to look at the man who had brought him to this place, not wanting to see the mirror-image of what he had become. He did not know it, but he was lucky. He was alive.

Foster felt good again as he left. Dawn was showing over the roof tops as a faint pink glimmer in the eastern sky as he made his way on foot to the Gare Centrale. He had a train to catch and there was work to be done.

Eighteen

In the week following the funeral, Jim Prendergast drove himself unmercifully. He spent the days trudging over miles of rocky beaches in a vain search of every inch of the coastline where he thought there was a chance of finding Susan's body, or even a scrap of wreckage from the *Larinita*. He sought anything that might offer some clue that would lead to identifying the ship that had run them down, but each evening he returned to the cottage, even more weary and disconsolate than the day before.

He even borrowed a local fishing boat and spent an entire day from dawn until dark patrolling off the Skerd rocks all the way to Roundstone, but without avail. On several occasions he saw blue lobster boats either out on the sea or close inshore, but they all looked the same, and he knew that he would be unable to identify the boat even if he came upon it. It was an impossible task.

Numerous telephone calls to the Aran Islands had simply confirmed that the island fishermen were continuing to watch their seas and coastline, but they had come upon nothing of any significance. The police in Galway had also turned up nothing. Iain McQuaid continued to be helpful whenever he spoke to him, but Prendergast already sensed that their investigation had begun to wind down. The police had many other things to occupy their time, and his, after all, was only an accident in their eyes.

Despair came and with it, hope slipped away like blood oozing from a wound. Prendergast was barely conscious that he was drinking and smoking too much. If it hadn't been for the enduring kindness of Mary McGonigal, he probably would have forgotten to eat.

A week later he returned to Galway to pay for the costs of the funeral. While he was there he also called to his insurance broker in Augustine Street to fill in the claim forms for the loss of his yacht.

The broker was painfully correct in his queries into the sinking, and was unhappy with Prendergast's inability to identify the ship. 'If what you say is correct, Mr. Prendergast, and I have no reason to disbelieve you, the other party is liable. It may be some time before the insurers process your claim.' His manner was prim.

Prendergast's temper boiled. It was going to be a protracted process. 'You're not slow to increase my premiums whenever you feel like it,' he retorted. He leaned across the desk. 'Just settle it. I'll sue if you don't.'

The broker gave a noncommittal sniff and showed him to the door. 'I'll do whatever I can.'

By the time he reached the street outside the broker's office, Prendergast had almost made up his mind to go and get blind drunk. Instead, he decided to call on Vincent Kelly at the Harbour Master's office.

He drove over and parked his car outside Kelly's office. The building, situated on the dockside, looked more like a portocabin than a permanent structure. Inside, however, it was comfortably well equipped, revealing a number of offices and a large conference room that was used for meetings of the Harbour Board.

He enquired for Kelly at the receptionist's office just inside the entrance. The woman smiled politely. 'I'm sorry but he's not here. He is bringing in a tanker, but if you care to wait ...'

'Thanks, I'll call back later.'

Jim again considered going for a drink, but forced the idea out of his mind. It was becoming a problem that he could do without. Instead, he crossed the dock to the lock gates at the entrance to watch the tanker coming in. He could see that there were no ships in the docks except for the old *Bullfinch* that traded between Galway and the Aran Islands. Mostly she carried building materials, food supplies and Guinness for the island shops and pubs, but it would be doing her a favour to refer to her as a merchant ship at all. She was tiny in comparison to modern coasters, and like a venerable old lady, was already showing her wrinkles.

Standing near the lock gates, he saw that he didn't have long to wait. A fully-laden Shell tanker was already in the channel inside Nimmo's Pier, moving slowly towards the entrance. In direct contrast to the *Bullfinch*, she was a modern well-kept ship, and he watched with interest as she slid through the narrow entrance without fuss, her deck crew competently preparing to dock alongside a festoon of black hoses in front of the tank farm.

His bitterness savagely returned as he imagined what a disparity there must be between this crew and the one which ran him down just a short couple of weeks ago. Two weeks, he thought. Could it be only that long? It seemed more like a year.

Vincent Kelly waved from the navigation bridge as the ship passed through the locks. The Harbour Master cupped his hands and shouted something unintelligible as a sudden burst of sound from the ship's square red funnel drowned out his words. Then her powerful engine went astern to slow the ship's swing as her propeller churned up the dirty brown waters of the dock, bringing to the surface a disgusting collection of plastic bags and other debris. The crew expertly passed ashore her mooring lines and she secured alongside the oil terminal. Within minutes, the cargo hoses connected and the ship began discharging her cargo.

Jim felt suddenly envious of Kelly. There he was, still able to command a ship, doing something worthwhile. What the hell am I doing? he thought viciously, except going round and round in circles getting nowhere. His self-esteem plummeted to a new low, and he realised that he was going to have to do something about it, soon.

Presently, Vincent Kelly joined him on the dockside and they walked together the short distance to the office. Kelly was a short muscular man. He was entirely bald but his face sported a neatly trimmed red beard. Jim liked his slow spoken manner, and there was a quiet confidence about the man that suggested reliability.

The receptionist served them tea in Kelly's office. It was a large comfortable room furnished with a big mahogany desk and a scattering of chairs. The walls held several framed charts of Galway Bay, and the bookshelves contained various technical reference books on ship handling and loading procedures. A single window, with venetian blinds for privacy, overlooked the docks outside. The room had a satisfying nautical air to it and it reflected Kelly's business-like professionalism.

'Help yourself to the biscuits,' Vincent said after they settled in their chairs. 'I've been meaning to give you a call.' Seeing the expectant look on Prendergast's face, he hastened to add, 'I haven't any real news for you, I'm sorry to say. I have made a few enquiries, though. I contacted Valentia radio station, the Shannon pilots – any place on the west coast that might have handled your ship. I drew an absolute blank, I'm afraid. She simply disappeared. What about you, have you managed to turn up anything?'

'No,' Prendergast replied, lighting a cigarette. He felt disappointed, but he hadn't really expected to hear anything else. 'Thanks for doing that much anyway, Vincent. It was probably a lot more constructive than anything I've done. A while back the police told me that divers had located the wreck but they couldn't find a body. Since then I've been wandering the beaches, looking for Susan. Not a fucking trace of anything.' His voice sounded flat. 'Between you and me, I think the Guards have given up as well. I'm going round and round in circles, Vincent. I'm certainly no bloody use as a detective, that's for sure!'

'Are you going to get yourself another yacht?'

Vincent's question surprised him. 'I haven't thought about it, but the answer is, probably not.' He stubbed out his cigarette in an ashtray. 'Not yet, anyway. The insurance people are giving me a hard time. It'll probably be a few months before I see any money from them.'

Kelly poured himself another cup of tea and stirred two spoons of sugar into it. 'Have you thought about getting away for a while, a holiday perhaps?'

'It's crossed my mind a few times. I think the winter will be the worst. A few weeks in the sun then might not be such a bad idea.'

Vincent nodded. He got up from his chair, walked over to the window and stood for a while staring out across the docks. A sudden flurry of rain spattered against the glass, heralding a change in what had, until then, been a fine day. He didn't speak for a moment, contemplating the litter being swirled across the quay by the squall. Further down the harbour a bulky red trawler had entered the docks and was having difficulty coming alongside.

Turning away from the window, Vincent said, 'You're not too old yet you know, and you still have your master's ticket. It's just an idea, something to consider.'

'Vincent, are you offering me a job?' Jim laughed. His laughter sounded hollow in the panelled office, but it felt good.

Kelly sat down again and faced him, his weather beaten face quite serious. 'No. Well, not exactly. I'm just thinking aloud, I suppose, but the *Bullfinch* out there is laid up. She failed her annual survey last month. As far as I know she has been sold and will probably be going to a breaker's yard somewhere. She's going to need a delivery crew. I might be able to put in a word for you if you fancied getting away for a while.'

Prendergast got to his feet and went to the window. The rain had stopped as quickly as it had begun. Now sunshine washed over the docks to where it was reflected by the superstructure of the tanker on the far side. He stared at the forlorn hulk of the *Bullfinch*. 'Jesus, Vincent, she's a bloody wreck!'

Kelly laughed. 'You're right, of course. It was only a thought.'

Prendergast moved towards the door. He didn't want to sound ungrateful. 'Look, don't get me wrong Vincent, I appreciate the thought and I'm not throwing it out. Give me time to think about it. You can let me know if anything else turns up.'

Vincent smiled. 'Of course I will. This might not come to anything anyway.' They shook hands and Kelly saw him to the door.

After he left the harbour office, Jim drove to Brennan's pub on the other side of the docks and had several drinks while he pondered over what Kelly had said. He couldn't make a decision that fast, he thought. Leaving Brennan's, he drove home unsteadily.

A Garda squad car was waiting outside the cottage, and Iain McQuaid got out as he pulled in. Prendergast climbed out of his car and staggered slightly. McQuaid's face was serious and he knew it was bad news. 'I'm sorry,' he said. 'I've had a few drinks.'

'I didn't hear that,' McQuaid replied. 'Jim, I need you to come into Galway with me. Your daughter's body has been found.'

Prendergast's jaw sagged. He felt as though he had just been punched in the kidneys, the pain was so bad. 'Where?'

'Down off the coast of Clare, near the Cliffs of Moher.' The detective took a pace forward and rested his hand on Prendergast's shoulder. 'I need you to identify her, Jim.' He hesitated for a second. 'She's been in the water for a long time – it will be difficult for you.'

Prendergast's face was ashen. 'Let's do it,' he replied. 'I'm glad she's been found. It's a relief. Just not knowing, that was the worst.'

He dreamt that night, a terrible dream of the sea where he was chained to the decks of the sinking *Bullfinch*, and the ship dragged him screaming on an interminable plunge to the abyssal depths of the ocean. Jane and Susan were reaching for him with outstretched arms from the bottom slime. Over the tortured scream of rending metal came the sound of laughing voices, and a lone black sailor beckoned him downwards, ever downwards.

Prendergast awoke in the early hours before dawn, in a sweating panic and finished what was left in a bottle of brandy from the night before.

Susan's funeral was a blurred memory in Prendergast's mind. Each day became hazy with alcohol and he rarely left the house except to buy more. Even Mary McGonigal had stopped calling to the house. Then he heard from Vincent Kelly again. The telephone call came as he opened his second bottle of the day. With weaving footsteps he went to the phone and picked it up.

'Jim?'

'Yeah.'

'Vincent Kelly here. I've just been approached by the new owners of the *Bullfinch*. They want to move the ship within a couple of weeks and will need a delivery crew for a trip to either northern Europe or the Mediterranean, it hasn't been decided yet. Do you want the job?'

Prendergast tried to concentrate. 'I'm not sure,' he replied. He was conscious that he was slurring his words.

'Jim, pull yourself together! I'm sure the job will be yours if you want it, but there's little time. You have to make your mind up.'

'Can I have until tomorrow? I need to think about it.'

He heard Kelly's impatience at the other end. 'Yes,' Kelly replied. 'But only until tomorrow. They want to move fast, and there's a lot of work to be done to get the ship ready for sea. I expect to hear from you before lunch time tomorrow.' There was a click as the line went dead.

Prendergast dropped the telephone into its cradle and staggered to the settee where he had left the bottle. He sat there late into the night, the bottle of brandy beside him, mulling over the prospect in his befuddled mind. He had nothing now. Susan was buried beside her mother and he was drinking his way to joining them. Facing him was an opportunity to escape his self-destruction. He would be well paid for the trip and the money would be useful. At the back of his mind also lurked the hope that he might encounter the freighter. No matter how hard he drank, he could not shake off the hope of somehow finding those responsible. When he eventually closed his eyes that night, his last thought was of the tired old *Bullfinch*.

Early the next morning Prendergast drove to Galway. Vincent Kelly invited him straight into his office. Kelly was shocked at the change in Prendergast since he had last seen him. Prendergast was unshaven and his clothes were rumpled as though he had slept in them. Briefly, he wondered if he was doing the right thing. 'I'm sorry I couldn't make it to Susan's funeral, Jim. I was away in England.'

Prendergast sat down and closed his eyes for a moment. 'I'll do it,' he said. 'I'll take her wherever they want her to go.'

Kelly looked startled for an instant. 'Good,' he said. 'Let's see if we can settle it right now while you're here.' He reached for the telephone on his desk and dialled a number. 'Mr. Pavlides, please,' he said. 'Ah! Good morning to you, Sir, this is Captain Kelly here in Galway. I might have a master for your ship, a Captain Prendergast, master's foreign-going ticket .... Yes, he's a good man.' He placed his hand over the receiver and looked at Prendergast. 'Can you meet him in Dublin on Wednesday next?'

Jim nodded his assent.

'Okay, Mr. Pavlides, three o'clock Wednesday afternoon at the Gresham Hotel. Thank you.'

Kelly replaced the telephone. 'Well, that's it. It's up to you now. Pavlides is flying over from London on Tuesday to arrange the transfer of registration. He'll meet you Wednesday, before he goes back.'

Prendergast wasn't sure whether to feel pleased or not. 'Vincent, I really appreciate all of your help in this. I really don't know what to say.'

Kelly dismissed his remark with a wave of his hand. 'Think nothing of it,' he replied. 'You're doing me a favour. I want to see that tub out of the docks before she sinks there.' He smiled broadly. 'Besides, I get a fee for acting as the local agent.' He reached into a desk drawer and produced a bottle of whiskey and two glasses. 'Let's drink on it,' he said.

Prendergast eyed the bottle hungrily. One drink might quell the churning of his stomach, but only one, he thought. It was time to start straightening himself out. 'Make it a small one,

Vincent. I've been turning that stuff into a habit.'

'I'm glad you said that, Jim. I had a few worries on that score.' Kelly raised his glass. 'To a successful voyage!'

'To a successful voyage!' Jim repeated, realising he meant it. 'By the way, did Pavlides say where the ship is going?'

Vincent sipped his drink before answering. 'No, he didn't mention it, but he's not the real owner. He's a go-between. From the sounds of it she might not be going straight to the breakers. You know what the Greeks are like, they can always squeeze a profit out of any ships that we can't run any longer. Sounds to me as if she might trade for a while yet before they break her up, but it's hard to say. It wouldn't surprise me if you have to deliver her to a Med port somewhere.'

Prendergast felt a twinge of excitement. 'What about the crew?'

'That's up to you, but my advice is to keep the number to an absolute minimum, just enough to carry out the delivery voyage. If you're smart you will negotiate a flat delivery fee and pay the men out of that. You should come out of it very well that way. When you're ready to hire a crew I can point you in the right direction. '

Kelly finished his drink. 'I'm sorry Jim, but I'll have to cut you short. I've got a meeting with the Harbour Board in half an hour. If you get the job, we'll see a lot of each other, but you'll have your work cut out getting that bitch ready for sea.'

They shook hands and Kelly walked with him to the door of the office. 'Let me know how you get on after your meeting.'

'Of course I will. I'll give you a call on Thursday probably; and Vincent, thanks again.'

Jim left the harbour office feeling better than he had for a long time. He strolled slowly across to the *Bullfinch*. She looked even worse when you got close, he thought. Jesus! What a bloody mess. He studied the ship with renewed interest. Some of her hatch boards were missing from the single cargo hold on the well deck and he could see the glint of water sloshing about far below in the darkness. Her anchor windlass was a mass of rust and obviously had not been used for years. The navigation bridge was a peeling shambles, and her funnel looked more like a collander riddled with rust holes. Prendergast couldn't even bring himself to think what her engine must be like. He began to have doubts whether he would get her out of Galway Bay, never mind to the Mediterranean, or wherever was to be her ultimate destination.

From across the dockside, Vincent Kelly watched him for a while through a slit in his office window blinds. Then he picked up his telephone and dialled a number.

Nineteen

Jim Prendergast rose early on Wednesday morning. As the first rays of morning sunlight streaked the bay he stood by the window and smoked a cigarette while he waited for the kettle to boil in the kitchen. Directly below him the sea scratched at the shingle and further out, ruffled by a gusty breeze, the waters were flecked with waves that seemed to wink their approval of his thoughts. It came to him that he was looking out over the sea for the first time since the sinking, without experiencing those darting pangs of black anguish that he had become accustomed to.

He stretched his fingers and studied his hands. They were steady. He had cut back on the booze since his last meeting with Vincent Kelly and could see that it was having the desired effect. He felt good about himself and he was ready to face Pavlides, whatever might be the outcome.

The kettle shrieked as he turned away from the window, confident that he was doing the right thing.

As the train rattled slowly across the bridge outside the Galway station, Prendergast relaxed in his seat and scanned the morning newspaper headlines. The front page was taken up with warnings of an imminent breakdown in the Northern Ireland peace talks. A Loyalist backlash was predicted in response to recently renewed activity on the part of the IRA, while the British Government were denying that the Unionists now controlled the parliamentary process and claimed that peace in the North was never closer. On page two, he read without much interest a report that the German Chancellor, Helmut Kohl, was considering an invitation to meet in Ireland later that summer with the British Prime Minister, the Irish Taoiseach and the President of the United States. The proposed meeting was already leading to a spate of rumours that the British had been engaged in secret meetings with Sinn Fein, the political wing of the IRA. Heated denials of this had been made in Parliament, but the editorial on page six was full of hope that the American President could influence a continuation of the peace process.

Prendergast skipped through the rest of the day's news without enthusiasm. He couldn't help thinking that Ireland was rapidly losing its innocent isolation, hell-bent on joining the rest of the world in an increasing surge of violence. Soon he tired of the paper altogether and turned to the window as the train sped through the flat bogland of the midlands.

For a moment the blurred hedgerows mesmerised him and he could see Jane's smiling face reflected in the glass. She looked happy, just as on the first day he had seen her. He never did tell her what he saw in her. It had never seemed necessary. She knew, that's all that mattered. Now he regretted all the wasted opportunities, and he wished he could tell her over and over how much he loved her.

He remembered the excitement of his retirement when the shipping company he worked for finally sold their last ship and went out of business. It was a time when the last remaining great British ship owners finally surrendered to the pressures of world commerce and threw in the towel.

Jane's face had flushed with pleasure in the knowledge that he would now be home all the time. On a holiday that summer, they fell in love with Connemara and it took only a particularly dismal September in London to persuade them to sell up and return.

Not long afterwards, they found their new home in Kiggaul and spent a year rebuilding the cottage. It had been their home ever since. With the house finished, they bought *Larinita* and sailed her back from Devon. Then came Susan, an unexpected joy. It was like a dream, and now that dream had been destroyed by his stubborn insistence on one stinking race. They were gone forever.

The train's siren blared a warning as they flashed through a deserted crossing. He shut his ears to the sounds around him and closed his eyes.

The rattle of the train clanking slowly across the points woke him as the train entered the semi-darkness of Heuston Station. Once outside, he hailed a taxi, and settled into the back of an old battered Datsun. He fell to watching at the shoppers crowding the streets, a curious mixture of the poor and the glamourous that was synonymous with Dublin.

As usual in the city, the day seemed warmer than on the west coast, where the air was clear and crisp. To him, the noise and smell of the bustling city streets were disturbing, and the buildings crowded in on each other, bringing a mild feeling of claustrophobia. At the same time, he welcomed the change. One could achieve an anonymity in the city crowds that the sparsely populated beauty of Connemara always denied. He half wondered if that was not what he was really seeking; somewhere to lose himself for a while.

He paid off the cab on O'Connells bridge and walked the short distance past Trinity College to Grafton Street where he passed the next couple of hours browsing in the shops. On impulse, he bought a brightly coloured silk scarf for Mary McGonigal. It was expensive. But, he thought, richly deserved for all the help and support she had so freely given him. He smiled at the thought of her generosity, and hoped that it was not too late to repair the damage his drinking had done.

Just before three o'clock, he stepped into the opulent lobby of the Gresham Hotel and enquired at the check-in desk for Mr. Pavlides. An attractive woman rewarded him with a brilliant smile and informed him that Pavlides was expecting him, and was waiting for him in the lounge.

It was easy to spot Pavlides. He was the only male seated in the lounge and was pouring coffee from a silver pot that a waiter had placed on a low table before him. No one else in the room looked anything like him. He was exactly as Prendergast had imagined a Greek ship owner to be.

Prendergast hesitated only for a moment before crossing the expensive royal blue carpet that separated them. The carpet alone would pay for a new yacht, he surmised.

'Mr. Pavlides?'

The other man rose to his feet. He was considerably shorter than Prendergast. His smile was expansive. 'Ah! Captain Prendergast, I'm pleased to meet you, please sit down.'

'I'm sorry, am I late?'

'Not at all, Captain. I have finished my business in Dublin earlier than I expected. I am now relaxing, and enjoying your beautiful city immensely. I find that your people are so friendly and courteous, I hardly want to return to London tonight. I'm only sorry that this has been my first visit. It will not be my last, I hope.' He signalled to a waiter hovering near the marble fireplace on the opposite side of the room. 'You will join me for coffee, of course?'

Jim accepted and thanked him. While he lit a cigarette he had time to take in the other man. Pavlides was short and stocky, with sleek pommaded hair, and a black moustache set over rather fleshy lips. He smiled a lot, revealing a number of gold capped teeth. He wore a severe charcoal pin-striped business suit that was a bit too tight on his ample waist. He also sported a white shirt and a black tie on which there was a gold crest. Pavlides might easily have just stepped off the set of a Hollywood Twenties movie, Prendergast thought. On second glance, he noticed that the gold crest on Pavlides' tie was really an egg stain. He stifled an urge to laugh.

The Greek helped himself to several heaped spoons of sugar. He smiled again and said, 'Perhaps you could tell me a little about yourself, Captain?' His was friendly and matter-of-fact.

Jim gave him a detailed account of his experience and seagoing career, at the end of which he reached for his briefcase and extracted some papers. 'I have my Master's ticket here.' It came to him that he had omitted to mention his recent tragedy. Pavlides had not even asked him if he was married.

Pavlides waved the papers aside. 'Hardly necessary, Captain. I've been in the shipping business long enough to know a professional seaman when I see one.' He lit a cigar and exhaled a cloud of smoke towards the lofty ceiling. 'So, you were with the MacAndrews Line before you retired. I knew them well. They were a fine company with beautiful ships. A great pity so many of those grand old British companies have gone out of business.' He sipped his coffee. 'You must be well acquainted with the Mediterranean, Captain?'

'Yes. I've been in and out of just about every port between Gib and Istanbul at one time or another, if that's what you're asking.' Jim was not sure whether he liked Pavlides or not. The man didn't quite ring true, and he certainly did not like the flashy gold rings that the Greek sported on the podgy fingers of each hand. Or, for that matter, the ostentatious gold Rolex on his left wrist. It didn't really go with the egg stained tie, he thought.

'Captain, let me explain what we have in mind. The ship in Galway is not mine. I am only acting as agent for a business acquaintance. Her true owners are the Pegasus Shipping Company registered in Liberia. My job is simply to arrange for her delivery to the Mediterranean, nothing more.'

Jim's face registered his surprise, 'Oh! She's going to be re-flagged? I was under the impression that she was destined to be broken up in Europe.'

Pavlides flashed his gold teeth again. 'I believe that was the original intention, but I think the owners have decided to trade her for a little longer. She has been re-registered in Monrovia and has been re-named *Maria B*. I haven't seen the ship myself, but I have studied her survey reports. I gather from those that she is, ah, somewhat well used.' He gave a dry laugh. 'She will be refitted in either Malta or Piraeus. Your job will be to deliver her there, after which the crew will be flown back.'

Pavlides flicked the ash from his cigar and stole a glance at his watch. 'Are you interested, Captain?'

Prendergast nodded. 'That would suit me fine. A short voyage is what interests me right now.'

Pavlides seemed relieved. He relaxed, and sat more comfortably in his chair. 'Excellent!' he said. 'Excellent! We will pay you well of course. Now, on the question of your salary ...'

Prendergast quickly interrupted him. 'I would prefer a flat delivery fee. I can raise a crew here in Ireland and will pay them from my fee.'

'Even better,' said Pavlides. 'I don't mind admitting, Captain, that you will save me considerable trouble, and of course, the cost of transporting a crew over here.' He lapsed into silent thought for a moment. 'Twenty thousand, Captain. American dollars, plus expenses of course. You will obviously have to prepare the ship for sea, the costs for which you will submit through my London office.'

Prendergast hid his surprise. It was a generous offer, one that he could hardly refuse. He calculated that he would have a week or two to prepare the ship, perhaps the same again to reach the delivery port. If he kept the crew to a minimum, he could clear a substantial sum for less than a month's work. Better still, he would be active and the work involved would help to clear his mind. He smiled his agreement. 'I'm willing to shake hands on that, Mr. Pavlides. Your terms are fine with me.'

The Greek extracted a brown sealed envelope from his inside pocket and slid it across the table. 'Five thousand dollars, on account, Captain. We will pay the balance into your bank account on your arrival in the Mediterranean.' His handclasp was limp and clammy. Prendergast felt like washing his hands after it.

'How long will it take you to prepare the ship for sea, Captain?'

Prendergast smiled cautiously. 'You did say that you haven't seen her?'

'That is correct. Can she be as bad as your tone suggests?'

'Possibly a little worse than that. Her engine will be my biggest worry. I'll need to find a good engineer.'

'I am sure you will find such a man, Captain. I have every confidence in you. I must reiterate at this point that costs are to be kept low. Any major repairs will be undertaken in the Mediterranean.'

Prendergast frowned. To some extent, this made sense to him as he knew that Galway did not have the facilities to carry out major ship repairs, but he was equally concerned that he would not put to sea until the ship was adequately prepared to his satisfaction. It was bad enough knowing that the ship had failed a survey; her vital equipment would have to be in working order. 'I will not take her to sea until I am satisfied that she is capable of it,' he replied forcefully.

'I understand your concerns, Captain. That is your prerogative of course, and I wouldn't suggest anything different. Perhaps we could continue our conversation in the bar? I would like to seal our agreement over a drink.'

Over several drinks in the hotel bar, Pavlides made it clear to Prendergast that he must ensure that the *Maria B* was made ready without delay. 'Two weeks at the outside,' he emphasised. 'I will advise you of your destination before you sail from Galway.' He handed Jim a business card. 'You can contact me at any time.'

'Thank you, Mr. Pavlides. I understand the urgency perfectly.' Pavlides escorted him through the reception area to the front door and they shook hands on the steps of the hotel.

Prendergast took a taxi to the station from outside the hotel. The drive along O'Connell Street was slow in the mounting rush hour traffic, but he barely noticed. He paid scant attention to a small group of stragglers with little else to do except loiter on the steps of the GPO, listening to nationalist speakers haranguing the passing crowds from beneath their fluttering tricolours. His mind was already in a whirl of activity.

The crowds on the evening train to Galway made it difficult to find a seat on the return journey. A large group filled the bar and there was no dining car. Jim spent most of the trip wedged in a corner of the swaying carriage, drinking silently from a paper cup. There were many things occupying his mind. His days were going to be hectic if he stood any chance of having the old *Bullfinch* ready for her new role as the *Maria B*, but he felt elated and confident, although his thoughts soured and wandered to the mystery ship and her whereabouts many times during the journey.

It rained persistently on the way home, forcing him to concentrate and drive carefully to stay on the road. He was tired, but in a satisfied way. He would not have to resort to a bottle of brandy to sleep tonight.

Twenty

Sir Harold Webster was concerned. He paced the thick Indian carpet of his office for more than fifteen minutes after replacing the telephone receiver.

Why doesn't life remain simple and uncomplicated, he thought. He had enough to occupy his day without early morning calls like that one from London. Besides, he was now going to have to cancel his morning golfing appointment. Monday morning blues perhaps, but the day was definitely not taking the course he had planned for it.

He stood for a while in the large bay window of the room, slowly gathering his thoughts. On either side of him, tasselled maroon curtains draped elegantly to the floor at the edge of the alcove. Outside, the morning traffic was moving spasmodically and a haze of exhaust fumes hung over Merrion Road. The ritual daily snarl-up was already starting but the double glazing of the Georgian windows muted the noise of the traffic.

He really liked Dublin, he mused. It was far better than his last posting to Beijing. Come to think of it, it was even better than many of his overseas diplomatic posts. That was a sobering thought. Perhaps he really was getting too old for the job.

Old Etonian and a career diplomat, it had come as something of a surprise when he found the Irish to be genuinely likeable after he took over as Ambassador in Dublin. His father had always said that the Irish made great soldiers providing they had British officers to control them. If he was honest with himself, he thought, England had not exactly played a fair game in the history of Ireland. To some extent, he could understand the reasoning and the desire amongst some for a united country.

Although the occasional rabble-rousing of demonstrators in the street outside the embassy was irksome, he regretted the need for guards. The high security and the need for constant vigilance in everyday life galled him and he wished that it could be otherwise.

Quite frankly, he had no love for the posturing of the Northern Unionists either. If anything, they were far worse than the demonstrators and added to the morass of bitterness. Most of the time he just wished the problems would simply disappear and permit him to enjoy his final posting before his retirement in another year's time. He had already bought a place in Devon for that eventuality and he looked forward to moving into the quiet backwater of retirement. Right now, it seemed a very attractive option.

Returning to his desk, he picked up the telephone again and made an internal call to the communications centre elsewhere in the building. 'Jonathan old boy, you might pop up for a chat if you are free.' He put down the telephone and turned his attention to the file on his desk marked "Top Secret".

The summons did not surprise Lieutenant Colonel Jonathan Cooke. It was quite usual. The "old man" probably had nothing better to do, he surmised.

He had already sifted through the copies of decoded messages that had come in to the communications centre overnight. Those that were classified he had consigned to security to be placed in their appropriate classification folders. One folder marked "Confidential" he tucked under his arm to take with him.

Jonathan picked up his walking stick and made his way stiffly downstairs. He still had trouble with the stairs. It was a lot worse going up, although he had to admit that the pain was decreasing. The doctors had been right. It was a matter of time.

Three years had passed since a bullet had torn away his knee cap and shattered the bone in his thigh. He was lucky to have a leg at all, he knew, never mind being able to walk on it. He had the surgeons in the Belfast Royal Hospital to thank for its rescue. Perhaps he should thank the terrorists too, whose actions had enabled the doctors and nurses to hone their techniques to perfection over the years of mayhem. His abiding regret, however, was that it was not a terrorist bullet that did the damage, but an accidental discharge of a rifle by a young, over-enthusiastic paratrooper from his own battalion.

Whatever about it, the event had prematurely finished his career in the Parachute Regiment. By now, given his commitment and ability, he should have been a full Colonel, perhaps even a Brigadier. He was not only a good soldier, he had all the right connections. Those same connections had directed him to C-13, the Anti-Terrorist Unit. A number of diplomatic postings abroad had followed. Life had not been all bad since then, but he sometimes found his duties boring and he missed the army immensely.

The Ambassador closed the file on his desk as the knock came to the door. He crossed the large room to a rosewood table on which was a silver tray, an ornate coffee pot and a china tea service. 'Do come in.' He was pouring coffee as the door opened. 'Good morning, Jonathan.' He did not look up, nor did he smile.

'You wanted to see me, Ambassador?' Cooke remained standing in the doorway.

'Come in man, close the door and sit down.' Sir Harold sounded tetchy. Cooke crossed the room and seated himself in a comfortable arm chair close to a coffee table set near the window. The room was familiar to him but the simple elegance of its furnishings still impressed him.

Sir Harold seated himself opposite. 'How's the leg, Jonathan? Still bothering you?'

'Not really, Sir. In fact, it's improving all the time and I'm finding that it also has its compensations.' He chuckled. 'I am much more accurate than the Met people at forecasting rain!'

The Ambassador laughed. 'Yes of course, I hadn't thought of that.' He picked up the sugar bowl. 'One sugar or two?'

'Black, no sugar, if you don't mind.'

Sir Harold stirred his coffee. 'I've just heard that the PM has definitely decided to visit us. Bloody nuisance really. Bang go my holiday plans.'

Jonathan selected a biscuit. 'We have been preparing for that for some time now, and the security arrangements are almost complete. We have already had a number of meetings both with the local people and with the U.S. and German embassies. I feel confident that we have covered all eventualities.'

The Ambassador frowned and said, 'It's not the official visit that concerns me so much, at least, not in Dublin. It's the President. You know that he has fired himself up about his Irish roots and all that rubbish. To complicate things, he's heading into an election year and wants to be seen as the one that solves this mess in the North of Ireland. Now he's got a bee in his bonnet that he wants them all to have a weekend break somewhere in the country after the meeting in Dublin Castle. There are no final agreements yet, mind you, and Kohl is saying he is far too busy; but if the President gets his way it puts a totally new dimension on the security angle.'

'Well,' said Cooke, 'If I know the Yanks, they will have that one well and truly sussed out. Their security people have a phobia about walk-abouts. I doubt that they will let him do it.'

The Ambassador gazed at a portrait of the Queen on a far wall, thinking of next year's honours list. It would be rather nice to be included before he retired, just to round things off, so to speak. 'I hope you're right, but perhaps you would go through the planning again so that we are completely prepared. Meticulously so, I might add. By the way, now that I have got you here, what is new in your spooky world?'

Cooke did not like the way Sir Harold always referred to him as a spook. It irritated him and he tried to ignore it. 'Not a lot, Sir. Things have been relatively quiet of late. A man named McGinty blew himself up with his own car bomb recently. The Godfathers gave him the full treatment. Even Gerry Adams turned out, so he must have been of some importance. He had a record of course, bit of a thug if you ask me. In the end, there was very little left of the car. Or him, for that matter. The only thing interesting to come out of it was that the detonator and the timing mechanism were a new type.

Sir Harold shifted in this chair and crossed his legs. 'Is that important?'

Cooke sighed and shrugged his shoulders. 'Maybe. Their bombs are getting to be more sophisticated. They obviously have a new source in Europe for the timers. That's being looked into of course, but their devices are becoming so good that it is rather surprising this one went off accidentally.'

The Ambassador looked at him with renewed interest. 'You're not suggesting that they might have blown him up themselves? Why would they do that?'

'We have no idea. Anything is possible with these people. They are constantly warring amongst themselves. It might even have been the work of the Loyalists, but I don't think so. So far they are holding the line, even if it is strained to breaking point.

Sir Harold got up and walked over to his desk. He selected a pipe. Although he no longer smoked, he still liked to chew on a pipe stem, especially when he felt perturbed. He returned and said, 'It doesn't seem to affect us down here.'

'No, perhaps not. There is one other thing, though.'

'What's that?' Webster sucked on his pipe, half wishing he had some tobacco, sensing a complication that he could do without.

Jonathan shifted uncomfortably and scratched at an imaginary itch on the back of his neck. 'You might have read of that yachtsman down in Galway who claimed he had been sunk off the Aran Islands by a freighter?'

Sir Harold was thoughtful for a moment. 'Yes, I remember reading about that. It was an unfortunate incident, very unfortunate. The man's wife and child drowned, didn't they?'

'They did. The sailor, Prendergast. He's an ex-Merchant Navy Captain. We have contrived to have him offered a job. Our liaison, Vincent Kelly, made the connection. There is an old ship in Galway which has been laid up for some time and is by all accounts, quite a wreck. They say that she will go to the breaker's yard, but I have doubts about that. Kelly sent

Prendergast to meet with a Greek last week in Dublin. A man named Pavlides, who hired him to captain the ship. This Pavlides has been mixed up in some very shady activities, including shipping toxic chemicals from Italy to West Africa. The Greenpeace people started taking an interest in him a long time ago.'

The Ambassador raised his hand, 'Good God! Jonathan, what on earth has this got to do with us? Quite frankly, Greenpeace I can do without. They have stirred up quite enough bother for us with the Sellafield problem.'

'I was about to come to that,' Jonathan said. 'I suspect that Prendergast really was run down by a cargo ship, just like he said. If so, and presuming it really was an accident, why didn't the ship hang around the area? I think that there might be some connection with these new timers and detonators. We know, for instance that Semtex is available to them now. They have to be getting the stuff shipped in here somehow. The most likely route is down here in the south with distribution taking place from here. I suspect that Pavlides is somehow involved and that another arms run is imminent.'

'What about the Irish Special Branch, do they share your viewpoint?'

'No, they don't, or if they do, they're not saying so. Of course, they get embarrassed when one suggests that anything comes through here without their knowledge. Frankly, they don't have the resources and it's a big coastline. In any case, anything that smacks of the *Claudia* affair is de rigueur, I'm afraid.'

'Hmmm.' The Ambassador stroked his chin for a second. 'Is that all you've got?'

'No,' Cooke said. 'There is something else.'

'I thought there might be!' Webster was no fool and he knew that Cooke had his finger on most of the scraps of information that filtered through the embassy, no matter how insubstantial. He motioned for him to continue.

'Two weeks ago, two Greek seamen were murdered on board a ship called the *Georgios* in Ceuta. That ship matches the description Prendergast gave after he was rescued.'

'How on earth do you know that?' The Ambassador felt confused. Diplomacy was difficult enough without all the cloak and dagger stuff.

'Our people do not have a presence in Ceuta but we are in Gib as you know. We got the word from Mossad. They have an abiding interest in that part of the Arab world.'

Webster felt even more perplexed. Good God, he thought, who else was mixed up in this mess? After a while he said grudgingly, 'Well, one should never ignore an input from the Israelis, I suppose. I think we have learnt that by now.'

'I absolutely agree,' replied Cooke. 'Mossad have the best eyes and ears in the Arab world. Way ahead of the Americans, I would suggest, apart from their satellite intelligence. We are trying to run a check on both ships to see if there is a connection, and you know how difficult that might be. Foreign flags, companies within companies and all that sort of thing. It could take quite a while to come up with something.'

Sir Harold's eyes narrowed. 'Where does Prendergast fit into this?'

'He is certainly not mixed up with anything illegal. Purely a sailor, you understand. I thought that if we handled him right, he might be useful enough to keep an eye on things for us without having to involve our own people directly.'

'Too dangerous, far too dangerous.' The Ambassador responded immediately. He already had visions of the possible repercussions with the Irish government and his tone was emphatic. 'We certainly don't want to risk being compromised in some way with the government here.' He tapped his finger on the file marked "Secret" lying on his desk. 'Especially at this point in time. We really are on the brink, Jonathan. It is very delicate and could swing either way. Everything is in the balance. Peace in the North has never been in greater jeopardy. We cannot afford risks, not now.'

Cooke's disappointment showed on his face. 'By the way, there is one other thing that I forgot to mention.' Jonathan paused for a moment and slid a manila signals folder across the desk. 'Two weeks ago the emigration people at Heathrow picked up a Chinese seaman named Yun See who they thought might be trying to slip in illegally. They questioned him at the time but in the end they let him go. It turned out he had a legitimate entry visa. The interesting thing is that we now know he left the *Georgios* in Ceuta the day after the murders. We're trying to track him down right now. If that ship was ever on the Irish coast we'll know about it soon enough'

The Ambassador opened the folder and read the single sheet of paper inside; closing it, he passed it back across the desk. 'Let it stew for a while, Jonathan. We'll talk about it again.' Sir Harold had heard enough for one morning and he got to his feet. The chat was over.

'Thank you, Sir. I'll let you know if there are any developments.' Jonathan walked towards the door, feeling deflated. His job was difficult enough without having to deal with Sir Harold Webster.

Sir Harold's voice stopped him just as he placed his hand on the brass handle of the door. 'One moment, Colonel!'

'Yes Sir?'

'You're fond of fishing aren't you?'

Jonathan turned around in surprise. The Ambassador was standing with his hands folded behind his back staring out of the window.

'Yes Sir, but ...'

'Why don't you take a couple of days off? I'm told the fishing is good in Galway at this time of the year.'

Cooke smiled inwardly. Maybe he had underestimated the "old man" after all. 'Of course Ambassador, I would enjoy that.'

'Nothing big you understand, just a bit of gentle trolling perhaps.'

Jonathan Cooke closed the door behind him. Grasping his stick firmly, he gritted his teeth and tackled the stairs.

Twenty-One

Jim Prendergast had never worked so hard in his life. The labour absorbed him and he felt fulfilled. Since he had returned from Dublin he had little time to dwell on the tragedy, and sheer exhaustion enabled him to sleep without the nightmares that had plagued him. He had even taken to staying on board the ship to save the long drive home to the cottage.

He had spent the first day clearing an accumulation of rubbish from the tiny captain's cabin behind the wheel house, but he had failed in all his efforts to fix either of the showers located on the lower poop deck. Neither was he able to power up the generator for electricity. For the present, he made do with an oil lamp in his cabin.

The weather had remained fine and warm since his meeting with Pavlides, and in spite of the ship owner's warning to keep costs low he had hired a gang of men to paint the ship. The rust streaked hull of the *Maria B* already looked transformed by fresh paint that hid the ravages of time.

Built in Goole in 1936, 413 tons and 156 feet in length, the ship floated high in the water in the confines of the inner harbour, ladylike in her new finery. Whenever he looked at her, Prendergast was proud of his accomplishment.

The lunch time hooter from Rynne's engineering works on the other side of the docks penetrated to the dark confines of the engine room and Prendergast wearily climbed the short iron ladder to the poop deck. Emerging at the afterend of the bridge accommodation, he stood for a moment blinking in the sunshine. He was glad of the break. His knuckles were sore and skinned beneath oily grime after struggling all morning to dismantle a cooling pump. His efforts left him in no doubt that he needed an engineer badly and he had better concentrate on getting one soon.

The gang of labourers he had hired from the dole office around the corner were already filing ashore to the Harbour Bar, leaving behind their paint tins and brushes scattered about the decks.

Prendergast saw Vincent Kelly coming out of the Harbour Master's office directly across the quay. Prendergast went to the wing of the bridge and shouted across to him. 'Vincent, I need an engineer badly. Got any ideas where I might find one?'

Kelly strolled across to the quay side and squinted up against the sun. 'It might not be that easy, unless you get someone off a trawler. Have you tried the dole office?'

'Yeah, I've left word with them but they have nobody on their books at the moment. I'd like to get a local man if I could. What happened to the guy who was here before she laid up?'

'He lives over in the Claddagh, third house on the right after the Dominican church. He's getting on a bit, though. His name is Eddie Molloy. I think he's packed it in and retired, but you could try him, I suppose. If that doesn't work out, let me know and I'm sure we'll find someone up in Dublin. The way things are, there must be a rake of engineers with no jobs in the country.'

'I'll try Molloy after lunch. Got time for a pint?'

Kelly shook his head. 'No, I'm meeting someone. Maybe tomorrow, if you've got time. By the way, when do you plan on sailing, or is that an embarrassing question?'

Prendergast shrugged. 'Next week, if I can get her ready. I haven't fired up the engine yet. A lot depends on getting an engineer now.'

Kelly surveyed the ship with a practiced eye. 'Well, you've worked a miracle on her so far. She's looking like a ship again. Best of luck.'

Prendergast stripped off his overalls. 'Thanks. Talk to you later.'

Vincent waved and retraced his steps to his office.

Jim went back inside the wheel house. His cabin off the chart room smelled of the fresh paint, but at least it was clean. He changed into shore-going clothes. Through an open port-hole he was able to see across to the other side of the dock where a man was standing at the end of the pier. The man had a camera slung around his neck and was focusing it on the ship. He was leaning on a walking stick and using the camera with one hand. This ship was worth a photo, Prendergast thought. It was one for the record books. Prendergast finished dressing and made his way ashore for lunch.

A high tide had flooded the Claddagh basin by the time Prendergast walked across the Wolfe Tone bridge. He circled left by the church overlooking the stone piers of the old fishing harbour. Dozens of swans dotted the broad expanse of water that now covered the mud and stones of the lower reaches of the River Corrib, and nearby, a group of backpackers was pitching a pair of tents on one of the grass topped piers.

Eddie Molloy's house was semidetached, but neatly kept in comparison to its neighbour that sported a couple of rusty half-dismembered cars in its front garden. The garden of Molloy's house reflected care and attention, and in the centre, a large bed of roses flowered in profusion.

A short concrete path led to the front door that stood open, allowing the afternoon sunshine to penetrate the narrow hall. Jim was about to knock, but he hesitated for a moment as voices rose in anger from behind a door at the end of the hall. Maybe, this wasn't a very good time, he thought. He could do without becoming embroiled in a domestic row. Prendergast was about to turn away when the kitchen door opened and a man hurried out. He was followed by a woman in hair curlers wearing a floral print apron who continued to hurl abuse at him. The man grabbed a jacket from a hall stand and hurried past him without stopping.

'Mr. Molloy?' Jim enquired. The woman had already slammed the front door shut.

The other man stopped halfway down the garden path and turned to face him. 'Who're you? What do you want?'

'My name is Jim Prendergast. I wonder if we could have a word together?'

'Never heard of you!' Molloy started off again toward the open gate.

Jim followed and fell into step beside him. 'If you are Eddie Molloy, I have a favour to ask of you. Perhaps we could have a chat over a couple of drinks.'

The man stopped walking and glared at him. 'Are you buying?'

'Of course.' Jim laughed.

'Good, because I've got no money.' Molloy's voice was still testy. 'Let's go to Taylor's, it's handy enough.'

Taylor's was just a short distance away, on Dominick Street. The interior of the bar was comfortably dark and quiet that afternoon. Normally Jim would expect to find a gang of students draped around the place sipping pints or coffees, stretching their money. Jim fetched two pints from the bar and joined Eddie Molloy at a corner table.

'Cheers!' Jim raised his glass.

'G' luck!' Molloy muttered.

'Vincent Kelly told me you used to be an engineer on the old *Bullfinch*,' began Prendergast.

'Chief Engineer,' Molloy corrected him, wiping a line of froth from his upper lip. 'Hold on a minute ... Prendergast. Are you the man who lost his wife and daughter a few weeks ago?'

'Yes I am.' Prendergast frowned.

'I'm sorry about that,' said Molloy, the belligerence gone from his voice. 'I read about it in the papers. 'T'was a sad business.' He took a swallow from his glass and smiled for the first time. 'Take no notice of the missus back there. She's a bit pissed off having me around her feet all the time. Just hasn't got used to it. Forty years at sea before I paid off the *Bullfinch*. Can't say I blame her, I suppose she's used to having the place to herself.'

Jim liked Molloy already. He judged him to be over sixty; his silvered hair and badly fitting false teeth were a giveaway. Molloy had pleasant features and Prendergast could see that the lines on his face came mostly from laughter. He came directly to the point. 'I'm looking for an engineer. I'm taking her back to sea.'

Molloy drained his pint in silence and pushed his empty glass across the table. Prendergast signalled to the barman for a refill.

Molloy placed his elbows on the table and leaned toward Jim. 'I heard she was sold and re-named. Are you going to run her out to the islands again?' Not waiting for a reply, he went on. 'She's an absolute bitch below, you know. I think I'm too old for her, but nobody knows that bloody engine the way I do.' For a moment a wistful look came into Molloy's eyes and Jim did not miss it. He waited for him to continue.

'It's German – Humbolt-Deutz – six cylinders. They built them well, the Jerries. I was on her for the last five years. I suppose you know her bottom plates are shot to hell?'

'Don't get me wrong, it's nothing permanent, just a delivery voyage to the Med.' Molloy's eyes glinted and Prendergast knew he had said the right thing. 'Sunshine and good pay for a couple of week's work, that's all,' he added. Eddie Molloy's face told him he'd hit the right chord.

Molloy drained his second pint and wiped his mouth with the back of his hand. 'Where in the Med?'

'I don't know yet, probably Malta or Piraeus. Does it matter? Either way, there's a thousand dollars in it for you and your airfare back.' Prendergast glanced towards the barman.

Molloy eyed him for a moment, then he smiled broadly. Tapping his glass, he said, 'Fill that up, Cap'n. You've got a deal!'

It was late when they left the pub. Jim hardly remembered finding his way back on board the darkened ship. He climbed into his bunk that night, secure in the knowledge that he had accomplished a lot that day. All he needed now was a deck hand or two. He knew he had a good man in Molloy. Providing I can keep him sober, he thought, just before sleep overcame him.

Prendergast awoke the next morning to the sound of a generator whirring into life below in the engine room. He opened his eyes to see that the bare electric light bulb over his bunk was glowing and the blower fans were breathing cool air through the ventilation piping. The ship was coming alive!

He pulled on his working clothes and clattered down the ladder into the engine room. A grease-stained Eddie Molloy grinned at him and shouted to make himself heard above the whine of the generator beside the main engine. 'Mornin' Cap'n! Thought I'd put a bit of life into the old girl.'

Jim slapped him on the shoulder. 'Cut the captain shit and call me Jim. I'll get the coffee going now that we have power.'

Prendergast felt that a load had gone from his shoulders. He could forget the engine room. The shore gang were already appearing on board and work was starting on the last of the hull painting. Now that there was electricity, he could concentrate on getting the bridge sorted out and he could check out the radio gear in the chart room.

For a small coaster, the ship was well equipped electronically. In one corner of the wheel house stood a venerable Decca radar together with a more modern automatic pilot that appeared to have been recently fitted. The chart room held a Decca navigator system and on the bulkhead beside the entrance to the captain's cabin was an old Marconi radio telephone that looked as though it had not seen use in years. There was no VHF radio. Prendergast determined that he would try and get Pavlides to agree to the purchase of one before they sailed.

By lunch time, Jim had established that the radar and the autohelm were both operational. However, there was no life in the radio telephone. The Decca navigator appeared to be working, although it was not locking onto signals properly. Instead, it gave various positions, which, when plotted on the chart, put the ship high in the hills on the other side of Galway Bay. He was going to have to call in a technician to help him sort out that problem.

Later, he joined Eddie Molloy for lunch in the Harbour Bar. Lunch for Eddie consisted of four or five pints of Guinness.

Prendergast chose not to notice. The man's company was refreshing. He laughed and joked continuously and had certainly proved his worth in the engine room during the morning. Molloy was already predicting that the cooling pump problem would be fixed by the evening and the engine would be ready for testing the next day.

When they got back to the ship a truck was unloading new hatch boards and the shore gang was transferring them on to the main deck.

Prendergast peered down into the hold. 'Eddie, you might try and get the pumps working. It's full of water down there.'

Molloy belched. 'Leave it to me, Skipper!' He went off whistling towards the engine room.

Vincent Kelly was unlocking his car outside his office as Jim crossed the gang plank. Kelly shouted at him, 'Jim, hold on a minute, your boss has been trying to get you on my phone.' A clatter of falling hatch boards on the deck drowned out his voice.

Cupping a hand to his ear, Jim shouted, 'Who?'

'Your boss – Pavlides, in London. You can call him back from my office if you want.'

Jim walked over to the harbour office. Kelly was about to get into his car. Another man was with him and the Harbour Master waited for him. 'Jim, I'd like you to meet a friend of mine, Jonathan Cooke.'

Jim shook hands with the other man. 'Pleased to meet you.'

Cooke leaned heavily on his walking stick and said, 'I'm delighted to meet you, Captain. Vincent has been telling me all about your ship. Ships have always interested me. You could say that they are a passion of mine.' His accent was clipped and precisely English.

Prendergast grinned. 'I'm not sure you could be passionate about this lady. She's breaking my heart! Were you at sea yourself?'

'Unfortunately not. I wanted to go to sea when I was young but my father had other ideas for me. Vincent tells me you are heading for warmer climes. I envy you.'

'Perhaps you would like to sign on. I'm looking for a deck hand.'

Cooke laughed heartily and tapped his leg with his stick. 'Don't think this bloody leg of mine would be any use to you, but thanks for the offer. Look, I'm on holidays here for the next few days. Perhaps you would care to have dinner with me? You can tell me all about your voyage. I'd like to know more about your trip.'

Prendergast hesitated, 'That's very kind of you, but ...'

Cooke buttoned up his sports coat and climbed into the car. 'No buts, Captain. I'm sure Vincent will join us too, won't you, Vincent?' Kelly nodded his agreement. 'That's settled then,' Cooke said. 'We'll make a night of it, the three of us. Eight o'clock in the Great Southern bar?'

It would be a welcome break to have a night away from the ship, Prendergast thought. 'Thank you very much, Jonathan. I accept.'

'That's excellent. I'll see you later.'

Jim watched them drive away. Quite suddenly he realised that he had been talking to the same man who he had seen photographing the ship from the other side of the dock. Made sense, he thought. Cooke had said that he was passionate about ships. He went into the office to call Pavlides in London.

Pavlides sounded delighted with the progress that Prendergast had made in readying the ship for sea. He readily agreed to the purchase of a VHF radio set but the most important news was that he confirmed the ship would dry dock in Malta. Prendergast could go ahead and order the charts he would need. Pavlides also agreed that Jim could provision the ship and take on fuel as soon as the ship was ready.

Crossing the quay in the afternoon sunshine Prendergast made out the new name painted in white on the ship's forecastle. *Maria B* was certainly coming together. He came on board with a spring in his step as an explosion of water through an outlet in the ship's side confirmed that Eddie Molloy had the pumps working. Prendergast was whistling when he climbed the ladder to the bridge.

By the time the old engineer went ashore in the evening, Prendergast could have kissed him. The showers were working as well.

Vincent Kelly and Jonathan Cooke were already at the bar in the Great Southern Hotel when Prendergast got there. The Englishman wore a brown tweed suit, with a yellow silk handkerchief in his breast pocket. Over a number of pre-dinner drinks Prendergast noticed that Cooke's speech, although jovial, had a military ring to it. He gave the impression that he was used to exercising authority.

Cooke had booked a table in a restaurant at the far end of the town. The evening was fine and warm; most people were in shirt sleeves and the street buskers were out in force, filling the evening air with music as the three men made their way through the crowds thronging Shop Street.

The dinner was excellent and the conversation relaxed. Prompted by Cooke, Jim and Vincent did most of the talking, reminiscing about their early days at sea. Cooke showed great interest. He made sure that their glasses were never empty, and several brandies at the end of the meal ensured that they were staggering when they left the restaurant. Outside, they shook hands. Jim refused an offer of a nightcap at the hotel. 'Lot of work to do in the morning, I'm afraid. It's all very well for you, Jonathan. You're on holiday.'

'I have thoroughly enjoyed your company, Captain,' Cooke replied. 'I hope we can do it again sometime.'

Walking down Quay Street alone on his way back to the docks, Prendergast became aware in a fuddled sort of way that Cooke had gleaned his entire life story but had divulged nothing of himself. All that Prendergast knew of the man was that he was English, a close friend of Vincent Kelly's, and was on holiday. Fishing on the lake, he had said. If Prendergast had thought about it, he might have remembered that he knew that much when he first met the man outside Kelly's office.

Twenty-Two

The ferry from Rosslare to Le Havre was late leaving: *For tech - nical reasons*, a disembodied voice announced in robot-like tones over the ship's tannoy system. Liam was not impressed. He was not a good sea traveller and the thought of spending a night on a ferry did not appeal to him.

Lisa, however, had told him how much she was looking forward to the journey. For her, a return to the Continent signalled action. She was tired of hanging around Connemara, waiting for something to happen.

When the summons came, Liam had been unable to understand why he needed to accompany her. It had taken a visit from Jim Hogan to convince him that the meeting they were to attend with Foster was crucial and there could be far-reaching consequences if he was not there. Liam formed the distinct impression that Hogan was not entirely happy having Foster working for them. Something was going on that had Hogan worried. And if it was serious enough to worry Hogan, Liam had every right to be worried, too.

After depositing an overnight bag in a small two-berth cabin, they joined the crowds of holiday makers on deck. As the ferry glided swiftly from the harbour, Liam cheered up a little when he found that the sea outside the entrance was calm and benign. The surface of the water was a translucent blue, streaked with gold by the late evening sunset. On the horizon, a ragged line of white clouds presented no threat and within minutes the dark shadow of land behind them receded, the deck barely moving under foot.

Lisa clutched his arm. He could feel the soft thrust of her breast against his bare forearm. There was something comforting about the unaccustomed intimacy, making him feel happy to be with her.

'I'm getting cold here,' she said. 'Let's go to the bar and get a drink. I feel like celebrating.'

Liam's smile faded. 'There's nothing to celebrate as far as I'm concerned. I don't understand what's going on.'

'Don't worry,' Lisa said. 'You're on your way to meet some very interesting people. My sort of people, for a change. I think you will be pleasantly surprised.'

Since they had taken to sleeping together their relationship had improved. The past few days in Connemara had been free of tension. He had dismissed the thought of love. He was too much aware of her lethal hardness for that, and he knew he could never control a woman like Lisa. But her sexuality excited him.

Turning towards her, Liam kissed her lightly on the forehead. 'Okay, you be boss for now. Let's go.'

She seemed surprised by the kiss. Liam realised that his flash of tenderness had come and gone in an instant, embarrassing him a bit. He was already retreating.

Liam had never been with a woman like Lisa. She seemed to find his inhibitions amusing and found them a challenge. She irritated him, but he found solace in having her to cling to when his sweat-soaked dreams came in the night. At least, he thought, until the nature of their business took that small comfort away, as surely it would.

Lisa was a woman who knew what she wanted. She craved notoriety and success. Love didn't even rank. Sexual gratification was like eating or drinking, something she took when she wanted, from whomever she wanted. Love did not come into it.

Later, she approached Liam in the cramped confines of their cabin, rubbing her body against his as they undressed, willing him to drop his reserve. He responded by taking her almost brutally, standing up, hammering her against the cabin bulkhead until their sweat mingled and her orgasm came in sobs. She used his body as much as he used hers. They only stopped when someone in the next cabin pounded on the thin walls.

The Mercedes camper rolled down the ramp of the ferry early next morning and climbed the narrow walled tunnel leading up to a square of blue sky marking the entrance. Liam had a hangover, as was usual whenever he drank too much wine. He had vague recollections of making love to Lisa the night before but he was not sure whether he had climbed into her bunk or whether she had joined him in his. Whatever had happened, he had woken up on the thin carpet of the cabin floor just before dawn, alone, his mind a blur.

Driving fast, they soon left behind the urban sprawl of Le Havre as they took the flat road to Amiens, then moved swiftly on to the motorway leading to Lille. Skirting the cities and towns, they eventually crossed the Dutch border at Breda on the E10 motor way. It was late evening. From there they sped across the flat lowlands of Holland, reaching the outskirts of Amsterdam near Schipol airport at nightfall.

Liam struggled through the revolving door with two suitcases and looked around with growing impatience. The hotel was a modern day disaster, part of a French-owned chain providing low cost accommodation. Built too close to the runways of the airport, its sole purpose was to cater for the limited needs of a host of transit passengers who only required a bed for one night, or even less.

'Give me the Ardilaun any day,' he said. 'This is a kip!' Lisa pushed him towards the check-in desk.

The receptionist demanded advance payment for their night's stay, then handed Liam a plastic key-card. He found their room on the first floor, right next to a bank of stainless steel escalators that whirred in constant use, operating throughout the night like a pair of voracious monsters, spewing out their human cargo into the early hours.

The packed bar where they finally located Foster vibrated to the sounds of heavy rock music. In one corner, a noisy group of children crowded around a bank of shrieking video games and added to the din.

Liam shuddered. 'Jesus, this is a nightmare!'

'Relax,' Lisa said. 'It's only for one night.'

Seated at a littered table as far away from the noise as he could get, Foster looked pale. His fleshy features were drawn and tired. He managed a smile when they joined him and after shaking hands, signalled to a blonde waitress dressed in a minuscule black skirt and an almost transparent white blouse. 'Three beers, please.'

The waitress tossed her head and disappeared. When she returned she slopped three foaming glasses of good Dutch beer onto the table. 'Twelve guilders,' she said, swaying to the music.

'I'm glad you were able to make it, Liam,' Foster began. He grimaced at a creamy white hole high up on the waitress's black tights as he threw some money onto her tray. 'We have a busy day ahead of us tomorrow and there is a lot to be done. Lisa's people are flying in from Hamburg in the morning.'

Lisa looked up. 'Who is coming? Will Hans Dietrich be there? I hope this trip is not going to be another waste of time.' She sounded pettish.

'I don't know,' replied Foster. 'Someone I met in Brussels is driving up tonight, but he won't be here until late.' He glanced around the crowded room. 'I don't think we should discuss any of this here. Why don't we have dinner? I'll fill you in on what's been happening since I got off that damned ship.'

'That suits me,' Liam replied. He was in no mood to listen to one of Foster's schemes. It had been a long and tedious drive. In spite of himself, he could already feel his eyes closing and he still had a headache.

The hotel restaurant matched the rest of the place, he thought. Even the lobsters in the tank at the entrance were plastic. The food was unpalatable. Lisa picked at her plate and left Foster to finish her leathery steak while Liam fought to stay awake.

They retired to Foster's room where they finished most of a bottle of whiskey as they listened to him droning on about the next day's meeting with Ghalboun and the Germans. It would be a turning point Foster said, one that was going to shake up the Brits like they had never been shaken before. He also told them at length what had happened on the ship, describing how he had slipped away in Ceuta with no one being the wiser.

Liam could not believe that what he was hearing was real. 'Foster! Have you gone fucking nuts! What kind of a clown are you?'

Foster's face turned puce, but he didn't reply. In contrast, Lisa seemed to gain a new source of energy. Foster's plans and adventures excited her. 'Let's not fight amongst ourselves,' she pleaded. 'We're all tired.'

Liam made up his mind that he would sleep alone in one of their single beds that night. 'If you ask me, we're more than tired. We're mad to even be here. This is a waste of time.'

As it turned out, Liam did not have to reject any advances from Lisa. She slipped into her own bed and left him to switch off the bedside lights. He lay for a long time listening to her heavy breathing. His mind was active, a restless jumble of thoughts. How much did Hogan already know of this? Surely he was not condoning Foster's scheme?

Liam woke early. He climbed out of bed and gently shook Lisa's shoulder. Her skin felt cool and silky, tempting him for a second to climb into bed beside her, but the clatter of the escalators and the early morning room cleaning services prompted him to dress. The meeting started soon after eight o'clock in Foster's room. By noon, the arguments had ranged backwards and forwards, sometimes turning to fury when they reached sticking points. The atmosphere remained tense and expectant.

'That's settled, then? You agree as well, Liam? I assure you there is no other way forward from here. We are prepared to give you more than you ever dreamed of. Think about it, Liam.'

Colonel Ghalboun finished speaking and got up from the table. The shoulders of his well-cut suit reflected a shaft of sunlight from the window. He looked out at the sprawl of Schipol airport, then turned and faced them again. 'We are talking missiles and launchers,' he said. 'All the toys that you have always wanted, but which we have never been prepared to give you. Until now, that is. You will never again see such an offer. Walk away from it if you like, but be assured, many of your own people will reject you. Your own survival is at stake.'

Liam looked slowly at the faces crowding in on him, waiting for him to reply. He had fought against it all morning. The price was too high. Now it was time for him to decide. He knew that everyone there ranged against him. Like vultures waiting to pick at his carcass, they had him cornered, and he knew it.

Foster glared. Lisa remained icily distant. The three Germans from Hamburg simply looked bored. He could tell from their comments and criticisms throughout the morning that they were beginning to see the Irish in the same way Lisa did, as shiftless and blundering, an anchor to which they never should have become attached. Hans Dietrich, the leader of the group, fingered a pen knife and lowered his eyes.

Liam felt naked. 'I agree,' he finally said in defeat.

Ghalboun nodded at Foster. 'I think we have a consensus, gentlemen.'

Liam held up a warning hand as the tangible silence in the room exploded. 'I'll have to go back to Belfast to sell it to my people. I must discuss it with Jim Hogan.' He had to raise his voice above the babble.

'That's not necessary,' snapped Foster. 'I'll go. It's not going to be difficult. He knows a lot about it already.'

The Libyan looked at Liam and said, 'Mr. Foster is correct, I think. There is very little time in which to put this together. Your job now is to get a pilot for the helicopter. That is essential.'

Hans Dietrich slipped his coat on. 'That's where we can help you. There is a man in the States who has worked for us before. He will do the job if the price is right.' He took a business card from his wallet and handed it to Liam, 'He is now in Mexico, you will find him at that address. His name is Buckholtz.' The card gave an address of a bar in Puerto Vallarta.

Dietrich took two sets of airline tickets from his briefcase and passed them across the table. 'You can leave with Lisa tomorrow. It's best if you both go. A couple travelling together always attracts less attention.'

Liam picked up the tickets. 'Supposing I had not agreed?'

The German laughed. 'Then someone else would have gone in your place.'

And I would be dead, Liam thought. Perhaps that would be preferable to this lunacy.

Mohammed Ghalboun was already leaving the room. He shook hands with Liam. 'You have made the right decision my friend. You will not regret it. There is now an open budget.'

The Libyan handed Liam a bulky envelope that he had extracted from his briefcase. 'Expenses to get you going,' he said. Almost as an afterthought, he added, 'Good luck!' With an imperceptible bow he left the room.

The three German men huddled in a corner with Lisa and spoke their native tongue in lowered tones. Liam caught a glance from Lisa only once. He knew they were talking about him and he wished he could understand the language.

Foster was already making flight reservations to Belfast by way of London. His face beamed with satisfaction. Liam hated him. Foster had dragged them into a whirlpool of intrigue. Peace in the North was never so far away.

Amsterdam that summer evening was sultry, inviting people to linger along the canals. The evening air was filled with the youthful vigour that was the essence of the city and, like a drug, it beckoned seductively.

Lisa and Liam travelled into the city on a courtesy coach operated by the hotel. They just had time to pay a brief visit to the Rijksmuseum on Stadhouderskade before it closed. Liam had been reluctant to go there, but Lisa had insisted. Now he stood in awe before Rembrandt's painting of *The Night Watch* as its size and delicate intricacy took his breath away. 'My God,' he whispered, 'it really is magnificent. Just as you said.' He had never seen anything quite like it. For that matter, he had never before been in an art gallery. For a short while the painting made him forget why they were in Holland.

Lisa squeezed his arm. 'I thought you might like it,' she breathed. 'There is sensuality here, can't you feel it?' She rubbed against him. 'It will prepare you for what I plan for you later.'

The museum closed at five o'clock, leaving them no time to see more. Tripping down the steps outside, they became tourists again and Liam's spirits lifted as the evening turned to night.

On a canal bank outside the museum they strolled beneath trees festooned with fairy lights. Lisa gripped his hand. 'Come on, run!'

'Where to?' Liam protested.

'Never mind, just run!'

Piling aboard a glass-topped barge, they sailed along the Herengracht, craning their necks to see the magnificent seventeenth century splendour spilling down to the canal banks on either side. Later, after an expensive dinner in the Five Flies restaurant, they wandered the tree-lined streets and gravitated down the tourist path through Dam Square and into the red light district stretching across its two canals. There, they lost themselves for several hours in a warren of alleys. On impulse, Lisa bought him a pair of red beach shorts from a street vendor. 'You'll need them in Mexico, on the beach!' Her laughter became infectious.

But in the early hours of the morning back at the hotel, his worry and fears returned. Frustrated, Lisa turned away from him in the bed and padded back across the room to her own.

Sleep eluded him. He lay awake tracing the pattern made on the ceiling by the airport searchlight a mile away. It was inconceivable that Hogan had agreed to this. But he must have. Otherwise, Foster would never have dared – not now – not with the cease-fire, not when they had a chance of respite from all the bloodshed. Daylight diffused the window blinds in gold before slumber finally came.

Twenty-Three

Jim Prendergast did not see Jonathan Cooke again for a number of days. He was so engrossed in the final fitting out of the ship that he had almost forgotten the man entirely. Now that the work was finished and he had paid off the shore labourers there was time for a respite. He lit a cigarette and wandered out onto the bridge. Everything on the foredeck looked neat and ship-shape. At last he felt satisfied.

It was raining for the first time in a week, but the shore gang had finished the last of the painting the day before. Prendergast let the soft rain drizzle on his face. It felt good. The decks were now green and the ventilators and masts a buff colour. The original red funnel was black. Even in the wet afternoon, he could see the *Maria B* showing something of her old elegance. Her fuel tanks were full and the flooded ballast tanks trimmed her nicely.

Vincent Kelly had been most helpful. He had even found two fishermen in need of work who had agreed to sign on for the voyage. A third crew member, who would act as an engine room greaser, was due to arrive the next day from Limerick, where he had been working on a dredger.

Eddie Molloy continued to be an innovative dynamo and a tireless worker for a man of his years. He seemed almost as driven and enthusiastic as Prendergast with the preparations for sea. Nothing was too much for him.

Prendergast was about to stow the last of the new charts in the chart room when Molloy arrived dressed in shore-going clothes. 'She's as ready as I can get her down below, Jim. With any luck that brute of mine will take you wherever you want, now ... well, as far as Malta, anyways.' He smiled. 'If it's all the same to you, I'm heading off home early to placate the missus. If she doesn't let up on me, I won't bother coming back from the Med!'

Jim laughed. He had recently met Nora Molloy and she was certainly not the ogre that Eddie made out. A lifetime spent at sea had simply kept them apart for too long and she was not used to tripping over her man around the house. If the truth was known, she probably looked forward to Eddie going away again. Prendergast suspected it would be as good for her as for her husband.

'That's all I've been waiting to hear. We'll sail on the tide the day after tomorrow. You go right ahead. You deserve a break. I'd never have got this far without you, and bloody well you know it!'

'Okay, Jim, as long as you're sure.'

'Yes, I'm sure. All the gear is up and running. We'll take on stores tomorrow and that will be it. I'm going out to my own place shortly to see the neighbours before we leave.'

'Right, I'll see you tomorrow.' Molloy crossed the wing of the bridge and vaulted ashore.

Jim lit a cigarette and watched him from the wheel house windows. Molloy was jaunty as he walked down the dockside. He's like myself, Prendergast thought. Eddie has risen to the occasion simply because he's got something to do, instead of dreaming what might have been. His face clouded as his thoughts flew back to Jane and Susan. The pain and anger was never far away. They lurked just beneath the surface waiting to bubble up. He exhaled and went back to work fitting the new VHF radio.

Prendergast drove out to Gorumna Island that evening and saw that Mary McGonigal had been in several times since he had taken to living aboard the ship. Everything was neat and tidy and his collection of empty bottles had disappeared. He felt a stranger in his own home already. It was almost as if he were not meant to be there. He left again quickly, taking with him a few books and his sextant in its mahogany brassbound case.

The boreen leading back to the road looked neglected. He hadn't really noticed it on the way in. Blackberry briars, shining from recent rain, encroached from the stone walls and scratched at the sides of the car. They would need cutting back soon, he thought. They might even have taken the place over by the time he returned. He continued on down the road to the McGonigals' cottage.

Mary McGonigal appeared in the doorway as he got out of the car. Jim hugged her, holding her for a moment. Eventually he said, 'I've been a pig during the last few weeks, Mary. I'm sorry. I hope you'll forgive me.'

She squeezed his hand and led him inside.

Bertie McGonigal was sitting in the kitchen eating his evening meal. Two of the children curled up on a threadbare sofa, intent on a television at the far end of the room. Bertie stood up. 'Jim! You're looking great. All that work must be doing you good!'

Mary studied Prendergast for a moment in the fluorescent light of the kitchen, her face serious. 'I think you've lost weight. You're not eating properly, are you?' She didn't wait for a reply. 'You can have a good dinner with us now, there's plenty in the pot.' She went over to the range and lifted a lid from a saucepan, and the smell of a fine stew enveloped the kitchen.

'You know I'd never turn down an offer like that, Mary. I've been eating in pubs down on the docks most of the time. I just came out to let you know that we're heading off the day after tomorrow.' Jim seated himself at the kitchen table. He was delighted to see them all and a little guilty that he had not called out before this.

Mary ladled stew onto a plate. When she spoke, her voice was disapproving. 'Are you sure you're doing the right thing, going off on that damned ship? Bertie told me it was an old tub of a thing.'

Jim smiled at her. 'Oh, she's not that bad. Anyway, it's not for long. I'd go mad if I didn't have it to occupy me right now.'

'Aye, you're probably right, Jim, if it keeps your mind off things,' commented Bertie, mopping his plate with a piece of bread. 'No point in you hanging around here moping. It's just a damned pity that the Guards haven't been able to do anything about those bastards.'

'No chance,' replied Jim. 'I think we can forget all about that.' He changed the subject. 'I don't know for sure when I'll be back, so if you could continue to keep an eye on the house, I would appreciate it.'

Mary slipped a steaming plate in front of him. 'Eat that while it's hot,' she said, 'and forget the house for now.'

He ate his food, savouring each bite until he finally pushed back the empty plate. 'That was delicious, Mary,' he said. 'Thank you. I'll remember to come again.

'You'd better,' she replied. 'Think of this as your second home from now on.'

Jim pondered how he could repay such kindness. 'I won't be needing my car while I'm away. Why don't you use it, Mary? It's taxed and insured for the year.'

Her face reddened with pleasure. 'Are you sure?'

'Of course I am. It's no use sitting down in the docks.'

'I won't know myself, Bertie,' she said to her husband.

Jim rose to get up from the table, but Bertie motioned for him to sit down. 'Time enough, Jim. You'll have a drink before you go. Mary, fetch that bottle of whiskey from the sitting room.'

When he got back to the docks in Galway, except for a couple of dim deck lights, the ship lay shrouded in darkness and the quays looked deserted. Below in the engine room the generator hummed quietly. The lock gates were open to the high tide still flooding the dock and the ship floated higher than usual, making her look bigger and more purposeful. Prendergast was glad to be back on board again. It was almost time. Already he could feel a sea wind tugging at his coat, drawing him away.

As he made his way to the bridge ladder, he noticed a light showing in the messroom on the lower deck. Prendergast poked his head through the open door. To his astonishment, Jonathan Cooke was sitting at the table, reading a newspaper.

'Jonathan! What are you doing here?' Jim's voice reflected the surprise on his face.

Cooke rose from his seat and extended his hand. 'I heard you were off soon and I wanted to wish you *bon voyage*. I had hoped that we might have another evening together before you sailed, but unfortunately I have to go to London tomorrow.'

'Oh! Holidays over already? How was the fishing?'

'Yes, over far too soon I'm afraid, but the fishing was very good. I landed a four-pound trout this afternoon.' Cooke sounded pleased with himself.

Prendergast busied himself with a coffee pot near the serving hatch to the galley. He wondered what was Cooke doing on board. It was obvious that he had been waiting for some time. There was certainly something odd about Cooke. On a very first casual meeting the man had invited him to dinner and now here he was, waiting to say good-bye as though they were life long-friends.

'Coffee will be ready in a minute.' Prendergast turned to face his visitor and studied him for a moment. 'So now it's back to work. What business did you say you were in, Jonathan?'

Cooke's voice sounded distant when he replied. 'I didn't, but now that you ask, I'm a civil servant.'

The coffee bubbled in the percolator, filling the cabin with its aroma. Prendergast turned to face Cooke. 'Oh! I see. Over in London, I presume?'

Cooke blew his nose into a spotless white linen handkerchief. 'Yes, some of the time at least.' He sniffed and dabbed at his nose again. 'You know, I really think I am going to go back with a damned cold.'

Jim was annoyed. Cooke was being evasive. 'Look, Jonathan, let's get to the point. What have you really come to see me about?'

Cooke did not flinch. His eyes bored into Prendergast. With one hand he smoothed back his hair, and with the other he placed his walking stick on the table. 'I've already told you. I'm interested in ships. Particular ships, that is.' Some of the warmth disappeared from his voice.

'Come off it, Jonathan!' Jim sounded disgusted. 'You can't tell me that a rusty old bucket like this holds any interest for you!'

'On the contrary. I am as much interested in this ship as in the *Georgios*.'

'The *Georgios*? What ship is that?' Jim was perplexed. Cooke's response had taken him by surprise.

Cooke's reply was matter-of-fact. 'She's the ship that ran down your yacht, or so I am led to believe.'

For one brief moment Prendergast wondered if he was losing his sanity. He was not even sure that he had heard correctly. His hand shook as he poured coffee and placed the mugs on the table. Pulling himself together, he tried to control a quiver in his voice. 'If you know that, why don't the police?'

Cooke stirred sugar into his coffee and added some milk. 'Because I have made it my business to find out. I took an interest in what happened to you, and one or two things fell into place.'

'Just like that!' Jim's eyes flashed with anger.

Cooke's tone softened slightly. 'There is a little more to it than that, Jim. I have access to certain other information that helped.'

Prendergast's eyes widened. How could Cooke know so much? *Who* was he? 'What other information are you talking about? Look, Jonathan, I don't know what all this is about, but if it isn't some kind of sick joke, you're coming to the Guards with me!'

'I would prefer not to at the moment. I believe that the person or persons who owned the *Georgios* also own your ship. You might be able to help us establish that.'

'Help who? For Christ's sake! Who in the hell is *us*?'

The silence between them crackled with tension.

'The department I work with is interested in terrorist activities. It is our belief that the ship that ran you down was involved in an illegal operation. Furthermore, we believe that it is a possibility that your ship may be used in a subsequent operation.' Cooke stared at Prendergast. 'I can't put it any plainer than that!'

Cooke's clipped military accent suddenly made sense to Jim. 'You're not a bloody civil servant at all. What are you ... SAS, MI5, MI6, what?' He felt that he was about to crack as he resisted a desire to punch Cooke in the mouth.

'Something like that,' replied Cooke evenly. 'It doesn't really matter.' He gave a polite cough. 'Those that you mentioned are all civil servants in their own way.'

Prendergast boiled. 'I think I've had enough of this! You're giving me a line of total bullshit!' He pushed his chair back from the table and made to get up.

Jonathan reached over and held his forearm, restraining him. His grip was surprisingly strong, his steely eyes steady and uncompromising. 'I'm going to be truthful with you. It is very unlikely that the Gardai will ever apprehend the people responsible for the deaths of your wife and daughter. You must have already realised that yourself. Two members of that ship's crew were found murdered since, and a third died during her last voyage in, to say the least, mysterious circumstances. If we are correct in our assumptions, it may be possible, with your help, to circumvent the illegal use of this ship, if that is the plan for her. At best, we may be able to arrest or get to grips with the people who rammed your yacht.'

Cooke paused for a moment before continuing. 'It may be all theory on my part, of course. But if I am right, you could well be able to do a great service for your country and save a large number of lives. You must have read the papers recently. You know that there are rumours of behind the scene talks. I can tell you now that the rumours are true. We are doing our utmost to keep the peace initiative on track, but others are not satisfied and want a return to violence. If that comes, it will be like nothing we have experienced before. I think it could even engulf the South. If my information is correct, your ship could plunge us all straight to hell!'

Jim wanted to pinch himself. There was a dream-like quality

to Cooke's words and they remained floating in the air. Except for the hum from the ventilation blowers the stark messroom was quiet. Prendergast stared at Cooke until the man's grip on his forearm relaxed. 'I don't know what to say to you,' he said. 'I'm dumbfounded by all of this and I find it extremely hard to believe.' He raised his eyes to the ceiling. 'Beam me up, Scottie, for Christ's sake!'

Cooke laughed and the tension between them evaporated. 'I know how this must sound to you,' he said.

Prendergast lit a cigarette and inhaled deeply. 'I'm not sure that you do. If you're who you say you are, you're more used to this type of shit than I am. What makes you so sure you're right?'

Cooke frowned and poured himself another mug of coffee. 'I'm not sure at all. That's the trouble. Much of it is theory and guesswork, but I am convinced about the other ship. An emigration official at Heathrow picked out a Chinese seaman who arrived from North Africa a few weeks ago – they are tightening up a lot on illegal immigrants these days. As it turned out, the man had a visa and they let him go, but he told them the name of his last ship. Afterwards we received a report that two officers had been murdered on the same ship in Ceuta before he paid off. We got lucky and spotted the connection. We tracked him down a few days later and had a chat with him. He didn't know much, but he got scared that we might kick him out of the country. He told us that his ship was involved in something peculiar on the west coast of Ireland at the time your yacht was sunk. He also told us that the ship carried a passenger, an Irishman, who left the ship the night she arrived in Ceuta. A few more enquiries led us to your Mr. Pavlides, who had an interest in the *Georgios*. He has a history of shipping dodgy cargoes. Some of the ships that he had connections with have been lost at sea in circumstances that worry the Lloyds insurers quite a bit. Perhaps you should take note of that,' he added.

'What about the rest of the crew? Have you questioned them?'

Cooke frowned again. 'That's the biggest problem. The

owners sold the ship while she was in Ceuta. The crew paid off and scattered before we got on to it. The ship's crew records were minimal. To be perfectly honest, we haven't yet established the true owners.'

'What about the men who were murdered?' Prendergast's voice still registered his disbelief.

'The police in Ceuta believe it was a local robbery that went wrong. They are not very forthcoming. Our contacts in the area think there is a cover-up operation going on. We may never know what really happened. Personally, I think there is far more to it. The Irishman that I mentioned was not on any of the ship's records. It is possible that the IRA or a similar group was involved, especially if an arms shipment did take place. Maybe something went wrong and it was some kind of punishment killing. We may never know.'

It was evident to Prendergast that Cooke was serious about what he was telling him. He began to believe the man. Hesitantly he asked, 'What exactly do you expect of me?'

Cooke thought about his reply for a moment, then said, 'I think that after your arrival in Malta you might be presented with an opportunity to remain on the ship. If it's an innocent commercial voyage, that's fine, but on the other hand, if it's not, you could pass on information that could be valuable to us. We know that limited quantities of arms have been shipped in here successfully by sea already. If we stop another shipment getting through, that is a success. There is also the slim chance that this could lead to identifying those who were responsible for the deaths of your wife and daughter. No guarantees, you understand, but a chance nonetheless. I'm sure you would want that.'

Cooke had played his trump card. Prendergast's face was grim; he didn't hesitate. 'I'll do it,' he said. 'Anything you want.'

'I thought you might.' Cooke looked serious. 'There will be no heroics required or suggested. Please understand that. Just a telephone contact in Malta at this number.' Cooke handed him a card on which he had written a name and a number in Valletta. 'We will take any action that may be necessary if you strike lucky. The number on the other side is for my office. You can reach me there at any time.'

Prendergast glanced at the card and raised his eyebrows. 'Your number is in Dublin?'

'Yes, I am based at the British Embassy.'

Prendergast put the card in his wallet. 'That's it then, as simple as that?' He sounded as though he didn't expect an answer.

Cooke pushed back his chair from the table. 'Yes. Of course, I need not remind you that all of this is more than confidential. You must not discuss it with anyone else.'

'Not even with Vincent Kelly?'

'Not even with Vincent Kelly.' Cooke's eyes answered the hidden question.

'Jonathan, how long have you known all this?'

'I didn't know all of it when I first met you, if that is what you are asking. I'd like you to believe that. I only had suspicions then.'

Jonathan reached under the table. Straightening up, he placed a shoe box on the table and pushed it towards Prendergast. 'You don't have to take this if you don't want to,' he said, 'but you might be safer with it.'

Prendergast lifted the lid from the box. Inside under tissue paper lay a black pistol and two ammunition clips.

Cooke leaned forward. 'Browning 9mm. Thirteen shot clip. Very reliable. I'll show you how to strip it, if you want to keep it.'

Jim lifted the gun from the box. It felt heavy but well balanced. 'I'll take it,' he said.

'Good,' said Cooke. 'You'll notice that the serial number has been removed. For obvious reasons the weapon is not traceable to us. It is unlikely you will need it, but one never knows. If the whole affair turns out to be a wild goose chase, I suggest you dump it overboard.'

Cooke took the pistol from him. 'Please .... Let me demonstrate ...'

Twenty-Four

Foster only stayed in Belfast for one day before travelling to Wexford for a visit to his mother. Belfast depressed him as it always had, and he felt ill at ease. It was far too easy to run into some half-baked Protestant hit squad, and the very sight of British troops infuriated him so much that it impaired his reason.

His meeting with Big Jim Hogan had not gone well. Hogan would not even listen to the plan and refused outright to allow him to take it further.

'No!' Hogan turned to Foster as the car in which they were driving stopped at traffic lights. 'This scheme is utter madness,' he spat. 'I won't sanction it, and I'm not prepared to discuss it with the Army Council.'

'It's the way the Libyans want it,' Foster protested.

'I don't give a shit what the fucking Libyans want!' Hogan's face turned crimson. 'Find some other way, Foster. You're not short of contacts in Europe. Talk to the Russian Mafia, for fuck's sake! They'd sell their grandmothers, the state they're in. The ammunition is there, right under your bloody nose!'

'But the missiles ...'

'To hell with the damned missiles,' Hogan snapped. 'It's too high a price!'

Hogan signalled for the driver to pull in by a cab rank near the Central Station. 'I'll drop you here,' he said.

As Foster opened the rear door of the car, Hogan gripped his wrist tightly. 'Do it, Foster. That's a direct order. Pull back Liam and the German from wherever they are. This is to go no further, you understand?'

Foster nodded and Hogan released him. He stood for a few minutes on the pavement until the car lost itself in the traffic. Fuck Hogan, he thought. There had to be a way to continue with his plans in spite of the danger. Then he thought of Harry Trent. Harry would understand. He strode into the station and searched for a telephone booth.

Seething with frustration, he listened to the phone ringing at the other end of the line. He was about to give up when Trent answered.

'Harry? It's Foster. I haven't got much time but it is important that I see you.'

'Where are you?'

'I'm in Belfast.'

'There's a club on the Falls ...'

'I know it, Harry.'

'Be there in fifteen minutes.' Trent hung up.

Foster's heart raced at the risk he was about to take. He hurried to a taxi and climbed inside.

Of late, Foster had found himself increasingly drawn towards Trent, seeing in him a kindred spirit. He knew the type, he thought. It would be a question of salesmanship. There was always more than one way of getting things done, and Trent was his angle. Foster felt sure of that. Besides, he needed encouragement. Perhaps he was overstepping the mark this time.

Trent listened patiently until Foster had finished. At the end, he lit one of his cheap cigars and watched the smoke spiralling toward the ceiling. 'I believe in what you're trying to do,' he said. 'I think you know that already, but without Hogan's agreement it's a lost cause. You might have got him to agree a couple of years ago, but not now. There's too much at stake. Between you and me, Hogan hasn't got the guts for it anymore. He wants the cease-fire to continue, even though he doesn't mind giving the Brits a prod now and again to keep their interest up.'

Foster sensed danger. 'Hogan is getting old, Harry. He should retire. You know that as well as I do.'

Trent smiled. His teeth looked yellow in the light. 'Nobody

retires from this job, Foster. Least of all, Jim Hogan.'

Foster glanced at his watch. He had suspected that this would not be easy and he still wasn't sure how much he could trust Trent. 'This isn't just about the ammunition that we lost, Harry. That was peanuts. I tried to explain that to Hogan. We will never again have such an opportunity; the Libyans will give us Stingers this time. He doesn't seem to understand the importance of that. Also, there's enough Semtex on offer to last us for years. It's even possible that we might not have to go through with the entire plan.'

Trent shifted. 'You don't fuck with these people, you know that. You deliver, or else. Don't try to cod me, Foster. Besides,' he said, 'I agree Hogan should take a second look at it.'

At last, Foster thought, a chink of light. 'Harry, get him to change his mind. The Brits will never survive this. They'll have to get out this time.' He paused. 'You do realise, of course, that all the credit will go to you for having the foresight to see it.'

Trent said nothing. He studied Foster closely for a moment. He didn't like the man. There was something about Foster that gave him a creepy feeling, but he forced the thought aside. 'Okay,' he said. 'Leave it with me. I'll talk to him again and see if I can persuade him. Call me tomorrow. I'll try to have an answer by then.'

Foster brightened. 'You won't regret it,' he said firmly. 'It's a golden opportunity and one not to be missed, I assure you. I'm going down to Wexford tonight, but I'll call you before I go back to Madrid.' He stood up to leave. Trent followed him to the door.

Outside, a chill wind swirled a cloud of dust into the air, magnifying the desolation and squalor of their surroundings. It was a forbidding street of gaunt terraced houses, the nearest of which had a glaring Republican mural on its gable end that depicted a hooded man brandishing an Armalite against a background of a fluttering Republican flag. Foster shivered even though it was summer and a thrill ran up his spine as he stepped into a waiting taxi. He was glad to be leaving.

Hogan belched and slammed down the telephone. What the hell did Harry Trent want now? It had to have something to do with that ridiculous dream of Foster's. Put those two together and it spelled trouble, he thought. Ever since he found out that Liam was off on some crack-pot trip to Mexico, his blood pressure had gone wild. Why couldn't the bastards be content with an occasional foray into London, just to keep the pressure on? He was beginning to detect a shift towards the mad antics of the INLA and the mayhem they brought to everything they touched. Surely Liam, of all people, was not a party to this stupidity?

Hogan called on one of his best local men to drive him to Cookstown for the meeting. Chalky White had been with him for years and remained totally loyal. He was also a close friend of Liam's, close enough to be one of the men who had helped to dispose of McGinty's body. Before Hogan left the house he tucked a Smith and Wesson forty-five into his waistband under his anorak. Just in case, he thought, he needed to stamp on Trent once and for all.

They had plenty of time and took the meandering A505 without having to speed, but it was no time to enjoy the scenic countryside or the evening sunshine. Throughout the drive Hogan remained morose and remote, confiding none of his thoughts.

The pub Trent had selected for the meeting was a sprawling building known as the Ranch House. Built at a crossroads a few miles outside Cookstown, it was popular for its country music sessions, but tonight it was quiet, and only a few cars stood in the car park facing onto the road.

Hogan rolled down his window. The trees at the rear of the building's mock Tudor facings were alive with crows settling for the night. Their raucous cawing only served to heighten Hogan's unease. He remained in the car for several minutes warily surveying the scattering of cars outside. 'Chalky, stay out here in the car. Keep an eye on who's coming and going while I'm inside. If you see anything odd, come and get me.'

'Okay boss.' Chalky extracted a machine pistol from under the driver's seat and rested it on his lap.

Harry Trent was waiting inside at the bar. He had said he would be alone, and he was. Somehow Hogan had expected he would have someone else with him; Harry didn't usually like being on the front line when there was something difficult to do.

Hogan recognised the barman as he approached. 'It's quiet tonight, Max,' he commented. 'No music?'

'No, not at midweek. Nobody's got any money these days, so we've cut it out except at weekends. What are you having?'

Hogan glanced to the far end of the vast room. In spite of the money that had been lavished on its decor and furnishings, it was seedy and in need of cleaning. 'Give me a Blackbush on the rocks.'

'I'll bring it over to you if you want a bit of privacy. It's on the house.'

'Thanks, Max, we'll go up to the far end. Bring your drink, Harry.' Hogan was in no mood to waste time. They selected a table in a darkened corner well away from the other customers. Hogan checked the place. Most of the drinkers were farmers, all probably locals. He didn't know any of them, but it had always been a safe pub and he began to feel a little bit easier. 'Let's get on with it, Harry. What's this all about, or do I need to ask?'

'It's about Foster,' Harry said. 'He asked me to try and get you to change your mind.'

'Forget it!' Hogan snapped. 'Between the two of you, you will bring the whole bloody world down on top of us. We'll lose every bit of sympathy we have in the States, and as far as I am concerned, we don't need fucking Arabs to fight our wars!'

There was an unmistakable finality in Hogan's words. The man was like a rock, unshakeable, and to Harry, just as stupid. 'You don't understand, we get Stingers out of this,' he faltered.

Hogan seethed. 'And what the bloody hell would you do with a Stinger, Harry, bring down a British Airways plane with a load of women and children aboard? You're supposed to be an Intelligence Officer; try to act like one!'

Harry ignored the remark. 'Anyone can make mistakes. Look at what happened to McGinty on whatever kind of mission you sent him on. One hell of a transfer, if you ask me. All I'm asking is that you discuss it with the Army Council and let them decide,' he said. 'That's all I want.'

Hogan unzipped his anorak. The wooden butt of his revolver was visible in his waistband. 'No, what you really want, Harry, is my fucking job. I can tell you now that you will never see it, unless you get to know one of these.' He tapped the butt of the gun. 'Get out of this while you are still ahead. If I go to the Army Council, it will be your bloody court-martial I will look for.'

Trent couldn't take his eyes from the gun butt. He was not going to achieve anything, he realised. There was no point in pushing this any further. 'I meant no offense. I promised Foster to try, that's all.'

Hogan grunted. 'Okay. Enough said. You get on to Liam, wherever he is, and pull him back.' He zipped up his anorak and finished his drink. 'Do it right away. I'll expect a call from you in the morning. Just get it into your head, Harry – Adams is talking right now, to both governments. At last there is a chance of a settlement, and we might not have another opportunity. Bring in the ammunition if you like, but cut out this shit with the Libyans.'

Trent nodded and looked at his watch. 'Okay, you win,' he said. 'This has nothing to do with me, you understand? Foster insisted, that's all.'

'Stop acting the maggot, Harry, and get some sense!' Hogan ignored Trent's proffered hand. As Harry walked with bowed shoulders towards the door, Hogan went to the toilets at the back of the bar and relieved himself. He could see out the small open window across the wide expanse of the car park and he noticed that two of the floodlights were not working, but he could see Chalky White sitting in the car where he had left him. He saw Harry Trent walking quickly across the open space. He didn't stop and no one met him. Minutes later Trent drove away at speed, spinning the rear wheels of the car in the loose gravel and leaving a blue cloud of exhaust to hover in the still air.

Hogan straightened his trousers, loosened the revolver in his waistband and zipped up his anorak. It was time to get out.

Hogan left the pub by a back door near the kitchen. He stepped out into the cool night air and stood for a moment in the shadows, breathing slowly, preparing himself. Nothing moved. Everything looked normal. He started across the car park to where he could see Chalky still sitting in the driver's seat of the car. Suddenly, the engine of a car off to one side came to life, and the car rolled forwards. Fear came to him in an instant. He started to run, screaming for Chalky, then turned to face the headlights of the oncoming car.

He tugged desperately at the zipper of his jacket as the first bullet struck his hand, tearing off his finger and imbedding his wedding ring in his chest cavity just as his fist closed around the butt of the Smith and Wesson. He switched the gun quickly to his other hand and got one shot off before a second bullet tore through his larynx, forcing him to his knees. In the car's lights he could see his own blood spurting in front of him. His gun went off, sending a shot whining harmlessly into the night sky. He was already dead when the third bullet hit him in the stomach, sending him sprawling backwards in the dust.

Hogan had not got close enough to his own car to see that Chalky White sat rigidly upright in front of the steering wheel, blood trickling steadily from a gaping wound behind his ear, his face already pallid in death.

The car stopped and a man in the passenger seat leaned out and shot Hogan in the temple at close range. Then the driver gunned the engine and the car careered out into the road, leaving a trail of sparks as the exhaust pipe bottomed on the asphalt.

Foster telephoned Harry Trent from Wexford the next morning. Trent simply confirmed that they now had the go-ahead. He suggested that Foster check page three of that day's *Irish Times* for news of a mutual friend. His voice told Foster all he needed to know. He replaced the receiver with smug satisfaction, his face flushed with elation at being given the green light. Quickly packing a hold-all, he checked out of the hotel, paying his bill in cash.

In a quiet cafe near the harbour, Foster ate a late breakfast.

He opened his newspaper at the page mentioned. A single column of text contained the report he was looking for. Both Hogan and Chalky White had already been identified as the victims of a hit and run shooting by what was suspected to be a UVF hit squad, although there had been no coded confirmation from the UVF themselves. The reporter quoted from an RUC police statement that reflected muted satisfaction in the knowledge that two known IRA suspects were no longer a threat to the peace and security of Northern Ireland. The police spokesman who had worded the statement was obviously pleased with the outcome and probably wished he had done the job himself.

Foster breathed out in quiet satisfaction. He folded the paper and ordered more coffee. Hogan deserved it, he told himself. He had always believed the man to be an encumbrance, lacking in imagination. In a world where imagination was vital, Hogan was weighed down by his father's archaic dreams and too old for the job.

Before leaving the cafe, Foster carried his overnight bag into the toilet and changed his clothes. He left by a side door leading onto a municipal car park.

The nursing home stood on a wooded hill outside the town of Wexford. It was really an extended split-level bungalow with all the upstairs bedrooms opening onto a long teak-railed balcony that looked out over the sea. The house was modern and comfortably equipped. It was a haven in which each of its elderly clientele led a leisurely, if strictly controlled, routine existence. To Foster, the house represented freedom to pursue his travels and ambitions, secure in the knowledge that his mother received the attention that he could never provide.

He parked the car outside in a gravelled forecourt and stood for a while gazing up at the balcony. There was no sign of movement outside his mother's room. On such a fine day he would have expected to see her there in a wheelchair wrapped in the handwoven Andalusian rug he had brought her after one of his trips away. Her absence from the balcony frightened him, and he felt a dread emptiness, his fear causing him to stumble in the loose gravel as he hurried towards the terracotta steps leading to the front door.

The door stood open. Inside, the entrance hall smelled of floor polish and the oak floor cleanly reflected the sunlight. Mrs. Morgan had an unnatural devotion to floor polish that came from years of hospital work. Foster had never seen a speck of dust anywhere. Even a cobweb would be attacked with instantaneous aggression.

No one was in the hall. He rang the bell on an antique buffet table and waited. From somewhere at the rear of the house he could hear a clatter of dishes and the sounds of a radio tuned to the *Pat Kenny Show*. He rang the bell again and listened to the chimes ringing from the walls. A distant door opened and he turned to face the gargantuan form of the owner striding towards him on white rubber soled shoes that squeaked on the polished floor. She greeted him with a special smile that she reserved for those who always paid their bills on time. 'Good morning, Father Foster! Thank you for telephoning. Your mother is looking forward to seeing you. I have already told her that you were coming.'

At the use of his title, Foster's fingers flicked to the unaccustomed constriction of his white clerical collar. He gave a slight cough and clasped her extended hand. 'Is she all right, Mrs. Morgan?' His voice sounded hesitant and unsure. The sheer size of the woman always intimidated him.

Guinneth Morgan patted a large red hand at her hair, which was trapped under a ridiculous looking white nurse's cap. 'Of course she is, Father. At least, she's as well as can be expected at her age.' She studied his face earnestly for a moment. 'Although you must realise that she is not always in our world anymore. Senility is a dreadful word, I know, but we have to face it, don't we?'

Foster felt a twinge of relief, but an instant sense of distaste also. At nine hundred pounds a month, he suspected Morgan was willing to face a lot. 'I got worried when I didn't see her on the balcony.' He looked towards the stairway.

'There is no need to worry yourself, Father. Your mother is

fine, but she hasn't been well enough to go outside for the past few days. Why don't we go straight up and see her now?'

Mrs. Morgan led the way upstairs. Encased in thick white tights, her legs flashed ominously in front of him, while her enormous buttocks undulated out of control beneath the starched preciseness of her nurse's uniform. For all her bulk, she reached the upper floor breathing far less heavily than Foster. She opened the last door in the corridor. 'Take all the time you need,' she said. 'But please don't expect too much from the poor dear.'

Foster closed the door quietly and looked about the room, inhaling the usual scent of lavender. Beneath a white counterpane, the woman in the bed lay propped by snow-white pillows, eyes half closed, her breathing shallow. Her thin arms lay stretched on top of the covers. A set of rosary beads were entwined around the clenched fingers of her right hand. Pale curtains moved slightly at the open doors to the balcony. Outside, in the far distance, the sea glittered like burnished steel. Except for a picture of the Sacred Heart on one wall, the only colour in the room was from her high-necked blue night-dress.

Foster crossed the room tiptoeing in the silence. He could almost hear his own heartbeat. 'Mother, it's me, Jimmy. I've come to see you again.' He placed the flowers he carried on the bedside table and bent over to kiss her cheek. 'I've brought you flowers.' Her skin felt cool and she made no sound but he fancied that her eyelids fluttered in silent recognition. He pulled up a chair and sat quietly by the bedside, holding her hand, a glint of steel from the empty wheelchair in the corner bringing a lump to his throat. The room was oppressive and the claustrophobic imminence of her death overcame him, sweeping him up in a black tide. He broke away and knelt by the bed where he intoned the prayers of the rosary without the need of beads, his voice loud and crashing like surf on the barren walls of the room.

When he finished, he held her hand again, stroking it gently. It was like a dried leaf; blue veins pulsated slowly beneath the waxy skin. He wondered what it would be like to caress the hand of another woman. He had never tried it. Nor would he.

At last he broke the silence. 'I have to go soon, Mother.' Mother, he thought. Why had she always insisted on the formality of the word, just as she had always insisted on calling him James and not Jim, or even Jimmy, as he would have preferred. When he was young all the other children called their mothers Mammy, but his mother had been aloof and formal, absorbed by her passion for prayer and the Holy Mass. Later, he too allowed himself to be grasped into the arms of the Church like an insignificant ant being swept down a drain. But for once, he had pleased her. His ordination was a source of joy and her crowning glory. Only at that moment had he ever seen love in her eyes.

She stirred in the bed and saliva trickled from the corner of her mouth. He dabbed it away with a moistened cloth as her eyelids opened to reveal her translucent eyes. Her brittle stick-like fingers tightened on his and her mouth sagged open. 'Go and do God's work, James, take with you the blessings of the Saints.' Exhausted, she sank back into the pillows and closed her eyes.

Foster crunched across the drive to the car. His black suit constricted him, trapping the warmth of the sun, and he felt sweat trickling down the insides of his arms. Yes, he would do God's work. For Ireland, just as she asked. He started the engine, ripped off the clerical collar as if it was a leech sucking his life's blood, and flung it angrily into the back seat.

Twenty-Five

The sand became hot at midday, burning the soles of Liam's feet and forcing him to scuttle back to his lounger, but the beer cans he carried from the hotel beach bar were ice cold, chilling his fingers.

Lisa sprawled full-length, her body supine, already tanned golden-brown after only two days in the sun. She wore a straw hat pulled down low over her forehead to shade her eyes. Her white bikini clung to her silkily, whiter than the curve of the vast beach that swept for miles in either direction. Liam drew in his breath as he approached her. Lisa was a vision, her sexuality heightened by the minuteness of her costume. He plonked himself down beside her, wincing as the backs of his thighs touched the hot plastic of the lounger.

'You should be careful, you're burning up,' she said.

Liam laughed, 'How come you go brown and I go red?'

She smiled and took one of the beers from him, her nails manicured and blood red against the metal can, the same colour as her lipstick. He couldn't see her eyes behind her dark sunglasses. 'Because you're a Celt and I'm an Aryan.'

Liam placed a towel across his sunburnt shins and chuckled. 'What the bloody hell has that got to do with it!'

'Probably nothing. It was the first thing that came into my mind.' She lay back and stretched. 'You know, I could stay here forever.'

He leaned over her and kissed her. Her lips tasted slightly salty. 'Why don't we? We've got the money to do it,' he whispered. He had spoken without thinking, and the enormity of his suggestion shot through his brain.

Lisa sat upright, her face no longer beautiful. 'Liam, we're here to do a job. Don't even think about it!' Her voice was as harsh as her features. 'The world is not big enough for that.' She removed her sunglasses and peered intently into his face. 'Don't even think about getting serious about me, either. It's not going to last. It never does. And I don't want it to.'

'Forget I said it.' Liam knew his voice sounded unconvincing and he felt like a scolded schoolboy caught without excuses. He lay back and closed his eyes, not wanting to say anything else. His thoughts drifted to the flight out two days ago.

He had never been on a 747 Jumbo jet, and like an excited teenager had drunk too much and refused to sleep, enjoying every minute of the flight. Somewhere high over the Caribbean in a cloudless sky while others slept, Lisa, after a whispered discussion of the merits of the Mile High Club, had even suggested he join her for a quickie in one of the rear toilets, but he hadn't been ready for that . Now, he wasn't so sure. Maybe on the way back, he thought. They had flown from Amsterdam to Caracas, then on to Mexico City to avoid New York and the prying eyes of an over-zealous emigration service. He smiled inwardly. Join the IRA and see the world, the long way round, he thought.

'Liam, how long are we going to wait for this guy Buckholtz?'

He rolled over onto his stomach and looked at her. She lay on her back with her eyes closed, a thin trickle of perspiration rolling softly down her neck where a blood vessel pulsed. 'You heard what they said in the bar. He's away sport fishing or something.'

She sat up again. 'Or something,' she repeated.

He watched the trickle of perspiration disappear inside one satin cupped breast as her eyes flashed. 'Well, don't you think we should start giving it some thought? Two days, they said. That means he should be back today. We can't just sit here waiting for him to appear.'

'Right now I don't give a shit if he never shows up. A few more days like this suits me just fine.'

'That's what worries me,' she said. 'Don't go soft on me,

Liam.' There was a threatening tone in her voice before she smiled. 'I'm going for a swim.'

Liam lit a cigarette and watched her run down the sloping sand to the sea. Bloody Germans, he thought. Always wanting to be the super race. Why can't they learn to relax and enjoy life?

Lisa hit the cool blue Pacific on the run, cleaving through a rolling breaker. Surfacing, she swam in a steady crawl straight out away from the crowds in the shallows. Further out on the bay a speedboat cut a white swath in the blue water, dragging a para-glider higher into the sky. She rolled onto her back and floated, watching the green and red parachutes. Maybe Liam was right, she thought, enjoy it while you can. This was way better than that stinking Connemara. Another day or two might not be so bad.

'Amigo, you like a tequila marguerita?'

Liam squinted up at a white-coated waiter hovering with an empty tray. 'Yeah, why not!' He spotted Lisa coming out of the sea. 'Make it two, pal. By the way, what's your name?'

'Mario, Senor.' He smiled and there was a flash of gold beneath his black moustache.

'Okay Mario, two margueritas.'

Lisa picked up a towel and dabbed at her hair. 'You know what someone told me down at the water?'

'What?'

'Richard Burton and Liz Taylor used to live near here.'

'Is that so?' Liam said dryly. 'That's an earth-shattering piece of information and no mistake.'

Lisa leaned over and kissed him on the lips. 'No need to be sarcastic. I'm sorry I flew off at you.'

'Forget it. It never happened. Give me the towel, I'll dry your back.' He took the towel from her as she lay down on her lounger.

Mario padded across the dance floor in the open-air bar and ordered the drinks. He collected two frosted glasses and nodded at two men drinking beer at the bar before returning to the beach.

'Your drinks, amigo.' Mario extended the tray.

'Thanks, Mario. How much?' Liam took the salt-rimmed glasses.

'Twelve thousand pesos, Senor.'

'I'll get it,' said Lisa, reaching for her purse.

They sat side by side sipping their drinks. 'Christ, I could get used to this stuff,' said Liam. 'It's a good job we didn't bring Johnny out here with us. He'd be pissed all day, poor bastard!'

Before Lisa could make a reply, a shadow fell over them, blotting out the sun. Liam looked up and squinted. Two men stared down at them.

'Your name Liam, buddy?' The voice was coarse and American.

Liam sat up, suddenly alert, his eyes suspicious. 'Who's asking?'

'The name's Buckholtz – Gene Buckholtz. I heard you were looking for me.'

Liam glanced around. No one was sitting close by. 'That's right, we've been waiting for you.' He stood up and extended his hand. 'Dietrich sent us.' Jesus, Liam thought. He's a big bastard. His own eyes only came level with the other man's shoulders. Buckholtz was dressed in a pair of black shorts which showed-off his massive mahogany-skinned torso. His black close-cropped hair receded slightly at the temples, and his face was hard looking. Powerful jaws chewed on a wad of gum, and dark sunglasses hid his eyes. He gave off an aura of aggression.

'Maybe I know Dietrich, maybe not. What's important is, I don't know you. What do you want to see me about?' Buckholtz sucked in his breath and flexed the sinews on his arms as he caught sight of a young woman in a fluorescent-green bikini making her way down to the water. 'Hey! Nice ass, I like that!'

The second man stood back a few paces. Of smaller build, he wore khaki shorts and a straw hat. His face and shoulders were heavily pock-marked. His mouth was wide with thin lips. Liam judged him to be Cuban, and immediately formed the impression that he rarely smiled. He stood silently like a sphinx, remote from them, eyes roaming cautiously over the beach, taking in every movement.

'That goes for both of us,' Liam replied. 'I want to know that you are who you say you are before we take this any further.'

Buckholtz laughed. His laughter was deeply resonant, but humourless. He slapped his big hands against his tight shorts. 'I don't usually carry a passport or a driving licence on the beach, buddy!'

'Then I suggest we satisfy ourselves later. I like careful people.'

Buckholtz stared down at Lisa, his eyes roaming over her slowly, not missing a curve. 'Nice body. Who's the lady?' His voice held a mocking tone.

Lisa stood up. 'Lisa Schmitt,' she said coldly.

Buckholtz extended his hand and she shook it reluctantly, feeling her hand enveloped in the hugeness of his fist. He held it for a moment, until it was more of a caress than a handshake. Then he let her go and gestured towards the other man. 'This here is Chico Gonzales. Nothing gets done without him, just remember that. Where are you guys staying?'

'Right here in Los Arcos.'

Buckholtz spat a wad of gum onto the sand. 'Great! Then we can talk over dinner. You know Andale's bar, right? Just up the street at eight o'clock.'

Liam watched them walk away, Buckholtz with his exaggerated muscle-bound swagger and Gonzales one step behind like a cur dog. He exhaled and picked up his towel. 'Let's go back to the room. I feel like taking a shower.'

Later, as the sun sank like a great red stone and became extinguished far out to sea, Liam stood bare-chested on the second floor balcony of their room sipping a beer, his mind evaluating the meeting on the beach with Buckholtz. He was sure that the man was who he claimed to be. But he fought against being lulled into a sense of false security, even though Lisa had assured him that Buckholtz matched the description given to her by Hans Dietrich before they left Amsterdam.

The balcony overlooked a promenade above the beach that ran in a wide circle to the centre of Puerto Vallarta three miles away. The path was crowded with people strolling and planning another lazy evening's entertainment. The smell of cooking wafted on a gentle breeze, tantalising his nostrils.

Directly below him a tiny arched bridge led the path over a trickling muddy stream that flowed onto the sands, nourishing a line of palm trees on its way. He idly watched a slim elderly man dressed in white trousers and a pink shirt dawdling on the bridge like a Kentucky dandy, hand in hand with his aged baby doll wife. Wisps of silver hair showed beneath a braided black western style hat. His silver moustache glowed against a tanned leather skin. His wife was a fluffy powder puff of white lace and elaborately coiffured blonde hair. Her silicon breasts jutted beneath wrinkled skin. Creatures of habit, they had appeared there every night at the same time. Liam tried to imagine them strolling like that through the bleakness of Pettigoe village in Donegal. The idea was so ridiculous that he collapsed into a deck chair laughing.

Lisa crossed the darkening bedroom and switched on a low bedside light. 'What are you laughing at?' she called.

He glanced inside the room through the open balcony doors. She was naked except for a towel around her waist. In the dim light her breasts bobbed whitely against the rest of her golden-brown expanse of skin and he felt a surge of desire.

'Wild Bill Cody is back again with his dolly. Her name has to be Mary Lou something or other.' He laughed again, 'Jesus! Americans!' Liam finished his beer and went into the room. Lisa slipped into a pair of powder-blue panties and he drew in his breath to the snick of a bra strap. He walked over and ran a finger down her spine to the small of her back.

'Don't you think you should have that shower? We don't have much time.' She smiled. 'You've changed since we got here,' she said.

'How do you mean, I've changed?'

She laughed and pointed at the bulge in his red beach shorts. 'That,' she said.

'It must be the weather or something,' he grunted, blushing. Stepping into the bathroom, he stripped and turned on the shower. He remained in the cubicle for a long time, tingling to the cold needles of water probing his skin. He felt better than he had in years.

Changing into slacks and short-sleeved shirt, he joined Lisa on the balcony. Silhouetted against the lights outside, she looked ravishing in a pale blue silk dress. She twirled in front of him so that the diaphanous material floated up around her tanned legs. 'What do you think?'

'You look bloody great,' he said, snapping a can of beer.

'Coming from an Irishman, I'll take that as the finest compliment I've ever had!' she mocked.

Liam swallowed the beer in a long series of thirsty gulps. 'You're the one that said I shouldn't get too interested.' He smiled. 'Let's go. Bring your passport.'

Gene Buckholtz stood at the bar in Andale's Tavern waiting for them. Dressed in jeans and a long-sleeved teeshirt that seemed tailored to emphasis his muscles, he looked bullish and mean. Chico Gonzales was less sinister without his sunglasses and straw hat.

Liam looked around. The bar was a great barn of a place with a lofty smoke-blackened timber ceiling supported by what seemed to be the trunks of old trees. They had both been there many times since their arrival.

Buckholtz looked Lisa over minutely. 'You look good enough to eat, honey!'

'Let's get on with it, Buckholtz,' Liam snapped.

'Follow me, pal!' Buckholtz led them upstairs to an open air balcony which balanced over the street.

A waiter handed them leather-bound menus. Buckholtz spoke rapidly to him in Spanish and he immediately began to drag away the nearest tables. 'Just to ensure our privacy,' Buckholtz drawled. 'Try the spareribs; they're the best in town.'

'You seem to have a bit of clout around here, Gene,' Liam commented.

'I should do!' Buckholtz slapped Gonzales on the shoulder. 'Me and Chico here must have spent enough to buy the place at least ten times over during the past five years.'

'You live here then?' Lisa asked.

'I guess you could say that. When we're not busy doing other things.' Buckholtz laughed. 'Uncle Sam didn't like to have us around Miami, so we moved, eh, Chico?'

Lisa stared at Buckholtz for a moment. Then she said, 'Roll up your right sleeve, please.'

'Sure lady, I'll take the lot off if you like.' His voice was sardonic. Buckholtz rolled up the sleeve of his teeshirt and bared a forearm. 'You like tattoos, right? I got this one in 'Nam – nice ain't it?'

The tattoo was a grotesque caricature of a helicopter, head on, spitting two red bolts of lightening. A scroll ran through it with the words "Canned Heat" emblazoned in blue.

'That's good enough for me.' Lisa shot Liam a sidelong glance. It confirmed what Dietrich had told her.

Buckholtz stretched across the table and ran the back of his hand lightly across Lisa's left breast. In spite of herself, her nipples hardened as she reached for a dagger-like steak knife on the table. 'And you, sweetheart, have a mole right under your left tit!' Buckholtz's laughter followed like a roll of thunder.

Chico's mouth tightened in a thin line, the nearest he could get to a smile. He shook as if laughing, but he uttered no sound.

A slight smile played at the corner of Liam's mouth. Buckholtz had checked them out already. 'We seem to have established our credentials to each other's satisfaction,' he commented. 'Looks like there's no need to exchange passports.'

Their conversation lapsed as the waiter brought two pitchers of cold beer to the table and took their orders. After he had gone, Buckholtz said, 'I can do better than that, buddy. I called Dietrich this afternoon just to check on you two. He gave me a message for you from some guy called Foster. Your old pal Hogan is dead. He said to tell you that the UVF got to him two days ago.'

Liam slumped in his chair as his whole world turned upside

down. Not Big Jim Hogan. Liam felt as though he had lost his own father. He had always looked upon that great brute of a man as indestructible, out of reach of anything or anyone. The grinning face of Buckholtz swirled before him like a disembodied skull. He clenched his fists, wanting to smash it to pieces. As if from a distance, he heard the others talking; muffled sounds. Slowly he pulled himself together and, although white-faced, regained his composure.

'We're looking for a pilot.' He spat the words out, hearing the shake in his voice.

'You've found one, buddy, the best in the business. What do you want me to fly?' Buckholtz, self-assured and bragging, swam before his eyes like a mirage.

Liam heard Lisa saying, 'We want you to fly a chopper.'

Buckholtz picked up a sparerib from his plate and chewed on it noisily, sucking chili sauce from banana-sized fingers. 'What kind of chopper, and where?'

Liam pushed his plate away untouched, his hunger gone. The balcony finally came back into focus. He took a long drink from his glass. 'We want you to fly a Hughes Cayuse in Europe,' he said. 'We want some people put out of business permanently.'

For the first time Gonzales opened his mouth to speak. His voice had a low hissing quality to it, like a snake about to strike. 'That kind of job doesn't come cheap, Senor. Who's to be hit?'

Lisa scribbled a figure on a paper napkin and pushed it across the table. 'You get two per cent up front, the balance when the job is done, lodged in any bank you choose. That's all you get to know until you arrive in Europe.'

Buckholtz dropped his eyes to the napkin and whistled through his teeth. 'If you're paying money like that, it must be someone very important.'

Liam placed his hands on the table and leaned forward. 'It's make your mind up time, pal,' he said. 'If you say yes, you're out of here within two days.'

Buckholtz glanced at Chico and raised his eyebrows in an unspoken question. Gonzales nodded slowly. 'We'll take the contract.'

'Just one proviso,' said Buckholtz. 'You tell your people that we get to choose the weapons.' His lip curled into a sneer. 'I don't want any fucking Micks pissing about calling the shots when it's our skin on the line.'

Liam nodded his assent. 'That's okay, Yank, just so long as we don't have to burn ourselves pulling you out of the fire.'

The waiter appeared with the bill. He wore a giant Mexican sombrero and two leather bandoleers that had bottles swinging in holsters at his hips. Liam fished in his pockets for money as the waiter handed out small glasses of brown liquid. 'Uno! Dos! Tres! Andale!' roared the waiter, slamming his fist onto the table and sending the dishes bouncing. Gonzales tipped back his tiny glass and swallowed in a single gulp.

Buckholtz roared with laughter. 'Speciality of the house. Slammers, for all of you,' he shouted.

Liam downed his drink to a second encore from the waiter, feeling the fiery liquid hitting his empty stomach like a time bomb. 'What the hell is it?' he choked.

'Tequila, Kahlua and 7-Up.' Chico's thin lips stretched into his interpretation of a smile.

Downstairs, the bar had filled up. Two huge wall-mounted speakers vibrated to full volume rock music. Overhead, a couple of television sets showed two different baseball matches in the smokey haze.

Liam swayed on his feet, wishing now that he had eaten something. Alcohol blurred his vision. Buckholtz ordered more tequila. It might as well have been water; it seemed to have such little effect on him.

The crowd pushed back and formed a noisy circle. In the centre, a diminutive Mexican with a Zapata moustache took a huge breath and pulled a condom down over his head. Puffing his cheeks, he exhaled and blew the condom into a swirling orbit around the bar to a roar of cheers. An obese American woman with wild blonde hair joined in. Every time the Mexican extracted a condom and pulled it down over her head, it burst. Failure was soon attributed to her earrings. Once they were removed the condom held and she received a round of hilarious applause.

Liam saw none of it. His mind was thousands of miles away in his own rain-drenched mountains, the ghost of Hogan stretched out in a coffin before him.

Buckholtz circled round Lisa several times, posturing and brushing himself against her. Each time, she moved away, until he finally tired of it. He pulled Liam close and shouted into his ear, 'Chico and me are going to split. Not enough action here. When do we get the two per cent?'

'You get it in the morning. Pick us up at ten. You can drive us to the airport.'

Buckholtz grinned. 'Okay, buddy. We'll be there.' He turned to Lisa and winked. 'Have a nice evening, honey.' With that he pushed his way roughly through the crowd towards the entrance, Gonzales two steps behind him.

Not long after they left, Liam took Lisa by the arm. 'Let's get out of here,' he shouted. 'We've done what we came for. I can't stand the racket any longer.'

Their room was in darkness when Liam opened the door, but immediately he was alert, forcing himself sober. He remembered leaving a light on in the bathroom, but it was off now. He switched on the main light. 'Stay here, by the door,' he told Lisa. He checked the room quickly, but found no one within or on the balcony. He motioned for Lisa to enter.

'What's the matter?' she asked.

'Nothing,' he said. 'My imagination playing tricks, maybe.' He opened a can of beer, feeling thirsty after the tequila, and stood on the balcony watching the pale orb of the moon and allowing the fretful sound of the surf to wash over him.

Lisa undressed. She staggered and almost fell removing her shoes as she pulled a nightdress from a drawer. Slipping it over her head, she went out onto the balcony.

'Someone has been through my things,' she said.

Liam stared at the moon. 'Yeah, I know. You don't get points for guessing who. It's a fucking good job we put the money in the hotel safe.'

Lisa put a cool hand on his arm and stroked it. Softly she said, 'Come to bed. Forget Hogan.'

He thought of Buckholtz touching her and felt a pang of jealousy. 'No,' he said. 'You go ahead. I'll stay up for a while. I need to think.'

Lisa slid into the bed and switched off the light. She could see him outside, outlined in moonlight, lonely and withdrawn. Then she fell asleep, thinking of Gene Buckholtz and his fingers against her nipples.

Twenty-Six

Eddie Molloy kissed his wife good-bye on the scrubbed front step of their house. It was something they had done through all the years whenever he left for the sea. Not for the first time, Nora Molloy contemplated that it was the only time he ever kissed her outside their own four walls.

'Take care of yourself, love. I'll be in touch.' He picked up his bag, and without another word he turned and walked to the front gate. His farewell words still hadn't changed. For forty years they had been the same. She knew he wouldn't look back, but she watched him just for a while as she always did, until he turned the corner. Then she closed the door and went back to bed.

Once around the corner, Eddie stepped inside the Dominican church and walked self-consciously up the centre aisle to the second pew from the front on the right hand side. Nora didn't know it, but it was also another habit that went back through the years.

A priest was busy preparing the altar for seven o'clock mass and paid no attention to him. Molloy knelt and mumbled the same words that he always did. 'Dear God, you don't know me too well, I don't come here often, but I'd like you to look after the missus while I'm gone. Thanks very much.'

He thought for a moment of asking God to keep an eye on the *Maria B* as well, but at the last moment thought better of it and walked quickly from the church. He had only one last ritual call to make and that was to a harbourside pub that had an early licence for the dockers working on the day shift. There was time for a couple of pints before going on board.

The aroma of frying bacon woke Prendergast at eight o'clock. He didn't rush to get up, but lay in his bunk for a few minutes gathering his thoughts. Today was the day he had worked for. In a few short hours he would take the ship to sea.

By the time he had dressed, Eddie Molloy was already in overalls and busy below with his beloved engine. The three paid hands were tucking in to rashers and eggs when he got below to the messroom.

'Mornin' lads!' he said, pouring himself a mug of coffee. 'Glad to see you mucking in and looking after yourselves. Which one of you is the best cook?'

The engine room greaser cleared his throat and took a sip of tea. 'It ain't me, Skipper, that's for sure!'

Matty Lyons was a wizened little man with eyes that begged for sympathy. His neck looked as if it could do with a good scrub, and Prendergast noticed he had two fingers missing on his left hand. His accent wasn't Irish.

Prendergast lit a cigarette. 'Where are you from, Matty?'

'I'm a Geordie; from Sunderland, originally. I've been over here for a couple of years, I couldn't get a ship on the other side, and the mines are fucked.' Matty's voice faltered and he dried up as though he felt he had said too much already.

'You did a bit of time down the pits, then?' That explained the man's neck, Prendergast thought. He'd seen miners with skin ingrained with coal dust before.

'Aye, I did. In between trips to sea. That's where I lost these.' He held up his left hand. 'Got 'em trapped in a bloody conveyor belt.'

Prendergast turned his attention to the other two. The youngest, a big raw-boned man in his twenties had a great shock of red hair and his face was heavily freckled. There was something about him that reminded Jim of a drawing he had seen once, he couldn't remember where, of a recruit signing up for the Irish Rangers at the turn of the century. Seeing Prendergast looking directly at him, the young man announced 'I'm Jimmy Lafferty, from Spiddal,' his freckles forming one great blotch on his skin. 'Were you ever in deep sea before, Jimmy?'

question only served to increase Lafferty's embarrassment and his face became an inferno. 'N-No,' he stammered, 'I was a f-f-fish-erman.'

Jim smiled at him, 'Don't let that worry you, lad, you'll enjoy the trip and the work might not be so tough.'

The third crew member reached for the teapot. 'I suppose you want to know about me, next?'

Prendergast sensed the sarcasm in the man's voice but he smiled and said, 'There's no harm in us getting to know one another since we're going to be living in each other's pockets for the next couple of weeks.'

The other man slurped at his tea. 'The name's John Reynolds, the Chief knows me, I'm from the Claddagh as well. I've been to sea before. I was a quartermaster in the old Port Line.' He paused for a moment and then said, 'I suppose you know that the Seamen's Union don't like what you're up to.'

Prendergast sighed. There had to be one, didn't there? All he needed was a sea lawyer on board. 'What do you mean by that?' He fixed an icy stare on Reynolds.

'This tub failed her survey, didn't she? Me and the lads have been talking about that.'

Prendergast interrupted him quickly. 'You know exactly what the deal is. We're doing an undermanned delivery trip, and that's what you signed on for. You will be paid a bonus before you fly back. I must also remind you that this ship is Liberian, regis-tered in Monrovia. If you don't like the conditions, there's the door. You can fuck off ashore right now.' He fixed his eyes on the other two. 'That goes for anyone.'

Matty Lyons shrugged and looked away. 'You can count me in, Skipper,' he said. 'I need the job.'

Lafferty went red and mumbled, 'M-Me too.' For the first time Jim noticed that Lafferty had a squint in his right eye and his eyeball appeared to have gone into orbit inside his skull.

Reynolds placed his big hands on the table. 'Just testing the water, Skipper, thought we might squeeze a bit more out of you, that's all.'

Prendergast stared at him for a moment longer. Reynolds'

face held a self-satisfied smirk. He was a big man with a distended belly, across which his seaman's jersey stretched like a membrane. His hair was unnaturally dark for a man of his age. Prendergast decided that he used a dye on it. 'I'm not out to screw anybody, just remember that. You'll be well paid for what I'm asking you to do. Meanwhile, you have until three o'clock to walk ashore. Is that clear?' Prendergast stood up and walked to the door, not waiting for an answer.

He paused in the doorway and turned to face them. 'Just one other thing, so that you all know the score,' he said. 'We're short-handed and there isn't a cook. We'll be working watches four hours on and four off. The watch below cooks for the watch on deck.' All three nodded assent.

Prendergast went out on deck and shouted down into the engine room, 'Eddie, grab yourself a cup of coffee and come up on the bridge!'

A few minutes later Molloy joined him in the wheel house. 'What's up, Skipper?'

'That deck hand, Reynolds. He seems to be a bit of a trouble-maker, Eddie, what do you know about him?' Prendergast sounded angry.

Molloy wiped his hands on a piece of cotton waste. 'Aye, he's a bit of a rough bugger, Skipper. Likes his drink and beats up on his wife every now and then. He did a month in jail for assault a year ago, by all accounts. He was working on tugs for a good while before that. All I can say, other than that, is that he's probably a good deck hand, maybe the best we have.'

Prendergast rummaged in a flag locker and found the Blue Peter he had been looking for. 'Okay. We'll just have to keep an eye on him, but let me know if you hear him stirring up the rest of them. By the way, the pilot will be aboard just before three. Are you all set down below?'

Molloy thought Prendergast sounded as though he was in some private world. He had sensed a difference in the man during the past couple of days. Some of the spark seemed to have gone out of him. He had put it down to last minute nerves. 'I'm changing a fuel filter at the moment, but I'll be ready, all right.'

'Good.' Prendergast managed a wan smile. 'Okay, Eddie, you get on with that. I'll go ashore and clear with the agents and the customs.'

Prendergast hoisted the Blue Peter flag on the signal mast over the wheel house, then he walked aft and hoisted a brand new red and white striped Liberian flag on the ensign staff on the stern. It hung limply in the calm air, its white star on a blue square hidden in the folds of the flag.

Just before three o'clock Vincent Kelly came on board to pilot the ship out of the docks. Shortly afterwards, a dull explosion of sound from the engine room followed by a plume of black smoke from the ship's funnel announced the starting up of the engine. Kelly joined Prendergast on the bridge and stared down the length of the decks to where Reynolds was standing on the forecastle by the windlass waiting for orders to take in the mooring lines. Lafferty was on the afterdeck for the same purpose. Matty Lyons, the greaser, was standing by in the wheel house to take the wheel. 'All set, Jim?' Kelly looked relaxed and cheerful.

Prendergast walked over to the engine room telegraph where its brass pedestal picked up the sunlight flooding through the open door. 'Aye, we're all set, Vincent. Let's get on with it.'

Kelly went to the wing of the bridge and roared at Reynolds, 'Take in your bow line and for'ard spring!' Then turning aft he shouted to Lafferty to take in his stern line. A docker on the quay side let go the mooring ropes. 'Slow ahead!' he ordered.

Jim rang the telegraph and an answering tinkle followed by an increase in vibration announced that Molloy had put the engine into *ahead*. The bow swung slowly off the quayside as the ship, still held by her after spring, nudged the quay wall with her stern.

'Stop engines!' Kelly walked to the bridge wing and looked aft. 'Let go your back spring, slow ahead.'

With little fuss, they were under way, 'Hard a starboard,' Kelly called to the helmsman and Matty Lyons swung the wheel. Turning into the open lock gates, they could see the harbour outside opening up to them and the black and white pilot launch already moving swiftly ahead. The lock keeper waved as they passed through the gates and then they were clear.

Kelly lined the ship up with the leading marks to the channel, then turned to Jim. 'Well, Jim, you're on your way. How do you feel?'

Prendergast leaned on the bridge coaming as he gazed into the distance. 'Better than I have in ages. I've been looking forward to it.' He looked at a bank of fog that lay outside Mutton Island where the pilot launch waited in frozen stillness. 'Looks like we might have fog for a while.'

'It's just a heat haze. You might have it for a few miles till you get out near the islands, but you have a good forecast for the next few days.' Kelly moved further away from the wheel house door out of earshot of the helmsman. 'I hear you met Jonathan Cooke the other night.'

Prendergast frowned, the remark reminding him of the pistol lying in a drawer in his cabin. 'Yeah, he was waiting for me when I got back on board.' He didn't know whether Kelly knew of his agreement with Jonathan Cooke. 'How much do you know about Jonathan, Vincent?' he asked.

Kelly studied the swing of the ship's bow against the tide running up river into the Corrib estuary. He poked his head inside the wheel house door and said to the helmsman, 'Steady as she goes, keep her on the buoy now.' Coming back, he said, 'I know enough about him to know that he thinks he's on to something. You can rely on him. He won't let you down.'

'How long have you been involved with him, Vincent?'

Kelly shook his head, 'Don't ask so many questions, Jim. It's better that way. Anyway, does it matter? I just tell him a few things that I hear from time to time. Other than that I don't see much of him.'

The ship was approaching the pilot boat fast. Prendergast knew that whatever he asked Kelly, the answers would tell him nothing. Maybe the man didn't even have the sort of answers he wanted to hear.

'Okay, Jim. Stop engines.' Kelly was ready to leave. The ship slowed to the ring of the engine room telegraph and a few minutes later became motionless on the calm water at the edge of the fog bank. The pilot cutter came towards them, looking like a black beetle on the glassy surface of the sea.

Kelly extended his hand. 'Safe passage, Jim. Hopefully I will see you in a few weeks.' A few minutes later he was crossing the main cargo deck and had hoisted himself over the bulwarks to climb down the rope ladder to the waiting pilot boat.

Jim rang for *slow ahead* and the ship entered the bank of fog seconds later. Galway and Kelly disappeared astern as the ship became enveloped in a cocoon of candy floss mist, only the single long blast of her siren every few minutes announcing her presence.

Prendergast studied the radar screen in silence for a few minutes. He could already pick out the three Aran Islands on the forty-five mile range. Satisfied that no other ships were in range, he altered course for the North Sound rather than opting for the shorter route to the south. Switching on the automatic pilot, he ordered Matty Lyons to go below. He remained on the bridge alone.

At eight o'clock in the evening the *Maria B* broke through the fog blanket and rounded the Eeragh lighthouse in a blaze of late sunlight. Here and there small patches of fog still floated wraith-like, low over the water.

Eddie Molloy came up on the bridge and found Prendergast standing out on the bridge wing staring at the thin black and white spire. He knew they should normally have passed the islands on the southern course. Clearly, Prendergast was out here on some pilgrimage of his own. Molloy felt as though he was intruding. 'There's boiled bacon and cabbage below, Jim, if you want to have it,' he said quietly.

'No. You go ahead without me. I'm not hungry.' His eyes held a haunted emptiness. 'You can tell Reynolds to take over from me at midnight.'

Molloy made no answer as he left the bridge. As soon as he had gone, Jim went to his cabin and collected a bunch of red roses tied with a white ribbon. He went to the wing of the bridge and dropped them over the side and watched them bob away into the wash. The tears came then. He couldn't stop thinking that even now he was sailing over the wreck of the *Larinita*. That somewhere far below in the depths beneath that glassy surface covered in long fronds of sea wrack, lay the yacht that had crippled his life. He looked again at the pinnacle of the lighthouse two miles away before another bank of fog closed around it. Then he squared his shoulders and went into the chart room to lay off the course that would take them south past the Blasket Islands.

Twenty-Seven

The sun peeked over the horizon just before six o'clock in the morning, spreading its light in long tentacles through the palm trees fringing the beach. Within minutes the air heated, and the sea donned a glistening mantle of blue as though millions of sapphires had decided to make its surface their home.

The first rays of sunshine, hesitant at first, penetrated the room and focused on Liam's face, waking him instantly. He felt disorientated and unsure of where he was as he watched the ceiling fan circle. Gradually the events of the previous day fell into place and the stark fact of Hogan's death took over, plummeting him into tomb-like blackness, leaving only desolation.

A vision of Harry Trent taking over as Brigade Commander flashed into his mind. Foster lurked in the background like a Shakespearean wraith. The certainty that those two were somehow involved numbed him. He left the bed and pulled on his red beach shorts. Lisa was still sleeping peacefully. Her hair tumbled on the pillow, reflecting the sunlight that slanted across the room. She had thrown the sheet back during the night and one of her breasts was exposed above the lace-edged cleft of her satin nightdress. At that moment, he wanted desperately to take her in his arms and lose himself in the valley of her breasts. The thought startled him; it was not a sexual one. It was more of a yearning for long-lost innocence; a need to be comforted so that the dark events of both the past and the future could be washed clean. But for Lisa to respond in the way he wanted, there would have to be love. For her, he knew there probably never would be.

He left the room without waking her and went downstairs.

He walked along the edge of the pool and out onto the beach where the sand was already becoming warm. Over near the bar, Juan, the pool attendant, dragged loungers out onto the sand in preparation for his day's work. His malformed feet looked grotesque in his oversized runners. 'Buenos dias, Senor,' Juan grunted. Liam had the impression that Juan couldn't care less. To the Mexican, he was just another gringo with more money than sense. Liam ran straight down the beach to the water's edge and plunged into the surf.

The water was cool and bracing. He dove under the next breaker and swam out into deeper water. Floating on his back he gazed back at the hotel. He could see Lisa standing on the balcony, waving at him. He raised a hand to beckon her down, and she held up ten fingers and went back inside.

The mosquito bites on his ankle that had awakened him during the night stopped itching under the water's balm and he floated, allowing his mind to clear, closing his eyes to the sting of salt and sun. He rolled over and swam into deeper waters. Off at the edge of the bay he could see a sport fishing boat trolling for early morning marlin, its hull moving swiftly through the water, throwing spray astern. Soon, he realised, this place would be a memory.

Liam was already eating breakfast beside the pool when Lisa finally came down. She was conscious of several pairs of eyes following her as she teetered toward him on high-heeled sandals, which exaggerated her golden legs. An elderly man stopped eating, his fork poised between his plate and his gaping mouth, until a piece of hot omelette fell and scalded his belly.

Lisa kissed Liam lightly on the cheek and ran her fingers through his wet hair. 'Feel good after your swim?'

Her question, for some reason that she couldn't fathom, irritated him and his response was surly. 'Yes, but right now I'd rather be at home finding out what happened to Jim Hogan.'

'Liam, you must forget him, at least for now. When this is over you can go back. Meanwhile, we have a job to do.'

'Look Lisa, let's get something straight. I'm not backing out, if that's what you think. I'll go through with it, but one thing is for certain; I don't forget my friends. Hogan was more than a friend to me, and whoever killed him will find that out. I can assure you of that.'

Lisa felt the passion in his voice and noticed the grim lines that had set on his face. She touched his hand. 'I'll help you when the time comes, if I can.' She paused and examined him. 'You know, the sun suits you. You're quite a handsome beast at times, especially when you're angry.'

'Sit down and have your breakfast!' He withdrew his hand from hers and she could sense, almost taste, the gulf that opened between them.

Lisa devoured a plate of papaya and guava, occasionally looking up at him as he smoked a cigarette and helped himself to more coffee. She realized that he was becoming an enigma. One minute he was unnaturally soft and tender, then hard and uncompromising, with a cruel and pitiless streak running through him. Perhaps that's what makes up the Irish, she thought. They are mixed up; senselessly romantic and, at times, totally illogical.

Liam walked away from her and flopped down on a lounger out on the beach. A few yards away from him, a pelican waddled with ungainly steps on the sand, its human-like manner downcast, as though it carried the weight of the world on its nonexistent shoulders. Only in flight could it achieve any semblance of grace. Maybe it too, in some strange way, was mourning Hogan, he thought. He lay back and closed his eyes.

Gene Buckholtz arrived in the hotel at ten o'clock. If anything, Liam thought, his figure seemed to have grown overnight. The only indication that he might not have slept was in the dark rings around his eyes.

Close on his heels, terrier-like, came Chico Gonzales, his smoke-black eyes constantly roving, seeking something that was of interest only to himself.

Buckholtz sat down in the sand next to Liam and grinned. 'Hi buddy! This is the big day, eh? What time is your flight?'

Liam rolled over onto his side. 'Not until three o'clock.'

'Plenty of time then?' Chico noted.

Nearby, a well-preserved and tanned woman in a metallic bikini preened herself and entered into a loud-voiced monologue with a woman further down the beach. 'Darling, guess what! Bill bought me a condo last night ... can you believe it? Right on the beach, darling!' Her nasal Chicago twang reached a shriek. 'They won't even talk to you for less than a hundred and twenty thousand, my dear!' She sat up and settled her breasts more comfortably in their cups as though waiting for a round of applause.

Liam scowled, 'Another member of your great nation, Buckholtz? Is noise what makes you number one? Let's go over to the bar. Maybe there you'll be able to hear what I have to say.'

Buckholtz smiled and flexed the sinews of his arms, his eyes falling to his chest. 'Yeah, I guess you can say that we are the best, Paddy. That's why you're here, right?' His smile was sardonic as he followed Liam towards the thatched bar, Gonzales slinking in the background like a vulture waiting to pick at the remains.

Lisa came down the steps into the bar as they reached a vacant table. She was still wearing her highheeled sandals, forever the show-off. Liam could not help feeling that one day her exhibitionism would prove her downfall. She drew far too much attention to herself.

Buckholtz whistled softly through his teeth and let his eyes roam freely. 'Hi, honey! How are you today? See a bit of action last night?'

Lisa looked through him. 'I'll go and pack, Liam, and leave you to deal with these two monkeys.' She took an envelope from her handbag and handed it to him. 'No doubt you'll need this.' She turned and tottered up a path lined by potted palms, her heels clicking on the tiles.

Buckholtz's belly laugh followed her. 'I've got to hand it to you, Liam,' he sneered. 'That's some broad you have there.' He pulled a chair back from the table and roared at Mario to bring three Coronas. 'You got just thirty seconds, amigo,' he bellowed at the waiter, 'or I'll wring your scrawny little neck!'

'Cut out the shit, Buckholtz!' Liam passed him the envelope. 'Today's Wednesday. There's a flight on Friday night out of Mexico City to Rome. We'll meet you at the airport on Saturday morning.'

Buckholtz opened the envelope just enough to see inside it. His eyes hardened and any semblance of humour vanished from his face. 'What the fuck is this? This ain't no two per cent!' Chico Gonzales tensed himself, preparing to strike.

Unable to hide his satisfaction, Liam fished a small stainless steel key from the pocket of his shorts. 'For that, you need this,' he said tersely. 'What you have there is airfare and expenses. The key opens a safe-deposit box in a Rome bank. I'll take you there on Monday, before you leave Rome for your training.'

Gonzales pushed his pockmarked face forward aggressively. His voice was barely a whisper. 'What fucking training you talking about? We don't need none. We can fly a Cayuse in our sleep.'

'I'm sure you can,' Liam replied. 'That's why we came all this way to hire you. But for this operation we need to be sure, so you get training whether you like it or not. It's all part of the package.'

Buckholtz had the appearance of Goliath being faced down by David, but he took one last stab at truculence. 'Okay, so you want to be a smart ass, how do we know you'll be in Rome on Saturday?'

'We'll be there,' Liam replied. 'You can count on it.' He lit a cigarette and sat back in his chair. 'If we're not, you get an all expenses weekend in Rome. There are a lot of Lisas there at this time of the year!' His smile was taunting.

Buckholtz lowered his eyes and concentrated on two large black ants on the tiles by his feet. They were locked together in some mysterious struggle. Two microscopic monsters engaged in an undefined primeval rite. He touched them with his toe. They separated, but instantly re-engaged. 'What do you think they're doing, Liam, fucking or fighting?' He stared coldly at Liam across the table.

Liam shrugged. 'I don't give a shit,' he said.

Buckholtz stood up and motioned for Gonzales to follow. 'They remind me of you and me, amigo. One day we will have to find out.' Smiling, he ground the ants under his foot.

Gonzales grimaced as though he was in pain and shook silently. For a moment Liam imagined a forked tongue flicking between his lips.

'This whole thing better go just like you say, buddy. We'll pick you up outside the hotel at two o'clock.' Buckholtz turned on his heel and led Gonzales away through the palms.

Liam remained where he was and drank all three Coronas. Suddenly he felt good. He would do the job as planned. He put all thoughts of Jim Hogan on the back burner. That matter would be taken care of later.

At exactly three minutes past three in the afternoon, the pilot of the Mexicana jet started his engines, released the brakes and applied full thrust from the powerful McDonnell engines. Seconds later, the plane left the sun-baked runway, skimmed low over the burnt scrub, then banked swiftly in a climbing turn over the sea, leaving behind a transparent haze.

As they reached cruising altitude the terrain gave way to jungle-clad mountainous rifts along the Great Continental Divide.

Lisa reclined her seat and unclipped her safety belt as the warning lights went out. She stroked Liam's bare arm, her fingers toying with the thick mat of black hairs. 'That was good,' she said.

'Yeah, I enjoy the take-off, too.'

She smiled. 'I wasn't talking about the take-off, you fool. I meant before – in the hotel.'

He leaned over and kissed her on the lips, and she wriggled her tongue into his mouth. 'More please,' she said before releasing him.

Liam closed his eyes. The few days in the sun had rejuvenated him. He let his mind dwell on the morning's events. He was satisfied that he now had the measure of Buckholtz and his friend Chico. After they left he had returned to the room to find that Lisa had finished the packing and was waiting for him.

She lay on the bed in a transparent slip. Her travelling clothes were neatly folded on a nearby chair. She noted the air of satisfaction with which he closed the door and capitalised on it immediately, raising one leg, allowing the hem of her slip to slide back down one long thigh.

He had bent his head to kiss her parted lips and she smelt the odour of beer on his breath. Pulling him down beside her, she helped him remove his shorts, her eyes wide and excited by how erect and ready he was. Her fingers fluttered over the sinews of his stomach to that black triangle where his manhood stood proudly. Cupping his testicles she sucked first one, then the other, before moving over him in one sinuous movement. Already she was wet and open, and their mating became the ritual of two young animals, devouring one another in a sensuous feast.

Liam stirred in his seat. 'I'm happy,' he said. 'We did what we had to do.'

'Yes,' she replied softly, 'and now there is more.' She entwined her fingers in his. 'We will do that together, also.'

Twenty-Eight

Colonel Mohammed Ghalboun glanced around the hotel room with distaste. Compared to his own air conditioned suite in the airport Hilton, this place was a slum. There was no accounting for taste, he thought. Foster spent money as though each penny needed accounting for in triplicate. Even his clothes were nothing but rags, in Ghalboun's eyes.

Gingerly, he sat down on the edge of an armchair and adjusted his trouser legs before flicking an imaginary fleck of dust from the cuff of his Christian Dior jacket. He took a packet of Gauloise cigarettes from his pocket and lit one. 'So, Mr. Foster,' he began, 'you had a successful visit to your homeland?' His smile was quizzical.

Foster slopped whiskey into two cloudy-looking glasses. 'There's no ice, I'm afraid. Good Irish should be drunk without it, anyway.' He handed Ghalboun a glass, but remained standing in the centre of the room, two large sweat stains showing at the armpits of his cheap striped shirt.

Ghalboun wrinkled his nose. 'I prefer Scotch myself, with ice of course. I'm sorry, I mean no offense.'

'No offense taken, Colonel,' replied Foster. 'Every man to his own poison.' He cleared his throat. 'Yes,' he said. 'Everything went very satisfactorily, and as a result there has been a small but important change in our organisation. I am happy to say that we have silenced one of our more conservative voices.' He paused. 'Permanently silenced, I should add. We have reached a unanimous agreement and I expect to hear from Liam by tonight, at the latest.'

'I am delighted to hear that, because your weapons are already on the dockside in Tripoli and we are now organising a ship for their transportation.' Ghalboun massaged his cheek with his thumb. 'We need two further ingredients before we proceed. Final confirmation of the meeting with the exact time and place, and, of course, the helicopter crew in place. It is my belief that neither will be a problem, providing that your man, Liam, does his job.' He sipped his drink and shuddered. It was definitely not as good as Scotch.

Foster sipped his drink. 'Liam will do just what we ask of him. I know we had to pressure him, but once he agrees to something, he does it. Whatever else one might think, Liam remains dedicated and I have total confidence in him.'

'I'm glad of that,' Ghalboun replied. 'Your words are comforting.' He looked around the room again. The window offered a view of a rubbish-filled alleyway and the wall of a crumbling warehouse. The Hotel Trocadero, Ghalboun thought. Like calling a pile of shit a chocolate mousse. 'Are you sure, Mr. Foster, that you would not prefer another hotel?'

Foster gave a short laugh. 'Absolutely not, this suits me fine. I am a man of simple needs. Besides, this is where Liam knows that he can contact me.' He could have added that the basement housed a very interesting gay bar, but decided it was something better left unsaid.

Ghalboun fixed Foster in a penetrating gaze. 'What have you to say about the rumours of a new peace agreement in your country?'

'I would discount them,' Foster replied without hesitation. 'There have always been rumours. It will come to nothing, I assure you.'

Ghalboun finished his drink. 'There's nothing left to say then.' He extended his hand, 'Until we meet again, Mr. Foster. In Tripoli I think?'

'Yes, of course, in Tripoli. That is where our work will really begin.' Foster looked pleased. His eyes shone with anticipation.

Ghalboun was lucky. A taxi had already parked outside the hotel and it carried him quickly into the afternoon traffic. Through his dark glasses he noticed the driver studying him in the rear view mirror. He sank lower into a corner of the rear seat to escape the disconcerting brown eyes and turned his face away.

Arriving at his own hotel, Ghalboun alighted and walked into the reception lobby. He suspected that the surly Italian had added insult to injury by overcharging him exorbitantly, but what the hell, that was what money was for. Tomorrow he would be in the desert and there would be no need for it. It was time for one last extravagance.

A uniformed hall porter recognised him and directed him to one side of the vestibule. From there, he could view a lounge bar that was screened from the lobby by a small forest of tropical plants. Fed by a fountain, an ornamental stream wandered through the lush vegetation so that the cascading water caught the light from lofty windows set high overhead, filling the air with a melody of its own.

Ghalboun studied the young woman pointed out to him. She sat in a low cane chair sipping what appeared to be a Martini. An unopened novel lay in her lap. He noted appreciatively that she had red hair, and her simple cream silk suit had an elegance that came only with a high price tag. With matching handbag and shoes, she looked anything but the professional that he knew her to be.

Ghalboun smiled broadly and handed the porter a substantial tip. 'Excellent,' he said. 'I could not have been more selective myself. Does the lady have a name?'

The porter pocketed his tip with appreciation. 'Signora Ricardi,' he replied. 'Anna Ricardi.'

Ghalboun smiled. 'Delightful,' he whispered.

Ghalboun approached her from the far end of the bar. The moment he came into the room their eyes met, as each appraised the other.

A faint smile of surprise hovered on the woman's lips. Too often, her customers were fat and fumbling business men, more concerned with how they could hide her fee in their expense accounts than in anything else.

Ghalboun glided swiftly across the intervening space. 'Anna! How nice of you to call!' He extended his hand.

She returned a dazzling smile. Certainly this afternoon would not be a chore. She took his arm when he offered it, and allowed him to steer her gallantly towards the elevators.

Opening the door to his suite, Ghalboun glanced at his watch. Plenty of time, he thought. Four hours, before his plane hurtled him back into a desert where redheads and blondes were nonexistent. The slithering sound of silk falling to the floor announced that she had already shed her skirt. He closed the door and turned to face her.

When the call came through to Foster's room in Rome, it was late. He had already eaten and was ready to go downstairs to the disco bar in the basement. He was looking forward to the night's hunting. Fuelled by the excitement of what the night promised, he regarded the call as an unwanted interruption.

It was Liam. The call was very brief. 'We're on our way,' he said. 'The contract is in place. Meet the flight from Mexico City in the morning.'

'Good, I'll do that,' Foster replied and replaced the receiver. His good humour immediately returned. It mattered little that they were behind schedule. Perhaps the news would also calm any remaining fears Colonel Ghalboun might still harbour.

On the ground floor of GCHQ in Cheltenham, England, Fred Pilkington took off his headphones and rewound the tape. He was tired and bored. Nearing the end of his shift, he disliked having to face something that needed further investigation, perhaps even requiring a report.

Monitoring other people's conversations that bounced through space from lonely satellites had seemed exciting five years ago, but now he couldn't care less. Even the odd salacious conversation failed to raise his spirits these days.

He had picked up the call by pure chance, but it was the language used that caused him to home in on it. It was a language he had never heard before, and in spite of his lethargy, it intrigued him. He fed it through the computers for a second time and again came up with a blank. Damn it, he thought. I'm going to have to write a bloody report. He swivelled his chair in the direction of the keyboard and started thumping the keys with increasing frustration.

Early on Saturday morning an Alitalia 747 dived swiftly through the cloud layer over Rome and seconds later touched down in a perfect landing. The muted sound of politely reserved clapping from the rear of the plane drowned the hostess's welcome to Rome, as a group of Japanese tourists announced their pleasure that the long flight was over.

Gene Buckholtz released his seat belt and glanced towards the aisle seat six rows back. Chico Gonzales nodded and stood up in the aisle. They had agreed to travel separately and had avoided contact throughout the flight. It would be the same until they were clear of the airport terminal.

At the baggage pickup they stood at each side of the carousel without so much as the briefest of eye contact. Buckholtz was the first passenger to go through the arrivals door. Close behind, embedded in the group of excited Japanese, followed Gonzales.

Buckholtz slowed his pace as he came through the door. His eyes searched the waiting crowd until they met those of Liam, but he showed no sign of recognition. He saw Liam turn on his heel and walk towards the exit doors. Buckholtz glanced back at Gonzales and received an imperceptible nod. At a discreet distance they followed Liam outside and joined him in a waiting taxi.

Yet another brick was in place. Soon the final road would open before them.

Twenty-Nine

Ghalboun watched the brown arid desert fly past outside the closed windows of his speeding car. Although the road was good and the car had air conditioning, the simmering heat of the barren landscape penetrated. He perspired in spite of the cool interior of the Mercedes limousine.

Colonel Younis Bilgasim, co-ordinator of Libyan intelligence at home and abroad sat beside him in the back seat. Bilgasim controlled a huge empire. At a click of his fingers, he could call on Libyan front men scattered in companies across the world to carry out his wishes. He was also a close confidante of Moammar Ghaddaffi. That knowledge only served to increase Ghalboun's discomfiture. They were on their way to personally brief Ghaddaffi on the status of the operation, and to secure his final approval before they projected it like an unstoppable missile into its final phase. Ghalboun pondered what he should say to justify it.

Ahead, the black asphalt shimmered under the heat of the noonday sun and far in the distance, the buff walls that surrounded Azizya barracks floated above the sand like a mirage. Enclosed by high walls fitted with alarms and remote controlled infrared sensors, the teardrop-shaped compound stretched across the desert for nearly six miles. Ghalboun knew that the guards at the main entrance gates would already be monitoring their approach and preparing themselves.

The army driver slowed the car as they passed through several batteries of French-made Crotale anti-aircraft missiles that lay embedded on either side of the road. Ghalboun noted that there were more of them since his last visit. Ever since the massive US raid from England and from units of the Sixth Fleet which killed his fifteen month old daughter, Ghaddaffi had concentrated his efforts in forestalling any repetition.

Colonel Bilgasim smiled in satisfaction. The defensive perimeter was his achievement, and all of its sophisticated technology was chosen by him. He was a man obsessed by gadgetry. In his pocket rested his latest acquisition, an expensive pen containing a radio microphone, a well-chosen gift from Ghalboun. Perhaps, he thought hopefully, it would not be long before he could put it to use.

The car slowed to a crawl and threaded its way through a maze of huge concrete blocks that formed a chicane leading to the main gates. Placed in position to deter would-be suicide bombers, the blocks formed an effective deterrent against any speeding vehicle attempting such a mission.

The guards on the gate recognised Bilgasim long before the car came to a halt. Even so, they went through the full routine of checking their passes through electronic sensors linked to the main security room. Each of the guards was acutely aware that Bilgasim watched their every movement. They had learned by experience that the slightest deviation in procedure or any sign of laxness would result in instant retribution.

Two of the guards were women, Ghalboun noted. Both were hand-picked members of Ghaddaffi's own personal bodyguard. They wore sand-coloured uniforms and swung their automatic weapons in an accomplished way that suggested their skill in useing them. Their brown eyes were deep with mistrust.

Ghalboun thought of the red-headed Anna Ricardi, who was probably still asleep in Rome. Suddenly, he was no longer pleased to be home. He felt like a stranger in his own land.

Once through the main gates, the driver steered the car through ranks of drawn up tanks and armoured personnel carriers, sinister in their drab desert camouflage. Off to one side, a group of sweating maintenance mechanics struggled to manoeuvre one of the tanks onto a flat-bed transporter.

The omnipresent weaponry soon gave way to a deserted football pitch and gardens with watered lawns, leading to the front of a two-storey building that was home to Ghaddaffi's family. Shaded by trees near the tennis courts, two hundred yards from the main dwelling, lay a large drab-green Bedouin tent outside which two camels stood tethered to a stake. Born in just such a tent, near Sirte, Ghaddaffi had erected this one as a source of pride and a constant reminder of his Bedouin origins.

The car stopped near the tent entrance and the driver got out to open the doors for the two men. It was surprisingly cool in the shade of the trees and the murmur of water from numerous sprinklers lent serenity to an oasis that defied the relentless sun. Bilgasim, who had spoken very little during the journey, squared his uniform cap and faced Ghalboun. 'This could be a long session, my friend, but don't let it worry you. Watch your words and all will be well.'

Ghalboun stretched and smoothed down the creases that had formed in his uniform trousers. He would have felt more comfortable in one of his European summer suits, but for the purposes of this visit, uniform had seemed more appropriate. A movement in the trees caught his attention and he noticed the black snout of a machine gun swinging lazily towards him from a slit in a bunker set deep in the sandy soil. Behind it, a satellite dish peered into the sky.

A female guard with a holstered Colt 45 appeared and escorted them inside the tent. Her trousers were tailored to emphasise the graceful proportions of her limbs. Ghalboun noted that she was better looking than either of the two at the main gate. It was a small thing, but it showed Ghaddaffi's vanity. Everyone knew that he was a womaniser, and even female foreign journalists had received his attentions in the past.

Ghalboun removed his sunglasses and put them into his breast pocket. He looked around with interest. The tent unexpectedly revealed an inside lining of patchwork colours. Simple mats covered the floor, and there were comfortable cushions for guests to sit on. A large coffee table dominated the centre of the tent. On it rested a small gold globe of the world. Jewels marked various capitals. Mecca was a red ruby; Amsterdam, a diamond; Washington was marked with an amethyst. It was a priceless example of the skills of some unknown Swiss craftsman. A green telephone sat alongside the globe.

Off to one side, a large colour television was tuned to a CNN news broadcast. Beneath it, a cabinet contained a video recorder and a stack of tapes. From somewhere else in the tent, taped music escaped from unseen speakers. He recognised the female singer as a popular Egyptian. A favourite, it seemed, of Ghaddaffi's.

The guard left them standing alone in the centre of the tent and withdrew. Minutes later she returned with coffee and placed it on the table before taking up position outside the entrance.

A small sound from a screened-off area caught their attention and they turned expectantly. Ghaddaffi seemed to float towards them, his slippers soundlessly gliding over the carpeted floor. He wore white Pierre Cardin pyjamas. The scent of a Givenchy cologne preceded him and the air became heavy with its fragrance.

A deep rumble issued from his throat, his voice at once resonant and powerful as he welcomed them. 'Gentlemen, please be seated,' he continued. He spoke in Arabic, the sound guttural and harsh. Ghalboun felt overawed as he mumbled a greeting and sank onto one of the cushions.

Ghaddaffi ran a heavy hand through his thick mane of hair. Pouring tiny cups of treacle-like coffee, he pushed small plates of dates and sticky cakes towards them, gesturing for them to help themselves.

'Colonel Bilgasim has told me much about you, Colonel.' For a moment, Ghaddaffi's heavy features radiated light. 'You have done well, my friend. The Libyan people and all our Arab brothers are in your debt.' Just as quickly, his smile evaporated and the dark brown eyes narrowed, riveting Ghalboun. 'Tell me in your own words the details of this operation. Please omit nothing, not even your personal thoughts and feelings. The decisions we make depend upon the value of your analysis.'

Ghalboun began talking slowly and clearly, soon losing any vestige of apprehension. Both of the other men listened intently, without interruption, watching him for signs of indecision. He held nothing back. At the end, he summarised the risks and the consequences as he saw them.

Ghaddaffi's face remained clouded throughout. He said nothing after Ghalboun finished, but reached across the table and pulled the golden globe towards him. His thick fingers spun it until his index finger rested on the twinkling sapphire marking London. He ran his finger to the small raised shape of Ireland. There was no jewel marking Dublin.

Ghaddaffi smiled. 'I think an emerald might be appropriate for the Emerald Isle, Colonel Ghalboun.' On the other side of the Atlantic Ocean, the amethyst of Washington seemed to glow hypnotically and captured his gaze. His face became hard and his dark eyes, fixed on the winking jewel of Washington, were fathomless in their intensity. His cruel lips tightened as he remembered the American F1-11 fighter bombers streaking low over the sea before jerking to five hundred feet at five hundred miles an hour, the subsequent trembling crunch of their bombs followed by the smoke and confusion everywhere, and the screams, yes, the screams of his own children, as the Americans tried their best to kill him. A military failure perhaps, but it had taken the life of his daughter, Hanna.

When he finally spoke, Ghaddaffi's voice was almost a whisper. 'I agree,' he said. 'It is worth the risk. We have remained inactive far too long and they will not expect it.' His next words came like the cold night wind of the desert. 'Give me the blood of these people, Ghalboun, and I will give you a place in our glorious history!'

Ghaddaffi got to his feet without waiting for a reply. He went to a small bookcase where he selected a green leather bound book, a history of the Arab people. Selecting a page, he read in silence for a considerable time. Replacing the book, he spoke at great length, a rambling monologue on Arab unity in the face of threatening Western power and imperialism, his voice thundering and reverberating from the confining tent walls.

Ghalboun sat in stunned silence, trying to follow the incomprehensible discourse. Only on television had he ever seen

Ghaddaffi in full spate. Once during the tirade, he caught a glimpse of Bilgasim stifling a yawn, obviously more used to such rhetoric than he.

When Ghaddaffi stopped, perspiration covered his face and his silk pyjama jacket clung to his powerful shoulders like a rag. He was drained by his own oration. Ghalboun risked a peek at his watch. He could hardly believe his eyes; they had been in the tent for over three hours. Ghaddaffi slumped heavily into a cushion. His eyes held a haunted look as though he could see into the past and the future simultaneously, and whatever he saw in that vision mesmerised him. His voice was normal when he eventually spoke. 'When do our Irish friends arrive here?'

Ghalboun shifted uncomfortably. He was unused to sitting on a low cushion and his legs were cramped. 'They will arrive in Tripoli tonight. Do you wish to meet them?'

Ghaddaffi looked at him in surprise. 'There is no need,' he said. 'This is your operation, Colonel Ghalboun, yours alone. There must be no direct Libyan involvement other than the supply of weapons and training, and I expect you to take steps to ensure that that assistance is untraceable.' His eyes drilled into Ghalboun with laser-like intensity. 'You have sole responsibility for its success. Failure is unthinkable, but the rewards will be more than you can dream of.'

Abruptly, Ghaddaffi rose to his feet. The meeting was over. He accompanied them outside and stood watching them from the doorway of his tent as they drove away.

Ghalboun looked back through the rear window as they passed the tennis courts. Ghaddaffi was still standing in the doorway, a mystical figure with a dry breeze whipping at the legs of his pyjama trousers.

It was still daylight, but the sun was sinking rapidly in the West as the Libyan Airways jet swept in low over the sea. Buckholtz fastened his seat belt as the warning lights came on, and waited for the thud of the landing gear locking into position. Next to him, Gonzales extinguished his cigarette and glanced across the aisle to where Lisa was applying her lipstick. She wore a pale pink cotton suit, simple and exquisitely tailored. Anyone else might need jewellery to complement it, but Lisa provided all the glamour the suit needed.

Foster sat behind Lisa and Liam, quietly absorbing himself in his breviary. Most of the other passengers were ex-patriot British, returning for yet another lonely stint working the black gold that lay in hidden caverns beneath the desert sands. Some of them were big rawboned Scots, fresh from the North Sea oil fields.

The plane seemed to hover momentarily as if reluctant to land, and an urgent whine came from its engines as the pilot applied more thrust for a few seconds. Buckholtz's knuckles showed white on his seat arm rests. 'Flaps!' he muttered savagely. 'Flaps, you son of a bitch!'

The plane hit the runway with a jarring crunch. Twice it bounced back into the air before settling to slew madly down the runway, a great roar of noise from the engines as their cowlings dropped back to provide drag.

'Fuck!' Buckholtz roared, 'Give these fucking A-Rabs good U.S. machinery and what do they do with it? They fuck it up, that's what they do!' Gonzales enjoyed the outburst, but his yellow-brown features looked slightly paler and the pockmarks on his cheeks seemed to glow in the cabin lights.

Foster was the first out of the aircraft door. He stood for a moment on the top of the steps, sucking in deep breaths of air, annoyed that Buckholtz might have drawn unnecessary attention to them.

He need not have worried. Fifty yards away a bus waited to transport the passengers to the terminal, and directly under the steps a small mini-bus waited. Colonel Ghalboun climbed out and waved. 'At your service, Mr Foster,' he called. 'Welcome to Libya!'

Thirty

For the tenth time that morning, Jonathan Cooke spread the photographs out on his desk and used a magnifying glass to study them. Rain pattered softly against the window panes, making his small office seem unusually dreary and cold. He switched on a desk lamp to throw more light on the glossy black and white prints and hunched forward, engrossed in his task.

From a desk drawer he took a small pad of yellow glued labels and wrote brief notes before attaching one label to the back of each photograph. Satisfied, he placed the photographs in a manila envelope before picking up his cane to limp his way downstairs to the Ambassador's office. His leg bothered him more today, as it always did when it rained.

Sir Harold Webster placed a paper cup against the wall on the carpet and took twelve paces backwards. He dropped the golf ball and picked up his new Ping putter. He positioned his feet, gripped the club, and lined himself up.

The knock came to the door a split second before the club connected with the ball. 'Damn!' Webster exclaimed aloud as the door opened and the ball missed the cup by a mile. 'Come in, Jonathan, blast you! You've just ruined my stroke!'

'Sorry, Sir!' Jonathan struggled to hide his amusement. Now fishing, that was different, he thought. That was a proper sport!

The Ambassador let his putter drop lightly to the floor and retrieved the ball. 'Emily bought me this damned putter as a peace offering for her three weeks alone in Florida. I just can't seem to get the hang of the bloody thing!'

Cooke smiled politely. The entire staff knew that Emily Webster had a drinking problem. Her solo holiday trips were an excuse for a good binge and she always returned consumed by guilt. 'This won't take long, Sir,' he said. 'I presume you're playing today?'

Sir Harold walked around his huge desk and flopped into his chair. 'Yes, I'm having lunch with the new Irish Foreign Minister; David ... eh ... what's-his-name?'

'David Delaney?'

'Yes, that's the chap. Afterwards, we're meeting up in Portmarnock with the Papal Nuncio and Takayama, the director of that new Japanese bank that is going up by The Point.'

Cooke grimaced. 'An interesting combination,' he commented.

Sir Harold frowned. 'How do you mean?'

'Well, two Catholics, a Buddhist and a Protestant, all playing golf together. It knocks sectarianism right on the head, I would think! A little more of that in the North of Ireland might not be a bad thing.'

The Ambassador chuckled. 'I hadn't thought of it quite like that,' he said.

'This new man, Delaney, he seems to say all the right things,' Cooke offered.

'I agree. I get the feeling that he is honest and we'll be able to do business with him in the long run. Of course, he was a barrister, so he speaks well and he knows when not to be controversial.' Sir Harold looked hopefully towards the ceiling. 'Maybe we will yet be able to solve this damnable problem in the North.'

Webster looked at his watch and realised that there was not much time if he was to master the damned putter before he left the embassy. 'What's on your mind, Jonathan?'

'I think we are on to something, Ambassador.'

Webster raised his eyebrows. There he goes again, he thought sadly. Whenever Cooke referred to him as Ambassador, it spelt trouble. 'Your man, Prendergast, I presume?'

'No,' Cooke replied. 'He's still at sea. He's not due in Malta for a few days, but we do know that he and his ship passed through the Straits a few days ago.' He selected a photograph from the manila envelope and placed it on the desk in front of the Ambassador. 'Take a look at this.'

Sir Harold studied the print for a moment, 'Looks Arab to me, who is he?'

'You're quite right, Sir. Meet Colonel Mohammed Ghalboun, a Libyan Intelligence officer. He controls the Libyan People's Bureau in Brussels. We've known about him for some time. This particular photograph shows him outside a hotel in Rome three days ago.'

Cooke selected a second photograph and placed it on the desk. 'He met with this man briefly before flying to Tripoli.'

Sir Harold studied the second photograph. It showed the short podgy figure of a man sitting at a bar in what appeared to be a night-club. The face was in profile, partly in shadow, and not very clear, obviously taken without the aid of a flash.

Cooke did not wait for the inevitable question. 'We don't know who he is yet, but he's definitely Irish. It was also taken in Rome five days ago, in a gay disco underneath the hotel he stayed at. A place called the Trocadero. He registered under the name of Bailey. Ghalboun met with him there. We also know that he went to see Ghalboun in Brussels, not once, but on a number of occasions during the past year. I've passed a copy of this to the Irish Special Branch but they don't have a record of him and they are still checking.'

Cooke jabbed his finger on the photograph. 'See this young man here, at the end of the bar? The police found him dead in an alley outside the hotel yesterday. Two days after Bailey checked out and also flew to Tripoli. He died from a broken neck, but his lower torso was covered in cigarette burns.'

'You mean someone tortured him before he died?' Webster visibly recoiled at the thought.

Cooke's reply was matter of fact: 'Tortured and then murdered. Yes, that's right. The Italian police identified him as a homosexual known to frequent the club; there are many of them in Rome, Sir Harold. So one less didn't make any difference. They lost interest after that, and closed the case.'

Sir Harold Webster felt confused. 'Jonathan, I fail to see a connection.'

Cooke produced a third photograph with almost a flourish. 'The body was found right under the third floor window of the room that Bailey occupied.'

The Ambassador interrupted him before he could continue, 'Did you get these photographs from the Italian police or from our own people? Surely they have ....'

'We got them from our friends in Mossad. The Italian police do not have copies.' Cooke smiled cynically. 'Our Israeli friends are only interested in Ghalboun. Once they established an Irish connection they handed them over to us, as a favour, if you like. They don't wish to compromise themselves with the Italians. They even went so far as to have one of their female agents sleep with Ghalboun at his hotel in Rome.'

There was silence in the room for several minutes as Sir Harold digested what he had heard. Outside, the rain had stopped and weak sunshine broke through the cloud. Webster glanced at his watch again and thought of Portmarnock for an instant. When he did speak, he sounded scornful. 'Really, Jonathan, you do live in a murky world. I don't envy you one bit. What's in your third photograph?'

Cooke placed the third black and white print on top of the others on the desk. Whether you like it or not chum, you are right up to your ears in my murky world, he thought. I'd like to know what sort of nonsense you intend to concoct with the Papal Nuncio, the Japanese and God knows who else this afternoon on the golf course. Diplomacy was only another word for trickery, after all, he thought; hoodwinking one's adversaries with carefully thought platitudes.

'This picture,' he said, 'is of a man that we have identified as Liam Sweeney from Donegal. It shows him arriving in Rome on a flight from Mexico City. You can just make out the man, Bailey, off to one side in the crowd waiting for him.' He paused for a moment and added, 'It's a slightly better shot of Bailey's face this time.'

Webster picked up his empty pipe and clamped his teeth on

the stem. For an instant his thoughts wandered and a vision of Emily flashed into his mind. He wondered if he would find her drunk when he got home. Maybe not, he mused. She was still trying to behave after her trip to Florida.

The photograph showed Liam looking suntanned and relaxed coming through the arrivals door at the Rome airport. It was a good picture and captured his swarthy, handsome features. He looked like a businessman. At the least, a well-dressed tourist. Behind him in the crowd, jostling to come through the doors, was a very striking blonde woman. 'What do you know of him, Jonathan?'

'Not very much, Sir. The Special Branch have him on file but there is no hard evidence of a connection with a terrorist organisation. He comes and goes frequently to a farm worked by his brother in Donegal. The police only took a passing interest in him because of its proximity to the border and because he doesn't seem to have any regular job that would provide an income.'

Webster removed the pipe from his mouth for a moment. 'Sum it up for me, Jonathan.'

Cooke knew he was treading on unsure ground. He took a deep breath. 'Well, Sir, GCHQ in Cheltenham intercepted a telephone call from Mexico City to Bailey the night before he arrived in Rome. The conversation was in Irish, which, in itself, is unusual. It simply confirmed that a contract was in place. I believe that we are looking at two IRA activists. We are seeing an arms shipment in the making. Both Sweeney and Bailey flew to Libya three days ago; and if you want a wild guess, our friend Prendergast, or at least his ship, will meet up with them very soon.'

Sir Harold sighed. 'What do you propose we do about it, if that is the case?'

The telephone on the desk rang an interruption. 'Please excuse me, Colonel.' The Ambassador picked it up. 'Yes, he's here.' He handed the phone to Cooke. 'For you, Jonathan,' he said.

Cooke took the receiver from him. 'Cooke here.' He listened intently for a few minutes, 'Thank you for your co-operation Superintendent, it is most appreciated.' He paused. 'No there is nothing to add, purely routine. Yes, the same to you, good-bye.' He replaced the receiver and stared at it for a moment almost as though he expected it to ring again. 'That was the Irish Special Branch,' he said. 'Our man Bailey is really a James Foster; or rather – Father James Foster.'

Sir Harold clenched his teeth and the pipe stem cracked. He spat out a piece of broken stem. 'A bloody priest!'

'Yes Sir, exactly. A bloody priest.'

'Explain it to me, Jonathan, please.' The Ambassador seemed to be choking. For a moment Cooke wondered if Webster had swallowed a piece of his pipe stem.

'A Father Foster disappeared four years ago from a missionary order. His superior is naturally reluctant to discuss the matter. Apparently there was an earlier scandal involving boys in a school in Florida where Foster was teaching. Foster was transferred back to Ireland before any action was taken. Such matters tend to be swept under the carpet by the religious authorities. Our enquiries have revealed that Foster spends most of his time on the Continent, but turns up in Ireland every now and then. The Special Branch say he visited Belfast last week.'

Webster stared at him as Cooke raised his eyes. 'What was it you were asking me, Ambassador, just before that call?'

Sir Harold sensed Cooke's amusement and found it irritating. 'I asked you, Jonathan, if this is an arms shipment, what do you propose we do about it?' He sounded as though he was in pain.

Cooke stared into the far distance for a moment as if seeking inspiration. 'I suggest we wait for a while longer and see if the *Maria B* becomes involved. Once we have proof, we can take appropriate action.'

Webster ground the words out. 'What precisely, do you mean by appropriate action, Jonathan?'

Cooke felt a stabbing pain in his knee. It would rain again soon. 'I suggest that we sink her.'

'Are you seriously suggesting that we get Her Majesty's Navy to sink an Irish merchant ship?' Sir Harold's eyes bulged in an apoplectic way.

Cooke sounded calm. 'That would be one method. There are others, of course. I must remindyou, Sir, that she is not Irish but Liberian, and we will contemplate no action until we are absolutely sure of her cargo and intentions.' He paused for a moment and rubbed his knee. When he finally spoke, his voice was disarmingly quiet. 'Please understand, Ambassador, I am a soldier, not a diplomat. My response to this is purely a military one.'

'I haven't forgotten that for one moment,' the Ambassador replied. 'I might remind you also, that I am golfing this afternoon with the Irish Foreign Minister and the Papal Nuncio. What do you think their response would be if I told them that one of their priests had not only joined the IRA, but had killed a homosexual in Rome and was now busy organising an arms shipment from Libya? Add to that, that the British Government planned to sink a neutral merchant ship if necessary!'

Put that way, the whole idea sounded preposterous. Cooke laughed and the sound of his laughter relieved the tension. 'I understand your concern, Sir. It is a delicate matter, but one that I am sure we can handle.

Sir Harold calmed down, but it was some time before he spoke again. 'Jonathan, sometimes fact really is stranger than fiction. I want you to go to London today and brief the Foreign Office. If they decide to take this matter further, I will personally talk to the Prime Minister.'

Cooke felt relieved. Once again, Webster had confounded him. It satisfied him that Webster had not totally rejected his theories, but had simply shelved them for further analysis. 'Thank you, Sir,' he said. 'I'll get the first available flight.'

For a moment Webster seemed withdrawn. Then he said, 'I suppose you have considered this man, Prendergast, not to mention his crew, in all of this?'

Cooke got to his feet. His look was steady and uncompromising. 'Yes Sir, I have. It's regretful, but should they be on board the ship in such an eventuality, I consider them to be expendable.' He picked up his walking stick and added, 'For the purpose of military strategy, you understand.'

Webster nodded slowly and said nothing. He watched Cooke limp stiffly to the door. When the door closed behind him, he picked up his Ping putter and dropped the golf ball onto the carpet. For an instant, but for only an instant, he forgot Emily, Cooke, Foster and the whole damn lot of them and braced his feet. Click! The ball sped neatly into the plastic cup. He felt considerably better.

Thirty-One

The *Maria B* slipped towards Valletta at five knots through a sea that resembled a pool of India ink. A city of stars stretched across the horizon. The moon, with all its strange shadows in clear relief, lay suspended in infinity, making a gift of light almost bright enough to read by. On such a night, Prendergast mused, it was hard to imagine that men had already walked on its dusty surface but had found little to reward their efforts.

Jim rested his arms on the teak spray board of the bridge coaming. He would remain awake for the rest of the night, with the engine throttled back, timing his arrival off the Valletta pilot station for daybreak. Dreamily he watched a star streaking on some mysterious voyage.

Malta lay before him. A barren archipelago of small rocky islands set in the narrows between Sicily and Tunisia, in the centre of the Mediterranean. Only three of these islands were habitable: Pantelleria, Linosa and Lampedusa. Valletta, on Pantelleria, was built by the Knights during the Crusades. A fortified city, Valletta was home to a series of conquerors down through the centuries who prized it as a means of controlling the Mediterranean Sea.

Prendergast had the warm feeling of satisfaction that comes to all seamen making a safe landfall at the end of a voyage. The only thing that marred it was the knowledge that for him it also meant a return to a world that had been narrowed by death. A vision of Jane formed before him. She seemed so close that he thought of reaching out to touch her. His sense of loss and insecurity became more acute; he swallowed to hold back his tears.

He gazed at the sky for a long time, wondering if there really was a heaven. If there was, he wondered, were Jane and Susan happy there together? Were they watching him now?

Ever since entering the crowded shipping lanes in the Straits of Gibraltar he had rarely left the bridge in case he might miss sighting the *Georgios*, and every ship that appeared over the horizon became a subject for investigation through his binoculars. On several occasions he had even altered course to be doubly sure, but it always proved fruitless.

The further they sailed into the Mediterranean the more he could sense her presence. He knew she was there somewhere; he felt that he could smell her. More and more, he was at a loss to know what he would do if he did sight the ship. As far as he knew, the four winds had long since scattered those responsible.

Quite unexpectedly his thoughts went to the pistol lying in his bureau. Here he was, about to arrive in a foreign port with all that that entailed – customs, police, emigration and God knows what else – and he had an unauthorised firearm. He wondered if he should throw the damned thing overboard and be done with it.

Instead, he went inside to his cabin and unscrewed the ventilation louver in the trunking over his bunk. He stuffed the weapon and its ammunition clips inside. As he rescrewed the cover in place, the sound of metal on metal masked a soft footstep in the chart room outside the open cabin door.

'Trouble with the ventilation system, Jim?'

Startled, Prendergast stepped down off the settee and grazed his bare shin on the open drawer to the bureau. The air was oppressive and he was half blinded by sweat running into his eyes.

Eddie Molloy stood in the doorway, rivulets of perspiration trickling down the reddened skin of his belly. Around his neck he wore a sweat rag, and like Prendergast, a pair of khaki shorts and flip-flops.

'Sorry, Eddie, you startled me. I didn't hear you come in.' Prendergast wondered if Molloy would detect anything amiss. 'There's no problem except that a lot of dust seems to be coming through the ventilator. I thought it might need cleaning out.'

Molloy nodded, but he looked puzzled. He gave Prendergast a strange look before wandering outside to search for cooler air on deck

Jesus! Prendergast thought angrily. Had he seen the gun? Throwing aside the screwdriver in disgust, he followed Molloy outside.

Directly ahead, the lights of a ship showed brightly on the horizon. Prendergast made a two-degree adjustment to the auto-pilot and went outside to the wing of the bridge.

Molloy was just a dark shadow in a corner trying to catch the cooling breeze made by the ship's forward movement. 'Bloody hot down below,' he said. 'I couldn't sleep in it. I even moved my mattress up on deck, but the whole bloody crew is up there, and that bastard, Reynolds, is snoring like a pig!'

There was something odd about Molloy's voice. Jim looked at him in the moonlight and realised what it was. The man didn't have his false teeth in. He started to laugh, but it sounded contrived and unnecessary, so he stopped. 'This ship wasn't designed for warm climates,' he said.

Molloy grinned. 'If you think back, Jim, half the ships we ever sailed on weren't, either. Remember the Liberty ships and the Fort boats?'

Prendergast studied the lights ahead and didn't answer imme-diately. The approaching ship was coming up fast, but would pass safely to starboard. 'You're right, I suppose. A lot has changed in a short few years. Maybe we already saw the best of it.' Jim paused. 'Are you glad that it's almost over? This trip, I mean.'

Molloy stayed silent for a while, thinking about it. 'I dunno, really,' he said. 'Maybe I wouldn't mind going on a bit longer. I get a bit pissed off hanging around the house with nothing to do. It's as if you're finished, all washed up, and waiting to die. I've enjoyed the trip down. What about you?'

'I was thinking of approaching Pavlides about staying on for a while after we get to Malta. I've nothing better to do right now anyway, since ....' His voice trailed away.

Molloy knew that Prendergast was thinking about the yacht again. 'I've never lost anybody in the same way that you have. Maybe, for you, it would be the right thing to do, but Christ knows what sort of crew you will pick up in Valletta.'

Jim thought about that. Was it the right thing for him to do? He couldn't come up with an answer, but he knew that he had nothing to go back to.

The approaching ship was now almost abeam. A great long shadow loaded down in the water, bulky and ungraceful, so unlike the ships of years gone by. The milky foam of her bow wave glimmered in the darkness and they could hear the steady thud of her diesel driving her at almost seventeen knots. A tanker bound from the Gulf with a cargo of crude for God knows where. She passed quickly and he picked up a waft of oily fumes in the night air long before her wash lifted the tiny *Maria B*, rocking her gently.

'Ships in the night,' Prendergast whispered, as though he was talking to himself.

'What was that you said?'

The darkness hid Jim's frown. He gazed after the disappearing white stern light of the tanker, 'We're all like that, I think. People, I mean, like ships in the night, passing by.' He sighed wearily. 'You know Eddie, I read somewhere once that when a man dies, his woman simply straightens her skirt, fixes her hair and gets on with her life in the best way she can. She might grieve, but she gets on with it. But when a woman dies, half of her man dies with her and never comes back. I think that just about sums up how I feel.'

Prendergast felt the pressure of Molloy's big hand on his shoulder. 'If you decide to stay on, Skipper, let me know. You're going to need someone who knows that bloody engine of ours.' Molloy turned to go back down the ladder from the bridge.

Jim stopped him as he was halfway down to the deck below. 'Eddie – thanks.'

'For nothing,' came the reply. 'I can spare the time.'

'Send up Reynolds to relieve me for an hour or so.'

'Okay, Jim.'

Prendergast watched the old engineer making his way along the afterdeck. He realised just how much he had come to depend on him, but he also knew that he was not being fair. He would have to tell him, all about Cooke and the whole damned thing. Maybe it would make Molloy change his mind, but that didn't matter. Fuck Cooke and his secrecy; he had to tell him. He owed Molloy that, at least. If anything happened to the old man through his stubbornness, he would never forgive himself.

Vittorio Cassar sat patiently on the terrace of the Grand Harbour Hotel on St Ursula Street sipping his third cup of morning coffee. On his knee lay a forgotten newspaper, still folded.

Below him in the Grand Harbour itself, the clanging sounds of activity in the old naval dockyard on the opposite side were announcing that the day shift had started work. A scattering of ships lay at buoys, and early morning Dghajje water taxis were beginning to flit like flies across the shimmering water. Cassar looked up at the palest of blue skies, unblemished by cloud. It promised to be hot today, perhaps even in the high nineties. He slung a pair of binoculars over his shoulder before picking up his coffee and moving to a more shaded table on the terrace.

Vittorio was an old man now, but his figure was like that of a young boy. He wore a neatly pressed white open-necked shirt and faded red cotton sailing trousers. A straw hat hid his crinkly grey hair and shaded his nut-brown features. He un-slung his binoculars and trained them on the ships below in the harbour. Nothing of any interest there. Gone were the graceful shapes of the warships of his youth when the might of the Royal Navy was a source of pride and employment to every Maltese. In their place, just the rusty hulls of timeworn merchantmen.

Even the crews now were different, he thought, mostly underpaid Phillipinos, Koreans and Indians who knew nothing of the proud history of Malta, nothing of the blood, the terror and the privation of those days in 1942, when the combined might of Germany and Italy failed to wrest the island away from them.

Those were proud days in Vittorio's mind. Even now he

could remember the high-pitched scream of the Stuka dive bombers over the harbour. Yes, they were the worst, he thought. The Germans flying out of Sicily were fearsome and far worse than the Italians. Not for nothing had Malta received the honour of a George Cross.

A movement out beyond the great fortress commanding the approaches to the harbour caught his attention. He went to the edge of the balcony and re-focused his binoculars.

They had told him to expect a small ship, but this one looked ridiculously tiny in comparison to all the others in the harbour below. Slowly, like a bug on the water, she approached until she passed directly below his vantage point and rounded up to a pair of black mooring buoys. A puff of black smoke from her funnel came like a sigh of relief from the ancient engine as though the ship had grown suddenly weary, and could go on no further.

Vittorio put away his binoculars and finished his coffee. He strolled to a telephone at the entrance to the hotel and placed an international call, asking for Lieutenant-Colonel Cooke. 'Vittorio Cassar here,' he said when Cooke answered. 'Your ship has arrived.'

'Thank you, Vittorio, please inform me of any developments.' Then the line went dead as the receiver in Dublin dropped into its cradle.

Prendergast lowered the yellow quarantine flag. Folding it carefully, he stowed it in the flag locker inside the wheel house. The police and Customs officials had already left and the ship's Maltese agent was now boarding his launch to return to the shore.

To Prendergast's surprise, the agent had no orders except to declare that Pavlides would fly in from London the next day. Until then, Prendergast and his crew were to wait. But he provided a security watchman and made arrangements to advance them money, suggesting that Valletta had much to offer.

Prendergast gathered the crew on the afterdeck soon afterwards. 'Right lads!' he announced cheerfully. 'We have a day off, and the first drinks are on me!'

Eddie Molloy positively beamed. Even Reynolds lost his belligerence. Jimmy Lafferty stood looking around the harbour with disbelieving eyes; never away from Ireland before, the whole thing seemed like a dream to him.

An hour later they piled noisily into a water taxi and made their way ashore.

For Prendergast and Molloy, it was like the old days all over again. They roamed the dusty streets in a group until darkness came and each bar became a fuddled, distant memory. Back on board at the end of it, Prendergast slept as if he was in a coma, which to some degree, was true.

He awoke in a pool of sweat shortly after sunrise as the harbour heat started to build towards an intensity that would turn the ship into a cauldron by noon. When it became too hot to lie there any longer, he pulled on a pair of shorts and went out on deck, gripped by the depression of a hangover. He felt listless and still tired and wished that he had had the sense to come back to the ship earlier the night before. Seeing Eddie Molloy sitting on a bollard on the afterdeck drinking from a mug of coffee, he made his way unsteadily towards him.

'Mornin', Jim! It's going to be a hot one today.' Molloy sounded cheerful but his bleary eyes gave him away.

'You look worse than I feel,' Jim replied morosely. 'Where're the lads?'

'In there, having breakfast.' Molloy nodded towards the mess room door.

The thought of two-week old eggs and greasy bacon made Prendergast's stomach churn. 'I was going to ask them if any of them want to stay on, but it can wait, I suppose.'

'You already did. Last night, don't you remember?' Molloy smiled. 'We really tied one on yesterday! Reynolds is packing his gear, can't say that I'll miss him. The other two will stay on if they can, same as us – nothing to go back to except the dole queue.'

Prendergast scowled. What else didn't he remember, he wondered. He worried that he might have let his mouth run away with him. 'It's time for us to have a chat, Eddie. Finish your coffee, then come on up on the bridge where there's a bit of privacy.'

Reaching the security of the bridge, Jim waited for Molloy and mulled over in his mind what he should tell him. One part of him told him to bare his soul and tell Molloy everything, but he worried that it might be too much for Eddie to take. He wanted him to stay. Molloy was already puffing up the ladder; there was little time in which to decide.

'Something's on your mind, Skipper.' Molloy spread his arms along the bridge coaming.

Prendergast studied his face for a moment. All he saw was honesty reflected in his eyes. Christ! he thought savagely. The man has a wife waiting for him to come home. What right have I to jeopardise that?

'I know the name of the ship that sank my yacht, Eddie.'

Molloy's eyes widened in surprise, but he made no comment.

'She was the *Georgios*, and Pavlides was connected with her, too.'

'You mean ...'

'Yes, the same guy who is due aboard here at any minute.'

'What's this all about, Jim? How do you know...?' Molloy looked bewildered.

'I can't answer that. What I'm trying to say is that we might have to follow in her footsteps if we get the opportunity to stay on the ship. It might be dangerous.'

'How dangerous?' Molloy was wary now.

'We might have to take a cargo back to Ireland.'

'Not drugs! I'm not prepared to do that at any price!' The engineer became indignant. 'I'll not condone that shit, Jim!'

'Nor would I,' Prendergast replied firmly. 'It will probably be weapons.'

'Is that what the *Georgios* carried?'

'Possibly. I don't know.'

Eddie stayed silent for a moment while he thought about what he had heard. 'Tell me who told you,' he demanded.

Prendergast sighed. 'A man called Cooke, from the British

Embassy in Dublin. I don't know what he does, he's probably some kind of spy. Shit! I don't really care what he is if there's a chance of finding who killed my wife and daughter! Look, Eddie, don't get involved. There's nothing to hold you here.'

Molloy shrugged and spat over the side. 'Doesn't really change anything as far as I'm concerned,' he replied. 'This Cooke is probably full of shit anyway. His type have to justify their existence.' He cocked his head at Jim. 'By the way, I saw you hiding the gun the other night. I'm glad you told me.'

There was a flurry of activity over by the steps at the Customs House and Prendergast recognised the agent's launch detaching itself from a fleet of small boats.

'Looks like our visitor has arrived,' Molloy commented. He turned towards the ladder. 'I'll leave you to it,' he said. 'Are you going to tell the other two the whole story?'

'Not yet. Let's wait and see what Pavlides has to say for himself.'

'It might be wiser not to tell them at all, Jim. Just in case Cooke really is on the ball, the less they know, the less they have to talk about. If the worst comes to the worst, all that's going to happen is that the ship gets arrested when you tell the Brits.' Molloy thought about what he had just said and started to laugh, 'Just make sure they understand that none of us are to blame if it comes to that!'

Prendergast smiled. He felt better for having confided in Molloy. 'Eddie, why is it that I'm always thanking you for something?'

Eddie grinned at him and backed down the ladder.

Pavlides climbed the pilot ladder with an agility that belied his weight but he was puffing by the time he joined Prendergast on the navigation bridge. Jim extended his hand and walked towards him. The man looked somehow different from the one he had met in Dublin. A bit heavier perhaps? No, it was the moustache! Pavlides had shaved off his moustache, and it didn't suit him. It made his features look even more petulant and self satisfied. His handshake was still the same, limp and clammy, as though Prendergast had grasped a piece of dead meat.

'Good morning, Captain. You had a good voyage I trust?' Pavlides smiled with an intensity that failed to impress Prendergast. If he really did have a connection with the *Georgios*, that meant he was an accessory to Jane and Susan's murder. 'Yes, all things considered. It was an easy trip, no heavy weather and no serious machinery problems.'

Pavlides peered over the bridge coaming and looked out over the foredeck. 'This is the first time I have seen the ship, as you know, Captain.' He ran an appreciative hand over the polished brass telegraph. 'She is a fine vessel and a credit to your preparations in Galway.'

Prendergast frowned. Either the man is mad, or he knows little about ships, he thought. 'She's an old ship, Mr. Pavlides, a tired ship, and one in need of a major refit. We had light weather all the way but she is making water forward, much more than when we left Galway.'

Pavlides looked displeased. 'I had hoped that maybe I could delay her dry-docking. There is an opportunity for a quick cargo at very good rates.'

'There is no need for me to remind you that the previous owners sold her because she failed a Lloyds survey and repairs were not economic. There is massive play in the steering linkage and apart from leaking bottom plates, she is very foul beneath the water line. The best speed we could get out of her on the way down was seven knots. She's designed to do ten.'

The mention of speed seemed to make a distinct impression on Pavlides. 'And dry-docking would increase her speed, in your estimation?'

'I am sure of it,' replied Prendergast. 'She's like a farm field underneath.'

'Very well, Captain,' said Pavlides. 'We will dry-dock here in Valletta as planned. Ten knots, you say? My associates will be pleased! Yes indeed, she is a fine vessel!' Pavlides picked up his briefcase. 'Now, Captain, let us settle the question of your delivery fee. Perhaps the chart room would give us more privacy?'

Prendergast was not sure why he felt surprised. Pavlides was honouring the contract. In the chart room he handed him a deposit receipt to his bank in Galway and sufficient cash for him to pay the crew as promised. 'Mr. Pavlides,' he said, 'I have a proposition for you.'

Pavlides gave him a searching look. 'What is that, Captain?'

'Myself and the crew are interested in staying on if that suits you. With the exception of a seaman called Reynolds, that is.'

Pavlides looked at him quizzically. Prendergast knew that the mind behind those brown expressionless eyes was computing this new equation, looking for the hidden snag, while simplifying the problem so that the answer came out in dollars and cents.

'You could manage with the same number of crew?'

'Not quite,' Prendergast said. 'Reynolds will have to be replaced, of course, and we need a cook.' Jim smiled. 'We didn't eat too well on the last trip. A cook is essential.'

Pavlides brightened. 'You continue to find ways to save money for us, Captain Prendergast, I am impressed. We will pay Greek union rates, plus bonuses.' The gold teeth flashed for a second. 'Sometimes the bonuses will be good, sometimes, not so good.' He shrugged. 'It depends on the cargo, it is the nature of our business, you understand?'

Jim nodded. 'That sounds fine, Mr. Pavlides. I'm sure the lads will agree to it, too. Maybe you will get the agent to arrange for the crew that we need?'

Pavlides snapped shut the catches on his briefcase. 'I'll see to hiring a cook immediately and arrange for dry-docking without delay. I, personally, will replace the crew member who is leaving. Just until your first port of call.'

Prendergast could not hide his surprise. 'You will?'

'Yes, why not? I have a master's ticket, Captain, and it is only a short voyage.'

Prendergast fiddled with a cigarette and tried to sound non-chalant. He fumbled a match before lighting the cigarette. 'Where are we going?'

'I'm sorry, Captain. I should have mentioned it before. You are to load a cargo of hides in Iskenderun for Savona.'

If Pavlides had punched him in the mouth, Prendergast could

not have felt more shocked. All his suspicions, all his hopes, evaporated like a sea mist. He covered it well. 'Turkey eh? Haven't been there for a long time. This will delight the Chief. He likes belly dancers!'

Still in a state of disbelief, he accompanied Pavlides to the boarding ladder and watched the launch carry him away towards the Customs House quay. So much for that idiot Jonathan Cooke and his madcap ideas. He went off to tell Molloy that the whole thing was a hoax. There was nothing that needed to be said to the crew. The ship was just a tramp after all. Hides, he thought, his nostrils already filling with their stench.

Thirty-Two

Liam woke to the sound of the overhead ceiling fan grinding to a stop. As its swirl ceased, perspiration started to ooze from each pore in his body, swamping him in a cloying embrace.

He reached to the floor at the side of his camp bed, found a shoe, and hurled it towards the ceiling in fury. His aim was improving. It hit the base of the fan and immediately the motor squeaked back to life, sending the blades rattling into orbit, at least until the next time. The breeze slowly picked up and gradually his sweat became a trickle rather than a torrent.

Naked, he lay on the bed and stared dejectedly at the bare wooden walls of the room. The furnishings were minimal, just a metal locker, a bed, a small metal table and a folding chair. A thin layer of sand covered the floor and no matter how often he swept it clean, it always came back. The builders of the camp at Sidi Bilal, not far from Benghazi, did not intend it to cocoon its occupants in luxury. Instead, the room was purely functional and transient.

In the far corner of the room, a gap between the wall and the roof allowed a shaft of sunlight to penetrate the gloom. More sand lay suspended in its beam, as though stopped in time. He knew that in another hour the room would be untenable as the scorching sun rose higher, even though a short few hours ago he had been scrabbling for a blanket, shivering in the cold grip of a desert night.

Outside, the whine of a helicopter engine coming to life told him that Buckholtz and Gonzales were off on yet another training flight. He had to hand it to those two. Although they bitched and moaned continuously, they were true professionals and flew that damned chopper as though there was no tomorrow. Already their Cuban instructors had largely given up on being able to teach them anything, which had driven Buckholtz to new heights of exhibitionism. Night-flying exercises were scheduled again tonight.

The last ten days had passed quickly, he thought. During the past three, he had hardly seen Lisa and she had not come to his room. Her period, she had said. During the day she was always away somewhere else in the camp, one minute learning Arabic from the Palestinians and the next, engrossed in a training course for potential aircraft hijackers. The trouble was, he missed her, and although he knew that she seemed not to respond to any of Buckholtz's crude remarks, there was something in her manner that told him otherwise. Jealousy gnawed at him like a fever. Maybe she was already sleeping with the bastard, he thought. So what? But nothing seemed to assuage the tight knot in his stomach.

The rising temperature in the hut forced Liam to get up. After a shower, he pulled on a pair of shorts and stepped outside into the white haze of the central parade ground.

The camp consisted of a series of sand-coloured pre-fabricated huts stretching into the near distance to where a high wire fence ringed the camp. Beyond the defensive fence, by the beach, the sea shimmered like a mirror. Far out, the speck of the helicopter droned low over the surface, its tadpole shape homing in on the dark bulk of a barge moored off-shore.

Close to the central parade ground were the larger training huts and a big mess-hall, towards which he could see the squat form of Foster waddling to breakfast. Liam's stomach rumbled at the thought of food but the camp meals bordered on being deplorable. For the past few days, visions of grilled pork chops or bacon and cabbage had tormented him. Reaching the mess-hall he selected some figs and a goat's milk yoghurt before escaping to a shaded corner on a veranda overlooking the parade ground.

Foster joined him there sometime later. 'Ghalboun was here

earlier this morning,' he opened.

Liam glanced up at him distastefully. Foster was so pale that he looked ill. His face was a jaundiced. 'Is that so? What did he want?'

Foster's eyes gleamed. 'He said he has arranged for a ship. It will be here in four days.'

Liam raised his eyebrows. 'Good,' he said. 'Then we can get on with it and go home.'

Foster scowled. 'You don't like this job do you, Liam? You don't understand what it means to us.'

'It doesn't matter what I like or dislike. I've told you that before. I've given it my commitment, and it goes ahead, but mark my words, it will ruin us in the end.' He glared at the helicopter out over the sea where it was settling on the barge like a malevolent wasp. 'The most important thing on my personal agenda is to find out what really happened to Hogan and Chalky White. The sooner this is over, the sooner I get to that.'

He stood up. 'I've got work to do,' he muttered. Each time he came into close contact with Foster he disliked the man more. He strode away towards a group of Palestinians who crowded around the entrance to one of the long training huts. Somewhere out of sight amongst the dunes the clatter of small arms fire shattered the stillness, announcing that the real work of the camp was starting in earnest.

Foster settled into a chair on the veranda and watched Liam through narrowed eyes. Slowly his nervousness dissipated and his stomach ceased to churn. Liam was one of the very few people who frightened him. His efficiency was disturbing and Foster didn't like his offhand coldness. But his fear was not sufficient to prevent his thoughts turning to murder. You'll get yours, you bastard, he thought.

In the late afternoon, as Liam left the hut where he had been instructing a group of Palestinians in the techniques of urban bomb making, he saw the helicopter return and settle on the parade ground in a swirl of dust. The shrill whine of its Allison turbo-shaft engine died slowly away as Buckholtz and Gonzales jumped down from the cockpit and expertly dodged the turning rotors. They were laughing and in high spirits. The whole training side of the operation seemed to fill them both with amusement. They acted more like wartime flyers, brimming with the intensity of their own invincibility, disdainful of the ragtag brigade that surrounded them.

Seeing Liam emerging from the hut, Buckholtz, with a fit of affability, invited him to join them for a drink. The offer took Liam by surprise. The Libyans were strict when it came to alcohol, and as far as he knew, there was none available, but the thought of a cold beer or any form of alcoholic drink for that matter, was wickedly tempting. 'Why not!' he replied. 'You guys are obviously better organised than I am!'

Buckholtz and Gonzales occupied two rooms in a hut on their own. Liam released a low whistle of approval. 'Holy shit!' They had contrived to furnish their quarters to a far higher standard than his own. They even had a radio and a stereo system fitted in one corner, and a strip of carpet covered the floor. Always one step ahead, Buckholtz was at his patronising best as his companion delved into a cool box and produced a bottle of Scotch and a plastic bag of ice cubes.

Liam chuckled. 'I've got to hand it to you two bastards,' he said. 'You obviously made the right connections.'

Buckholtz smiled and handed him a glass. 'You've never been in a real war have you, Mick? You should have been with us in Nam, pal. You would have got hot pussy and cool pot to go with it!'

Chico flopped into a cane chair and snorted. 'As much as you could handle, amigo. We got some good grass coming in the next delivery.' His brown eyes twinkled. 'But so far, you've cornered the market on the pussy.'

'I'm glad there is something I can do better.' Liam risked a smile and added, 'Let's just call the score even, one all at half time.'

Buckholtz swallowed his whiskey. Grinning, he poured another. 'It's all to play for in the second half, right?'

Liam played the game and raised his glass. 'Cheers!' he said, feeling the cool whiskey catch his throat. He smacked his lips. 'Christ, that tastes good!'

Chico selected a tape and inserted it in the tape player and the room filled with the voice of Diana Ross. He lowered the volume and returned to sit on the edge of one of the camp beds. 'I want to know when this goddamn charade is going to end so that we can get out of here.'

Liam appraised him for a moment. Buckholtz might be a bully and a braggart, but Gonzales gave the impression of being more deadly. Liam finished his drink and held it out for a refill. 'In five days, no more than that. The ship is due on Wednesday.'

Buckholtz fisted ice into the proffered glass and poured a generous tot of whiskey. 'Now we have something to celebrate, pal,' he said. 'I was beginning to wonder if you guys knew your ass from a hole in the wall. Last night we heard on the World News that there were peace talks still going on between your lot and the British, but right afterwards they said that a bomb had gone off somewhere in England. Sounds to me like you guys don't know which end is up!'

Liam swirled the ice in his glass and looked away. He wished he knew what the hell was going on at home. From outside, the dull crunch of a mortar explosion announced that the work of the camp had still not come to a halt. 'You don't know much about us, do you? We don't give up halfway. We're in for the long haul and we do it for a fucking sight less than the money we pay you bastards.'

Buckholtz enjoyed baiting Liam. His response was always predictable. He was like a trout rising to the bait. 'That's your loss, buddy. Someday you'll get sense,' he sneered. 'The almighty dollar is what counts at the end of the day.'

Liam forced himself to remain calm. 'Look, Buckholtz, I didn't come in here to have a row with you. In any case, your whiskey is too good for that. You're going to have to prove that you can earn those dollars pretty soon. The time for talking is almost over.'

Gonzales shifted and the camp bed creaked under his weight. 'You've still got to tell us who we are going to hit and where.'

'There's plenty of time for that.' Liam sipped at his drink. 'You'll find out all about that once we're at sea, not before.'

Buckholtz grunted. 'Being kept in the dark pisses us off, Mick. It's our hides that are going to be on the line. We got more to lose than you do.'

Liam lit a cigarette and drew on it calmly, exhaling the smoke in a grey cloud. He felt better already. These two were still in his pocket and the thought was comforting. 'That's the way it is,' he said quietly. 'Just fly that chopper – get used to it in the dark, and fly it low.'

'Fuck you!' Buckholtz fixed his eyes on a point on the wall over Liam's head. 'Take care of that little bastard, Chico!' he snapped.

Chico's hand snaked to the top of his Western boot and a black combat dagger appeared in his hand. He flicked his wrist and Liam felt the wind of it as the blade sped past his ear and thudded into the wall. He flinched and turned his head to where a pink-white scorpion twitched once before falling in two halves to the dusty floor.

'That'll teach the little fucker!' Buckholtz spat. Gonzales hugged his knees, rocking backwards and forwards on the low bed, eyeing Liam's face with obvious pleasure.

Liam swallowed. 'I'll take another drink, if it's in it.' He held out his glass in a steady hand.

Thirty-Three

Even at nine o'clock in the morning the dry dock in French Creek was an inferno. There was little shadow in which to escape the summer sun and no wind to counteract the soaring temperature. The incessant noise of rivet guns and machinery penetrated to the bowels of the *Maria B*, wedged in astern of a monstrous Greek oil tanker that was missing a portion of her bulbous bow following a collision in the Straits of Messina. Prendergast stared at the huge tanker overshadowing his tiny ship. The agent had assured him that it would finish repairs in time to sail with the *Maria B*, but somehow he doubted it.

Prendergast laboured up a long gangplank stretching from the ship to the dockside and stood for a while looking down into the cavern below him. Already a swarm of dock workers was scurrying about, preparing to start de-scaling the hull below the water line. Near the bow of the ship, an oxyacetylene cutter spluttered into life as the operator cut into the corroded fore-foot plating.

Molloy was down there somewhere too, supervising the removal of the ship's rudder. Wisely, Pavlides had long since removed himself ashore to the comforts of the Phoenicia Hotel. The rest of the crew had the onerous task of bilge cleaning below in the holds. In this heat Prendergast didn't envy them.

Finding a water taxi moored at the steps outside the dock gates, Prendergast flopped into its cushioned seats for the short trip across the harbour to the steps by the Customs House. He took the lift up to Barracca Gardens, then made his way through the crowds of Kingsway, until he found a bank where he changed some money into Maltese pounds. In a shop further along the street, he bought a spear gun together with a set of fins, a snorkel and a diving mask, promising himself a few hours diving from the rocks outside the harbour later in the evening.

Near the Law Courts he found a public telephone. The card on which Jonathan Cooke had written the number, although stained by sea water, was still legible. Someone on the receiver at the other end answered in guttural Maltese.

'I'd like to speak to Vittorio Cassar,' he said hesitantly. 'This is Captain Prendergast of the ship *Maria B.*'

The voice switched to English. 'This is Cassar speaking, Captain. Where are you calling from?'

Prendergast formed the impression that the owner of the voice was well educated. The man's English sounded refined and held little in the way of an accent. 'I'm calling from a public telephone, near the Law Courts.'

'Good,' replied Cassar. 'It is urgent that I speak with you, but not over the telephone, please. You are not far from Straits Street. Meet me in the Resolution Bar in half an hour. I will be waiting for you.'

'But ...' The line went dead as Cassar hung up. Damn the man! He was typical of the Jonathan Cooke genre, playing the same imaginary game of intrigue. Prendergast slammed the telephone back on its cradle and left the kiosk fuming.

The Resolution Bar was not difficult to find, even in the cramped confines of The Gut, which for centuries had been the naval name for Straits Street. Prendergast had been there years before. Here, sailors of the Royal Navy had caroused while the Empire reached the apex of its greatness, being offered anything from a tattoo to a bellyful of fish and chips to remind them of home.

The solitary man sitting at a rusty circular steel table on the pavement outside the bar was not exactly what Prendergast expected. This skinny little creature in faded red sailing trousers and a straw hat could hardly be a British agent. Had the Empire deteriorated so much that this was all they had left?

From beneath his wide-brimmed straw hat Vittorio Cassar watched Prendergast approach. He rose from the table in a single fluid movement that belied his age. 'Captain Prendergast? Vittorio Cassar, at your service. Please join me for a drink, or at least a coffee if you would prefer.'

Prendergast shook hands without interest. 'A beer, if you don't mind. It's too damned hot for walking. If you had not hung up I could have told you all you needed to know without having to come down here.' He sounded irritated.

Cassar said something in Maltese to a waiter lurking inside the doorway. 'My apologies, Captain, but I have learned to have a certain respect for telephones. As the Americans say, it goes with the territory.' The Maltese went silent for a moment as the waiter delivered two bottles of cold beer. 'Your good health, Captain.' He raised his glass.

Prendergast took a long swallow from his glass and wiped the back of his hand across his mouth. 'You need not have worried,' he said finally. 'Your Colonel Cooke is simply paranoid. In my book he's slightly off the wall. So are you, probably.' Jim smiled. 'No offense intended,' he added.

Vittorio returned him a wan smile but there was little humour in his brown eyes. He removed his hat and ran his fingers through his hair. 'It is of no consequence to me,' he said stiffly. 'But you appear to have information which I don't.' He relaxed in his chair and waited.

'You can tell Colonel Cooke that he was wrong all along. His suspicions were totally without foundation. My ship is sailing for Iskenderun in two days time. We are to load a cargo of hides for Savona in Italy, nothing more than that.' Prendergast paused, 'Tell him too,' he said, 'that Pavlides is coming with us. That should make the silly bugger sit up and take notice!'

Vittorio sighed and replaced his hat. 'It may surprise you to know, Captain, that I do not know the background to your relationship with Colonel Cooke. My orders are to simply pass on any information that you might give me.' He threw a handful of coins on the table and finished his drink. 'I will, of course, relay your message. When do you expect to reach Iskenderun?'

'Perhaps in ten or twelve days. Does it really matter?'

Vittorio got to his feet. 'No, of course not,' he said wearily. 'I'm sorry to have troubled you, Captain.'

They shook hands and Prendergast watched him kick a battered Vespa scooter into life at the edge of the narrow pavement. The engine died and Cassar fiddled with the fuel filter for a moment before turning to face him again. 'I will do my best to be of assistance.' He raised his heel and kicked the starter again. The engine roared as Cassar waved and sped off.

Two days later the *Maria B* sailed. The agent was correct after all. In spite of Prendergast's earlier misgivings, the Greek tanker emerged from the dry dock behind her and moved slowly like a behemoth out into the Grand Harbour.

It was late afternoon and already the buildings on the far side of the harbour were falling into shadow. Pavlides joined Prendergast on the bridge as he rang down for *slow ahead* on the engine and edged the ship out towards the harbour entrance to where the pilot boat waited.

The Greek breathed deeply, stretching the material of his newly purchased denim shirt. 'Ah!' he exclaimed, 'It is good to be going back to sea! You have no idea, Captain, of the frustrations for a seaman confined to a desk in a London office. This will be a holiday for me that I will not forget.'

Jim felt he could do without Pavlides at the moment, but in deference he said, 'I know exactly what you mean.' After all, the man was the owner, he thought. Even if he was trying to dress like an ordinary sailor. Prendergast smiled at that. Italian designer jeans, no less!

Thirty minutes later, they dropped the pilot into his launch and after a farewell blast on the ship's whistle to the Greek tanker, set course for Turkey. A gong sounded on the afterdeck when the new cook was ready to serve the evening meal. It relieved Prendergast from the attentions of Pavlides. Happy to be left to himself, his spirits rose and he smoked a cigarette as he watched the sun sink and waited for soft-hued darkness to surround them. Yes, Pavlides was right. It was good to be back at sea.

It was midnight before Pavlides reappeared again, the heavy scent of his cologne announcing his presence. 'I am happy to relieve you for a few hours, Captain, if you wish,' he announced.

To Prendergast, it sounded more like an order than a suggestion. Jim tried to read his face in the darkness. 'If you are sure,' he said. 'The course is zero-five-zero, autopilot is on and there is no traffic to worry about. That Greek tanker has gone hull-down ahead of us.'

'Very good, Captain, zero-five-zero. Enjoy your watch below.'

Prendergast descended the bridge ladder and went aft to make himself coffee in the galley. He found Molloy sitting in his customary spot on a mooring bollard.

'Everything all right below, Eddie?'

'Aye, Jim, no problems.'

Molloy belched. 'Did you try the spaghetti? I ain't too sure about that cook Pavlides hired. I'm not into wop food meself.'

Prendergast laughed. 'If the only thing that worries you is your belly, you have little to be worrying about.'

Molloy produced a bottle from behind the bollard. 'Ah, fuck you!' he said. 'Put a dollop of this in your coffee. We're back doing what we both like best, aren't we? I'm looking forward to a run ashore in Iskenderun.'

'God save us!' Jim drained his mug. 'I'm going to get my head down for a few hours, Eddie. I suggest you do the same yourself. That heap of shit in the engine room needs all the TLC you can give it.'

'Okay,' Molloy said. 'Sleep well and quit worrying.'

Back on the bridge, Jim fussed around for a while in the chart room. He noticed that Pavlides had already taken running bearings of a lighthouse on one of the islands and had pencilled their position neatly on the chart. He had even done a radar cross-check. Good, he thought. At least the Greek was demonstrating an ability to navigate.

He undressed and lay on his bunk, willing sleep to come. His eyes focused on the ventilation louver just before he dropped off. Shit! That damned pistol was still in there. He would have to get rid of it tomorrow when he had the bridge to himself.

Prendergast woke in the morning knowing that something was wrong. He looked at his watch. Six o'clock! Someone should have called him long before this.

Cursing, he sat up in the bunk. Then he noticed the sun. Light was slanting through the port side porthole. It was on the wrong side. He pulled on his shorts and dashed out into the wheel house where he found Jimmy Lafferty outside the door. Prendergast rounded up to him. 'We're off course, you cock-eyed idiot,' he roared. 'Or haven't you bloody well noticed?'

Lafferty flushed an even deeper crimson than the sunburnt peeling skin of his face and his bad eye rocketed off into a tangent. 'T-t-the course is as given to m-m-me by Mr. Pavlides,' he stammered.

Prendergast went ice cold. 'Okay, it's not your fault, lad,' he murmured. He returned to the chart room to estimate their position before adjusting the autopilot to bring them back on to what, as far as he could judge, was the correct course.

Coming back to the wing of the bridge, he met Pavlides carrying a cup of coffee in his hand. 'Would you mind telling me what is going on, Mr. Pavlides? I understand that you authorised a change in course without my knowledge?'

Pavlides seemed relaxed, but his piggy brown eyes were cold, his smile unfriendly and uncompromising. 'That is correct Captain, there is a change in our plans and we are now en route to Tripoli.' It was a flat statement delivered in a way that suggested it was not open to negotiation.

'Tripoli! What happened to Iskenderun?'

'Captain, you are an experienced seafarer. You know only too well that owners change their plans in the face of better opportunities. Ships are diverted for many reasons, as you well know. Be so kind as to bring the ship around again onto her new heading of one-eight-zero.' Pavlides' voice became harsh as he added, 'That is a direct order!'

'I'm damned if I like this one bit, Mr. Pavlides!'

'Please do as I say, Captain Prendergast. Correct me if I am wrong, but I understood we agreed to our terms for the operation of this ship. Those terms can be rescinded on our arrival in

Tripoli, should you so wish.'

Prendergast's mind raced. How could he have been so stupid! Cooke was right after all. There was far more to this voyage than he expected. Pavlides was simply covering his tracks out of Malta. Since he had taken pains to reassure Vittorio Cassar that there was nothing untoward, it would be at least twelve days before anyone became aware of their non-arrival in Iskenderun, if they ever did. By then it would be too late. The *Maria B* would have loaded and would be away at sea. He was aware, too, that Libya did not report the movements of ships in its territorial waters to Lloyds of London. For all practical purposes the ship had disappeared, at least for the next twelve days.

Jim found himself blurting an apology. 'I'm sorry, Mr.. Pavlides, of course we have an agreement. It is your ship, to do with as you wish.'

Pavlides studied him for a moment before replying, then came that familiar flash of gold teeth. 'Thank you, Captain', he said. 'For a moment I thought I had misjudged you.' He followed this with a harsh laugh. 'There is still room in the world for those such as us. Profit is a remarkable spur , don't you think? Perhaps now we can return to our course and continue to enjoy our voyage?'

Jim nodded quietly and went inside to attend to the autopilot. He wondered what Molloy would say when he told him.

It came as no surprise to Prendergast when just after dawn on the following morning, the slim grey shape of a gunboat took station just off their port bow with the plain green flag of Libya rippling at her stern.

Directly ahead the low brown desert shores beckoned.

- 272 -

Thirty-Four

Lieutenant Colonel Jonathan Cooke was fortunate to possess a mild-mannered perspective on life and was not given to allowing outside influences to dictate his temper, except when he cut himself shaving, which didn't happen often.

The morning started badly. Not only was he up late and suffering from the effects of one of Sir Harold's interminable embassy parties, but he had already cut himself twice.

Furiously he dabbed another small wad of orange toilet paper over the wound and grimaced into the mirror, watching the blood spread in a neat circle at the centre of the tissue.

Damn! Damn! He was already late and he would have to forego breakfast. For years he had intended to buy one of those styptic pencils, but he could never remember to do so. Perhaps if he had married, his wife would have remembered to do it for him. But he didn't have a wife, did he? Instead, he had blood on his shirt! With rising irritation he applied more tissue and hoped he had remembered to pick up his other shirts from the laundry.

Halfway down the dual carriageway from Dun Laoghaire Cooke suddenly remembered that he had not looked under the car that morning, something that he did without fail since his service in the North of Ireland. His temper intensified. He really was slipping. He could have lost his good leg this time.

By the time Cooke manoeuvred out of the morning traffic clogging Merrion Road and drove into the Embassy carpark he had convinced himself that today was a day for fishing and nothing else. He walked through the numbered carpark and met the

Ambassador alighting from his Jaguar. 'Good morning, Sir!' he said, without much enthusiasm.

Sir Harold Webster stopped and waited for him, briefcase in hand. 'Good morning, Jonathan, I hope you enjoyed yourself last evening?' The Ambassador looked at him more closely and raised his eyebrows. 'I say old chap, if you don't mind me saying so, you do look a bloody mess.'

Cooke remembered the toilet paper sticking to the cuts on his chin. 'Cut myself shaving, nothing that a trip to the washroom won't take care of.' He refrained from asking after the welfare of Emily Webster that morning. Instead, he contented himself with the knowledge that her hangover was probably worse than his own.

'Yes, of course. I'd like us to have a chat about the security arrangements for the PM's visit later this morning. Perhaps at eleven? That should give you ample time to tidy up eh!' The Ambassador went to his office chuckling. Good God! he thought happily. Cooke, of all people, under the weather!

'Thank you, Vittorio. I am most obliged that you called. Goodbye.' Cooke replaced the telephone and sat drumming his fingers on his desk. He felt suddenly tired and listless. The pain in his leg gnawed at him. For once, it had nothing to do with the weather.

Jonathan re-opened the file and stared glumly at the collection of papers and photographs inside. He had felt so sure this time. Somehow, he felt that he was missing some vital connection. A younger man might take such disappointments in his stride, but he felt his age, and for the first time he thought of retirement, his mind wandering to some distant unfished lake.

He got up and walked over to the wall map in his office and found Iskenderun. It was a long way from Malta, the best part of fifteen hundred miles. His eyes dropped down to Tripoli, so temptingly near, a couple of hundred miles at the most. Even a ship like the *Maria B* could be there quite quickly. But hadn't Cassar told him that she had taken sufficient fuel, water and stores for a lengthy passage? And what about Pavlides? Would he risk his own skin on a run to Libya? He thought not. Pavlides was far too wily a fox for that. Prendergast himself had no suspicions, otherwise he would have told Vittorio Cassar. Of that, he felt certain. No. Finally, he had to admit that he was wrong.

He returned to his desk and reluctantly closed the file before locking it away in his safe. He glanced at his watch: ten minutes before he was due at the Ambassador's office. He knew he would be sticking his neck out, but it was worth a try. Picking up the phone he dialled a number and got straight through to Northwood.

'Toby! Is that you? Jonathan Cooke here!'

Deep below ground, near the operations room under the concrete buildings in Northwood that carried the incongruous name of *H.M.S. Warrior*, Commander Toby Sims R.N. was pleased to receive the call. His morning was turning out very much as all the others before it and he did not relish the next few hours of paper shuffling. 'Jonathan! You old rogue, how are you? Haven't seen you since Wimbledon! God! That must be four years ago!'

Jonathan gave a short laugh. 'It was. I suppose you know that I am in Dublin now?'

'Yes, I heard you were over there. How do you like it? I imagine you've taken to fishing again? I used to love Ireland before they started discouraging us from going over.'

'It has its compensations in that area, I must admit. I miss the Service though.' Cooke was silent for a moment, then he came out with the real purpose of his call. 'Toby, I need a favour.'

Sims hesitated just for a moment. 'I thought you might. What can I do for you? If it's cash, you can forget it!'

Jonathan laughed again. It was good to talk to his friend. He should do it more often he thought; the banter had not changed and it was a welcome relief. 'No, nothing like that, old chum. I presume the navy still has a few ships knocking about in the Med?'

'One or two.' Sims sounded noncommittal.

'Well, I've been working on a little problem over here. It concerns a Liberian merchant ship that left Valletta two days ago ostensibly en route to Iskenderun. I just thought you might ask your lads to keep an eye out for her.'

Sims frowned, sensing complications. 'Is this official, Jonathan? You know there are channels for this sort of thing, especially if you want her tracked or stopped, or whatever.'

Cooke quickly reassured him. 'Nothing like that at all. I'd simply like to know of any sighting, especially, if for instance, she comes out past Gibraltar at some stage.'

'Well, if you put it that way, I suppose I could do something. Just remember, we don't have much support of our own in the Eastern Med right now. The American Sixth fleet is covering that area as usual. Unless you get some official backing, I can't involve the Yanks.' His tone was final.

Cooke decided to push no further. 'I really appreciate this, Toby,' he said. 'I'll fax over the details.'

'Leave it to me old boy. After all, we are the senior service are we not? It's nice to know that you still need us now and again.'

'Thanks, Toby, I owe you one.' Cooke hung up. At least, he now felt satisfied that he had done all that could be expected of him.

Before going to his meeting with Sir Harold Webster, he faxed photographs of the *Maria B* to Northwood, together with a detailed description of the vessel.

Sir Harold studied Cooke's face carefully from across his rose-wood desk. He felt disappointed that there were no shaving scars, but that was probably just as well, he told himself. It would have been difficult to control his amusement.

'In conclusion,' Jonathan said, 'I have to admit, Sir, that I appear to have been incorrect in my assessment of the intentions of the *Maria B.*' There was an air of defeat contained in his words. Clearly Cooke did not enjoy admitting that he was wrong.

The Ambassador coughed politely and did his best not to sound smug. 'Frankly, Jonathan, this doesn't surprise me. I did feel that your ideas were a little far-fetched. At the same time, I'm glad you followed it up. These are taxing times and you were correct to be so vigilant. Now, let's get on to other things.' The Ambassador opened his desk diary and studied his neat hand-written notes. 'The meeting arrangements are agreed for the 28th of next month. That evening there will be a State dinner in Dublin Castle. The PM will fly over on the evening of the 27th and will be my guest that night. Are you entirely satisfied that the Irish security arrangements are up to par?'

Jonathan felt bored. They had been over this so many times that it made him sick, but he tried to conceal his feelings. 'I am quite satisfied, Ambassador,' he said.

Webster arched his eyebrows. There he goes again, he thought. 'No surprises, Jonathan, please,' he said harshly. 'Kohl has now confirmed his attendance. You are aware of that, aren't you?'

'Yes, Sir Harold, I am aware of that. I have already had a number of discussions with the German security people.'

'Good. The only worry I have left is this damned weekend at Ashford Castle. How comfortable do you feel about that?'

Webster sounded edgy and Jonathan risked a smile. 'The Yanks are in full control, as usual. A plane load of their secret service people came in yesterday. They are going to swamp the whole area, as only they can do. The Irish will hardly get a look in. They're a bit pissed-off about it, too.'

The Ambassador frowned. 'I'm not surprised. Scotland Yard was not exactly overjoyed to have all that weaponry loose in London when the President called there after his inauguration. Quite unnecessary, in my opinion.'

'Perhaps, but they have had a couple of Presidents shot at in recent years. One can't blame them for being a little paranoid.'

'Bunch of bloody cowboys, all wanting to be John Wayne!'

Jonathan felt pleased that he had managed to needle Webster. 'I understand the Americans are taking full responsibility for transportation as well as the security throughout the Ashford visit.'

Sir Harold sighed. 'Yes, three helicopters, one of which will be a decoy. The President, Kohl and the PM will leave the country from Shannon afterwards. Your duty, Jonathan, is to the PM. Make sure he gets on that RAF plane safely. I suggest you maintain a personal interest in this.'

'I wouldn't have it any other way, Ambassador. I have cancelled any plans for fishing that weekend.'

'This is hardly the time for sarcasm, Jonathan,' Webster flared.

'Of course not, Ambassador. I apologise if I gave you that impression. Rest assured I will give it my full attention.' Deep cover in a stagnant border ditch was far preferable to this, he thought.

Sir Harold glowered across the desk. 'Thank you, Colonel, I accept your apology.' His voice sounded like iron. 'You have total responsibility in this matter, that is clear, is it not? Whatever resources you need to be successful are entirely up to you. Do we understand one another?'

'Without question, Sir.' Jonathan was aware that Webster was hand washing as only he knew how.

'Thank you, Colonel Cooke, that is all.'

The Ambassador turned to some papers on his desk. Leaving the room, Cooke knew that he had better get this right. If he didn't, the axe would only fall on one neck, and that was his own.

Thirty-Five

Liam stood with Colonel Ghalboun on the end of the pier and watched the gunboat approaching. Following her was the *Maria B*, who stood in stark contrast to the neat naval ship. A group of ragged scarecrows in shorts clustered on her after- deck near the funnel.

Liam's throat constricted. The ferry to Le Havre was bad enough. Surely they didn't expect him to return to Ireland on this heap of scrap metal? 'Is that it? Don't tell me that is it!'

'Neither of us are seamen, my friend. Perhaps we should leave this to the experts, don't you think? Such a ship is hardly likely to attract attention,' Ghalboun said with approval.

Liam growled and flipped his cigarette into the blue Mediterranean. Foster had something to answer for. He turned on his heel and walked quickly towards the warehouses.

With the ship safely tied up in the dock, Prendergast rang down to the engine room. The monotonous throb of the diesel died away, leaving only the whir of the generator to break the stillness.

He left the bridge and joined Eddie Molloy on the afterdeck. Molloy handed him a cold can of beer and wiped the perspiration from his face with a rag. 'He didn't waste any time, did he?' He nodded towards the dockside.

Prendergast raised his eyebrows and looked towards the warehouses in time to see Pavlides joining two other men before all three drove off in a white Mercedes. 'I have a feeling, Eddie, that you and I are in deep shit,' he said in a low voice. He gestured with his beer towards the gunboat now coming alongside astern of them. 'We can't even leave this dock without that bastard letting us out.'

Molloy sucked noisily from his can and said nothing.

Jim waved his arm. 'Take a good look around, Eddie. This is a naval dock, not a commercial one. Mark my words, we're going to have a decidedly hot cargo when we leave here and there's sweet feck all we can do about it.'

'What're you going to tell the two lads?'

'I don't think I'll tell them anything. There's no point.' He looked crestfallen. 'It's gone too far for any of us to get out now.'

Matty Lyons and Jimmy Lafferty finished rigging lifelines to the gangway and joined the others on the afterdeck as a red-capped soldier in olive green took up station at the end of the gangway. The way he cradled his sub-machine gun was hardly inviting.

'What's up, Skipper? Don't they trust us or what?' asked Lyons.

Prendergast shrugged. 'I certainly don't think they want us to stretch our legs. You can forget any shore leave by the looks of things.' He shot Molloy a cautionary look and turned away toward the bridge ladder.

As Liam alighted from the car outside the Libya Palace Hotel, a movement on a second floor balcony caught his attention. He glanced upwards in time to see Lisa turning away from the railing towards the open bedroom doors. She seemed to be speaking to someone. Maybe he was mistaken, but he felt sure he saw the shadow of someone else just inside the curtains. He followed Pavlides and Colonel Ghalboun inside.

They joined Foster in a small airless ground floor room and minutes later Lisa came in followed by a waiter carrying a tray of iced soft drinks. 'Ah! Refreshments, gentlemen. Then down to business.' Ghalboun placed a sheaf of papers on the table and seated himself at the head.

Liam glanced at the tray as the waiter withdrew. 'I suppose you couldn't rustle up a beer or two?' His voice was heavy with sarcasm.

'Unfortunately not. I'm sure you know that I would prefer otherwise.' Ghalboun shrugged. 'This is, after all, Libya. We must abide by the rules, don't you think?' Liam recognised a genuine apology when he heard one. Perhaps Ghalboun wasn't so bad after all, he thought.

Lisa sat opposite to him. She looked quite beautiful at that moment, her open-necked blouse emphasising her suntan. She wore only the faintest hint of makeup. Liam drew in his breath and looked away from her for a second while he poured some iced lemonade into a tumbler. Was he mistaken, or had he picked up a scent of whiskey fumes on her?

At that instant, Foster sat down beside him. He seemed deathly pale by comparison to any of them and his skin had an unhealthy yellow tinge to it. The odour of his perspiration drove away the fumes of what might have been alcohol. Liam turned away from him to face Ghalboun. 'Let's get on with it then, shall we?'

Ghalboun flourished the sheaf of paper in his hand and said, 'This is a list of your cargo, some items of which will ensure your popularity on your return to your homeland. There are one hundred tons in all. Loading will start tonight and will be completed by morning. The container will be brought alongside and loaded tomorrow.'

Pavlides pricked up his ears. 'What container? Nobody said anything about a container before this. I hope someone has taken the trouble to measure the damned thing if it's to fit in the hold.'

Foster donned a pair of spectacles and reached eagerly for the cargo list. 'It will be carried on deck,' he said.

'You can't just stick a container on the deck!' The Greek's concern was obvious and they all looked in his direction expectantly.

'Containers normally require special stowage. Container ships are designed to carry them stacked on deck, my ship is not. It will have to go in the hold.'

'It goes on the deck,' rasped Foster.

Liam smiled. Foster had finally blown it. So much for their meticulous planning!'

Colonel Ghalboun got to his feet and lit a cigarette. 'Mr. Pavlides, for reasons I am not prepared to go into, the container must be carried on deck. It is a little larger than a standard container. What modifications are required to enable the ship to carry it?'

The Greek could sense jeopardy. Why they were so insistent in having the container on deck was really of no consequence, but his profit was. 'It's not a major problem. Had I known about it, we could have prepared the ship while in the dockyard in Malta. A steel framework welded to the decks would be sufficient to stow it safely over the main hold.'

'Is that all?' Ghalboun sounded surprised. Picking up a telephone, he spoke rapidly with someone in Arabic. Turning back to them, he said, 'Our engineers will start immediately. The ship will sail tomorrow night as planned.'

Foster sighed his relief and studied the cargo list. Ammunition, explosives, light and heavy machine guns, pistols, silencers, infrared sights for the AK47's. The list seemed endless and there at the bottom were the twenty-five cases containing the Stinger missiles. 'Just take a look at this,' he said with excitement, handing the list to Liam.

Liam had to admit that it was impressive. There were weapons here they had only dreamed about. Foster gave him a sideways nudge. 'Now, wasn't I right? Even Hogan would go for this.'

At the mention of Hogan, Liam hardened. 'The weapons are not an issue,' he shot back. 'In fact, the list is admirable. It's the rest of your scheme that I don't agree with, so shut the fuck up until its all over. And in case you've forgotten, Jim Hogan is dead.'

Foster averted his gaze. 'I haven't forgotten, God rest his soul.'

Ghalboun gave a polite cough and changed the subject. 'Gentlemen, as this is your last night perhaps you would be so kind as to join me for dinner.' He caught Lisa's eye and nodded politely. 'I'm sorry my dear, I should have said lady and gentlemen. Nine o'clock, outside the hotel. I will arrange for transport.'

Lisa linked her arm in Liam's as they walked back across the foyer towards the elevators. If he was surprised, he didn't show it. It was enough that she was close. They stepped into the elevator and Liam pressed the button for the third floor.

A brawny fist appeared just as the lift doors were about to close and forced them open again. Buckholtz stepped in beside them, a towel about his powerful shoulders. 'Hi guys! You should try the pool, real nice, and a big change from that fucking desert.'

Liam hit the door close button. 'What floor?'

'Two,' replied Buckholtz.

'Lisa?'

She gripped his arm and glanced at Buckholtz. 'Three. I'm right next to yours.'

Buckholtz got out on the second floor still grinning. 'See y'all later,' he drawled. 'The rag-head told me we're all having dinner together, on him.'

Liam inserted his key into the door marked 301. Lisa was doing the same right across the hall. 'Leave your door unlocked. I'll be back,' she said. 'I just need to shower.'

'Fine,' he said. In spite of himself, he felt a stir of excitement. It had been a long time.

The room was hot and oppressive. Someone had forgotten to switch on the air conditioner. He walked across and opened the French windows wide and stepped out onto the balcony.

The avenue below was still busy, filled with people homeward bound after a day's work. A mullah called from a minaret and people were laying prayer mats on the ground in a park across the street.

Liam looked over the edge of the balcony and saw a taxi just drawing up outside the entrance. He recognised Chico Gonzales getting out of it. A movement below him on a balcony on the second floor caught his attention and he saw Buckholtz. In an instant, his stomach tightened into a knot. Lisa's room was on the opposite side of the hotel from his, so why had he seen her earlier on a second floor balcony? He went inside and ripped off his clothes, hurling them on the floor, before stepping into a cold shower.

He didn't hear Lisa come in and was unaware of her presence until her hand reached inside the shower stall and led him reluctantly to the bed. She shed her robe and drew him down beside her, yellow hair cascading loose and still slightly damp on the pillows. 'Make love to me, Liam.' It was a whisper of urgency and she used a word that she had never used before.

Later, he lay beside her, the odour of Scotch heavy on his lips and watched the light fade outside, until the room became dusky and filled with the night sounds of a city winding down for the day. He lit a cigarette and dragged on it deeply as she stirred beside him.

'When did you start fucking him?'

She rolled away and stretched for her robe on the floor. Retrieving it, she slipped it around her shoulders and sat up in the bed, looking down at his darkened face. 'What does it matter? I told you in Mexico not to get close. You and I have chosen a transient life. I fuck who I like, when I like.'

For a moment he was silent, gazing up at her, her eyes hidden in the twilight. Then he heaved upwards and sent her sprawling from the bed. 'Yeah, you told me that. Now get the fuck out and leave me alone.'

With a tinkle of laughter she left the room and the door clicked shut.

Liam rolled into a tight naked ball on the bed. For the first time in many years, he prayed. He prayed for his brother Johnny, and for Hogan, and for release from this shitty world of his own making.

The thud of hatch boards being thrown onto the deck woke Prendergast. It was dark and oppressively hot. He reached up and switched on the reading light over his bunk. Covered in sweat, a half-remembered dream still in his mind, he lay for a while, trying to recall it. There were no visions, only sounds. The crash of waves and seabirds screaming, and a child's voice calling 'Daddy!'

Molloy was halfway up the ladder to the bridge when he got outside. 'They're starting to load, Jim,' he whispered.

They both went to the bridge dodger and peered down on the floodlit deck. The hatches were open and a crane on the dockside was already lifting the first pallet of neat metal boxes.

Over by the warehouse doors there was a heavy military presence and a number of jeeps had fanned out, guarding the approaches from the entrance gates to the dockyard. Each of them mounted a heavy calibre machine gun.

'We don't have to open those to know what's inside them.' Prendergast sounded calm and detached. He showed no signs of worry, as if he had expected it all along.

Molloy wondered whether he would have left Galway had he known what lay ahead of them, but he tried to put that thought aside. 'What are you going to do about it, Jim?'

He shrugged. 'The short answer is that I don't know. Not yet anyway.' He paused for a moment thinking about it. 'We probably have a few options. Time will tell. We could get a radio message off when we leave here and hand her over to the authorities; we could put into a port en route to wherever we're going and hand her over; or if everything else fails, we could scuttle her.'

Molloy did not sound convinced. 'What about Pavlides, do you honestly think he will let us out of here on our own?'

'It seems unlikely, but he is only one, and we are four, not including the cook. I don't see how he could stop us.'

Eddie contented himself with watching the second pallet of green boxes swinging down into the floodlit hold where a group of sweating soldiers manoeuvred it into position next to the first.

'I think we can be sure, though, where this is going,' Prendergast said. 'We are taking it home.'

'I suppose you're right. That Brit friend of yours from Dublin read all the signs.'

'The trouble is, our Colonel Jonathan Cooke believes that we are heading for Turkey right now. He has probably already scrubbed us off his agenda.' There was a hint of defeat in his words.

Eddie wiped under his arms with his sweat rag and hitched up his greasy shorts over his belly. 'If you had a choice in this,

Jim, what would you do?'

'Well', Prendergast sighed, 'Given that I believe we are dealing with the same people who sank my yacht,' he paused for a moment as if searching for words, 'and the same people who killed my wife and daughter, I'd play along in the hope that we could get the whole fucking bunch of them. Don't ask me how, but that's what I would really like to do. As a last resort we scuttle the bitch underneath us and send the lot to the bottom.'

'That might be our only option,' Molloy said.

'What about Matty Lyons and Jimmy Lafferty? They know nothing about this and I know I'm putting them at risk. I don't know what to do about that, either.'

A third pallet of boxes swung across the arc lights in front of the bridge and the crane jerked as it lowered the load into the hold.

'Take my advice, Jim, and leave well enough alone.' Molloy nodded toward the armed soldiers lolling around the quayside. 'There's nowhere they can go from here, even if they wanted to.'

'Well, we'd better convince Pavlides that we're all for it, then. And the best way to do that is to put a squeeze on him for a bonus payment.'

Molloy looked across at a jeep that had just swung to a halt near the warehouse doors. Four men climbed out, among them, Pavlides. 'Speak of the devil,' he said, 'Here he comes now, right on cue. You'd better go and meet the bastard.'

Pavlides stood for a while watching the activity on the deck below. The crane had stopped loading the pallets while three army engineers busied themselves with tape measures on the foredeck. Then he turned to Prendergast. 'As soon as loading is completed, welders will fit a framework to carry a container as deck cargo. You will be ready for sea tomorrow night.'

Prendergast raised his eyebrows in surprise. This put a different complexion on things. To discharge a container they would have to enter a port. It certainly couldn't easily be done at sea. 'Perhaps you could tell me where we are bound for?'

Pavlides shrugged. 'That is a matter for our charterers. Rotterdam maybe, who knows? You will get your orders at sea, Captain.'

Prendergast knew he was lying. The bastard knew all right but he wasn't telling him.

A forklift truck lowered a pallet load of circular containers in front of the crane. In the arc lights, the stencilled markings were clear. Danger – Explosives.

'Mr. Pavlides, I presume this cargo is legitimate?'

Pavlides smiled craftily and nudged him with his elbow. 'All cargoes are legitimate if the freight rates are right don't you think? You and your crew will be well rewarded for your efforts.'

'I was about to come to that,' said Jim. 'So long as that is clearly understood, we'll take it wherever you want.'

The Greek placed a fat hand on his shoulder and squeezed. 'Good,' he said. 'Have no worries on that account.' He turned towards the bridge ladder, 'I have an appointment ashore shortly, I must leave now.' He extended his hand. 'Have a safe passage, Captain.'

'You're not coming with us?'

'No, it is not necessary.'

Prendergast swallowed his distaste and shook hands. 'I'll see you before we sail?'

Pavlides shook his head, 'No, I leave tomorrow by plane, but I trust we will meet again to celebrate a successful voyage for both of us.'

Halfway down the ladder, Pavlides stopped and looked up at him, 'By the way, Captain, five supernumeraries will be joining you tomorrow evening before you leave. You will need to take account of that if you are provisioning the ship.'

'Supernumeraries?'

'Passengers if you like, charterer's agents, whatever.' With a wave Pavlides disappeared along the darkened deck and a few minutes later drove away in the army jeep.

Prendergast gaped after the disappearing vehicle. What next, he wondered, as he hurried below to tell Eddie Molloy about the container and their passengers.

Thirty-Six

The splutter of welding equipment continued all through the morning without respite as the Libyan army engineers worked on the foredeck of the *Maria B.* Prendergast spent the time in the seclusion of the chart room checking that he had sufficient charts for most of the ports in Northern Europe. Pavlides had certainly thrown a spanner in the works with his mention of Rotterdam as a discharge port, and although Jim was sure that it had been a lie, he felt that he needed to be ready for any eventuality.

By the time the lunch gong sounded on the afterdeck, the army engineers had already constructed a web of bolted steel supports on which the container would sit over the now closed cargo hold. Prendergast only gave it a cursory glance but it was apparent that the framework was carefully constructed so that it could easily be dismantled when no longer required.

The Maltese cook was beginning to prove his worth, so that by the time Jim got down to the messroom, Lafferty, Lyons and Eddie Molloy were already tucking into a meal of grilled fish that smelled delicious. The cook had even managed to do something with the oven that now allowed him to bake fresh bread.

'Pull up a chair, Skipper.' Matty forked food into his mouth. 'The grub's a lot better than on our way down.'

Molloy winked at Prendergast. 'He's right, Jim. A happy ship is a well fed one, and these lads are certainly happy.'

'I'm glad to hear it,' he said, accepting a steaming plate from the cook. He didn't say much during the rest of the meal. The food was certainly good and he concentrated on that, thinking carefully over what he should say to his crew. He had to be able to rely on their help when the time came.

Lafferty was the first to finish. As he got up to carry his empty plate into the galley, Prendergast pushed his plate away. 'Jimmy, come back here for a minute and sit down. There is something I want to say to you all.'

As usual, when spoken to directly, Lafferty's face turned crimson and his bad eye twitched into a squint, but he came back and sat down at the table. Jim lit a cigarette and rocked back on the legs of his chair, gathering his thoughts. The others waited expectantly for him to speak.

'We are sailing tonight, but first there is a deck container to load, which is the reason for the work on the foredeck.' He stopped and looked at the open serving hatch to the galley. Inside, the cook was banging pots about as he scrubbed them clean. Jim lowered his voice. 'Matty, would you mind closing that door?'

'Sure, Skipper.' Lyons reached over and closed the hatch.

Prendergast drew on his cigarette and continued. 'No doubt you have seen the cargo that came aboard during the night, so you must be aware that we are carrying weapons and explosives. The container is likely to have more of the same. We will not know our destination or discharging orders until we are at sea. Whether it is legitimate or not, I am unsure, but I suspect that it is not. There are probably risks for all of us.' He waited for that point to sink in.

Malloy picked unconcernedly at his fingernails with a penknife and waited.

Lyons shrugged. 'Is there extra money in this, Skipper?'

Jim stubbed out his cigarette and lit another. 'Yes, if we do as we are told. There is considerable money for all of us.'

'And if we d-d-don't?' Jimmy's face flamed, as if he was surprised that he had spoken.

Jim looked grim. 'I don't have a crystal ball,' he said flatly. 'Use your imagination. This is Libya, after all. No one knows we're here, as far as I know. Draw your own conclusions.'

Lyons looked at Eddie, 'What do you think, Chief?'

Molloy folded his pen knife and slipped it into his pocket. 'We don't have much choice, do we?'

'There is one thing more that I haven't told you yet.' All of them turned to Prendergast again. 'We have five passengers joining us for the trip. I don't know who they are, but they obviously have a direct interest in the welfare of this cargo.'

Matty sucked in a breath and scratched at his leathery neck. 'The Chief said it all, Skipper. We don't have a fucking choice. Anyway, if the money is right ...'

Prendergast waited but no one else spoke. 'That just about sums it up, I'll keep you posted of any changes. I suggest you keep him out of it.' Jim nodded toward the serving hatch. 'Pavlides hired him, not me.'

Something heavy bumped along the side of the ship. Molloy went to the open door and looked outside. 'Tug coming alongside with a barge, Jim. Looks as though our container is here.'

Jim smiled at the two seamen still seated at the table and got up to join Molloy. 'Just remember, lads, keep your mouths shut and your ears open. I don't know who is joining us, but they are unlikely to be family, if you get my meaning.'

The crane extended its jib to reach across the width of the ship's deck and a group of soldiers on the flat-topped barge attaching the slings signalled all clear for the hoist. Prendergast watched with interest from the bridge as the container swung into the air and passed in front of the wheel house.

To him, it didn't look different than any other container, having all the usual markings on its beat-up yellow sides. But as the crane set it down on its supports over the cargo hatch he noticed that it had a canvas top rather than one made of steel. That in itself made him take a closer look. There was something about it that he couldn't quite understand. Except that it seemed slightly longer and wider than a standard sized container, the crane had no difficulty lifting it, and the way the army engineers swung it quickly into position suggested that it did not weigh very much.

Once the container was secured in position with quick-release hooks he could just see over the top of it from the wheel house windows, although it would not be possible to see the anchor capstan or anyone on the forecastle. Otherwise, he knew that it would not present any major difficulty at sea unless the weather became really foul.

It was Molloy that pointed out something that he had not noticed. The engineer was down on the well deck but he hurried back up to the bridge. 'Those Arabs got their bloody measurements all wrong,' he said, panting when he got there.

'What do you mean, Eddie?'

'Well, take a look at it. They didn't need to put in all those steel supports. They go right out over the bulwarks on each side and there's more down ahead of the container over the rest of the hold, right up to the forecastle. They could have fitted four more containers if they wanted to.'

Perplexed, Jim lit a cigarette and stared down. 'Jesus! You're right, I hadn't noticed that.'

'There's more,' said Molloy. 'I gave it a belt of my spanner on my way past. I'd swear the bloody thing is empty!'

As the sun slowly sank in the western sky and the low desert shoreline cooled with the onset of evening, the *Maria B* stopped her engine two miles offshore. Close by, the same Libyan gunboat that had escorted them in, cruised in a tight circle around her. Prominent among the Army officers grouped on the small navigating bridge of the gunboat, Colonel Ghalboun anxiously awaited this final dress rehearsal.

Jim Prendergast sipped his coffee in the wheel house and watched in astonishment as a number of soldiers stripped off the canvas cover on the top of the container. He went outside and peered over the bridge dodger. There was nothing in it. Seconds later, the soldiers released clips on the side panels and with the gentle whine of electric motors lowered them carefully on their hinges. The final panel clanged down on to the supporting trestles so that now all that remained was a flat platform covering most of the forward part of the ship. The square platform surface had a white line painted around its outside edges and a white circle in the centre with diagonal white lines running from this to each corner. At any moment he half expected to see the start of a game of tennis.

It was only the dull throbbing sound of the approaching helicopter that made it all clear. He was looking down on a helicopter landing platform, right here on his ship!

Buckholtz flew in low, skimming the surface so that the downdraft formed small waves and kicked up a fine spray below him. Then he climbed sharply and banked in a circle over the ship, sizing up the landing area.

He and Chico had done it many times already in practice runs on the offshore barge, but this time there was no room for error and the bridge superstructure was an added constriction. The landing area was makeshift and there was no glide path. There wasn't even anyone with sufficient experience to hand signal him in. On an evening like this, with little wind and a flat sea it was not too difficult for a pilot of his experience, but in the dark, or in poor visibility with the ship rolling heavily below ... he didn't dwell on it.

Buckholtz grinned at Chico Gonzales seated beside him and gave the thumbs up sign. Reaching for the collective pitch lever, he swooped down in a gut-dropping action designed mainly to impress his three passengers crouched on the flat floor behind the pilots' seats.

Foster sweated profusely and made the sign of the cross as he felt the floor of the aircraft drop away underneath him. His fear was palpable, which encouraged Liam to appear even less concerned. Lisa concentrated on what she could see through the cockpit bubble and made no sound.

Nothing could be heard above the high-pitched whine of the engines. The chopper hovered for a second over the bridge and for a brief instant the downdraft tore at Prendergast's clothes and sprayed his shirt front with the contents of his coffee mug. Then, like a noisy insect, the helicopter settled its skids on the platform surface and the whine of its engines slowly died away.

The side doors in the matte-black fuselage opened. As the rotors slowed, the occupants climbed out and stood uncertainly on the landing platform, looking up at the bridge to where Prendergast stared back at them as though they were from another planet.

Chico Gonzales erected a small folding aluminium ladder and clambered up to release the quick-release pins that enabled him to fold the rotor blades. He was the last to leave the platform as the electric motors whirred and it became a container again.

Prendergast went down to meet them as they crowded on the afterdeck where Eddie Molloy and the crew had assembled, open-mouthed. 'Chief, please show these people below and be ready to get underway in five or ten minutes.' He didn't bother to ask their names. Molloy mumbled something and led them away.

The naval gunboat came alongside a few minutes later and took off the soldiers lining the welldeck. As she backed away a loudhailer blasted the still evening air. 'You are free to proceed now, Captain. *Bon Voyage!*'

Prendergast scowled at the military uniforms on the gunboat's navigation bridge and rang down for *full ahead* on the engine before setting course to clear Cap Bon on the northern tip of Tunisia.

Thirty-Seven

Harry Trent always worried. It was something that he was used to and his fingernails bore silent witness to it. Since the shooting of Jim Hogan he had fretted constantly that someone within the organisation would link him with the murder, but as time went on, no one had. Although the UVF denied all responsibility for it, everyone seemed to accept that it was their work.

The RUC had conveniently forgotten it. He knew that as far as they were concerned, Hogan was one less terrorist for them to worry about.

For the moment, Harry contented himself with the knowledge that now only Foster knew the real truth of the matter, and he could never divulge it without incriminating himself. As a bonus, he had just learned that the two men who had carried out the shooting had accidentally blown themselves up transporting a car bomb into Lisburn two nights ago. Things could not be better.

The news from Germany was also reassuring, he thought. The Libyans had made contact at last, confirming that the ship was on her way. It was just a matter of days now before he could bask in the reflected glory of the biggest strike for freedom in the history of his dirty little war. All he had to do now was to set up the arrangements with the fishing boat down in Galway. That should be relatively easy, and without too much risk to himself.

When he left his house to join the commuting traffic heading for the centre of Belfast, he basked in a feeling of near self-adulation until he turned on to the A20 at Newtownards. It was there at the road junction, waiting for a gap in the traffic, that he suddenly remembered that the ship was bringing Liam home as well. The worry started again.

He began to chew on a fingernail. Surely, Foster would recognise the dangers of that and take care of it? After all, the bastard had just as much to lose. Then again, maybe he was just imagining the worst. Liam may well have accepted Hogan's death and wish to do nothing about investigating it. The doubt in that thought would not leave him easily, and he carried it with him all the way to Lucky Harry's bookmaker's shop near the Strand Road.

Further south in Dublin, Jonathan Cooke drove through similar traffic. The summer high had come late this year, and in Dublin that day it was three degrees warmer than Belfast.

Jonathan, however, did not worry. He was finally beginning to accept that he had over-reacted to the *Maria B.* Toby Sims had not got back to him, meaning she must be still en route to Turkey. He put his thoughts aside. He had a busy day ahead refining the security arrangements for the Prime Minister's visit, and that, in itself, was enough to be getting on with.

Later on the same day, Vittorio Cassar decided to check on Pavlides. Although he had not voiced any of his feelings to Jonathan Cooke, ever since the *Maria B* sailed from Valletta, he had felt that he was missing something. Perhaps there was a simple answer. If he didn't sail on the ship as Prendergast said he would, Air Malta or one of the ferries must have a record of his arrival and departure. He called the airport.

Cassar's contact in Air Malta quickly confirmed that a Mr. Dimetrios Pavlides had arrived on a one way ticket from London the day after the ship arrived in Valletta. A quick check of the hotels revealed that he had stayed at the Phoenicia but had checked out on the same day that the ship sailed.

Cassar left the phone box and crossed the street to the shaded side and ordered a beer at a sidewalk table. Sipping his beer he mulled it over in his mind. If Pavlides did not fly out then he was either still on the island, or had sailed on the ship. But to where? There was no law against an owner sailing on his own ship, and after all, Prendergast had said that was his intention. Still, he decided to make a few more phone calls. He could see no point in alarming Jonathan Cooke, but just to satisfy himself, he would check the ferries and a few airlines. It would be interesting to know if Pavlides had found landfall since.

Hugging the Algerian coast that was visible three or four miles away on the port side, the *Maria B* settled into a sea passage routine and slipped westward towards the Straits of Gibraltar. Prendergast paced the bridge oblivious to the heat of the afternoon sun, racking his brains. Somewhere out there over the horizon on the starboard side were the shipping lanes that may have presented some opportunity to attract attention.

Rounding Cap Bon the previous night in the darkness of an unannounced levanter that blew steadily at forty knots out of the northeast, he thought he had an opportunity to try to get out a call on the VHF radio while most of his passengers succumbed to seasickness, only to find that the set was dead. He didn't have to be told that it had been tampered with.

Since then, as the seas had calmed, he had never been without company on the bridge. One of his passengers was always present, and the most watchful was Buckholtz, who was able to navigate. It was Buckholtz who had spotted his course that would lead them from Cap Bon out into the busiest shipping lanes leading to the Straits, and it was Buckholtz who insisted on going well inshore away from other ships. Now it was too late. His passengers were all finding their sea legs. The German woman had even resurrected a deck-chair from somewhere below, and was now sunning herself on the opposite bridge wing. They were all over the ship, or so it seemed, and there had been no opportunity to talk things through with Eddie Molloy.

For the moment Jim had to content himself with the knowledge that the narrow Straits of Gibraltar could yet provide the answer. Although no one had yet told him, he was sure that their destination was the Irish coast and that gave him a further eight days at least. He gave a fleeting thought to the distress flares in a locker inside the wheel house, but quickly dismissed it.

He knew that he no longer had full command of his ship.

'I thought you might appreciate a cold beer, Captain.'

Startled, Prendergast swung round to face Lisa as she came through the wheel house door.

'Thank you.' He tore his gaze away from her halter top, that, like her brief white shorts, did nothing to hide anything, and took the beer from her.

'It's magnificent, don't you think?' She stood beside him and gazed dreamily towards the bow cleaving through a sea as blue as her eyes. 'I've often wished for a Mediterranean cruise,' she gave a short laugh, 'but I always imagined it would be on a cruise liner.'

The faintest trace of her perfume tantalised Jim's nostrils. 'You could hardly call this old girl that,' he replied.

'Are you Irish, Captain?'

'Call me Jim. Yes ... well half, anyway.' Prendergast was aware that she was looking at him attentively. 'What about you? You speak English very well but I would guess you are German, right?'

Lisa arched her eyebrows. 'You'd hardly win a prize for that observation,' she said with a smile as she touched him lightly on the forearm. 'I'm more interested in knowing more about you, Jim. For instance, why you are doing what you do. You're not like the rest of us.'

The touch of her hand surprised him, like the sudden flaring of a match. 'I'm just a sailor,' he said quietly. 'But I have needs and like to make more money than some.'

Lisa studied his profiled face for a second or two. He was certainly still attractive, she thought. She liked men that took the trouble to shave each morning. He was a little older than she was used to, but what did the Irish say, the older the fiddle, the sweeter the tune. 'I thought for a moment, Jim, that you might have a more interesting answer.'

'Sorry to disappoint you, Lisa, I'm very ordinary.' He turned before adding. 'Just greedier than most.'

Before Lisa could respond, they were interrupted by the arrival of Liam munching on a sandwich. 'There's more below,

Lisa, I'll take over here.' Seeing the frown on Prendergast's face, he added mockingly, 'With your permission, Captain.'

Jim watched Lisa making her way back along the afterdeck. He wished she would cover her legs or at least wear shorts that were not quite so tight. Despite any attraction he felt, a sixth sense warned him that she could be more dangerous than any of the others.

Liam had gone into the chart room and was trying to make sense of the chart. He returned still eating his sandwich and flopped into the vacant deck-chair. It occured to Prendergast that this was as close as he had come to being hijacked. Angrily, he stormed through the wheel house and faced Liam. 'I would prefer that when you wander around on my bridge, you don't carry a weapon. It's not necessary.'

Liam remained expressionless for a moment, then got slowly to his feet. They were about the same height and build. His hand caressed the brand new shoulder holster under his left arm as though it was an extension of himself. 'I feel more comfortable dressed this way. We don't know you yet mister, so get used to it.' His look was bleak and unwavering.

Jim made no reply. Swallowing his pride and anger, he backed down and returned inside. This was no time for a confrontation. He fussed at the chart for a while before going out to the wheel house again, where he made a slight adjustment in course to the autopilot.

Liam watched the bows swing a degree or so further away from the shoreline. What was it Buckholtz had said? Something about making sure they did not edge out into the shipping lanes? He wasn't really sure. Prendergast sensed what Liam was thinking and joined him outside. 'Just in case you're wondering,' he said without smiling, 'I'm allowing for a current that is setting us inshore.'

Liam shrugged. 'You're the skipper, I assume you know what you're doing. Speaking of which, why are you doing this?'

Prendergast picked up a pair of binoculars and scanned the horizon slowly. 'Why am I doing what?'

'You know what I mean. Working with us. You don't sound Irish.

Jim replaced the binoculars in their holder and turned to face him. When he spoke, it was with a hint of irony. 'I didn't think Irish nationality was a prerequisite in your line of business. The rest of your group aren't all Irish either. I'm surprised you don't want to know my religion, but if it matters to you, I have expensive tastes, and the money is good.'

Liam laughed. 'I suppose I asked for that,' he said. 'What's your name?'

'Prendergast. Jim Prendergast.' He saw Liam open his mouth as though to say something, then hesitate.

Liam had a fleeting vision of his brother's farmhouse in Donegal. He couldn't think why. Then he remembered Lisa handing him the newspaper in the kitchen the morning he returned from Pettigoe after his last meeting with Jim Hogan. That guy from the yacht was a Jim Prendergast. Surely this was too much of a coincidence! Hadn't he overheard one of the crew telling Buckholtz they had sailed the ship from Galway? Lighting a cigarette, he drew the smoke deep into his lungs and said, 'Are you married, Jim?' He saw Prendergast flinch and he knew the answer before he heard the reply.

'Not anymore.' Jim's voice sounded vacant. 'She was drowned in an accident.'

Liam didn't need any more confirmation. 'I'm sorry to hear that.' He meant it, but before he could add anything else, Prendergast turned away.

Liam flicked his half-finished cigarette over the side and followed Prendergast inside the wheel house. 'I've got to take a piss,' he said. 'I'll be back.'

'Take as long as you like. I'm not going anywhere.' Jim stared at the horizon and ignored his departure. He was back on the yacht, reliving that dreadful day, and all he wanted was to be left alone.

Foster stripped and stepped into the cubicle. Turning on the water, he waited for the customary coughing of the pipes as the water made its reluctant way to the shower head.

The first hesitant gush of water struck him as a brawny hand grasped him roughly by the throat and rammed him backwards against the discoloured steel bulkhead. A gun barrel rammed into his mouth splitting his lower lip and almost breaking his front teeth. In terror, he recoiled from Liam as the hammer of the Smith and Wesson clicked into full cock.

'You stupid fucking shit!' Liam hissed. 'I'd like to blow your bloody brains out!'

Foster's eyes swam with abject fear. Even with cool water spraying on his body he could feel himself sweating, but there were no words, not with the barrel of gun bruising the roof of his mouth.

'You know who the skipper of this bloody ship is?' Liam's voice rose a notch. 'It's the guy who was on the yacht – the one that you fucking sank! You killed his wife and kid, Foster!'

Foster's eyes focused on the revolver and the fist holding it. He could see the trigger finger squeezing. His urge to urinate was compelling. Just before his panic became complete, he fainted.

Liam reluctantly let go of Foster's throat and allowed the body to collapse heavily inside the shower. He stuffed the revolver back in his holster and stood, breathing heavily, looking down on Foster's crumpled form as his rage subsided. A trickle of blood slowly dripped from Foster's mouth, mingling with the water trapped in the footwell. He spat at the prone body as he backed away, leaving Foster with the water spraying over him.

Thirty-Eight

The Third Officer of the Norwegian tanker *Sogneffell* again swept his binoculars through the massed cluster of lights on the horizon. Off to one side the lights of Gibraltar formed a backdrop in the night sky, adding complexity to a scene that had all the appearance of a busy motorway.

The ship was making all of seventeen knots on her final approach to the Straits, leaving little room for error, but nobody would thank him for slowing down without good reason.

Bound for Rotterdam, fully-laden with crude from the Persian Gulf, the ship was modern and well manned and he had every conceivable aid to navigation at his finger tips. He ran another radar plot. This time he was sure. Two miles ahead the echo showed green and phosphorescent as the radar beam swept over it. He went quickly back to the wheel house and adjusted the controls to the unmanned engine room to bring the ship to half speed. Raising his binoculars he swept the sea ahead of the huge bow that parted the seas six hundred feet from where he stood. He saw nothing, absolutely nothing at all, just darkness.

Captain Carlson, aware of his ship slowing, was on the bridge seconds later. 'What's up third mate, everything all right?'

The Third Officer allowed his tension to ebb. Having the captain on the bridge removed some of the responsibility that weighed heavily on his young shoulders. 'I think we have a rogue ship showing no lights up ahead. I've run a radar plot, we're overtaking and I've altered course to clear her. Probably a fishing boat or something.'

Carlson peered into the radar screen. It was a mass of echoes from the traffic moving into the Straits from both east and west. Two of the swift-moving blips crossing diagonally between Gibraltar and Ceuta were clearly ferries. The nearest echo was now only half a mile ahead and closing. Quickly, in the interests of safety, he ordered a further two degree change in course and walked to the extreme edge of the bridge wing. Even without binoculars, he was able to discern a small black shape on the sea travelling slowly in the same direction, heading westwards towards the Atlantic.

Still not down to half speed, the tanker overtook the blacked out ship less than quarter of a mile away. Carlson was able to look down on her shadowy shape. Not a single light showed, but she was definitely underway and as they drew abeam he could hear the dull throb of her engine across the narrow strip of water separating them. He switched on a powerful searchlight and swept its beam over her from end to end, picking out the single yellow container nestling on her foredeck. The light illuminated several white faces on her bridge staring back at him. Carlson shook his fist at them and returned to his own wheel house. Picking up the VHF microphone, he switched to the international Channel 16 distress frequency and pressed the transmit button. 'Ship without lights on my port side, this is the tanker *Sognefjell*, please identify yourself, over!' Three times he made the call and received no reply. Finally he gave up. Nothing would be gained by hanging around and he had a schedule to keep. His owners wouldn't take it kindly if he was half a day late arriving in Europort. Turning to his Third Officer, he said, 'Bring her back to full speed, if you please, and resume your course. By the way, good work, mister!'

In Gibraltar, the operator on duty in the radio station heard the call on Channel 16 and made a note of it in his log. It happened all the time. No wonder there were collisions at sea. Then he forgot it as another ship called, requesting a link call to her owners.

Prendergast had seen the overtaking ship long before it became a threat. Lit up like a Christmas tree, he could hardly miss her. He prepared for evasive action, until he saw the reassuring swing of her navigation lights as she altered course. They were lucky. Someone was keeping a careful radar watch. It came as no surprise to him when minutes later her searchlight picked them out, holding them in its powerful beam like petrified rabbits.

Everyone except Foster crowded his tiny bridge. Prendergast turned on Buckholtz, who had insisted that they enter the Straits without lights. 'You've just made a major mistake, mister. Not only were we close to being run down, I'll bet that the captain of that ship is now reporting us to Gibraltar. If we had an operational VHF you'd be able to hear it yourself, loud and clear.' Secretly he was delighted. They could expect company any time. When that happened, the voyage would be over.

'Go fuck yourself,' Buckholtz sneered. 'It ain't over till the fat lady sings!'

In the darkness Chico Gonzales rocked contentedly, backwards and forwards on the balls of his feet. Gene was the man to put manners on these clowns! Smiling to himself, he left the bridge to keep an eye on the engine room.

'Buckholtz, you better be right about this.' Liam was worried. It was clear even to him that Prendergast knew what he was doing, but he wasn't so sure about the American.

Lisa kept out of it. She hugged herself, trying to stay warm in her flimsy teeshirt, wishing the lights that surrounded them would go away.

Prendergast melted away into the background and concentrated on the radar. It was all up to Eddie Molloy now. Maybe he would think of arranging a convenient engine breakdown.

Two hours later the *Maria B* cleared the Straits of Gibraltar unscathed and Prendergast was allowed to switch on the lights. With the exception of Liam, the others left the bridge and went below to their beds.

'That's that then,' Liam said. 'Where to now?'

'Cape St Vincent and the Portuguese coast, then I need to

know where you want to go.' Prendergast sounded tired and despondent. He was disappointed that they had succeeded in sneaking through the narrows undetected. At the same time he had noticed a subtle change in Liam. It was almost imperceptible, but something was different since they had spoken two days ago. Even during the argument with Buckholtz about blackening out the lights, he had sensed Liam's support.

Liam made no reply. He lit a cigarette. 'Want one?' he asked.

Jim accepted as Matty Lyons arrived to take over the watch. He dragged on the cigarette. 'Are you and Lisa an item? Or is that a question I shouldn't ask?'

Liam didn't answer for a minute, then he said, 'Put it in the past tense, pal. Buckholtz is her latest.' Prendergast heard the bitterness and sensed the weakness. Now was perhaps not the time to exploit it. 'Sorry, I didn't mean to pry,' he said. He ground out his cigarette. 'If you don't mind, I'll turn in, I'm bushed. Matty, you've got the course?'

'Aye Skipper, I have her. Goodnight.'

Liam shifted in the dark, then said, 'You might as well know now. You're going home. Back to Galway.'

'Thank you. Goodnight, Liam.' There was no reply, just the glow of a cigarette in the dark.

Jim closed the door to his cabin. Pulling over a chair he climbed onto it and unscrewed the louver in the ventilation trunking. The pistol was still there, together with the two clips of ammunition. He extracted them and screwed the louver back into place. He loaded the pistol and wrapped the lot in some soiled underwear before hiding it in a drawer, then he stretched onto his bunk and slept.

Eddie Molloy finished his breakfast early, rushing it to be out of the mess room before the crowd arrived. He met Prendergast coming down the ladder from the bridge. They had had no opportunity to talk privately since leaving Tripoli. He inclined his head towards the engine room door. 'Get down here Jim, there's no one around right now.'

The engine room reverberated with the thunder of noise from the diesel, the spinning propeller shaft further aft, oiled and gleaming in the artificial lights. It was hot and stifling, the air heavy with the smell of heated machinery.

Jim followed Molloy past the engine right up to the bulkhead that separated the engine room from the main cargo hold. In a corner, hidden behind a collection of oil drums, was a small rusted watertight access door just large enough for a man to crawl through. It looked as though it had not opened in years. Molloy spun the clamps easily enough and led the way through, locking the door securely behind him. Inside, the hold was pitch black, but the bulkhead insulated them from the roar of the engine and only the noise of the sea outside the ship's plating echoed through the cargo area.

Eddie switched on a powerful torch and flashed it over the cargo. 'I've been working on that fucking door ever since we left Tripoli,' he said. 'The clamps were totally seized up. For a while I thought it might be welded shut. I had to do it without that bastard Gonzales seeing me.'

'Has he been watching you?'

'Yeah, all the time, like a bloody shadow he is. Trouble is, he's an engineer, did you know that? He understands that engine room almost as well as I do.' There was a trace of admiration in Molloy's voice.

Jim smiled. 'They have it well worked out, don't they? A guy watching you so that you don't pull any strokes in the engine room, and the rest of them watching me on the bridge!'

Molloy surveyed the neatly stacked boxes in the hold. 'You can bet on it,' he said. 'I thought of arranging a bit of a break-down in the Straits, but I couldn't do it. Gonzales was like a bird dog the whole time.'

'I was hoping you might try something like that. The funny thing is that they nearly fucked themselves. They switched off every light on the bloody ship and we nearly got run down by a tanker!' Jim gave a short laugh. 'You should have seen their faces! I was sure that the Navy would pay us a visit from Gib, but nothing happened.'

Molloy nodded toward the cargo. 'You see what's there? Missiles, no less. This is not just a shipment of bloody Lee-Enfield rifles. There's enough stuff down here to start a fucking war.'

'You haven't even mentioned the chopper up on deck.' Jim sounded crushed by the enormity of it all. 'Christ knows what they intend to do with that!'

'You've seen nothing yet, come over here.' Eddie shone his torch over the plating on the ship's side low down near the hold flooring. The light picked up a string of innocent looking black wires. 'See those little blobs there?'

'Yes, what the hell are they?'

'That's plastic explosive,' replied Molloy. 'This ship is wired so they can blow the bottom out of her anytime they want. It's just as well the Navy didn't pay us a visit.'

'How do you know?'

Molloy gave a short laugh. 'I've seen it in the movies! What the hell else can it be? It's not fucking liquorice!'

Jim examined the wiring. It didn't bear thinking about. She would go down like a stone even if the cargo didn't explode. The whole bottom of the ship would blow out in one go. 'Christ!' he rasped. 'They can send her to the bottom anytime they like. Where do the wires go?'

Eddie shone the torch upwards to the hatch boards high above. 'Somewhere up there near the deck, but God knows what controls it. I'm no explosives expert.'

Not for the first time, Prendergast felt frustrated. 'Liam told me last night that we are heading for Galway.' He looked at his watch. 'We'd better get out of here before we're missed.'

Molloy smiled. 'Well, if it's Galway, at least we might not have too far to swim if they decide to blow the bottom out of her.' He led the way back into the engine room, and carefully re-arranged the oil drums to hide the access door.

As Jim climbed the ladder out of the engine room, Chico Gonzales suddenly appeared in the doorway, his cold brown eyes full of suspicion. 'Got a problem, Skipper?'

Prendergast pushed passed him. 'No, just checking with the

Chief on our fuel.'

Chico stood back and watched him return to the bridge. Jim could feel his eyes boring into his back.

Foster lay on his bunk and watched the shapes flickering on the deckhead as the ship rolled in a beam swell. His lip was still sore and the slow forming scab was annoying. Except for venturing out for food and briefing Buckholtz on the operation earlier, he hid himself away, his mind poring over every detail of his plan.

None of the others shared his dedication. He could see that clearly now. They had no faith, no beliefs. God was meaningless to them. The Americans were mercenaries doing this for money; and that German tramp! Her wanton sensuality sickened him to the pit of his stomach. Even now she was probably rutting like an animal with that bastard Buckholtz. He'd heard them at it many times. Maybe all the men were sharing her. He shuddered at the thought, wanting to vomit.

He gloated that he held a trump card that none of them knew about. Thanks to his friend Ghalboun, he had in his pocket the power to dispense life or death. He looked again at the tiny black digital radio that Ghalboun had given him in Tripoli, turning it over and over in his hands. It looked like a small transistor radio receiver and even worked like one until it was programmed. All he needed to do was punch in a coded number and it was primed. Press the red button – and boom! The whole festering lot of them were no more; himself included, unless he was careful. There had to be a way that he could achieve his goal as well as take his vengeance when the time came. Setting the radio aside, he lay back and fixed his eyes on the deckhead while he thought about it.

Thirty-Nine

Harry McDonagh bought his own fishing boat in Donegal and sailed her home to Roundstone in a state of nervous excitement. It probably represented the greatest landmark in his life.

Even his arrival off the pier was exciting, with half the village turning out to meet him. He had timed his arrival for a Sunday evening high tide to make his home coming as heroic and spectacular as possible. The weather was on his side; a recent rain shower had cleared away, leaving the air fresh and clean smelling. The purple backdrop of the Twelve Pins mountains seemed to smile benevolently in the sunshine.

Throttling back the engine fifty yards out, he could already see his old friend and ex-skipper, Charlie Donovan, waiting amongst the crowd to take his mooring lines. He had to resist pinching himself. Perhaps it was all a dream.

A crowd of animated holiday makers watched from the street above the harbour outside O'Dowds pub wondering what the commotion was all about. None of them could understand why such a small, insignificant looking boat should be the centre of so much attention. A man with a Dublin accent squeezed his way into the crowd lining the stone wall. 'What's going on?' he asked his neighbour. She was a middle aged woman whom he had seen earlier working at the supermarket checkout desk further down the street.

'It's Harry McDonagh,' she said proudly. 'He's bought his own boat. We never thought he'd do it.'

'Doesn't look like much to me,' the Dubliner said before pushing his way back inside the pub. He found his companion at the bar. 'He's arrived,' he said, 'but the boat doesn't look as big as that bastard Donovan let on.'

The second man peered at him with rheumy eyes and called for two more pints. 'If he said it's bigger than his own boat, that's good enough for me. What do we know about it, anyway?' He laughed coarsely. 'It's a long way from boats that we were reared. Neither of us would know one end from the other! I'll tell Harry Trent that it's all set and we've done our job exactly like he asked. Drink your bloody pint and let's get out of here. If we leave now we can be back in Dublin in time for a drink with the lads.'

Charlie Donovan ran a practiced eye over the boat as he tied her up. A bit worn and in need of a coat of paint, but otherwise she was a useful looking craft and much bigger than his own. Harry was going to have to spend plenty of sea time to pay off his bank loan on this one. Still, he might be able to help him there. He hadn't expected another job quite so soon, and this time he needed two boats. Harry could not have timed his arrival better.

He jumped down on deck and shook hands with a grinning McDonagh. 'Congrats, Harry,' he said sincerely. 'Welcome home!' Donovan poked his head inside the wheel house, noticing the new looking Raytheon fish finder. 'Nice,' he said appreciatively. 'What's the engine like?'

Harry proudly removed the engine cover. 'Ford Sabre, eighty horsepower, runs like a clock.'

'You've done well, Harry lad,' Charlie smiled. 'Now all you've got to do is pay for the bitch.'

Harry frowned. On the way down from Donegal that fact had never really been out of his mind for long. 'First payment's not due for a month,' he said, trying to sound confident.

Donovan placed a friendly hand on his shoulder. 'You're going to have to pull a lot of lobsters,' he joked. Then he became serious. 'We have a job to do on Saturday night. That should help. The money is even better than last time.'

The risks frightened McDonagh, but if he was going to pay for the boat, he needed the money. It occurred to him that maybe he should have stayed crewing for Donovan. At least he didn't have so much to worry about then. 'I'll be ready,' he said, squaring his shoulders.

The crowd was already dispersing from the pier, drifting in small groups back to the pub. Donovan smiled. 'That's my boy,' he said. 'Now you'd better come up and buy your fans a few pints.'

Jonathan Cooke shed his raincoat and surveyed his small office without much enthusiasm. He felt disgruntled and unappreciated and it was difficult to feel motivated into tackling the day's routine, but with the arrangements for the Prime Minister's visit now in place, he had a little more time to concentrate on other things.

He had done as much as he could to ensure that the Prime Minister's overnight stay in Ashford Castle would be without incident, and that the transfer to the RAF aircraft in Shannon the following day would be no different. Security was mostly in the hands of the Americans, anyway. Even the Garda Commissioner seemed happy about that, and didn't trouble to hide his belief that the Americans could handle it without interference from the British. Cooke had been in Ireland long enough to know that the Irish assumed that everything American represented the best. As the old enemy, the British would never wield the same influence.

His eyes settled on the wall map in his office and travelled the length of the Mediterranean to Turkey. He glanced at his wrist watch calendar; the *Maria B* should be there by now. Even that thought did little to excite him or raise his interest in the morning's affairs.

Ten minutes later, all that had changed. Lloyds of London were adamant after a second check that the ship had not arrived in Iskenderun. The only news of her they had on file was her departure from Valletta twelve days ago. Angrily, he realised that he had allowed himself to be lulled into thinking all was well. He had allowed the visit of a bunch of bloody politicians to distract him at a critical time.

He grabbed the phone and punched in the number of Toby Sims in Northwood.

'Toby? Good morning, Jonathan here. You and I have a problem, old son, and I want you to do something about it immediately. Don't give me any bullshit about making it official. That will be coming, in triplicate if you like.'

Sims stifled a sigh. 'Jonathan, good to hear from you, but you sound a bit snappy old boy,' he drawled. 'If it's about your *Maria B* again, I'm afraid I've got nothing for you, no reports whatsoever.'

'Toby, I want that bloody ship found,' Cooke insisted. 'She hasn't turned up in Iskenderun, and she was due there yesterday at the latest. The damned thing could be anywhere by now, but I'm willing to bet my pension that she is on her way back here.'

'Jonathan, really old chap, there's not much I can do. I'll send out another signal. But quite frankly, it really is like looking for the proverbial needle. You must understand that.'

'Just do it, Toby, anything.' Cooke trailed off, realising that he was asking the impossible.

'Leave it with me. I'll do my best.' Sims did not sound too hopeful.

'Thanks, Toby. I'll call you later.' Jonathan replaced the telephone, trying to think of some way out of his dilemma. If she was on her way back, why had he not heard anything from Prendergast? He went over to the wall chart, willing it to give up the secret. Down at the bottom, Libya tantalised him. He got a ruler and did a few rough measurements. There was ample time for the ship to have loaded there. She might even be clear into the Atlantic right now. In desperation he picked up the phone again. It couldn't hurt to check with Cassar.

'Jonathan, I thought we had finished with this matter.' Sir Harold Webster paused for a moment to stare at the portrait of the Queen on the wall, as though he was expecting her to provide inspiration. 'Why don't you turn the whole damned affair over to the Irish? Let them do something about it.'

Cooke shook his head. 'If guns are on the way here, they are destined for use against British troops in the North. Forgive me, but it's not an Irish priority. Look what happened to the *Claudia*. The Irish navy failed to trap all of that shipment. More than half of her cargo was landed before they even intercepted her.'

The Ambassador remained unconvinced. 'We can't prove anything, and we don't even know where this damned ship of yours is. She could be anywhere, you've admitted that yourself. Why not have our people pick up this Pavlides fellow in London? He must know her whereabouts.'

'I've already thought of that,' Cooke retorted. 'But we still have to catch her in the act. There's no other way, as far as I am concerned. We can deal with Pavlides afterwards in our own time.'

Sir Harold doodled for a moment, drawing a series of interlocking circles with a red pen on his desk pad. When he did eventually speak, he did so slowly, enunciating each word. 'Colonel, I will agree to having the ship tracked. But once she enters Irish territorial limits, if she does, the Irish authorities must deal with the situation. Under no circumstances will I sanction a military solution on our part. Do you understand me, Jonathan?'

'I understand, Ambassador. There is only one snag with that, Sir. I already know that at this moment the Irish navy has five operational ships capable of interception. One is in dry-dock in Cork, the second is waiting with a bent propeller shaft to get into the same dry-dock and a third is on a goodwill visit to Sweden. The other two are engaged in fishery protection duties and won't be diverted unless we come up with very solid reasons. I suggest that hardly constitutes an interception capability.'

'I don't give a tuppenny damn, Jonathan! That is entirely a matter for the Irish authorities. I won't have it any other way. Damn it man! The PM will be here in a few days. We cannot risk a diplomatic incident at a time like this. '

Cooke knew that any further progress with the Ambassador in his present mood was impossible. He thanked him and left the room without another word.

H.M.S. Onslaught, a diesel-electric attack submarine, cruised silently five hundred feet beneath the black waters of the Atlantic. Homeward bound to Gosport from the South Atlantic, her twin 3,000 horse power English Electric motors drove her close to a soundless seventeen knots.

The evening meal was over, and in the galley the clatter of pots and pans announced that the cooks were in a hurry to finish up for the evening as off duty sailors drifted away from the mess-room.

In her sonar room, the operators sat with glazed eyes staring at their screens and listening intently to the sounds in their head-phones from the sensitive hydrophones. Except for a shoal of chirping shrimps they had heard nothing during the entire watch.

Further forward, in the torpedo room, a few off duty ratings from the crew of sixty-four started the evening game of uckers. Others sat on their cots reading or talking quietly amongst themselves about their fast approaching home leave.

Commander Timothy Bligh was completing his routine evening rounds of the control room. A big man, leaning towards being overweight thanks to the quality of the food on board, his flaming red beard picked up the reflected light from a myriad of dials and instruments. Unlike his namesake and early predecessor, Bligh's popularity with his crews bordered on something near to being God-like and was the talk of the submarine service. He epitomised the Elizabethan buccaneer in the modern navy.

Suddenly the quiet hum of the control room was shattered. 'Bridge – Sonar. Surface contact bearing zero-one-zero, speed one-zero knots, heading three-five-six.'

Bligh picked up a hand mike, speaking calmly in low tones. 'Sonar, bridge. Range as soon as you have it.'

'Bridge, sonar. Range one-five miles.'

'Thank you Sonar.' Bligh turned to the officer of the watch, 'Plot, Number One! Give me a solution when ready. Bring her to periscope depth if you please.'

'Aye-aye Sir, periscope depth! Coxswain, two degrees on fore and aft planes. Check all main vents shut!'

'Two degrees on fore and aft planes, Sir. All main vents shut!'

'Blow one and two!'

'Blowing one and two, Sir!'

In the bowels of the boat the sound of compressed air blowing water ballast preceded the slight incline to the main deck as the submarine headed for the surface. Minutes later the submarine levelled off thirty-five feet below the grey surface.

'Periscope depth, Sir! Thirty-five feet and steady. Course three-six-zero, speed sixteen decimal five.'

'Up search scope!'

With a gentle whoosh the great cylindrical tube of the periscope rose through the decking. Bligh removed his cap and peered through the eye-piece, turning the big Barr & Stroud periscope smoothly onto the known bearing.

It was not yet dark on the surface, but nightfall was only a short time away. A leaden sky brooded over sullen waves where half a mile ahead, the black shape of a small freighter wallowed in a quartering sea. As he watched, her navigation lights flickered on and he could see someone crossing along her boat deck.

'Bring her to three-five-five. Speed one-two, if you please Number One.'

Bligh watched carefully as he overtook the surface ship and slowly drew abeam of her. The light was fading rapidly now, but he could see a name on her bow every time a wave lifted it skywards. Squinting anxiously he deciphered it – *Maria B*, in rough white lettering.

'Down scope! With a hiss the periscope sped back into place. Bring her back on zero-nine-zero, speed one-six, at five-zero feet'

The First Lieutenant methodically carried out his instructions.

'Zero-nine-zero Sir, speed one-six, level at five-zero!'

Bligh left the Control Room and made for the communications centre. Whatever it meant, he had picked up the ship that Northwood was interested in, but having no orders to do otherwise, he was already back on course and speeding away from the scene at sixteen knots.

Fifteen minutes later, *Onslaught* extended her radio antenna above the surface and spat the signal into the atmosphere.

Forty

Commander Toby Sims worked his way through his morning in-tray methodically but without any great enthusiasm. The rumour mill had it that he was going back to sea duties. He couldn't wait, although so far he had been successful in hiding that from his superiors.

The signal from *H.M.S. Onslaught* came out from the bottom of the pile an hour later. It had been transmitted as a non-priority message the night before. Clutching the thin sheet of paper Sims hurried to the operations room.

'Jonathan? Toby here.' Sims didn't try to disguise his excitement.

Jonathan Cooke put down his pen. 'Get on with it, Toby, what have you got for me?'

'One of our subs picked up your *Maria B* last night just before dark.'

Cooke felt a rush of adrenaline. Got you, you bastards! 'Where?'

Toby paused to read the signal on his desk. 'I won't confuse you with latitude and longitude,' he said. 'Midway between Spain and Ireland, roughly three hundred miles south of The Fastnet heading north at ten knots.'

Cooke glanced up at his wall map. It all tied in, even the report from Gibraltar that an unlit ship passed through the Straits two nights ago. That had to be her. He had been right all along. 'Good work, old boy. I assume your sub is tracking her?'

Sims sighed, 'Unfortunately not. She didn't have orders to do so. We didn't see the report until a few minutes ago. The submarine is heading home to Gosport. At a rough guess she is approaching the Channel right now at least three hundred miles from the contact.'

'Damn it, Toby! We could lose her!' Cooke fought to control himself.

'We're working on it. If the sub has sufficient fuel, we'll turn her back. She is due to come to periscope depth and report an hour from now.'

Cooke struggled against his sense of impotence. He hated not being in control. 'I'm not going to say it again, Toby, we have to know what that ship is doing. Now that we've found her, I don't want to lose her.'

'Keep your hair on old boy. We'll find her again, don't worry.'

'I hope so.' Cooke put down his telephone. 'I bloody well hope so,' he said again, glaring at the wall map.

Combers driven by a near-gale followed the *Maria B*, helping her on her way. Only in an extra heavy roll did the waves manage to break inboard through the bulwark scuppers.

Prendergast watched from the bridge as Buckholtz and Gonzales waited for an opportunity to traverse the welldeck without getting wet feet. Seeing an opportunity as the bows reared skywards, they ran forward and clambered up onto the covered hatch and disappeared through a small door in the container.

It was already noticeably colder as they moved further northwards. They now needed to keep the wheel house doors closed, and the tiny compartment seemed cramped and unusually claustrophobic after weeks spent in the heat of the Mediterranean.

Jim hunched his shoulders as a bigger wave lifted them and the autopilot whirred desperately to counteract the force of the ship surging forward on the wave crest.

Liam clutched at the wheel pedestal trying to keep his footing on the sloping deck. 'Damn it!' he shouted, 'how do you stick this job, day in and day out?' His face looked pale as he fought off another wave of nausea.

Jim grinned at him, enjoying his discomfiture. 'Do it for long enough and you hardly notice it anymore. What are those two doing down there in the container?'

'Checking the chopper, I suppose. They're going to have to fly the thing off soon enough. Wouldn't you want to be sure it worked?' He gave a short laugh. 'If you ask me they're crazy. I'll be glad to see the backs of the pair of them.'

Jim tried to sound nonchalant. 'I thought we would be putting in somewhere to unload it .'

'Well,' Liam said, 'You're wrong. Those two nutters will fly it off, and the rest of the stuff will be unloaded at sea, six miles out.'

'That's going to be difficult with the container on deck, unless we do it after they take off.'

Liam shrugged, 'That's your problem. Once the chopper is off you can dump it overboard, if you like. That way, there's nothing to connect you with this once everything is landed.'

Prendergast thought about it for a moment. 'Are you all leaving with the cargo, then?'

'Yeah, that's the general idea.' Liam lit a cigarette but it made him feel seasick again. He stubbed it out and tottered toward an open window. Reaching the window, he held on to the ledge and breathed deeply, willing his stomach to settle.

'Try to look at the sky, not at the sea,' Jim said. 'You'll feel better.'

'Never,' replied Liam. 'I'll never get used to this.'

Below them, the truncated form of Foster appeared and scuttled along the deck towards the container. He timed it badly as a wave broke in front of him, soaking him waist high and almost sweeping him off his feet. Forgetting his seasickness, Liam laughed uncontrollably.

'You and he don't seem to get on too well,' Jim commented.

Liam's laughter died. 'Only the devil himself gets on with that bastard. Watch your back when that fucker is around.' He lapsed into silence for a moment and then added, 'You don't have to worry about me, but watch out for Foster, don't cross him.'

At that moment the door opened and a blast of wind preceded Lisa Schmitt. 'Lunch time!' she announced. 'Chili con carne! You can get yours now, Liam. I'll stay up here for a while.'

The thought of food made Liam's stomach churn. He left the bridge without another word.

Damn! Prendergast thought. Just as I was getting somewhere with Liam, she had to arrive. 'You sound cheerful.'

'That's because we'll be home soon. I'm looking forward to that. I might even take a holiday,' she replied. 'Would you like a coffee?' Not waiting for a reply, Lisa picked up the electric kettle and went into the chart room.

Prendergast listened to her humming for a while, but above it the faint sound of hammering from inside the container reached him and he turned back to the window. He didn't hear her return until she silently handed him a mug. 'Thank you,' he said.

'Don't mention it.' Lisa took a contemplative sip at her coffee. She saw Foster poking his head out of the container door. He glanced up at the bridge and then vomited onto the hatch cover before disappearing back inside. 'What's he doing down there,' she asked, frowning.

'How the hell should I know?' Prendergast sounded annoyed.

Lisa put her mug down and shrugged off her anorak, throwing it in a corner. Her sweater emphasised her breasts. She saw Prendergast look away immediately. She fluffed out her damp hair. 'Do I bother you, Captain?'

'Of course not,' Jim replied. He felt himself colouring and switched on the radar. He hid his discomfort behind the screen for some time; even on the forty-five mile range it showed nothing except specks of clutter from the sea.

'When do you think we will arrive?' She peeked at him over the rim of her mug.

'Tomorrow night, at this rate. We're making very good time with this wind and sea behind us.'

'Excellent.' She joined him by the radar set and placed her hand on his arm. 'Then you'll be rid of us. You'll like that, won't you?'

'I don't really give a damn.'

'Come now,' she pressed. 'I can feel how much you want that.'

Jim felt the warm pressure of her breast on his arm and jerked away. Just then he saw a quick flash on the radar screen dead astern of them. Something was back there, right at the limit of the range.

Lisa moved closer to the screen. He could feel her breath against his cheek.

'You must explain how this radar works,' she whispered.

At that moment he knew that if he wanted this woman, he could have her. Right now at this instant ... his cabin was only yards away. A second flash on the screen as the radar beam swept the sea behind them wiped desire from his mind. Something was there. He moved away from her and went outside into the wind.

Prendergast swept the horizon with his binoculars, but could see nothing. The wind whipped at him, chilling him. Nothing was back there except rolling seas with breaking white tops. The first patter of rain drove him back inside and he returned to the radar. This time, no echo showed on the screen. He watched the spot, waiting for a recurrence before he decided he must have imagined it.

Lisa waved at Buckholtz as he emerged and ran across the deck. Jim glanced at her. The moment was already lost. She had retreated as quickly as she had come, leaving him dissatisfied and irritable. It was just as well. Seconds later, a vision of Jane drifted past him, as though to admonish him for desiring another woman.

The black shape of the helicopter filling the inside of the container left little space to work in, but a series of powerful lights wired into the ship's power supply flooded the interior with light.

Foster sat on the floor feeling miserable. His clothes were soaking and he had already been sick twice. His misery seemed hilarious to Buckholtz and Gonzales, and any comments they directed to him were designed to magnify his discomfort. He tried to ignore them. Even the waves of nausea that gripped him could not diminish his feeling of exultation that the end was near. His eyes gleamed as he watched Gonzales unclip the lid of the first crate containing the missiles.

Gonzales and Buckholtz lifted the olive green twin missile pod from its container and clipped it into place on a small wing-like projection on the fuselage. They made the operation look incredibly simple.

Foster felt oddly disappointed. It did not look quite as lethal as he expected, just two simple tubes about three inches in diameter containing the five foot missiles. 'Is that it?' he asked, 'As simple as that?'

Buckholtz guffawed. 'That's it, buddy, simple as that. But if you got one of these babies up your ass, you'd wish your mommy had never fucked your daddy!'

Gonzales hoisted the second pair into place on the opposite side of the fuselage. He swung a boot at Foster. 'If you don't get out of the fucking way we might even let you taste one person-ally!'

Wiping a smear of grease from his hands on some cotton waste, Buckholtz turned to Gonzales. 'I'll leave the rest to you, Chico. I'm going to get my head down for a couple of hours. Just check the fire control instruments are green before you fin-ish up.' He gripped his crotch and leered at Foster. 'I might even have a hot date later. That Kraut broad can't get enough of this!'

Foster immediately felt sick and ran for the door. He could hear the two of them laughing as he dry-retched outside on the hatch cover.

When he got back inside, Buckholtz had gone and Gonzales was inside the Plexiglas dome of the cockpit. He lost his footing as the ship lurched crazily on an extra large wave, sending him sprawling across the floor of the container. His little black radio slipped out of his anorak pocket, skidding toward one of the helicopter landing skids. Foster scrambled to his feet and threw himself after it. Just as his fingers reached it, a heavy boot landed on his wrist and he screamed in pain. He didn't even see the combat knife until Gonzales pricked his throat with it, drawing a trickle of blood.

Gonzales reached down and snatched the radio from his hand. 'What the fuck is this?' he rasped.

Foster squirmed to free himself but he felt the boot grinding his wrist bone into the steel decking. 'Just a radio,' he gasped through the pain.

Gonzales slowly released him and the knife vanished magically into his boot. Turning the radio over in his hand he eyed it suspiciously for a moment, then, to Foster's horror he switched it on. There came the faint sound of music from a distant radio station that became louder as Gonzales adjusted the volume control. Gonzales dropped it onto Foster's chest. 'Just checking, buddy, just checking. Now get the fuck out of here!'

Foster pocketed the tiny radio and fled from the container, his hatred boiling.

Forty-One

Muffled by ornate dining room doors, the sound of applause signalled that the final after dinner speech was ending. In the oak-panelled lounge, Jonathan Cooke finished his brandy and straightened his bow tie. Thank God, he thought. This damned charade was almost over and he could finally go to bed.

Directly across the room from him, two men in identical navy blue suits stirred themselves in their armchairs and got to their feet. From their shiny black shoes to their short cut fair hair they were like clones. Even their white shirts and red ties were the same. Outside in the rain-swept grounds he knew there were more of them, cutouts drifting in pairs as darkness fell on Ashford Castle.

He tried to reject the thought that he was forming an intense dislike for the American Secret Service team, but it was becoming increasingly difficult. Heavy-handed and arrogant in their overblown sense of importance, they were a constant irritant that only the Irish seemed to be able to accept. Perhaps that was the price for being a second rate power in a shrinking world. If so, he wanted no more of it.

The doors opened wide and two more sharp-eyed agents appeared, followed by the President of the United States. His carefully cultivated smile was fixed in place, ready for the cameras. Beside him, was the Irish Taoiseach, looking pleased and self-important. Somewhere a flash camera exploded with light, and Cooke, leaning on his walking stick, watched with ill-concealed amusement as the Secret Service team went through their routine.

Behind the President came the British Prime Minister, looking relaxed but oddly donnish and unkempt, his hair in careful disarray, dandruff flecking the shoulders of his dinner jacket. At the back, towering over all of them, the formidable bulk of the German Chancellor appeared. As always, he was serious and haughty, and his features reflected an inimitable look of vague disapproval.

Minor dignitaries and their retinues filled the lounge. Here and there, a splash of colour from a scattering of ladies' dresses broke the sobriety of black dinner jackets. Handshakes and friendly farewells over with, the chief players retired to their rooms on the first floor, leaving the others to break into groups for post dinner brandies – and more bullshit, Cooke thought.

He remained only long enough to ensure that the Prime Minister had settled in his rooms. Passing the oil paintings and the suits of armour in the hallway without a second glance, he climbed the oak staircase as quickly as his cane would allow. Behind him, at the main entrance door, two uniformed Gardai looked on with bewilderment as the Americans sealed the ground floor into a fortress for the night.

The hallway outside the Prime Minister's rooms was quiet and well lit. Two vigilant MI5 agents sat alertly on either side of the door. Cooke spoke to them only briefly before ascending a further flight of stairs to his own room. Once inside, he closed the door and removed his dinner jacket and tie. He unbuttoned his shirt collar and limped over to the window. Opening it wide, he lit a cigar and exhaled into the night, satisfied that he could relax at last.

Except for the three huge Presidential helicopters bathed in floodlights below on the manicured lawns, there was an air of tranquillity and luxury to the castle and its grounds that few places could match. Away in the distance near the walled entrance gates, a few dim lights from Cong village twinkled in a faint drizzle of rain. Overhead the sky was heavy with cloud, and no stars showed. Somewhere in nearby trees a pheasant called into the night and down by the lake an unseen heron answered.

So far so good, Cooke mused. Puffing his cigar into life he watched the pale smoke idly rising into the damp night air, his thoughts turning to the *Maria B.*

Where was she right now, he wondered. The last he had heard was that the Royal Navy had picked her up again but she was remaining well out in international waters and making no attempt to close with the Irish coast. Of one thing he felt certain; the IRA would never penetrate Ashford Castle. Not tonight anyway. The joint press conference that afternoon had seen to that. Peace was really on the cards, and it was all up to Gerry Adams now. He had been given the final ultimatum. If he agreed to decommission weapons, the bloodshed and the years of agony would end. By six o'clock tomorrow morning it would no longer be Cooke's worry. Finishing his cigar, he half closed the window and went to bed.

The night was as black as any Prendergast had ever seen as he altered course eastwards towards an unseen coastline. An incessant drizzle hid both the powerful light on Slyne Head and the weaker one on the Eeragh rocks. There was little wind and only the residue of a heavy swell remained from the gale that had driven them north during the past two days.

He felt unbelievably weary. The strain was beginning to tell, and even Eddie Molloy seemed to have gone downhill in the past couple of days. At dinner time that night, he had been taciturn and looking older than Jim had ever seen him.

For the past hour Prendergast had hardly left the glowing radar screen. The first irradiant trace of the Aran Islands was already showing, but his eyes still flickered off to the southern quadrant where he thought he had seen the echoes the day before. The blip had never shown itself again.

The wheel house door slid open and Buckholtz and Gonzales squeezed through it. 'How's it going, Skip?' Buckholtz growled. Dressed in a zippered flying suit, he seemed bulkier than ever, filling the tiny space.

Jim answered him with a malevolent glare. 'It's like dipping for apples in a barrel,' he griped. 'Without a VHF the chances of finding the boats on a night like this aren't too good.'

Buckholtz nodded to Gonzales. 'Take care of it Chico,' he ordered.

Gonzales drew a screwdriver from his flying suit pocket and went into the chart room. Jim followed him and watched as he unscrewed the front panel of the VHF. He made an adjustment to something inside. 'That's it, Skipper,' he said, replacing the panel. 'It's all yours, but don't try anything funny with it. Otherwise ...' He drew his finger across his throat. 'Get my drift?'

Jim scowled. 'Do you think I'm crazy or what?' Gonzales withdrew to a dark corner of the wheel house.

A few minutes later, Liam joined them on the bridge. Prendergast felt glad to see him. Right then he seemed to be the only sane one amongst the lot of them. The combination of wet clothing and damp bodies began to steam up the wheel house windows. Jim opened two of them to let in more air.

Standing as far apart from the others as the confined space allowed, Liam appeared to be tense and ill at ease. Prendergast wandered over to him and said, 'Gonzales has fixed the VHF. I'll be making a call shortly and I need to know the name of the boat.'

Liam's face lit in the brief orange glow of a cigarette. His eyes looked puffy and tired. 'That's fine with me, but don't use the ship's name. Your code name is "Freedom One". The fishing boats will answer to "Freedom Two". Make the call only on channel 77, they have instructions to listen on that channel.'

A splatter of heavy rain rattled against the forward windows and sent rivulets of water spiralling down the glass. Below them, the decks took on an ebony sheen. 'Looks like we're home,' Liam said, slamming shut the windows. 'Always fucking raining, isn't it.'

Jim ignored him and searched the radar screen for movement. He found only the scattered echoes from the rock fringed island coastline twenty-five miles away. Maybe there was nobody waiting to meet them. He stifled a smile. Wouldn't that upset their apple cart!

The VHF hissed at him as he switched it to channel 77. He turned down the squelch control and spoke into the microphone. 'Freedom Two this is Freedom One, how do you read, over.' Silence returned to him. Perhaps they were still out of range. He made the call again. Still nothing. Hanging up the microphone, he turned up the volume on the set and went back to the others in the wheel house.

Buckholtz looked at him expectantly. 'Nothing?'

'Nothing,' Prendergast replied. 'If they're still well inshore, we might not be in range yet.'

Buckholtz swore under his breath and turned on Liam. 'I hope you guys haven't fucked this one up.'

Liam watched the rain coursing down the glass. 'They'll be here,' he said , moving closer to the windows.

In the darkness Chico Gonzales rocked on the balls of his feet trying to dispel the tension that always consumed him before action. Reaching into his pocket, he pulled out a small plastic wallet and dipped his finger inside. He rubbed some of the cocaine on his gums, massaging gently until calmness washed over him. Inhaling deeply, he returned the packet to his pocket and followed Buckholtz out into the rain.

Jim turned to Liam after they had gone. 'Those two are a bit jumpy,' he commented.

Liam shrugged his shoulders. 'We're all too bloody jumpy if you ask me.' He watched Gonzales and Buckholtz scurry across the foredeck towards the container. 'I've said it before and I'll say it again, I won't be sorry to see them gone.'

Jim couldn't make out Liam's features in the darkness. 'Why?'

A memory of Big Jim Hogan flitted into Liam's mind and he stiffened, clenching his fists. 'We've bitten off more than we can chew this time,' he muttered. 'Those two don't give a shit. They're like you, in it for the fucking money, not for any other reason.'

Prendergast fell silent and went over to the radar screen. The first trace of the mainland was showing as the beam picked up the finger of Slyne Head on the port bow. He adjusted the range cursor and measured a range of thirty-five miles. Another hour would see them twenty-five miles off, but still there was nothing moving out there, no sign of any boats. He looked up and studied the back of Liam's head. It didn't seem to matter to Liam that the guns were intended for the purpose of killing people, innocent people maybe. He swallowed hard. People perhaps like Jane and Susan. 'What happens to me and my crew after this is all over?'

Liam turned and faced him, 'What do you mean by that? You get your money and live happily ever after.'

'This ship is wired so that you can blow the bottom out of her anytime you like. How do I know you won't do that as soon as you get what you want?' Jim couldn't stop the words from coming out. The reaction he got was worth it.

Liam lit another cigarette. His cupped hands shook slightly. 'I don't know what you're fucking talking about.'

Prendergast turned on him. 'I've seen it down in the hold. Plastic explosive, all wired up and ready to go. If you don't know about that, who the hell does?'

Foster? Lisa? What the hell was this, Liam thought. His hands trembled as he sucked on his cigarette, trying to hide his emotions. Somewhere in the back of his mind Jim Hogan returned. There had to be a connection. 'You've nothing to fear from me,' he said gruffly to Jim. Then more softly, 'I know who you are. You've suffered enough already.'

Jim's mouth dropped open. He felt his heart racing. 'What does that mean?'

'It means that I know about your wife and kid. I'm sorry.'

Jim blinked his eyes trying to understand, struggling to get the words out. He felt like a man who had just stepped into a minefield. 'You were there ... on that ship – the *Georgios*?'

Liam gripped his arm with fingers like a vice. 'No, I wasn't.' His voice was hoarse. 'But I heard about it. It was an accident, nothing else. I wasn't going to tell you. I'm sorry.'

Prendergast shrugged him off roughly. 'You expect me to believe that you bastard!' Right then he wanted to kill the man, tear him with his bare hands, maim him, anything. 'We were run down deliberately, don't you fucking well understand that?' Blindly, he threw himself at Liam's dark shape, his hands groping out to throttle him.

Street-wise and more experienced, Liam sidestepped deftly and rammed his fist into Prendergast's groin. The pain brought Prendergast retching to his knees. The next moment he felt cold steel on his forehead and heard the hammer click back. 'Stop, or I'll drop you right now!' Liam's voice was icy. 'Now you fucking listen to me! How did you get into that bloody hold? I want you to ...' The engine room voice pipe whistled angrily. Liam hauled Prendergast to his feet. 'Answer that!'

Pulling the whistle from the voice pipe, Jim fought off a need to be sick. 'Bridge,' he coughed, putting his ear to the pipe.

Above the roar of the engine, Eddie Molloy's voice was faint but clear. 'Jim, I've got a fuel pump problem down here, I need to slow her down, and I might have to kill the engine for a while. It'll take me the best part of an hour. It's not an act, Jim, this is for real.'

'Do it Chief, but don't fuck around, be as quick as you can. Get Matty Lyons down there if you need help.' Prendergast stuffed the whistle back in the pipe and painfully turned to face Liam. 'We've got engine trouble. We're slowing down.'

'Shit!' Liam exclaimed, ramming the pistol into his ribs, 'Okay, make another call, no tricks.' He backed Jim towards the chart room and the VHF radio.

Close to the sweeping beam of the Slyne Head lighthouse Harry McDonagh bit his lip and stared into the blackness of Joyce's Sound. Picking up a rag, he mopped at a puddle of water forming on the instrument panel as a succession of rain drops found their way through a crack somewhere in the deck-head. With the engine stopped, the boat sat waiting in the darkness. Only the gentle hiss from his VHF and the slap of small waves against the wooden hull broke the eerie stillness that comes with rain on a windless night.

A few hundred yards away Charlie Donovan kept the same lonely vigil in his own boat. He did not share the same dread that wrapped Harry in its icy shroud. Patiently he sipped a mug of coffee and watched the radar screen for any sign of movement away to the south. He double checked that he had the VHF switched to the correct channel. An hour ago there had been a brief burst of static as if from an out of range transmission. Since then he'd heard nothing. Maybe they're not coming, he thought. He looked across at the dark shape of Harry's boat. Jesus! How was he going to keep Harry from cracking up if they had to wait out here every night like this? This was the second night. Another would drive him crazy.

Without warning, the VHF came to life. Charlie jumped. 'Freedom Two, Freedom Two this is Freedom One, how do you read, over!' The voice was faint as though coming from the maximum range. He picked up the microphone and replied, but there was no response. Damn! He was too close in among the rocks of Slyne Head. They must be blanketing his aerial. They needed to move out into clear water; he should have thought of it before. He slammed down the handset and went out on deck.

'Harry,' Donovan shouted, 'Did you get that? Start up, we're moving out. Keep close and head southwest!'

McDonagh had heard it all right, but he wished he hadn't. For the last hour he had been hoping that they were not coming. Now he knew he had to go. There was no avoiding it. He poked his head outside his wheel house trying to instill some confidence into his voice. 'Okay! Lead the way, I'll follow you.'

Two powerful diesel engines coughed into life and the pair of boats nosed their way through familiar black rocks for the open sea.

Eddie Molloy throttled back the engine of the *Maria B* and puffed his way up the ladder from the engine room to wake Matty Lyons. He hadn't told anyone, but for the past few days he had been getting recurring pains in his chest and he felt tired and dizzy most of the time. He hated to admit it, but maybe his age was finally catching up on him. Slowly he was beginning to accept that this might have to be his last voyage.

'Shake yourself, Matty! We've got work to do!' Matty Lyons

opened his eyes and blinked at Molloy in the harshness of the bare overhead light bulb. Reluctantly he swung his skinny legs over the edge of the bunk coaming and stood shivering bare-footed in his underpants. 'Okay, Chief. I'll be right down, just give me time to take a crap.'

In the other bunk in the tiny shared cabin, Jimmy Lafferty groaned and rolled over, stuffing his tousled head of red hair fur-ther down into the warm cocoon of his sleeping bag.

'You too, Lafferty!' Molloy roared. 'Get out of your bloody pit, I need both of you down below!'

Returning to the engine room, Molloy dragged a box of tools across the steel plates of the floor, towards the spasmodic diesel engine. Suddenly, he felt the stabbing pain in his chest again. It was like a red hot knife. He straightened up, seeking relief, and looked directly into Foster's piercing eyes. He held a pistol. 'What the fuck are you doing down here? Get out of my engine room and put that bloody gun away!' Eddie reached for the throttle and stilled the beat of the engine.

Foster took a step forward and raised the gun. 'More to the point, why is the engine stopping?' His voice sounded high-pitched and unnatural.

Molloy picked up a wrench from the tool box and raised it. 'Get out of my way, you bloody eejit!' As he swung the wrench, he saw the flash from the gun muzzle and suddenly the pain in his chest became excruciating as his ears registered the crack of the revolver. He crashed backwards and slid to a sitting position up against the hot engine casing, the spanner slipping from his grasp and spinning uselessly across the steel floor. With both hands he clutched his chest and stared numbly at the blood seep-ing through his fingers. 'You fucking mad bastard,' he muttered as a fit of coughing overtook him, and the pain intensified.

Foster's eyes were full of disbelief. He hadn't meant to shoot him, not yet anyway. A rattle of boots on the ladder leading to the deck diverted him and he whirled around to face the new threat. Self-preservation was all that mattered now.

Lafferty was still half asleep as he stepped off the last rung of the ladder, but he became wide-awake when he saw the sprawled figure of Molloy. Eddie's pain-filled eyes flickered a single warning as Lafferty swung round to see Foster crouching a yard away, wide-eyed and still clutching the gun.

'W-w-hat the ... ' His mouth sagged open. It was Jimmy's last stutter. The bullet hit him full in the mouth blasting four of his teeth out through the back of his head. Lafferty was already dead when his body crashed backwards and upset a half-full drum of lubricating oil. The trickling oil mingled with the blood spilling from his terrible head wound and spread in a widening pool on the deck.

Molloy lay there and watched in horror as Foster made the sign of the cross over Lafferty's body and mumbled what sounded like a short prayer. He slid into unconsciousness as Foster turned and scurried back up the ladder to the deck.

As the ship slowed to a stop, a distraught Matty Lyons burst into the wheel house, ashen white, and incoherently poured out his story. Then his legs weakened under him, and he stumbled to a stool in the corner. Slowly, he realised that maybe, he too, would be lying in the carnage of the engine room if he had not had to go to the lavatory.

Prendergast broke into a stumbling run across the slippery afterdeck the pain in his stomach but a memory. Behind him he could hear Liam's shoes thudding on the planking, following him. The old engineer opened his eyes as Jim bent over him. A thin trickle of blood dribbled through his bristle of beard as he tried to speak.

Jim heard Liam clattering down the ladder behind him. 'Take it easy, Eddie, don't try to move. What the hell happened, who did it?'

Eddie's voice was a faint croak. 'Foster ... the bastard,' he whispered. 'He's gone off his head.'

Prendergast stood up and whirled round on Liam. 'You hear that, you fucker! By Jesus, you bastards have a lot to answer for! Help me for Christ's sake, we've got to get him up on deck. He needs help and we're going to have to use the radio to get it.'

Liam took a step forward. His lips formed into a tight line in a face devoid of emotion. 'No radio,' he said.

Jim felt Molloy's hand tugging at his trouser leg and bent to put his ear closer. 'I don't want to be moved, Jim, there's not enough time for that. Send down Lyons, I can tell him what to do with the engine.' The old engineer broke into a spasm of coughing and a blob of unnaturally dark blood appeared at the corner of his mouth. He reached for Prendergast's arm. 'Just do what you're bloody told for once!' A faint smile played on his lips before he drifted off again.

When Prendergast next looked at Liam he could tell something had changed. The man seemed to have reached a decision. Liam fixed him in a steady gaze. 'Show me how you got into that cargo hold,' he said.

'Go to hell!' Jim screamed.

Liam bunched Jim's shirt in his fist and pulled him forwards until his face was only inches away. 'I'm trying to help you, damn it! Don't you understand that, you stupid bastard! There will be no more killing. I want my guns off, but no more killing. I promise you that.'

'What do you mean?' Prendergast asked, 'What the hell is going on? What are you doing with the helicopter anyway?'

'They're going to take out the President of the United States!'

Prendergast's mind went into overdrive as the enormity of Liam's admission hit him. 'You mean they're going to kill him? Where? How?'

Liam gave a harsh laugh, 'Right here in Ireland, pal. They're planning to shoot the fucker right out of the sky just before dawn. The British P.M. along with him, not that I give a shit about him, but this has gone too far. Now, do your friend Molloy one last favour and get me into that cargo hold.'

Stepping gingerly over Lafferty's body, Prendergast led the way through the inspection hatch hidden in the corner of the engine room.

Jim switched on a torch, flashing its light over the cargo and along the ship's hull plating. 'There's some of your plastic explosive,' he said bitterly, allowing the beam from the torch to rest for a moment on the rusty plating.

Liam brushed past him and ran a practiced eye along the wiring as far into the darkness as he could see. 'Forget that for the moment, there's time enough for that. Shine the torch over here on the weapons.' It took only a minute to find what he was looking for. He dragged out a five-foot long olive green alloy box. 'This will do,' he grunted.

The yellow pool of light wavered over the covering lid held in place by three locking catches. Jim read the yellow stencilled markings: *Rocket Ammunition with Explosive Projectile. Re-usable Container. Do not Destroy.*

'You lead the way,' Liam whispered. 'Warn me if there's anyone about up on deck.'

Lisa Schmitt woke as the noise of the engine died away. She had been dreaming but couldn't remember what about. Drowsily, she lay in the darkness for several minutes listening to the unnatural silence. For an instant she wondered if the ship was sinking. The thought galvanised her into action.

Jumping down from her bunk she pulled on her clothes. Then she realised that she could still hear the faint hum of the generator. Cursing, she switched on the cabin lights, catching a glimpse of her tousled hair in the mirror over the washbasin. There was no time to do anything about it now. She clicked a seven-shot magazine into the butt of a Walther PPK pistol and stuffed the gun into her anorak pocket before leaving the cabin.

She waited outside on deck for several moments. From somewhere forward she could hear noises coming from the deck container and she padded off in that direction.

The first greenish blip from a surface ship showed on Charlie Donovan's radar screen at a range of twelve miles. He had expected to pick it up much sooner as he was already further offshore than had been planned. Altering course more to the west he strained his eyes to see something, but ahead of him, all was blackness. Again, he tried the VHF and got no reply.

Fifty yards astern, Harry McDonagh followed, becoming

increasingly nervous with each revolution of his boat's engine. The only thing that kept him going was the thought that a bank payment on his boat was due in four day's time and he didn't have the money to meet it. He listened to Charlie's call on the VHF and worried about what no reply really meant.

The two approaching boats were showing on the radar now. This time the VHF radio got through to them, and the relief in Charlie Donovan's voice was palpable as he answered the call. Shakily, Jim replaced the microphone and returned to the wheel house. There was little to do now except wait. The boats would be alongside in an hour, maybe less. He had sent Lyons below to sort out the engine, and by that time, hopefully, it would be repaired.

He stood for a while looking down on the foredeck. Of Liam there was no sign. He hadn't seen him since he left him on the afterdeck. Foster and Lisa were both standing in the drizzle, watching Gonzales remove the canvas cover from the top of the container. He wondered what Liam was up to. The man was a terrorist, plain and simple. Not only that, one that had played a part in the death of Jane and Susan. And now he had to trust him. He shuddered and stared into the night towards the invisible Aran Islands. On a clearer night, the flash of Eeragh Lighthouse should be there somewhere in the east. It was time now to get the gun from his cabin. There might not be another opportunity.

As soon as he opened the drawer he knew there was something wrong. He scrabbled amongst the clothing, throwing it onto the floor until the drawer was empty. The gun was gone.

Swearing at his own stupidity he returned to the wheel house, taking up his station at the windows just as the first section of the container was lowered into position. The helicopter revealed itself, a dull sheen forming on its metal fuselage as the damp fingers of the night air caressed it. Nearby, Gonzales waited with his ladder to extend the rotor blades into position for flight.

Gene Buckholtz ran his fingers quickly over a line of switches and the instrument panel flickered to life, bathing the cramped cockpit in an eerie green light. Beside him, Gonzales eyed the instruments as the engine coughed just once before building its pitch into a powerful whine.

Buckholtz flicked another switch into its on position and a red light shone back, indicating that the missiles were activated and ready to fly. He adjusted his helmet microphone and spoke into the intercom. 'Looks good, Chico, she's ready. We'll go in two hours time.'

Chico scanned the engine monitors and replied with the thumbs up sign. Even in the faint light from the instruments, his dark eyes revealed the excitement that now consumed him.

Satisfied, Buckholtz shut down the engine and removed his helmet. Through the Plexiglas nose cone he could see Foster's fleshy white face staring anxiously from the deck below. Lisa stood a few feet away from him, her blonde hair hanging damply about her head. She looked cold and uncomfortable, and without make-up the blatant sexiness was gone.

Buckholtz switched on a cockpit light and swivelled to face Gonzales. 'I've been thinking a lot lately, Chico,' he growled. He nodded in Foster's direction. 'These fuckers are a bunch of amateurs and we've got a wad of money riding on this one. Enough to put us in clover, know what I mean?'

Chico's eyes slitted and his hand fidgeted at the hilt of his combat knife. 'You want me to take care of 'em?'

'Naw, nothing like that,' Buckholtz shook his head. 'I just think that maybe when its over we look after ourselves that's all. Once we do the job there is nowhere to fly to; with only enough fuel for two hundred and fifty miles we would be sitting ducks. The sky is going to be a fucking war zone! What I mean is, we don't bring the chopper back out here to ditch near the ship. We ditch her close inshore and get out of the country under our own steam.'

'Like a couple of tourists?' Gonzales smiled. The idea appealed to him.

'Yeah! Something like that.' Buckholtz grinned and patted him on the knee. 'We've been at this too long to get stung now, and I've got a gut feeling that tells me these monkeys are going to get themselves caught when the shit hits the fan. Something tells me we'd be right in the killing zone back out here on the ship.'

Chico felt relieved. He had been having exactly the same thoughts himself for a few days now. He was smart enough to realise that the Libyans were only interested in their own ends. What happened to the Irish didn't matter to them. As long as he and Gene carried out their contract the money would be paid. He gestured towards Lisa on the deck below. 'What about her?'

Buckholtz scowled. 'Fuck her! She's just a piece of ass. We can buy a dozen better than her back home.'

Gonzales sniggered and pulled his packet of cocaine from his pocket. 'You had me worried for a while, buddy. I thought maybe you had gone sweet on her.' He proffered the plastic packet. 'Want some?'

Buckholtz laughed and opened the door. 'No way, you know me better than that.' Still laughing, he stepped out into the drizzle. 'Come on,' he said, 'We've got packing to do.'

Forty-Two

Eddie Molloy died painfully with the smell of his beloved oil and grease clinging in his nostrils. His last breath rattled out of him as Matty Lyons brought the diesel engine thundering back into life and the noise of it stilled the fear in his heart.

Lyons had seen death in many violent forms, but before this, it had always been below ground in the dripping Durham coal fields that ran their subterranean skeletal fingers out under the North Sea. Accidental death, and because of that, acceptable to miners conditioned to it by the rigours of their existence. Nothing had prepared him for death wrought by a bullet. With a sick feeling he arranged the two bodies side by side and started to clean off the oil and gore with a pressure hose until the engine room regained a semblance of normality. Then he rang the bridge.

Prendergast replaced the voice pipe cover. He turned to face Liam. 'Molloy is dead.'

Liam hesitated for a minute before answering. 'I'm sorry.' His voice was little more than a whisper.

'Sorry!' Prendergast shouted. The word tortured him. 'You people are always sorry. You should read the papers sometime, every time a bomb goes off and someone gets killed, you say you're sorry, it was a mistake. You're even sorry you killed my wife and daughter. It's a small word in your vocabulary that means nothing.'

'Get off my fucking back!' Liam retreated into a corner as the ship vibrated up to full speed. He contemplated the treach-

- 337 -

ery he was about to commit, knowing he was signing his own death warrant. Hogan would approve, he told himself. The man had never wanted this, never even wanted to be a party to it, and he had paid for it with his life. To Liam at that moment, life seemed a reasonable price to pay.

Since finding out about the primed explosives in the hold and Foster's act of murder in the engine room, with every second that passed, Liam's certainty deepened. Foster had been on board the ship when it rammed Prendergast's yacht. Foster had murdered three men on the *Georgios*. Foster had undertaken to convince Hogan of the viability of the plan and he had ended up dead too. Foster would have needed help for that one, and only one man could have set it up. Only the combined efforts of that obsessive little shit, Harry Trent and that lunatic, Foster, could have brought them this far down a road leading to disaster.

For the next hour Prendergast left Liam alone with his thoughts. Absorbing himself with the radar he watched the yellow blips of the two approaching boats come closer. Had they been showing lights they should already be visible to the naked eye, even in the present murk that lay like a misty cloud over the sea. He willed another ship to come on the scene. Where was the Irish Navy? Probably off arresting some errant Spanish fisherman. Like a policeman, never there when wanted, he thought ferociously.

Charlie Donovan led the way and brought his boat alongside the blacked-out ship that lay stopped in the water. Somewhere on deck a torch flashed as heavy coir fenders were lowered into place. Whoever was up there fumbled Charlie's thrown mooring lines and it was some time before he secured alongside the rusting steel side of the *Maria B*.

Minutes later the rumble of hatch boards being hurled onto the deck signalled that someone was preparing to transfer the cargo, but it was some time before the first sling-load of boxes jerked erratically into the air overhead.

Prendergast looked on from the wing of the bridge. Thanks to the murders, no experienced crew members were available to handle the cargo so Matty Lyons was down in the hold with Foster and Lisa, helping to unload the weapons. Anxiously he watched the Maltese cook operating the cargo winch. In his inexperienced hands the first load hung suspended over the ship's side while he fiddled with the controls, then it hurtled down unchecked to crush a tangle of fish boxes and lobster pots on the boat's afterdeck. He heard Donovan shrieking for Harry McDonagh to come off his own boat tied astern and help him.

Prendergast could see that the situation had all the makings of a disaster. This was going to be a slow process. Working without lights, they would be lucky to escape without a fatality. He judged it to be two hours before dawn, with no glimmer of approaching daylight in the east. A gentle breeze that had sprung up earlier now sent cats paws flitting on the surface of the sea as the mist turned into fine rain. He shuddered. If the wind increased, so would the waves, and then the ship would roll, adding to the danger.

Buckholtz zipped up his flying suit and smiled confidently at Gonzales. 'Okay, buddy, let's go do what we do best.'

Chico picked up a small zippered bag. 'One for Muong Lan.'

Buckholtz stopped in the doorway. There was a distant far-away look in his eyes. 'Yeah, one for Muong Lan,' he echoed. 'That was down to another President, but this one ain't any different.' For an instant, Gonzales had transported him back to the steaming jungles of Laos, and he relived the crackling heat of burning jungle, smelling the roasting flesh and hearing again the screams of the dying. The memory of it primed him, and he was ready for what he had to do. He flashed a smile. 'Canned heat – that's our business, Chico baby! Two for the price of one this time, a chicken shit President and a dumb-ass Prime Minister! Kaboom! Courtesy of the Libyan government! Them A-Rabs will be having one hell of a party tonight! He laughed harshly and shouldered open the door to lead the way into the wet night.

The shrill whine of the Allison turbo-shaft engine drowned out the rumble of the cargo winch, and as the four blades of the helicopter started to revolve, all work on deck stopped.

Wearily, Foster allowed a metal box of ammunition to drop to the splintered wood floor and joined Lisa and Matty Lyons to stare up at the black hole of the cargo hold above their heads. Through the opening, a blast of moist air swept down on them as the chopper, hesitantly at first, lifted a few feet off the deck. Briefly, a powerful landing light bathed them in radiance, then with a thunderous roar the chopper soared upwards with a single light flashing beneath its belly until they could only see it as a blacker shape in the hatch opening.

Lisa felt a surge of excitement in the pit of her stomach and for the first time she saw Foster smiling. His features glowed in the single cargo light that shone on the remaining boxes of weapons in the hold. She raised her hand to wave, but the aircraft had already banked clear and the thud of its rotors became muted as it turned low over the sea.

Prendergast watched as the cargo derrick rattled back into life and another shadowy box jerked its way out of the hold. He could still hear the dull throb of the circling helicopter. His mouth felt dry as he fed it with yet another cigarette. Liam had been gone now for at least ten minutes but suddenly he saw him again, a black crouching shadow outside on the bridge wing fiddling with the top of a box lying on the deck.

Liam straightened up, and when he did so, a long tubular object rested on his shoulder. He searched the night sky, listening for the rotors.

Prendergast felt a choking feeling come over him. He could never accept the cold-blooded way these people prepared to kill. He took a step towards the door as though to stop it from happening, but his emotions became charged by anger. He remembered Susan sleeping in her bunk that night and hatred swept over him. Let them do their worst to each other, he thought, with a savagery that shocked him. But even so, when the flash and the explosion of the launched missile came, it left him shaking and rooted to the spot.

Flying on instruments, Buckholtz switched off all lights and swung the helicopter in a low arc looking for the ship. With some difficulty he picked out a faint glow from the open cargo hatch but in the darkness the ship with the fishing boats alongside was invisible. He spoke into the intercom. 'Okay. Chico, we got plenty of time, let's check everything one last time, then we'll go do the business!'

Gonzales turned his attention to the instruments and started calling out the checks. He glanced across at Buckholtz and raised his thumb. 'All green. You have a go, Gene!' he intoned.

Buckholtz levered the control column and banked the helicopter away to the east in a slow climbing turn. Suddenly a warning signal flashed on the instrument panel with blood red intensity. Gonzales felt the return of the same fear that had jabbed him so many times in the skies over Vietnam. 'Incoming,' he croaked. 'Incoming missile!' His voice rose to an urgent scream. 'Hit the deck!'

Buckholtz dived the helicopter wildly for the blackness below them, his eyes fixed on the twirling artificial horizon as the flickering altimeter beside it danced its maniacal jig. The roar of the engine reached a shriek as all three hundred horsepower was unleashed.

It was already too late. From behind them, the five-foot long Stinger missile jinked and wove, copying every movement of the helicopter, its infra-red sensors alert and locked on to the howling turbine engine. Like a pedigree hound, it didn't deviate from its task until the proximity fuse detonated a split second before impact.

The explosion and its fireball occurred a scant fifty feet above the surface of the Atlantic, briefly illuminating the motionless ship three thousand yards away. Then all was blackness again.

Seconds after the missile streaked over head, Foster came out of the hold like an unleashed demon. Lisa was right behind him, her heart pounding. Wiping away a bead of perspiration with the back of his hand, Liam slowly relaxed his hold on the pistol grip of the launcher. The second missile he had loaded was redundant, but it was some time before he could tear his eyes away from the spot where the helicopter had been. He was shaking slightly when he lowered the launcher to the deck.

As Lisa sped along the deck she saw Liam duck back below the bridge coaming. 'Traitor!' she screamed. She fell to one knee and fired two shots up into the darkness.

Liam felt the searing pain of a bullet ripping through his shoulder muscles. Ducking quickly, he avoided the second, which splintered the coaming just in front of his face and filled the air with jagged shards of hardened teak.

Prendergast glimpsed Lisa dropping to one knee at the side of the hatch coaming before a bullet shattered the window in front of him. He heard the whine of it ricocheting off the compass binnacle. An instant later she was racing ahead of Foster for the ladder leading to the afterdeck.

Liam stumbled through the door, a pistol in his hand, blood spattering his face. His eyes looked wild and his left arm swung uselessly by his side, blood dripping from the tips of his fingers. 'We don't have too much time,' he said. 'Watch the door on your side. I'll take care of this one.'

Before Prendergast could answer, a darker shadow showed itself at the top of the ladder outside. 'Watch out!' His eyes flashed a warning before the shout erupted from his lips.

Liam pivoted on his feet and brought up his pistol. Quickly he pumped off three shots and the shadow transformed itself into Lisa as she jack-knifed into a sitting position in a corner of the bridge wing, the small calibre Walther pistol in her hand cracking a single shot that gouged a harmless scar in the deck planking. Her eyes stared back, lifeless in the darkness, her face a mask of surprise. Slowly, breast high, inside the open anorak, the blood spread in a widening circle on her white angora sweater.

As the opposite wheel house door crashed open, Prendergast dived frantically for the open door leading to the chart room, but Liam was too late. A fusillade of bullets hurtled into the wheel house and instantly, the air was full of flying glass and wood splinters.

A sliver of glass ripped into Liam's right eye as he raised his hand in futile defence and a single bullet tore deep into his stomach bringing an intensity of pain that he could never have imagined.

Prendergast plunged through the door, lost his footing, and landed in a sprawling heap half inside his own cabin. He thought he heard a dull crack as his wrist twisted under him, and instantly he knew it was broken. He saw a gleam in the darkness, the underwater spear gun he had bought in Valletta. He reached for it and staggered to his feet.

Cautiously, Foster crept into the wheel house. His face reflected his terror, but his eyes burned with fanaticism. He tore his eyes away from Liam's crumpled figure lying opposite him. He half turned, catching a flash of reflected light as Prendergast raised the spear gun in the doorway. There was a metallic spring-like sound as the spear leapt from the gun. The barbed tip sped three feet to rip viciously through his chest pinning him to the wooden bulkhead. Dropping his gun, he brought up both hands to the quivering dart that impaled him. Then he screamed as agony transmitted itself to his brain.

Jim groped for a switch and lighted the wheel house, the spear-gun in one hand. His mouth went slack and hung open as he surveyed the carnage with disbelief.

Liam was trying to sit up, both hands clutching his stomach. His eyes reflected death as the blood pumped steadily through clutching fingers that tried to stem it and hold back his gut. Foster was screaming as his fingers twitched and tried to pluck out the barb from his chest.

Jim picked up Foster's fallen pistol from the floor. It was the gun that Cooke had given him.

Foster's eyes met those of Prendergast and he began to pray out loud. One hand searched for his jacket pocket and plucked out the tiny radio transmitter. He had already programmed it, and a red light showed above a single red button. His lips peeled back in a grotesque grimace. 'Now you can join Hogan,' he mouthed at Liam.

'Kill the bastard!' Liam screamed. 'He did your wife and kid, Prendergast!'

Prendergast raised the pistol and felt the gun explode in his hand. He wasn't conscious of squeezing the trigger, but he was so close that he could not miss.

Foster pressed the button a micro second before the single bullet hit him in the side of his head, blowing out a great chunk of bone and splattering the bulkhead with blood and tissue. His head flew back with his lips bared in what appeared to be a half smile, as the explosion ripped through the bottom of the ship.

Matty Lyons had no chance. He was still down in the hold, too afraid to go up on deck since the gunfire erupted. A great fire-ball of exploding ammunition consumed him long before the sea swept in through the shattered bottom plates. The *Maria B* lurched under the force of the explosion and immediately started to list. Far below in the bowels of the ship, a forward bulkhead collapsed as flame and pressure roared upwards through the open cargo hatch. The cargo winch cable snaked around the cook's legs and dragged him screaming into the flames.

Desperately, Charlie Donovan fought to let off his mooring lines. Harry McDonagh was useless, quivering down amongst the scattered ammunition cases in the fish hold. The ship's side towered over him and suddenly canted downwards at a hideous angle. A second explosion ripped through the ship and a great hole appeared back towards the engine room beneath the bridge. Burning fuel oil spurted through it, setting fire to McDonagh's boat tied astern of him. Moments later his own boat caught fire. He tried to jump for the side away from the ship just as the cargo derrick crashed over the ship's side and pinned him to the deck. He was already dead when the ammunition started to explode in his own fish hold, killing McDonagh instantly.

With difficulty, Prendergast dragged Liam across the sloping deck towards the door. He could already feel the heat of flames licking through the engine room beneath his feet. Behind him the chart room erupted in flame, cutting him off from the VHF. Suddenly, the lights went out as the flames reached the generator down below and a gust of flame shot up through the funnel into the darkness.

Liam regained consciousness as the wheel house bulkhead caught fire. Outside, flames were already licking at the deck and Lisa's body was beginning to smoulder. Desperately he tried to pry free of Jim's grip. 'I've done my job,' he croaked. His voice reached a whisper as the last of his strength ebbed away. 'Look after yourself. There's nothing left out there for me.' Searing pain again wrenched through his stomach and his single eye rolled whitely in his bloodied face as the flames licked closer.

Prendergast agonised only for a second longer before lunging for the open door. He fell halfway down the bridge ladder as the ship canted wildly. He felt something crack in his chest as he painfully slithered aft to where the inflatable dinghy rested in its canister. Fumbling at the lashings, he hoped desperately that the thing would inflate. Too late now to wonder if he had remembered to have it tested.

The deck reared skywards as he released the container and watched it splash into the sea twenty feet below. The sound of another bulkhead rupturing reverberated through the ship as though a tomb was slamming shut. Then, a thundering torrent of water forced a great cloud of steam to billow through the engine room skylights as the fires below in the engine room were swamped.

Prendergast launched himself overboard and hit the water a few feet away from the bobbing dinghy. Reaching it he held on and kicked out wildly as the *Maria B* reared skywards above him in her final death throes, rising even higher before plunging for the bottom in a great swirling gust of steam that hung in the night air.

With difficulty, Prendergast forced himself out of the water into the dinghy and lay exhausted on its rubber floor. He felt pain flooding through his body. Through the opening in the hood of the raft he saw a flicker of moonlight penetrate the low cloud and a star showed itself weakly. Except for the lapping of tiny waves as the dinghy bobbed on the surface of the sea, there was silence, then a fitful breeze picked up to become a light wind that teased the calm water. Somewhere far away in the east a flash lit the horizon and he knew he was looking at the Eeragh light for the first time since leaving Galway. For a second time he was a survivor, alone on the ocean.

The sky gradually lightened with the coming of dawn. It could have been minutes or even hours. He heard a noise close by, then he heard faint voices carried on the wind. Then the voices became clearer, English voices. He struggled to the opening in the canopy. No more than twenty yards away lay the dark outline of a submarine, motionless in the water.

Slowly the rising wind carried him closer until he bumped softly alongside, then he felt hands pulling at the canopy drawing him near. He felt pain stabbing in his chest as careful hands lowered him through a circular hatch in the deck, and he almost passed out with its intensity. He heard all around him the whir of well-oiled machinery and from somewhere overhead on deck came the voice of an officer calling for the dinghy to be brought aboard.

A hatch clanged shut. He felt his clothes being stripped from him, the warmth of wool blankets, then someone talking quietly in medical terms. As though from a great distance, he heard muffled orders, then the swishing noise of compressed air being released before he felt a slight incline to the bunk on which he lay, as the submarine slid quietly into the deep.

Forty-Three

In late September, summer deserted the west coast of Scotland like a migratory bird and broken weather replaced it with winds that held an autumnal hint of an early winter.

The single customer in the bar overlooking the pontoons of Troon Marina sipped a good malt whiskey and looked out over the yachts restlessly snubbing at their mooring lines. A cackle of chattering halyards penetrated the double-glazed windows adding a sense of loneliness to the small harbour. Few people were tending to their boats.

In a corner, near the harbour entrance, he could see a scattering of ugly warehouses surrounded with piles of rusting scrap metal that added to an air of dereliction.

Jonathan Cooke ordered another drink at the bar and returned to the window. The sea outside the harbour had a leaden colour matched only by the scudding clouds overhead. Here and there in the distance, breaking white wave tops driven by the wind added a splash of relief to a sombre scene that might well have been set in mid-January or February.

Cooke felt the familiar pain throbbing in his leg and he knew rain was not far away. Silently, he watched a small yacht speeding towards the harbour entrance. She was well reefed down, but sailing fast. Occasionally a flash of white showed a wave breaking along her weather decks.

The barman put down his newspaper and joined him at the window. 'That's the boat, Sir.' he said. 'She's the only one that goes out every day no matter what the weather.' He frowned and added disapprovingly, 'There's a lot of 'em down there that have more money than sense, floating caravans most of 'em, and some never move from the dock. He's different.' The barman obviously approved.

'Thank you.' Cooke finished his drink and picked up his cane, 'I'll stroll down and meet him.'

Expertly, Jim Prendergast rounded up to his berth and the headsail rolled away. The yacht gently nudged the pontoon and came to a stop with only the reefed mainsail flogging in the wind. He stepped lightly ashore and secured the mooring lines.

Even Cooke could appreciate that the whole manoeuvre had been carried out without the aid of the boat's engine. He reached the yacht just as Prendergast finished stowing the mainsail. 'Hello, Jim, you seem fit and well.'

'What are you doing here?' Prendergast was not friendly. He didn't stop covering the mainsail.

Cooke shuffled his feet. 'Can I come aboard? I've got a few things for you. Thought I'd drop them down in person, rather than post them.'

Prendergast nodded grudgingly. Perhaps he was being too hard on Cooke, he thought. The affair with the *Maria B* had not been entirely his fault, but it was difficult to forgive the loss of life and he still felt Cooke could have prevented it.

Climbing down the short ladder from the cockpit, Cooke noted that the cabin was surprisingly spacious. Everything was neat and in place. He unbuttoned his coat and seated himself on a narrow settee running the length of the cabin before placing a bulky brown envelope on the table. 'I know you've been waiting for these,' he began. 'Everything you need is there. How's your wrist, by the way? I see the plaster is off.'

Prendergast lifted a lid in the centre of the teak table. Rummaging inside, he extracted a bottle of Gordon's gin. 'Fine,' he said. He flexed his left hand. 'It's still a bit weak, but it'll toughen up.' He opened the envelope. Inside was a passport and a bank deposit book together with some other papers.

Opening the British passport, Jim flicked through it while he poured two generous measures of gin. 'James Broderick. Where did you find the name?'

Cooke poured a tonic water into his glass and listened as it hissed back at him. 'In the 'phone book. Everything you need is there, birth certificate, bank papers – the lot. You're even recorded correctly in Somerset House. Your house is up for sale, and I'm told there is a possible buyer. The proceeds will be lodged with your bank when the sale goes through.'

Jim frowned. 'Are you sure all of this is really necessary? I thought I had finished with this cloak and dagger nonsense!'

'It's certainly necessary.' Cooke sipped his gin and gazed out through the open hatch towards the stone breakwater opposite to them. Over that wall was the sea, he mused. Beyond that, the horizon, and beyond that again, the cauldron that was the North of Ireland. He felt his weak knee stiffen even as he thought of it. 'There are still people loose out there who would give a lot to know the full story of what happened on the *Maria B.* You can't go back to Ireland, not for a long while at least. I'm sorry, Jim, but you're dead. Get used to it. It's for your own good.'

'What about the others, did you do what I asked?' Jim's look was cold.

'Yes, Molloy and the rest of your men had accidental death insurance policies. We made sure of that. It was a simple marine disaster, if such things can be simple. Their next of kin were informed while you were in hospital. The Irish government know about it of course, the whole affair is classified as top secret by both governments.'

'And Reynolds?'

'He's at home. Thankfully, he knew nothing.'

An uncomfortable silence followed. Jonathan massaged his cheek and looked around the cabin, 'Nice boat, what is she?'

Jim lit a cigarette, 'Contessa thirty-two – a classic, sails like a dream. I've named her *Jane's Legacy.*'

Cooke coughed politely and said nothing for a moment. 'I'm sorry. I really mean it.'

Prendergast stood up and removed his sailing jacket. Underneath he wore a short sleeved polo shirt. Livid burn scars were still visible on his forearm. 'Too many good men died,

Jonathan. You sound like that bastard, Liam. He was sorry too. There's little to choose between either of you and I feel somehow responsible.' His despondency was tangible.

'You have to get it into your head that you performed a valuable service,' Cooke insisted. 'You prevented a huge arms shipment from getting through and a terrorist cell was virtually wiped out. The peace talks are continuing. That's without counting what might have happened if that helicopter got through ... damn it man! They intended to kill the Prime Minister and the President of the United States! Does that not mean anything to you? This had nothing to do with the Irish problem. The German and her friends were only interested in total anarchy, nothing else. Incidentally, I lost my job over this.' He smiled and shrugged. 'I never liked it much anyway.'

'My turn to be sorry,' Jim said quietly. 'I didn't know that. What happened to Pavlides?'

'May I have one of your cigarettes?' Cooke lit up and coughed. 'Haven't smoked a cigarette for years, just the odd cigar.' He paused and drew on his cigarette. 'Pavlides was found dead in his bath. Drowned. Obviously the Libyans got to him in London before we did. Incidentally, Colonel Ghalboun – the one who put all this together – he slipped back to Libya. He's probably still there, if he hasn't already faced a firing squad. For all practical purposes we have you to thank for that, too. He is unlikely to be seen again.'

'I didn't do anything.' Jim leaned forward speaking earnestly. 'Liam did it. He stopped it, not me.'

'You underestimate yourself Jim. You were the right man in the right place at the right time. Can't you understand that? Without you, we would never have known.'

'I can't help feeling that I was used by your people. You could have stopped it before people started getting killed. Christ! I killed a man myself! Don't you understand what that means? I blew his bloody head into bits without giving it a second thought. I find that hard to accept.' He looked away for a second. ' I have to live knowing that I enjoyed killing him, simply because it was revenge for what he did.'

Cooke gave him a penetrating look. 'Killing someone – even an enemy – is never easy. If I could have prevented it I would have done so. Circumstances kept us from knowing in time. The submarine was a lucky break, but she got there too late. We didn't know about the helicopter and it was all over too quickly for anything to be done. Whatever you think of us, even we can no longer get away with sinking unarmed merchant ships, especially inside someone else's territorial waters. Irish navy ships were on the way, but too far off to be of use. Either way people would have died. If we had tried to board you at sea, Foster would have blown your ship out of the water. Jim, Foster carried the responsibility for countless deaths, including those of your own family. You have to absolve yourself from guilt.'

'Perhaps. I'm not sure.' Prendergast fell silent.

Jonathan stubbed out his cigarette. 'Its unfortunate that we were lulled into a false sense of security after your report from Malta. Had we known in time that you were bound for Libya, perhaps we could have done more.' He stood up. 'There's nothing else to say, Jim, except to wish you good luck. I'll leave now. Thank you for the drink. When do you plan on leaving, by the way?'

Prendergast picked up the passport and other papers and slipped them into the chart table locker. 'I might as well go right now. I've only been waiting for these. The wind has gone north and the boat's ready.'

'Where to first?' Cooke asked, picking up his walking stick.

'Spain, I think. Then across to the Canaries. I'll be in time to pick up the Trades for the Caribbean in November.' There was a far away look in Jim's eyes, a gleam of anticipation, perhaps.

The two men shook hands in silence and he followed Cooke up into the cockpit.

For a long time Jonathan stood with the wind whipping around his trouser legs, staring after the yacht until it became a small speck out to sea. He found it difficult to comprehend what drove Prendergast to go out there alone. Perhaps it was the silence and peace of his own company. Whatever it was, he wished him well.